The Return of Glenn Miller

Other books by C O Lamp

Journey to a Star

Gentle Tigress

Distant Love, Lasting Love

The Return of Glenn Miller

C O Lamp

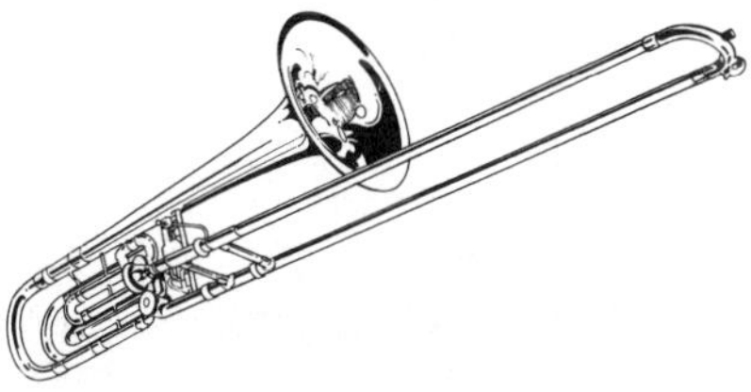

1999
Galde Press, Inc.
Lakeville, Minnesota, U.S.A.

First Edition
First Printing, 1999

Cover art by George Ostroushko

Library of Congress Cataloging-in-Publication Data
Lamp, C O 1927–
p. cm.
ISBN 1–880090–84–8
I. Title.
PS3562.A46485R48 1999
813'.54—dc21 99–27017
CIP

Galde Press, Inc.
PO Box 460
Lakeville, Minnesota 55044–0460

This book, a labor of love, is dedicated to anyone who enjoys music in the Miller mood, to all the friendly folks in Clarinda, with special thanks to the ladies of the Clarinda Public Library, the Clarinda Association of Business and Industry, and the Glenn Miller Birthplace Society, to Joanne Dunkerson, and super special thanks to my editor, Toni Lin Hengesteg, and Rosemary Joy, the Joy of My Life for all these years.

In fiction, anything is possible if you dare to dream.

In life, anything is possible if you dare to dream.

Beyond Diminuendo

He left Clarinda, sliphorn in hand,
To walk with destiny, to lead a band
On paths circuitous, of gouged travail,
With Pollock and Goodman, on Dorsey's trail.
Cold one-night stands, making Noble arrangements,
And Helen, his wife, knowing . . . hating estrangements.
When his first band failed, another came round
To caress clarinct and sax in the Miller sound.
Woodwinds zesty, flowing on mellow brass,
Made the band unique, alone in its class.
Romance from music, in dreams come alive,
The young learned to waltz, the old turned to jive.
In drab honky-tonks or in Carnegie Hall,
The sound was the same: he gave them his all.
Old and new, borrowed and blue, that was his rhyme,
As a nation listened for Glenn Miller time.
His songs touched the soul—a voice from the heart—
Fulfilling a need in a world ripped apart
By freedom defied, madmen lusting for war.
New rhythms in rivets, blast furnace roar,
Entering the conflict, he made marching men swing.
For Limey afoot and Yank on the wing.
Dissident chords over the channel whirred.
The C-64 then plunged like a bird
Breastshot, into the depths of mystery.
A white gull halo circled the misty sea.
His melody lingers in a world gone shrill.
For those who knew,
IT'S GLENN MILLER STILL!

Clarinda, Iowa, exists in the heartland of America, the birthplace of Glenn Miller on March 3, 1904. The population of Clarinda is about 5,100 and has remained relatively stable. As a local humorist put it, "Whenever a baby is born, a man leaves town." The joke sounds like Mark Twain and may have drifted over from Hannibal, Missouri. Who can say?

The Glenn Miller band captivated America and much of the world. Voted the nation's number one dance band, Miller formed an Air Force band about which General Eisenhower stated, "It was the next best thing to a letter from home." Ike could sometimes be wrong. For many the band was better than a letter from home.

Accordingly, the names of the original band members and their contemporary musicians and associates are real. All other names in this work of fiction are just that—fictional. The names of the characters portrayed in Clarinda and scenes alluded to in Phoenix and Dallas and members of later bands are purely fiction. Any relation to persons living or dead is purely coincidental.

Chapter One

Alex Barca tossed back his head to a thunderclap of laughter. Through dark, slitted eyes, he read the road sign: CLARINDA 2 MILES. A little hick town in the remote corner of a cornball state—who would think of looking for him here? Only a few miles from Missouri, all he had to do was cross the boundary to escape an Iowa warrant. Clarinda would provide a fertile ground for a man with ideas. More than fertile ground, he quickly amended. The place was ripe for picking. His thin, bloodless lips moved.

"Power."

The ultimate power resided in information—information that would land men in prison. He had gathered that kind of evidence against two higher-ups in the Federal Communication Commission when he'd worked there and had removed several incriminating files. Instead of resorting to pressure for cash, he had prudently decided to trade favors. He favored them by keeping their dirty secrets, and they favored him by losing letters, delaying documents, rerouting reports, and running interference.

Tips from the pair at Com-Com had enabled him to purchase flagging radio stations at bargain prices, pump them up, and sell them at a premium. That all changed in Hopkinsville, where the clamor of community spirit tempted him to employ an attorney and form a corporation. Each day he sold stock at slightly higher prices. Before long he had sold twice as many shares as were authorized. One afternoon he marched into the bank near closing time and withdrew the money. He stole away during the night, leaving the attorney—who had not been paid—to explain that a man had a right to sell his stock at any price he could obtain. Alex never stated how many shares existed. He'd let the yokels sort it out.

Unhampered by rigidity, he adapted his scheme to fit each new opportunity. Despite variation, he always attempted to retain one salient feature. He particularly relished leaving town with the attorney's bills unpaid. The best part of the operation—not the best part really, but certainly an important part—it didn't cost his contacts at the FCC a dime. It didn't matter whether Bush or Dukakis replaced President Reagan at the end of the year. The pair at Com-Com were entrenched bureaucrats, and he'd use them as long as either of them remained there.

Alex slowed the car when he saw the sign GLENN MILLER BIRTHPLACE. The music of Glenn Miller would provide a splendid format for the rebirth of the radio station. Because of his friends at Com-Com, the Clarinda radio station had remained dark long after the government should have reassigned the license or increased the power of other stations in the area. KNDA belonged to Cordelia Cooper.

Alex had checked local history. In the early days of radio, Henry Field had opened KFNF, and Earl E. May started station KMA in neighboring Shenandoah, Iowa. Jake Cooper had licensed a stronger rival station in Clarinda, but he had no seed or nursery business to sustain him as did Henry Field and Earl E. May. Jake's station failed. According to townsfolk, the station was the only poor investment he ever made. He'd scored successes with a chain of area dance halls, a couple of movie theaters, a shoe store, a saloon, and two car dealerships; in addition he owned farms and city real estate.

Jake sold most of the businesses at the height of their popularity and carried back the loans at a high rate of interest. He'd tell buyers up front, "If you can get a cheaper loan anywhere else, you hop to it." As a result, Jake became rich and merchants who otherwise would not have been able to obtain loans managed to start businesses of their own.

Jake Cooper had been dead for two years. Alex wondered if Jake's widow Cordelia had actually acquired any of her late husband's business acumen. The man at the station where he'd purchased gas remembered, "Jake was shrewd. He was a dealer. Cordelia is sharper and she has a lot more vision."

A friendly pharmacist said, "She's the town treasure or a pain in the ass, depending on the issue."

He had no trouble locating Cordelia Cooper's address on North Glenn Miller Avenue. The sprawling ranch-style home had become a local landmark. Built of high-grade brick not long after World War II, the house clung to the top of a hill, well back from the highway on a well-manicured lawn, flanked by a curtilage of farm buildings. He glanced at the nearby cemetery and winced. He'd hate to live where ghouls and goblins prowled at night, practicing their evil spells. During the day, on the adjacent golf course, duffers practiced their evil spirits on one another. Golf didn't appeal to him either.

He approached the house, knocked on the door, and waited. When there was no response he knocked again.

Cordelia Cooper prepared to meet a stranger. Friends came right in or knocked and entered. "C'mon in," she shouted. "The door isn't locked."

Alex passed through a foyer with an open door. His eyes swept the room. Cordelia restrained a large black dog with bared fangs and an endless throaty growl. Alex saw two wheelchairs, one battery powered. He saw a walker, and leaning against the overstuffed chair where Cordelia sat were Canadian crutches.

An old cripple. They never told me she was a cripple.

He appraised her in a glance. Her gray hair had been gently tinted with a blue rinse. Alex noticed that not one strand was out of place. Her lips were full, her large oval features had become flabby with age. Alex guessed that she'd been a heller in her younger days.

The dog barked twice and Cordelia pointed to a spot to the right and slightly behind her. "Buster. Sit."

The dog obeyed and continued to eye the stranger warily. Every time Alex stared at the dog, Buster would tighten his upper lip and expose his fangs.

Cordelia saw a delicate, fine-boned man who moved with the grace of a dancer. His cheeks were hollow, his eyes deep set, but she couldn't read them. They appeared as mere slits in a face of pasty dough. His lack of color told her he was not accustomed to being out in the sun.

He's a damn puma. "Well," Cordelia demanded. "Are you just going to stand there? State your business."

The pharmacist had told him she would be crisp and intimidating. "Don't mince words with her," he had advised. Alex made a mental note to use the pharmacist the next time he needed information.

"I came to talk about your franchise for the radio station."

"Just to talk?"

"Actually, I'd like to buy it."

It had been an eon since anyone had shown an interest in the station, but Cordelia feigned a sigh. "Another buyer."

"Yes, ma'am."

"Well, sit down." She diverted the conversation and talked about the weather the way Iowans do. There had been a dry spell. "How's the corn crop? What did you see on the way in?"

"Eh? I'm afraid I'm not much of a farmer. It all looks the same to me. About the radio station—"

Cordelia sighed wistfully. "Jake always wanted to get the station going again."

He picked up on the comment at once but let it pass. To work a scam, a guy had to be a good listener. A scammer played on the mark's hopes and dreams and, of course, mainly his greed.

When the time was right, he said, "We could announce at station breaks, 'This is a Jake Cooper Station.' Or perhaps the Jake Cooper Memorial Station."

"Splendid idea," Cordelia said. "The last fur ball who wanted to buy the station wanted nothing but rock 'n roll music."

"Oh, we wouldn't do that," Alex said. "I saw the sign GLENN MILLER BIRTHPLACE. My plan is to feature Glenn Miller music; music in the Miller manner; music in the Miller mood."

"Perhaps live performances too," Cordelia suggested. "Maybe the Mound City Blues Blowers?"

"Why sure," Alex said unctuously.

The fool, Cordelia thought. He doesn't know that some early Miller platters—before Glenn was known—had been pressed and released under the name of the Mound City Blues Blowers. Her eyes narrowed and she peered at him intently. Where were his pupils? He had dark lashes and his eyelids were heavily lined. The lines beneath his eyes enhanced the impression of dark eyes but she wanted to see them up close. *He's a weed. A noxious weed.* She reached for a pack of cigarettes, tapped one, and said casually, "The lighter is over there; would you do the honors?" He needed to open his eyes to bring the lighter carefully to the end of her cigarette. That's when she planned to see his eyes.

Alex charged forward and lit the cigarette. When the lighter flamed she made a quick appraisal. *I was right. He's a crook.*

In the instant before he averted his eyes, he stared into the mercurial depths of Cordelia's old and tired eyes. He saw a youthful vigor he had not expected. Her skin held an unhealthy pallor.

She cleared her throat. "I really am not inclined to sell."

"That's what I suspected," Alex said quickly. He knew the FCC had pressed her. He would roll with the punch. "Just now as I sat here, I had the idea that you might let go of half. You could be president. I could be a silent partner—or vice president. With the money required to get started, we probably need to take in some minor partners. I'm not going to quibble about the price. It would be nice to have the community involved. Jake Cooper is well thought of around town. He's an icon." *Playing on the Cooper legend he should be able to clear a bundle.*

"Then you would be working for me?" Cordelia said. "That's an idea. And getting the community involved? That's another good idea. I can see you are the kind of voltage I had in mind. I'm sure we can work something out. I'll need to have papers drawn up. I'll need a little information for the contract. I'm sure my attorney will ask. Date of birth, social security number, that sort of thing."

"I can give you prior references from a station I managed—" His pen moved across the back of an envelope and he handed it to her. She had not asked for references so he only wrote his address.

"Atlantic," Cordelia said when she'd glanced at the address he'd written. "Fine. I'll let you know when the papers are ready to be signed. Glenn Miller music appeals to me. A memorial to Jake Cooper. It sounds too good to be true. You have a deal, mister."

"It's a possible dream," Alex said. "Anything is possible if you dare to dream."

"You remind me of my late husband."

She's hooked. Alex turned to go. He glanced again at the dog and winced. Buster intercepted his gaze and bared his fangs.

Cornelia called after him. "Oh, Mr. Barker. Thanks for stopping by."

Barker? He halted with a sudden jerk that did not escape Cordelia's watchful eye. Pushing back an insincere smile to mount one of absolute sincerity with a hint of self-effacement, Alex managed, "It's Barca. A common mistake. I hear it often."

Arrogant little pipsqueak. Cordelia stubbed out the cigarette. She rarely smoked these days. He hadn't quibbled about the price. That carried with it an abundance of suspicion. He probably had a record—

Alex scowled as he started his car. On arrival he estimated the cripple couldn't last much longer. But she exhibited a surprising vitality and a keen mind. He had convinced her to sell and retain a half interest, which meant he'd only need to raise half the money. With her remaining as president, she would be responsible for whatever happened. If they got into trouble, she would take the heat. No big deal. She wouldn't be around long enough to see a courtroom. In the meantime he'd concentrate on selling the half interest in dozens of small parcels. That would probably be easier than selling three times the half. *With a block that size it would be touchy.* He decided to play it as it developed.

Alex continued to scowl. Cordelia Cooper had disarmed him with her request for a social security number. He hated giving it to her but she would have balked had he refused. Refusal would have torpedoed the entire transaction.

Cordelia heard his car kick up gravel before he sped down the hill and out of the driveway. Buster approached and she patted his head. "Well, what do you think? He's a cat isn't he? I noticed you didn't cotton to him any more than I did. I figure he's a puma. We'd better look into that." She at once dialed the number of the police department.

"Chief Wilbur Wendinger, please. This is Cordelia Cooper."

Ellen Iverson waved at the chief and said loudly in order that he might prepare, "Right away, Miz Cooper. I'll put you through." She silently mouthed the caller's name at her boss in case he had not heard. "Cordelia Cooper."

"This is Chief Wendinger."

"Cordelia Cooper calling."

"Hello, Miz Cooper. Long time no hear. How are you?"

"I need a favor, Wilbur. Run a check on an eel named Alex Barca. He might also use the name Barker." She remembered how he had stiffened at the name.

When the chief had written down the data, he said, "I'll get back to you as soon as I have something."

"Thank you, Wilbur."

Relieved, the chief closed his eyes as old images flooded his memory. He remembered he'd been in tenth grade when he and Orville Keane decided to raid Jake Cooper's barn. Earlier, he'd watched the Cooper farm from his window. Jake had a pattern. Ten o'clock: turn loose the dogs. Not long after the news, the house would go dark. Accordingly, he and Orville planned to be inside the barn a few minutes before ten.

When viewed from the house, the most visible side of the barn had two walk-in doors. One was heavily braced and padlocked from the outside. The other door remained unlocked.

One night at seven minutes before ten the boys crept toward the barn and approached the unlocked door. The moment they stepped inside—surprise!—the spring-activated door snapped shut behind them and locked.

"What's that?" Wilbur said anxiously. The flashlights they carried illuminated the bars. "Oh, God," he wailed. "We're trapped!"

"We're sunk," Orville agreed.

They saw a clever metal grill attached inside the door. Jake Cooper had taken a night-school welding class. Using the old radio tower and other metal scraps, he had welded a hidden room inside the barn. With bars on four sides, the cell had no windows and contained a toilet, a sink, a tap with running water, and a pile of straw.

They located a light switch they were afraid to turn on. They also found a sign in the beam of their flashlights. DON'T EVEN THINK OF STARTING A FIRE. YOU WILL BE THE FIRST TO COOK.

"I don't know why I let you talk me into this," Orville muttered.

"Me? It was all your idea!"

"What if they don't find us?" Orville worried.

"We can live a long time on water. At least a week."

They spent a long, miserable time before they managed to fall asleep.

Following his inquisitive dogs, Jake found them the next morning. "What a fine kettle of fish. Aren't you a pretty pair? What were you aiming to do?"

"Nothing," Orville squeaked. In reality they planned to lift some of the antiques they heard were stored in the barn, take them to Atlantic, and sell them for cash.

"Just looking around," said Wilbur.

"You could have asked me for a cook's tour. No, you're trespassing, plain and simple. You know that. Sneaking around like thieves in the night. That's just what you are. Well, it's time to call the police."

"Please don't," they wailed. They begged and pleaded.

"Well, all right," Jake said. "We can hold court right here and now. If you plead guilty we can work out a penalty and the police won't hear a word about it. Are you ready to admit to trespass, burglary, and attempted theft?"

They hesitated.

"Well," Jake prodded. "Make up your minds. I ain't got all day. Is it a plea or do I call the police?"

They hesitated.

"Speak up. I can't hear your words."

"Guilty," Orville said.

"Yeah, guilty," said Wilbur.

"All right. Now we move to the penalty. How many hours of work do you think it's worth?"

The boys discussed it and Orville offered, "Thirty-six hours. Weekends only. We have school—"

"Accepted," Jake said. "I won't interfere with school. You both have a lot to learn. You just picked the length of the penalty. I get to pick the time. I don't care if it's Homecoming week or some big prom. When I call, you come running. Understand?"

They nodded.

"Then the police won't hear a thing about it," Jake said.

"It would just be your word against ours," Wilbur said.

"Glad you reminded me." Jake turned and exited the door he'd unlocked.

"Now look what you did," Orville charged. "You and your big mouth."

"Who me? What about you?"

Minutes later, Jake returned with his wife and a flash camera. "Here's another witness. Admit your crime to Cordelia."

"We were going to steal something," said Orville.

"That's right," Wilbur said. He hid his face.

"Now don't turn away, boys," Jake said. You don't get out without a picture. Smile pretty for the camera. Nobody will see the picture if you hold to your agreement."

"We will be back to do the work," Orville promised.

"Wilbur and Orville," Jake deadpanned. "I guess you're no flight risk. One thing more. No one knows about this room. If I hear a word circulating downtown, I'll know who spread it and the deal is off. Understood?"

"Understood."

Jake had unlocked the cell and the boys scampered down the road.

Chief Wendinger opened a locked desk drawer. Inside a notebook he found a snapshot given to him by Jake Cooper the day he was sworn in as a police officer. On the back was written, "Always do right."

The chief noticed Ellen, his secretary, peeking at him out of the corner of her eye. He closed the notebook and returned it to the locked desk drawer.

"We haven't heard from Mrs. Cooper in a while," Ellen remarked.

The chief nodded. "I'm counting my blessings." He wondered if Cordelia ever called Orville Keane. He stared over Ellen's head into the distance and said, "I wonder what she's up to now?"

"You'd probably never guess," Ellen said. "You know Cordelia."

Cordelia had initiated another phone call. "I need some legal work done," she told Attorney Orville Keane. "Some papers prepared."

Orville Keane listened intently. "Anything. Any amount. Any time," Orville said cheerfully. He meant every word.

He remembered sleeping on straw in a barred room in Cooper's barn. The boys had worked up a sweat later, cutting weeds, shoveling earth, and one day Jake said, "The work's going to be easier this afternoon. I need someone to carry my tucker." He'd taken the boys fishing. Wilbur didn't care much for fishing but he'd kept up a friendship with Jake. They had often gone fishing. When it came time for college, Orville mentioned money problems.

Jake made an offer. "You get yourself through the first two years and I'll make sure you get through the second half."

Later, the same deal applied to law school. He'd repaid the loans in time—probably the only no-interest loans Jake had ever made—and he'd promised to do all their legal work free forever—as long as he could tell folks he was their attorney.

"I think he's a banana peel," Cordelia said of Alex. "He may try to sell six hundred percent of the mine. Tie him up so he can't take on more than two partners."

"That will be interesting," Orville predicted. "With you owning half and others owning half, you've lost control."

"I like life to be interesting," Cordelia insisted. "Our Mr. Barca has no idea as we speak that I'm limiting his sales potential. What do you think of setting up an escrow account at the Page County State Bank? I'd hate to tempt the man by putting cash in his pocket."

"Cordelia, you're something else," Orville chuckled. "I can build on that. When the ol' schemer wakes up and finds he's in the henhouse with a killer wolfhound, he's going to wonder what hit him."

"He was too eager and jumped at the price. And I didn't like what I saw in his eyes. And Buster didn't like him either."

When the call ended, Orville leaned back in his luxurious office chair. A lot of corn had passed through the grinder since Jake captured two snot-nosed boys in his trap. He vividly remembered the night he had spent on a mound of straw. Through the years he and Wilbur had grown apart. Now he represented clients that Wilbur had captured and brought to the bar of justice. He wondered, did Wilbur ever hear from Cordelia Cooper? Attorney Keane decided as he had in the past, he would never mention it. After all, a deal is a deal.

Alex Barca barely heard the drone of the engine as he drove north toward Atlantic, Iowa. Tree-lined fences reminded him of the *bocages,* the hedgerows of Normandy, a place he'd finally visited. Travelogues of France always fascinated him, especially of Paris.

After making a score in Texas, he hadn't plunked all of the cash into a Cayman Island account. He'd treated himself to a trip to Paris. The young woman with whom he shared an apartment during those weeks had not been right for him. She merely wanted a rich American to provide her with a meal ticket. In Paris a man might easily have a mistress. Clarinda was a friendly, conservative, mind-your-own-business kind of town. No one would care if he had a mistress as long as he did it very discreetly. Hadn't a man almost as wise as he ordained that discretion be considered the better part of valor?

He amended the idea and wondered if he'd meet the right woman in Clarinda. He had to admit that his get-the-money-and-run operation no longer held the fascination it once had. He sniffed. That was the second time he considered putting down a taproot. He wondered, had gravity settled in his guts?

It had been too easy selling the old cripple. Perhaps it had something to do with Glenn Miller. *Glenn Miller music. Would that play around here longer than six weeks?* He had to get in and get out. "Damn," he muttered. There was something wrong with the setup. He couldn't put his finger on it. He'd been turning it over in the back of his mind, resulting in an uneasiness he couldn't define. Things weren't coming together the way he planned. Perhaps conducting business within the aura of a cemetery might be blamed for the unpleasant feeling. No good would come from such profoundly negative vibes. "I wish I had never given her my social security number. No good can come of that either."

Maybe she won't use my social security number except for her own records. Crippled the way the way she is, she might not last long. She could check out any time.

That cuts two ways. Don't waste time. Get her name on the dotted line.

Chapter Two

Attorneys were always notoriously late. However, Alex guessed that Cordelia Cooper's attorney would arrive before the appointed time to discuss the proposed contract. To dilute their strategy, Alex arrived more than fifteen minutes early, but his ploy had not succeeded. He saw a Cadillac parked in the driveway. It had to belong to the attorney.

He approached the house and didn't knock. He eased open the front door and lingered, hoping to overhear their conversation. Instead he heard the throaty growl of Buster that announced his presence. He crossed the foyer and walked into the room with a confident "Good morning."

They returned his greeting and Cordelia introduced her attorney. Orville Keane stepped forward and extended his hand. He was a broad-shouldered man, and Alex envied his ability to make an off-the-rack suit appear tailor-made. The man was definitely model material. From his casual attitude, Alex decided Keane lacked the fire and drive of a big-city attorney. That could be expected here in Clarinda, where the pace seemed to be second gear.

"We might as well get started," Cordelia said, with a gesturing that Alex should seat himself in the empty chair.

"I prepared a contract," Orville Keane said, sliding it across the table. He thoroughly enjoyed working with Cordelia Cooper. Well read, well educated, she had put him onto some tax loopholes and was responsible for the trust business he'd developed.

Cordelia contrived to sit close to Attorney Keane. Whenever Alex Barca looked up from where he sat reading the proposed contract, he had to see them both. Cordelia had placed a Canadian crutch on the table and Alex stared at it fearfully, as if it was a giant pistol pointed directly at his heart.

For a long moment his eyes scanned the crutch, searching for a firing mechanism. *Bitch.* He mounted a deceptive grin calculated to tell them he had not lost the initiative. He continued to read and suddenly his head snapped. "What?" he exclaimed, voice straining into a protesting bleat. "I'm limited to only two partners?"

"That's correct," Cordelia acknowledged. "The most unwieldy entity in the whole world is a committee. Whether civil or political, secular or ecclesiastical, whether a church or a school, is there anything more inefficient than a committee? Certainly not! At my age, I do not wish to challenge fifty local citizens with one hundred different opinions, telling me how to run a radio station. Fifty sheep running off in a hundred directions? Thank you, no. Not at this stage in my life."

Maybe somebody should stage an accident. "I understand," Alex said blandly. He realized broad community participation was out. He had to find one or two pigeons. One or two very fat pigeons.

"The proceeds will be placed in escrow, in the Page County State Bank," Orville Keane explained. "The money won't be released to Mrs. Cooper until the total sum is raised. There's a condition precedent." Attorney Keane paused and continued. "The sale by Mrs. Cooper does not take place until all the funds are paid to her out of escrow. At that moment the transfer of half ownership occurs. Not until then."

"Which also protects you," Cordelia interrupted. "Because the same provision applies to any third party or fourth party. Which means they do not come aboard until they have paid into escrow as well."

"I see," Alex said. His tongue wetted his thin, bloodless lips. "Yes, I see."

"I thought you would appreciate that safeguard," the attorney said.

"A station needs a star, a personality," Alex said with an expansive gesture. "I was hoping to coax a couple to join us with minor ownership based on sales. I can't do that now. Well, no problem. I'll come up with something else."

"I don't doubt it for a minute," Cordelia said. *You're quicker than a cobra.*

"After the station becomes operational, we need a restriction. A partner—or his heirs—must give the first right of refusal to every other partner before offering stock to anyone else. That's only fair."

A growl emanated from the black dog's throat. "Quiet, Buster." Cordelia hesitated. She turned to her attorney. "Add a whereas."

Orville rose and placed a Remington portable typewriter on the table and selected another chair. He whirled two sheets and a carbon into the machine. His lean fingers moved with the speed of a secretary. "Think of it," he said. "In this day and age of high tech, an old portable and carbon paper still has utility."

Alex signed the document with a flourish. "You won't be sorry, Mrs. Cooper. I think you've made a decision you'll look back on with great satisfaction." He stared at the big black dog lying on its stomach. A totally obedient dog could also attack on command. He rolled up his copy of the agreement, grasped it like a baton, and strode out with a purposeful step.

They heard his car spew up gravel as he raced down the driveway.

Cordelia glanced at the typewriter. "Is that the machine Jake and I gave you when you were in college?"

"The very same," Orville said.

"It's holding up well. Better than I am."

"You're doing all right." His eyes came to rest on the dog. "As you said, Buster doesn't cotton to Mr. Barca. Buster kept showing his teeth. I'm surprised that he doesn't growl at me."

"Professional courtesy," Cordelia teased.

"Now you cut that out."

Cordelia assumed a pensive pose. "Somehow I think we just saved the community some embarrassment. Pardon me for saying so, but I think we roadblocked Alex Barca from selling three hundred percent of a radio station."

"Or more." Orville bobbed his head. His eyes widened. "Your intuition again. I've learned to respect that. Barca could still fleece several naive investors by inflating the price, but it's not likely. With that kind of money an investor would be inclined to check."

Orville left and Cordelia felt a rising uneasiness. She'd called in a favor from Chief Wilbur Wendinger and he'd reported, "No criminal convictions on an Alex Barca or Barker. He's not wanted for any crime."

Cordelia frowned. There was something about Alex Barca that disturbed her. He was artful, she had to give him that. On the other hand what she had seen in his eyes and detected from his manner might merely be her own prejudices. After all, his record revealed no convictions—

"Stop," she scolded herself. "You old frump. You have more to do than chase a whirlwind."

Alex Barca continued to assault the posted speed limit. "Damned old crone," he muttered and smacked a button on the dash that brought in rival Station KMA from nearby Shenandoah. "It will take more than a couple country hicks to sideline Alex Barca."

He swung into a vacant parking spot on the Square. Like many another town constructed in that era, the courthouse rose out of the prairie in glory and majesty, a monument to the rule of law, a constant reminder that "You'd better not get caught doing it."

Posing as a reporter, Alex accosted people passing by. "I'm from Associated Press. I'm doing a series on the concentration of female wealth in rural America. I've selected Clarinda as a typical small town. Could you identify local women of wealth?"

He heard the name of Cordelia Cooper with such frequency that pent-up anger at being outwitted on the contract finally flooded over the dam of restraint. "Not her," he snapped irritably.

"Well, if you don't want the answer," retorted a farmer, "why in hell did you ask the question?"

Now Alex included in his question, "About half the age of Cordelia Cooper, or possibly less."

People frequently responded, "Erin Ames."

"Erin Ames," Alex mused. The name had a certain ring to it. "Erin Ames."

He walked directly to the pharmacy and spoke to the pharmacist who had been so helpful supplying information about Cordelia Cooper. "If I didn't mention it before, I'm with the Associated Press. We're doing a series on modern women of wealth in rural America. I keep hearing the name of Erin Ames."

"Oh?"

"What's the hot skinny on her?"

Suspicions aroused, the pharmacist swallowed with difficulty and seized the opportunity to call to a woman who had just entered the store. "Your prescription is almost ready, Mrs. Wagoner. Have a seat. I'll call you just as soon as we have it enfarfillated." He turned to Alex. "I don't know a thing about Erin Ames or whatever her name is. Try Mr. Seligman at the chamber of commerce. He seems to know everything."

The man's attitude told him he knew a great deal about Erin Ames. A very great deal. *Is he a lover spurned?*

Alex decided a bar would be a better place to seek information. He hadn't noticed a tavern in his stroll around the Square and remembered seeing a couple of lounges on the highway. He imagined a Presbyterian city father long ago at a city council meeting telling those assembled, "There will be no liquor on the Square."

He headed back toward Highway 71 and parked at Bruner's.

"Whiskey sour," he told the bartender. "Pour a drink for yourself."

"Too early in the day for me."

"Pour yourself a Pepsi then." Alex looked around. The place was almost deserted. "What can you tell me about Erin Ames?"

"If you figure that one out, you're in line for the Nobel prize."

"She's complicated?"

"Why else would a dame wear high-fashion clothes here in Clarinda? They don't even wear that kind of stuff in K.C. Walking around in high heels. Sheesh!"

"They say she has money."

"So they say. I wouldn't know."

"What's her history? Married? Divorced?"

"What is this, twenty questions?"

"Oh, just curious." Alex paid for the drinks with a five-dollar bill and said mechanically, "Keep the change."

"Like I said. Cut yourself in for the Nobel prize. She went off to marry some Air Force officer. Some say she did. Some say she didn't. That's ancient history and none of my business. She comes in here, has a drink, and leaves."

"She comes in here?"

"All the time."

"She's a lush?"

"Erin? Hell no. She drops in after work. She never has more than one drink. Sometimes she orders a Pepsi." He held up the can from which he sipped. "Thanks."

The information Alex developed at the nearby Ice House Lounge was much the same except the younger bartender knew nothing about an Air Force officer. The young man searched for and found a note pad in which he had written what he called, "Vintage Erin."

Alex said, "That's unusual. Why did you do that?"

"Maybe some day I will develop into a part-time writer. It's educational. There's always somebody trying to put the move on her. I wrote down some of her come-backs." He read from the notebook. " 'Go home to your wife, George.' Here's a cute one. 'Why would you want to go out with a lezzie?' She'd found out that's what the guy called her behind her back. She faced him. 'That's what you said about me, isn't it?' He came right back, 'So sue me. That's how you act.' In about a week, in comes a process server with a million dollar lawsuit complaint and hands it to the guy, charging him with slander. Of course it's a fake, but he doesn't know that. He almost lost his wig. Erin has guts. The guy's brother-in-law, Henry Leighton, is her boss over at Washington Savings and Loan. I'd give a quarter to know what he said."

Alex nodded and smiled. Eyes narrowed, he knew he'd found his mark. Erin Ames. He decided it would be a fatal mistake to approach her in a bar. He'd see her at the savings and loan and offer to buy her a drink. He'd mention that he needed to find a man to invest in the radio station. Maybe he shouldn't mention the radio station at the first meeting. He'd ask her to assist him in the search, for a finder's fee, all the while begging her to keep it confidential. Mostly, he'd play it by ear. If she agreed, they would meet at a different lounge. He didn't want the bartender to come out with "I see you found Erin," or some equally devastating remark.

He returned to the Square and strolled into Washington Savings and Loan and saw a fashionably dressed woman, probably mid or late thirties, her hair drawn back in a bun, wearing no makeup. *You can't miss her. She looks like a well-scrubbed farm girl in foxy go-to-meeting clothes.*

"Hello. I'm Alex Barca," he said glibly. "And I need your help." He paused for a long moment, staring into eyes of Lake Okoboji blue and of the same unfathomable depth. "I talked to some people in the bank and they mentioned that I should see you, that you could point me in the right direction. Could you possibly assist me?"

Erin dispatched a generous smile. "I will if I can."

"I'm looking for men who might be interested in a really outstanding investment right here in Clarinda."

Erin's chin came up as she appraised him. His gaze remained unwavering, something he must have practiced. "Investment?" she exclaimed as if the term was totally foreign to her. "Interesting."

Behind the counter Alex could not see her toes slip out of flat shoes and into highly polished heels. He allowed a confident smile to build and froze it. "If this isn't a good time to meet, I could come back. I see you have customers now."

"I am rather busy at the moment."

"I don't wish to interfere with your business. Would it be possible to meet here when you close? We could walk over to J's Pizza Lounge on the other side of the Square, perhaps have a cocktail or a Pepsi." He'd found a lounge on the square he'd missed earlier. *Pizza isn't precisely Presbyterian, eh, Signorina?* He gestured for emphasis and spoke slowly. "No obligation on your part—but you might earn a few hundred dollars as a finder's fee."

Erin's voice lowered. "Meet me here at four o'clock. I'll have the bookkeeping done by then."

She's following the bait. "Fine. I'll be back."

Erin realized it would be an important meeting and she wanted to look her best. War paint was certainly in order. At the first opportunity she phoned her friend at the pharmacy.

"Hello, R-ex. Has that non-allergenic lipstick I wanted to try come in?"

"Not yet."

"It hasn't? Okay." *Damned allergy.*

"There was someone in here asking about you. A slick out-of-town dude."

"I think he found me. Thanks, R-ex."

"Okay."

He stopped at the pharmacy too? Barca had mentioned stopping at the bank. Erin wondered if he'd explained the investment there. If the bank hadn't been interested—

Alex appeared promptly at four and they strolled to J's Pizza Lounge. Alex lingered at the door and watched Erin's flawless legs scissoring toward a table as she walked ahead of him. He took another long, hard lecherous look and followed.

Erin seated herself and debated whether to order a cocktail or a Pepsi. *One drink will not fuzz your mind. Now don't be stampeded.*

"Vodka Collins," she said.

Alex said, "I'm glad you decided—" *to follow the bait* "—to meet me. I think you'll find it interesting."

Erin smiled. "You mentioned the investment would be located here in Clarinda. I'm always interested in something that will benefit the town."

"Believe me. This will. Tell me, what do you think about television?"

"Everyone watches TV."

"Right. The problem with television is that only a few big stars pull in the viewing audience. Radio is more reliable. And radio serves the local community. It may not be as glitzy, but radio is tried and true."

Erin's face mirrored surprise. "This is about radio? We had a station here sometime back. It failed."

"That was yesterday. Ancient history."

"A radio station in Clarinda again? If Jake Cooper couldn't make a go of it, how do you propose—?"

Alex interrupted. "People are always selling radio short. Yet they listen driving to and from work. At a place of business a radio is always humming in the background. I noticed you had a radio on. I'll admit that radio isn't hot like it was. It isn't exclusive, but—" He waved a didactic finger for emphasis. "It's virtually a gold mine. Name a station that went broke lately. Even a tiny one with a small trading area. You can't. Not one with a glitzy format." He spread his hands. "You just can't."

She raised an eyebrow. "Other than Jake Cooper's station you mean?"

"You need expertise to run a station. I have it." His tone at once became conspiratorial. "There's no way to keep a lid on this—I beg you to keep it confidential. I have purchased the local radio station from Cordelia Cooper. The natural thing would be to float a public stock offering and entice local businessmen and citizens to join me. As shareholders they'd be good customers. We don't have that luxury. We're pressed for time and must limit ourselves to one man, possibly two men. They need to be large investors."

"It does sound interesting," Erin conceded.

"More than interesting, I tell you it's a once in a lifetime opportunity."

"With radio stations all around us, isn't the market already somewhat congested?"

"Not at all." He lowered his voice to a whisper. "I have something planned. Keep it confidential. Where else in the world is a station better suited to feature Glenn Miller music than right here in Clarinda?"

"Now that does sound exciting."

"The Glenn Miller station of the nation!" His voice had raised and he at once resumed a whisper. "It's another spoke in the wheel leading to the birthplace of Glenn Miller. All we need is one or two investors. I could spend days looking for the right man or men. With your special knowledge of the financial community you could probably find the right man overnight. And earn a big finder's fee."

"Is that a flat fee, or a percentage?"

"Say five hundred dollars for any man you bring in who buys the big casino. Some man who would be willing to buy a one-fourth interest or more. Like I said, he comes in on the ground floor." He tore the corner off a napkin, wrote down a figure, and flashed it at her. He quickly wadded the paper scrap and stuffed it in his pocket.

"All I have to do is find a willing investor?"

"That's it."

"I might be able to do that."

"I know you can."

Erin finished her drink and rose. "I'm fascinated. I'll get to work on it."

"Remember," Alex whispered. "We need to keep it confidential."

"Mums the word."

He watched her beautiful legs marching toward the door. He kept focused on her until she was lost from view. *Hooked. But not landed.* He expelled a breath and said with unconcealed admiration, "There goes some lady."

"Hmmmpf! Her?" exclaimed the waitress who had come to retrieve the glasses. "She grew up on Twelfth Street. Gun Town. Her family didn't have the proverbial pot or a window to throw it out of. Her father was a bum. Her mother ran him off or he left them, depends on what you believe."

"She seems to have turned it around," Alex mused. The barmaid was obviously jealous.

"Much too suddenly," came the sullen and sarcastic response.

Alex refrained from further comment.

He drove at once to the Gun Town area and by six o'clock had rented a squalid room on Twelfth Street. The elderly landlady loved to talk and he engaged her in conversation.

"Do you remember the Ames family? Erin Ames? I understand they used to live around here."

"Sure, I remember the Ames family. Belle and her kid. The little urchin used to run around the neighborhood barefoot and in rags. Why are you asking about her?"

"No reason. I just wondered if money was important to her."

The landlady guffawed. "That's a rib tickler."

"Barefoot," Alex mused. That explained Erin's predilection for high-fashion clothes and high heels. "I guess they moved."

"As soon as they got two nickels to rub together. Belle bought a nice house on Nodaway with money left to her by her mother. From Atlantic they were."

He felt tempted to drive to Nodaway Street but Erin might see him. The last thing he wanted to do was give her the impression he was stalking her.

Erin would have seen him. Garden hose in hand, she stood watering the front lawn, debating whether or not she should make a phone call. At length she reached a decision, went indoors, and seated herself at the phone.

"Mrs. Cooper, this is Erin Ames. I don't know if you know me."

Cordelia's pulse quickened. *The daughter of Belle Ames calling me? That's a switch.* Her tone softened. "Yes, Erin, I know who you are." *The question is, do you know who you are?*

"I've been contacted by Alex Barca. He tells me that you have sold the radio station."

"So you're the pigeon," Cordelia said with amusement.

"Not I," Erin replied. "I'm supposed to find a pigeon."

"Nonsense. Let me ask you this. Would a falcon dive at a pigeon in anything but a straight line? If Alex Barca can find me in the whole of the United States, he certainly can find you in little old Clarinda."

Erin's shoulders rose and fell. She exhaled a weary breath. "I suppose so. If you put it that way."

"Just so you know, Erin. I still retain a half interest."

They talked at length about details. Cordelia explained about the escrow at the Page County State Bank.

"May I call you again?"

"Yes, girl. Any time," Cordelia said. "Remember Alex Barca is not from around here. We don't know a damn thing about him. You watch yourself, girl. Watch this way-too slick out-of-town dude."

Erin chuckled. "I think I've heard something like that before."

Cordelia replaced the phone and in a cupping motion rubbed her sallow cheeks. *Very interesting. Erin Ames, our paths finally cross. This should be very interesting. I wonder how much you know.* Cordelia felt a joyful optimism she hadn't felt in a long time.

Belle Ames casually listened to her daughter from the living room. Had she heard what she thought she heard? She padded in and asked, "Who were you calling, dear?"

Her mother always enjoyed hearing about business matters. The news about the radio station coming alive would interest her.

"I just spoke to Cordelia Cooper."

Belle Ames reacted as if slapped. "What?" she shouted. Color came into her features. "What could you possibly want with *her?"* She stormed out of the room.

Erin frowned. *Now what brought that on?* Of course her mother wouldn't tell her. Erin held the phone, entranced, until the buzzing on the line reminded her to return it to its carriage. Her eyes fixed on the wallpaper across the room. If Barca had sought her out, it was more than likely that he would ask whom she'd contacted. If she informed him that the prospects she spoke to were not interested, his ego might prompt him to conduct a personal follow-up to see if he could push them into sale territory. He'd mentioned a finder's fee. Maybe he'd try an end run to avoid paying the fee. One thing was certain, Cordelia did not relinquish the pertinent half interest until the money had been placed in escrow. If Alex Barca was looking for a buyer, it meant he was underfinanced. He didn't have the money. She reached for the phone.

"Harvey, this is Erin Ames." Harvey owned the very successful Harvey's Hardware. "Listen, this is confidential. I'm involved in a transaction with an Alex Barca who recently rolled into town. He's starting up the radio station again. If he contacts you about buying an interest, tell him you're not interested. You're out of money—a radio station is a bad idea. Whatever. If you hear anything, get back to me."

"But what if I really am interested?"

Her voice dropped an octave. "Har-vey," she scolded.

"All right. All right. Will do. I know you will square with me later."

"Of course."

"I know one thing. You've got me curious. The radio station again. That's wild."

"Thanks, Harv."

Erin made two more calls—to the owners of the variety store and the Super Valu—and made similar requests. She suspected that Alex would not wait until five o'clock of the following day to call her. Her estimate was on the mark. Early in the morning Alex requested that she meet him at Vaughn's Victuals during her first break.

He sat at a table far back and to the side. When Erin entered, more than one head turned in her direction. It had to be her fashion clothes and high heels. He wondered if she was aware that he had made her come to him. He watched her approaching with measured steps. She looked classy, acted a classy role, but she had to be just another dumb hick.

He did not rise and gestured for her to sit opposite. Without a preliminary greeting, he demanded, "Well, who have you contacted?"

"Whom," Erin corrected. "I spoke to three of the most promising men in the community. No luck. They have no imagination whatever."

"Keep trying," Alex said. "There has to be some man in the community who will take a flyer on an outstanding business. Some man who wants to get in on the ground floor. Some man who knows Clarinda needs a radio voice. Some man who can see that the Glenn Miller tie-in is a natural. Really it's a fantastic deal."

Erin nodded, aware that he had not asked for the names of the prospects. He kept emphasizing *some man.* Why didn't he ask for names of other prospects that he might contact?

"I'll keep trying," she said, aware now that he was more interested in her.

"It's better than money in the bank," Alex said and watched intently as she walked away. *Million dollar legs.*

Erin telephoned Cordelia at once. "I think you were right. I am the pigeon. It's easy to say it's only money, but I enjoy a bargain as well as the next MAN. Would you be willing to give me details?"

Cordelia chortled. "I knew you would call back. What a challenge. Hah. We'll put our heads together. Maybe we can outrun this sidewinder." *Erin, it's you who will have to do the running. Now, Cordelia, stop feeling sorry for yourself.*

Erin said, "At the very least we can make him squirm."

"Keep your eyes open. Remember, Erin, you're not toying with a night crawler." Cordelia felt her heart race. When the conversation ended she immersed herself in thought. Not all of it was fantasy. *I like that girl.*

When Erin again approached Alex, she wore a dour expression. "I feel really sad about not finding a man to invest in the station. I thought I could but I haven't had any luck. I wonder, would it be possible for me to be a substitute? I have a little money put away. I might be willing to invest."

"You?" Alex exclaimed in mock surprise. "I never thought for a moment that you would be interested."

"Well, I didn't either. Not really. But you are so enthusiastic, so persuasive—" She had decided not to flutter her lashes. One shouldn't go wading in deep water.

"You?" he said again.

"It's probably a mistake on my part. To me radio sounds exciting. But I know nothing at all about radio."

"The mistake is mine," he said graciously. "I never realized—I'm sorry. I should have asked you in the beginning. Generally investors are owners of businesses. You work—I'm sorry."

"The owners of businesses I contacted weren't interested," Erin said pointedly. "Not at all interested. Do you have a figure in mind?"

She listened patiently for his expansive presentation. Suddenly she rose. "That's out of the question," she said abruptly. "I'm sorry. That's too rich for my blood."

He watched her walking away and marveled. What a performance. He noticed she'd left her Pepsi unfinished. A nice touch. An alien idea surfaced. "We'd make a helluva team." He cautioned himself. "Remember, money is the priority." He shifted to watch her lovely legs as she crossed the street.

When he thought he had waited long enough to pique her interest, he phoned her at work. "Maybe we can negotiate," he said. "Would it be possible to meet again?"

"Perhaps."

This time they met at J's Pizza. Negotiations were repetitious, tenuous, and tedious. Once again he watched her walking away. *Bitch. She's playing the old cat-and-mouse game.* At the next meeting he would force her hand. He'd make liberal use of the word no. No. No! *No!*

He didn't have the opportunity. At the outset Erin made her final offer. A counterproposal. Having spoken with Cordelia, she knew precisely what Alex had paid for a half interest and she had computed the value of a one-third interest to the nearest cent—and made a small subtraction.

With an unyielding pose, little emotion on her well scrubbed face, she bit out the words, "Take it or leave it." Alex would lose two hundred fifty dollars if he accepted. It wasn't merely the money. She was rubbing his face in it and she knew he was painfully aware of that fact.

Alex nervously wet his thin lips and watched her heels clicking toward the door. "Don't be that way. Come back here. We have a deal."

She turned and slowly approached him, mounting just the hint of a smile. "And don't forget the finder's fee."

"No finder's fee," Alex said sharply. "Finder's fees are paid when the finder locates someone else—not himself."

"Herself," Erin corrected. "I distinctly recall you saying, 'No matter what.' That's what you promised. I'm the what. I'm the who."

"No," he said stubbornly. That's already been decided in court. There's a Michigan case on it. You need to find someone else to qualify."

"That's not what you said," she persisted. "Besides, This is Iowa, not Michigan." He had to be lying in his teeth about Michigan law.

"The same principle applies. Well, are you in or out? Make up your mind." *See how you like an ultimatum, bitch.*

She wanted to shout an enthusiastic "In!" but retained her calm demeanor. "All right," she said very slowly and in a low voice. "You win." It would be important for him to think he had won. "I'm in. It will take me a few days to get the money."

"Fair enough. But time is of the essence."

She almost said, "Let's shake on it," but realized she did not want to touch him. The mere thought made her cringe. She did not want to be betrayed by a look of revulsion and turned to go. *The game is over, Turkey.*

He watched her walk away with long, purposeful strides. "Delicious legs," he whispered as he watched the scissoring action. *Legs—there is always something at the other end.* When he had her money in hand—in escrow—maybe he could start thinking of her as a woman. He rubbed his thigh. Wonderful legs. He could almost *feel* them.

Although she had beaten down the price, Erin could not forget that Alex had reneged on the finder's fee. He hadn't come through with what he'd promised.

Fool me once, shame on you. Fool me twice, SHAME ON ME!

Eyes open, girl. She made a solemn promise. *There ain't gonna be a second time.*

Chapter Three

Anyone who resided in the United States during the last quarter of a century and listened to the radio would have heard the mellifluous voice of Downbeat Jackson. His voice was familiar if his name was not. After his Jive Five band of up to fourteen members had broken up, the peripatetic Jackson worked in radio stations "from the rockbound coasts of Maine to the sunny shores of Cal-i-for-ni-ay."

A person didn't need to be a certified public accountant to be aware of Jackson's relentless downward spiral. Each successive job had been a step down. Station owners were loath to retain an announcer addicted to alcohol, who sometimes put on an hour-long tape, locked the station door, and went "out to lunch." Federal Communication Commission directives mandated that a live body always be in control. Owners would tell him what a great guy he was, that he was fun to have around. Then the ax would fall. "I really like you. It's not personal. I just can't afford the risk of keeping you on."

Gray at the temples now, over the years Jackson had added a paunch and jowls, but he still had the ability to ad lib for twenty-four hours. His on-the-air ability could not be challenged.

"I've been on the wagon for thirty-five months, Mr. Barca," Jackson said. Beads of perspiration raised on his brow. His hands spread like a pair of hams. "You can check it out."

"I already have," Barca said curtly. He hadn't. The only reason he was hiring Jackson was because he came cheap and he was available. There might be a bonus. If the occasion demanded, Jackson would make an ideal fall guy.

"Can you work with a Glenn Miller format?"

"A Glenn Miller format? I can do that standing on my head."

"All the way back to the Mound City Blues Blowers?" Alex asked. He'd learned about the Blues Blowers since Cordelia Cooper sprung it on him and later made him feel like a fool.

Jackson leaned forward, his cherubic features intense. "Those records are scarce, virtually nonexistent. They'd have too much surface noise. We might be able to find some old recordings of when Glenn played with the Dorsey Brothers, Ray Noble, and Ben Pollock. Yeah. If I come here, I'll incur moving expenses. What kind of guarantee do I get? Twenty-six weeks?"

"Guarantee? One week," Alex said flatly. "No guarantees in this business. What do you have to move? Two suitcases?"

Wilted, Jackson chose not to speak. Actually he couldn't speak. *End of the line.* He'd known that sooner or later he'd come to the end of the line. What could he do? At his age he was too old to start a new line of work. New line of work? Hell, no one wanted a guy his age even with experience. They wanted kids who could rock and roll. He swallowed what felt like a whole lemon. "All right," he managed. "Sign me up. I'm on board."

What the hell, he'd go down in a blaze of glory. A guy couldn't do any better than go out with Glenn Miller music. "When do I start?"

"Ask me in a week," said Alex.

At that moment, across town, other plans were made that would dramatically affect station personnel. Erin Ames made a phone call.

"Cordelia," she said. "I need to make a trip to Omaha. I wonder, would you like to ride along?"

"Would I!" Cordelia exclaimed with enthusiasm. "I'd jump at the chance." *Over the moon if necessary.* "I need to level with you though. In addition to my stilts, I have to make frequent bladder stops."

Erin laughed. "I have one of those myself." She didn't inform Cordelia that she was picking up a check from her Omaha stockbroker in order to pay for her share of the radio station. Certainly it made abundant sense to be on good terms with the largest stockholder.

"My life is coming together," Cordelia exclaimed. "I've been taking vitamins and doing my exercises. Suddenly everything seems to be worthwhile. I don't drive much any more. Only around town here. I'll be ready whenever you are."

"A trip is a good way to outdistance depression," Erin observed.

"Who's depressed?" Cordelia demanded. "I'm fit as a fiddle and ready—oh well, never mind. I hope you're not depressed."

"Oh no."

When the conversation ended Erin wondered, had her voice betrayed her? That might have happened. Her thoughts had been focused on another trip she made to Omaha more than a dozen years ago. The remembrance engulfed her with unyielding persistence. Omaha had been the beginning of a dream. But a dream could suddenly turn into a nightmare.

She remembered that she had attended a convention and at the end of the day found herself attracted to spirited music emanating from the large hotel ballroom. She had seated herself near the door and glimpsed the bride dancing in the arms of the groom in the all-important ceremonial first dance of their marriage.

Presently their attendants joined them. She became aware that an Air Force officer had joined her.

"Enjoying the music?" he asked through a lopsided boyish smile.

"Very much."

"I have an idea," he said, elfin mirth dancing in his eyes. "The two of us. Let's crash the wedding."

"Not a good idea," she answered. "He's seen us sitting here." She gestured toward the hulking attendant at the door. "We would need an invitation."

"We might try the direct approach. Are you with me?"

"I'll try anything once," Erin said.

"Really?" His eyebrows arched.

"That's a firm maybe."

The officer—a captain—approached the burly bouncer and said with confidence, "We've been sitting here positively enjoying the music. Any way we can get inside—just to dance?"

The man stared at them appraisingly. "Thirty bucks gets you in—and you have the hospitality of the house. All you can eat and drink."

The captain opened his wallet and led her inside. While they were looking for a place to sit an old man wearing a white yarmulke approached, hand extended in welcome.

"Wayfaring strangers traveling from afar?"

"Not strangers for long, I hope," replied the captain.

"I am always happy to welcome the military. There was a time when I prayed that the American planes would drop their bombs on my head, but God had other ideas." A short laugh escaped him. "But let us not speak of rain. Welcome. Enjoy the hospitality of the house." He returned to his place at the end of the head table.

"He fascinates me," Erin said.

The captain nodded. "It's what he says. He makes one think."

Presently the old man moved to the center of the table and tapped a glass with a spoon. "Time for a speech," he said clearing his throat. "I know what it means to be free. Free to follow one's hopes and one's dreams."

A voice nearby said, "He was a prisoner of the Nazis. In a concentration camp."

The old man continued. "How difficult it is to grant that same freedom to someone else. It's hard. Now this has to be said. I call a spade what she is. When Sarah said she was going to accept a new faith, my heart broke. Part of it. Not all. I understand Robert's parents wanted to disown him because he is no longer

Catholic. Well, in this country people have a right to choose. Sometimes it's difficult. From the bottom of my heart I say Godspeed to the new Episcopalians. I wish them the joy and happiness I had on this day long ago—and I hope for them it lasts forever. Now," he said, turning to the band that had come all the way from New Ulm, Minnesota. "Turn on the Glenn Miller music. Grandpa wants to dance." The band struck up the refrain of "Moonlight Serenade." For a long moment the room fell reverently silent. Now the old man approached Erin. "Would you do me the honor? With your permission, captain."

The captain grinned and nodded. "You have it."

The old man was a rhythmic dancer, easy to follow. Erin said, "I thought you would prefer the bouncing old time music we heard earlier."

"I do. They brought in the band to honor me. What the young people really want is Glenn Miller. So I honor them. Look, everyone is dancing."

Erin learned that when the old man arrived in America he made his home in New Ulm where he played with the bands of Fez Fritsche, Six Fat Dutchmen, and Whoopee John. After his daughter and son-in-law were killed in a car crash, his granddaughter Sarah remained his only living relative. She had come to work for an Omaha radio station, a co-sponsor of the event.

When they stopped dancing, the old man held her hand and slowly looked her up and down. Erin appeared somewhat perplexed and embarrassed when he said, "I might have ignored you and the captain when you joined our celebration. Had I done so, I would not have been so richly rewarded."

He returned her to the captain and drew him aside. Erin did not learn until much later that the old man advised him, "You are a fool if you let her get away."

"Events are moving so swiftly I haven't had the opportunity to introduce myself," said the captain. "May I present Gaylord Haversham?"

Erin nodded. "May I present Erin Ames?"

They extended their hands in unison and laughed.

There was something about the captain that Erin liked. It was more than his mirthful eyes and boyish smile. The lopsided grin brought magic to his face. There was something in his manner that suggested good breeding. The bashfulness of a boy had been replaced by the confidence of maturity. His laugh was infectious, with happy lines wrapping his eyes with the warmth of a woolen blanket. When he donned his cap he wore it tilted back on his head at a rakish angle.

It was the kind of evening Erin hoped would never end. Captain Gaylord Haversham walked her to her room and said, "May I come in?"

"No," Erin said and at once relented. "Well, all right. But I'm drawing a line you cannot cross. If you cross the line, out you go."

"Would an officer and a gentleman do anything else?"

"I can think of a couple alternatives," she said. "Sit," indicating a chair. "This is the line." Her hand moved, as if to draw an imaginary line on the carpet. She seated herself on the bed, her back against the headboard, legs drawn up beneath her. Why the bed? she would ask herself later. Was that not an invitation? *Klutz.*

Captain Haversham was not a handsome man but when he grinned he became rather good looking. There was strength in his six-foot frame and yet a gentleness. She found it easy to be with him. He made her laugh. He loved to talk and she loved to listen.

"I'm glad I met you," he said.

"And I'm glad I met you."

"It's been a lovely evening. For me."

"For me too," she said.

She could love this man, she decided and wondered if her face betrayed her.

He rose and started for the bed.

"Stop," she shouted with such intensity that it surprised her. "You've crossed the line!"

He halted abruptly. "It's getting late. Thank you for a lovely evening." He turned, opened the door, and without looking back, walked out and closed it behind him.

Eyes on the door, she waited for him to knock. She waited for him to return. She waited. And waited. A wave of regret washed over her. She hadn't treated him right. She wanted to phone and apologize. Then she realized she did not have his phone number. He might not even be a guest at this hotel. The realization did nothing to assuage her guilt. On the other hand, he should have known the rules and not dared to cross the line. Rules were not meant to be broken. Except when they were.

Eventually she fell asleep and was awakened early in the morning by a rap-tapping on her door.

"Room service."

"I—I didn't order room service."

"Room service."

"Just a minute" She walked to the door, unlocked it, and seated herself on the bed. "It's open," she shouted. "Just put the tray—"

She halted. There stood Captain Haversham, bearing a steaming pot of coffee and enough food for six.

He saw her sitting cross legged on the bed. He put down the tray, flung his cap on a chair, and leaped for the bed with such grace that he appeared to be flying. He drew her into his arms and kissed her firmly. "That's what I wanted to do last night," he said breathlessly. "I had to do it now, before you drew another line."

"The line is still there," she said awkwardly.

"No," he insisted. "The line vanished a minute after I left. Lines have a way of doing that. They're temporary. Look at the world. Yesterday's enemies are today's friends."

"Well, now that you *have* crossed the line," she said. "Are you going to serve breakfast or what?"

"I know I'd prefer what—but that darn line."

She drew her hand through her tousled hair. "I must look a fright."

"You look just fine to me."

"What you see is what you get," she said and instantly regretted her words. What was he getting? Her? Why didn't she keep her stupid mouth shut? *Klutz.* "I hope I'm not giving you the wrong impression. I *would* like breakfast in bed."

"Breakfast in bed, it is." He couldn't help staring at her flimsy pajamas.

Erin became aware of his gaze and wished she'd brought a robe, but she never in her wildest dreams imagined anything like this happening to her.

"Orange juice first?"

She nodded. "Please." Her hand swept through her hair again. "Do you serve breakfast in bed to every Jane you meet."

"No," he said. "And you're no Jane."

"Only after you cross the line?"

"Honestly, I didn't know what to expect. I was ready for you to toss me out. Really, I'm not much good at relationships. You bowled me over. I had to try."

She smacked her well-kissed lips. "You try very well." There was something adorable about him. Was it the almost brotherly informality? His boyish smile? When he looked at her, she felt her heart turn handsprings.

"If I hadn't crossed the line to kiss you, I would have regretted it forever. The only things we really regret in life are the risks we didn't take."

Time raced by and they had to say farewell. She supplied her address and phone number. He shook her hand and said "Good-bye" through a lopsided grin and promised, "I'll be in touch. I'll phone. I'll write."

She had returned home to Clarinda, expecting to receive a phone call that very evening, but the call never came. She decided he must be a letter writer and waited several days for a letter. The letter never came.

Erin squelched the memory of all that. She raised her gaze from the phone and wondered how she could resist sharing her innermost thoughts if she and Cordelia drove past the Omaha hotel that held so many pleasant memories? She decided she would risk driving around the hotel block and if Cordelia asked why she had done that, she would have a ready response. The trip with Cordelia Cooper would be long and wearying. There might be frequent stops. It would require a great deal of patience. Certainly it would not be necessary to dredge up old memories.

At the appointed time, a sprightly Cordelia clicked toward the car on her crutches, obviously feeling elated.

"I'm glad you invited me on this outing, Erin. You can't know how I've been looking forward to it."

Erin toyed with the radio and failed to find a satisfactory program. She punched in a tape. "Wouldn't it be nice if we could dial in our own radio station and listen to Glenn Miller?"

"That would be nice," Cordelia said. She reached out and touched Erin's arm. "I need to say this. I didn't pressure you in any way to buy into the station. It's possible that you might lose your entire investment. I hope you don't blame me."

"I know I can lose my entire investment," Erin said.

"With this Alex Barca it's even likely."

"I hope not," Erin said.

"I know I don't trust Barca. We know nothing about him."

"I know he weaseled out of paying me a finder's fee. All because I didn't find someone other than me. He quoted Michigan law. He might be from Michigan."

Cordelia made a mental note to call Chief Wendinger and tell him, "Find out what is pending against Alex Barca in Michigan. Leave no sturgeon unturned." She smiled inwardly and wondered if the chief would find humor in the word she substituted for stone.

"How's your mother, Erin?"

"Retired. She has her card club and there's bingo. She cooks my supper, which is nice."

"And your father?"

"I never really knew my father. Mother had me a little later in life. What I know about my father is what I've heard. After a while, what I heard almost becomes almost a memory. I don't know were he is, or if he's even alive."

A disagreeable memory caused Cordelia's mouth to draw tight momentarily. *She doesn't know.* Cordelia lost herself in her own thoughts.

Erin drove in silence. It had been gracious of Cordelia to inquire about her mother.

Suddenly Cordelia spoke up. "Time to pee."

A Texaco service station loomed ahead. "I purposely didn't fill the tank before we left so I could stop for gas."

It was not the last stop they made. At length they arrived in Omaha. As she had planned, Erin drove around the hotel to spook whatever ghosts still lurked there.

"We used to come to Omaha a lot," Cordelia said. "Jake would meet with car dealers, broadcasters, theater owners—whatever association he happened to be involved in at the moment. I rather miss that. I hope I don't go maudlin on you, living old memories."

Erin said, "That's what I promised myself I wouldn't do."

"I didn't realize we are so much alike."

Erin located the electronic store that represented one of the reasons for the trip. She drove past and said, "I'd like to buy something for you. Let me treat you to a new pair of shoes. Yeah, I know, you don't walk a lot."

Shoes? Does she know about the shoes? "You'd be surprised how rough I am on shoes."

"I could drop you at the front door. I have an errand that won't take long. I'll be back."

Someone buying shoes for me? That's a switch. "Erin, I appreciate the thought, but what would Herb and Eloise Schecter say if I hobbled into their store with a pair of foreign shoes? If you insist on buying me something, if it's all the same to you, I would prefer a hat. Can you possibly make it a hat?"

"A new hat it is. I'll drop you."

Erin shopped the electronic specialty store, purchased a briefcase, and tossed it into the trunk. When she returned to the hat shop, Cordelia stood preening, tilting her head to get a better view of the large brimmed hat adorned with a single feather "Isn't this outrageous?"

"It's classic," said the saleslady.

"I love that hat." Erin said. "It's really you. Bold enough, daring enough, to be you."

"I'll take it," Cordelia told the sales lady. She said to Erin, "Now you must allow me to treat you to lunch at the Stockyard Inn. But first we need to stop and see an old friend. It's a place where Jake and I used to buy antiques."

The antique shop required a drive beyond the high-rent district, even beyond the low-rent district. They approached a dilapidated wooden building that needed paint. The windows were covered with grime, appearing as if they had not been washed for years.

"Hello, Abe," Cordelia caroled. "Are you still kicking?"

"Still kicking," said a short gnome of a man who limped out of a dark corner. "Mrs. Cooper, is that you?"

"None other. In the flesh."

"I can't believe my tired old eyes. Cordelia Cooper back in my shop. Has the sun come up in the west? Whatever did you do with all the antiques I sold you and Jake?"

"Still got them. Three basement bedrooms full. Didn't have kids. Had to use the bedrooms for something. We had antiques." Cordelia laughed from her depths. "That's a good one if I do say so myself. Listen, Abe, do you have any old seventy-eight phonograph records? Early jukebox era. Glenn Miller, if you know what I mean."

"There's a stack in the corner in my back room. Gathering dust. I can get them."

"Lead the way. I ain't helpless."

"You're the first real customer I had in a while," Abe said. "Now I get mostly out-of-towners. Old customers. Word of mouth."

Erin blew off the dust and exclaimed, "This has to be an omen. Glenn Miller right on top."

"Where would you expect to find Glenn Miller except on top? How much for the lot, Abe?"

"How about twenty bucks?"

"Okay. We're starting up the radio station again. I thought we might play some of the original platters."

Abe shook his head. "Not these. There's too much surface noise. Tell you what, why don't you just take the records and give me thirty dollars worth of advertising on your station. When are you going on the air?"

"Any day now. I'll send you a postcard so you can tune in."

"Just like old times," Abe mused.

"Old times, hell," Cordelia declared. "I stopped the clock sometime back."

"Let me know how that works. Be careful," Abe warned when Erin picked up a stack. "If you drop them they shatter like glass. Let me get you some boxes. I don't want to have to sweep out broken records. I swept the place just last year. Or was it the year before? I don't want to do it again."

"Look around the store, Erin. Make a list of what Abe has. You've just sold your first ad. You'll have to write the copy." Cordelia stalked to the door and waved a crutch. "You take care of yourself, Abe."

When they reached the Stockyard Inn, Erin announced, "I know I'm driving but I'm going to have a cocktail."

Cordelia said, "I know it will make me pee, but I'm going to have one too."

"You're incorrigible."

"Just like you."

"Hah."

Cordelia became pensively silent with an unfocused faraway look. At length she felt Erin touch her arm. "I'm sorry," she said. "I was reminiscing. Jake used to bring me here." She sighed wistfully. "The dear man. He used to lie to me and tell me he had never loved anyone else as much as he did me. But I'd sometimes catch him looking at the picture of his first wife. That was in the early days of our marriage. Later I came to believe what he said was true."

"You were lucky. You were married a long time."

"Thirty-seven years to a wonderful man. After I lost full use of my pins, we always thought I'd be the first to meet Saint Peter. It didn't turn out that way. Still, I have no regrets. Except one."

Erin gazed at her with a somewhat incredulous look. "Only one?"

"I wish I would have had a daughter." She stopped before she blurted an innermost thought. *Like you.*

"It might have turned out to be a son."

"No such luck either."

"You might have adopted."

"Jake's first wife couldn't give him a child. She died of leukemia. When I couldn't conceive, Jake thought God had decided that he would have no children." *At least that is how he tried to play it. He knew and I knew there were other reasons.* "Jake tried to compensate for that in other ways."

"Thirty-seven years?" Erin marveled. "I didn't get thirty-seven days."

"You're still young. Whatever you did get is better than nothing. They say it is better to have loved and lost than never to have loved at all."

"I didn't lose his love. I lost him. In a plane crash."

"Here we sit. Two old crocks, wallowing."

"Speak for yourself," Erin said. "I'm not a crock. I have put forth some effort convincing people that I'm a fruit jar."

Cordelia laughed so outrageously that everyone looked at her.

Erin said, "I think we just crossed the line."

Following lunch Erin purchased some cosmetics that the sales lady insisted were non-allergenic and "won't give you a bit of trouble."

"They better not," Erin said. "A rash that takes eight seconds to arrive takes eight weeks to disappear."

They made a final stop at the Piper Jaffray brokerage firm where Erin picked up a check to be deposited in the Page County State Bank to pay for her purchase of stock in the radio station.

"You know," Cordelia said. "I feel apprehensive about you buying stock in the station. I set a rather aggressive price."

"I would rather pay too much for something that's good than to pay too little for something that's not."

Approaching the Shenadoah junction, Cordelia said. "Hair of the dog. I need another drink. The last one has worn off. Are you with me?"

"With you through thick and thin." Erin turned the wheel. "Now if I get arrested for drunk driving on the way into Clarinda—"

Cordelia interrupted. "If that happens in Clarinda, just you leave Wilbur to me."

At the end of the day, an exhilarated Erin halted her car near Cordelia's front door. Cordelia stepped out and said, "Now Erin, don't you be a stranger. You come and see me any time. You don't need to call ahead. Just come. As far as I'm concerned, you're family." *If you only knew.* Cordelia gave her a searching look. Alcohol had loosened her tongue but she was glad she hadn't blurted, *You're the daughter I never had.* Private thoughts ought to remain private.

Erin telephoned Alex Barca and asked him to meet her at J's Pizza Parlor. She arrived a deliberate seven minutes late, walking with a jaunty gait, carrying the newly purchased briefcase. When she put it down flush with the table top, a tiny spool inside began to turn, recording their conversation.

"You arranged for the money in a hurry," Alex said approvingly.

"Let's go over the details," Erin said. "You told me I wouldn't get a finder's fee."

"That I did," Alex said with ample satisfaction. "There will be no finder's fee."

Erin waved to the bartender. "Gertie, we need some refills over here." She scratched notes on a napkin.

Alex marveled at the way she took charge. It was almost masculine the way she ordered drinks. "You certainly know how to do business."

Erin suppressed a smile. "Whatever else might be said about me."

Chapter Four

In the early days, the building housed a stable. Then the place became a repair shop for carriages, with horse stalls relegated to the rear. With the advent of horseless carriages, the building became a garage, sales and service. Not long after Jake Cooper purchased the building, he noticed that on an extremely humid day or when he hosed down the planks, along with the aroma of oil and grease he detected the odor of horse manure. One weekend he washed down the planks with formaldehyde solution and called in carpenters to lay a new floor over the planks. The floor had been carpeted when the building became a radio station. Now, when the rotund Downbeat Jackson plumped along the corridor, the floor shook.

"Take up the carpet," he cracked. "This floor is made for dancing."

Had there been dancing, a larger group might have collected on the sidewalk in front of the plate-glass window that extended across the face of the building. Only six people stood outside watching. From their location they could see over the heads of the spectators seated in the two rows of the audience area, over the two desks for receptionists, and through the glass of the soundproof broadcasting booth on the left. Along with Downbeat Jackson in the booth, the engineer sat with his back to the crowd. Behind the booth, at the distant end of the building, Alex Barca had installed himself in the deluxe suite, a rather plain office when measured by modern corporate standards. On the right were offices formerly occupied by car salesmen.

At one of the desks in the reception area lounged a willowy blonde, Jennifer Otley. A recent graduate of Clarinda High School, Jennifer had been homecoming queen. Accentuating her beauty, a flawless complexion over high cheeks had led some to conclude erroneously that she represented the stereotypical "beauty without brains." In Jennifer's case, it was a matter of immaturity and a lack of motivation. She had opted not to attend college because as she variously stated: (1) She had not settled on a major. (2) She could not decide which college to attend. (3) She needed to save money for college expenses. (4) Her applications had netted no invitations. (5) She hadn't actually applied. (6) She needed time out.

Jennifer possessed a certain ingenuity and had developed a system whereby the receptionists would hold up a flashcard in the shape of a bell to tell the announcer to pick up the phone for an on-the-air call in case the caller had not properly dialed the phone in the booth.

At the other desk sat Decorah Gordoncamp, called Doris by nearly everyone, hired to be a problem solver, erstwhile program director, and all-around girl Friday. No longer a girl, she had the salt-and-pepper hair that arrived during early middle age. Well known around Clarinda, folks described her as "You know, the mother of that delinquent." Her pleasant oval face provided a contrasting facade to the churning resentment within her depths, usually well concealed. She accepted President John Kennedy's pronouncement, "Life is basically unfair," but why in her case did life have to be so totally and wretchedly unfair? It certainly didn't help matters that every time something in town was stolen, Chief Wilbur Wendinger always included her son Keith among the usual suspects rounded up for interrogation.

When Sparks the engineer turned, folks saw a man with thick round spectacles, hair uncombed, in need of a shave. His grooming habits had prompted Doris to observe, "Why doesn't he clean up his act, starting with washing his face?"

With tension mounting, the moment approached when radio station KNDA would shine, glow, and become a beacon of light in a troubled world.

Downbeat Jackson turned to Alex Barca. "Do you want to take the opening, boss?"

"No," said Alex. "That's why we have you."

Jackson carried his ever-present baton, a prized possession that he waved to pretend he was leading the band. He became adept at faking the moment of the actual downbeat. Closer inspection revealed the baton was much heavier than an ordinary baton, more like the swagger stick carried by British officers at colonial outposts in the days of empire. Technically it wasn't a swagger stick. In reality it was the tanned penis of a Wiese and Son Hereford bull to which an ornate handle had been attached. Presented to Jackson by the National Hereford Association at a formal banquet, he would sometimes whap the table to generate enthusiasm, such as when he conducted an on-the-air auction.

The floor vibrated as he ran into the booth, whacked the table twice to get the attention of the imaginary orchestra, and said, "Radio station KNDA, Clarinda, Iowa, a Jake Cooper station, is on the air. Now—" His baton came up. "Glenn Miller!"

"Moonlight Serenade" filled the studio and went wafting over Missouri, Iowa, Kansas, and Nebraska. When the theme ended, without a word, Downbeat played another Miller recording.

"That was the famous Glenn Miller rendition of 'In the Mood.' Now if you're in the mood for a drive up Omaha way and have a hankering for antiques, you just stop at Abe's antique shop and visit with Abe who will tell you that he is also an antique."

Designed to entice area people to Omaha, the voice of Downbeat Jackson blanketed Omaha and soared far beyond. As instructed by Alex Barca, Sparks had KNDA radio broadcasting at the full power of fifty thousand watts, which had originally been authorized when Jake Cooper started the station. Current FCC specifications limited broadcasting to five thousand watts.

On the sidewalk outside, onlookers had grown to ten, then dwindled to three. Inside, among those seated on the two rows of spectator seats, Erin Ames rose, walked toward a desk, and shook hands with Jennifer Otley.

"Hello. I'm Erin. I own one-third of this radio station."

"Pleased to meet you," Jennifer murmured.

Alex Barca overheard the exchange and frowned. After Erin continued to the desk of Doris Gordoncamp and made the same assertion, he stepped forward.

"Come to my office. I have something for you."

Erin followed. She assumed he would present her with the stock certificate she'd been pestering him about for days.

He did not wait for her to be seated and remained standing. "I know you've been waiting to receive this," he said with a smirk, and handed her the document.

Erin glanced at the certificate and attempted to remain calm. "Sixty shares?" she exclaimed, completely shocked. "Only sixty shares?" Her lips turned down in an angry slash. Her hand moved swiftly to the phone on his desk. She spun it around and spanked the buttons.

"Cordelia, this is Erin. I'm standing in the office of Alex Barca here at the station. How many shares are there in the KNDA Corporation?"

"Three hundred," Cordelia answered. "Three hundred shares issued and outstanding."

"Of which you sold fifty percent?"

"That's correct. Barca has one hundred fifty shares representing a half interest, which he may sell part of, to not more than two investors."

"Thank you, Mrs. Cooper," Erin said with formality. She put down the phone and made steely eye contact with Barca. "There are three hundred shares outstanding. As owner of a one-third interest, I should receive one hundred shares. Where are the other forty shares?"

Aware that she knew Cordelia's number without looking it up in a book, Alex raised an eyebrow. "One-third?" he questioned. "Where do you get one-third? You purchased only twenty percent. That is what I just delivered."

Erin's voice sharpened. "What? How can you say that? I bought a one-third interest!"

"I'm sorry. I beg to differ. You bought twenty percent."

"I bought one-third," Erin persisted. A hot tongue of anger ascended her spine, crimson spread over her neck and diffused across her cheeks bringing heightened color. She felt a simmering at her armpits. Her fingers clenched. "One-third. I distinctly remember writing on a napkin. I still have it."

"Anyone can write on a napkin. I remember the transaction clearly. I guess it is my word against yours." His smirk deepened.

"Is that the way you want it?" she shouted.

"That's the way it is," he said calmly.

"Think it over. I demand the one-third I paid for."

"There was nothing written on your check—no indication that it was for one-third of the stock. I'm sorry you don't understand business."

I understand business well enough. So will you before I am through. Erin ran out of the office, slammed the door, and stormed down the corridor.

Alex raised an exultant fist in triumph and jerked his arm down sharply. "Yes!" And again. "Yes!"

His lips twisted in a sardonic sneer. "Ah, my bucolic prairie princess. Now you know how the game is really played."

If Erin did nothing, another forty shares were his. Then he would have ninety and be the second largest shareholder. If she complained to attorney Orville Keane, who seemed like a slow-rolling, agreeable country lawyer, and they settled by splitting the difference, he would still net twenty shares. If she wished to play the cloth-headed milkmaid and sue, by the time she reached the inside of a courthouse, he would have gathered his chips and been long gone. *Fan-doubleass-tastic!*

Whatever sounds soared out on the airwaves could also be heard throughout the office. Aware now that Cordelia Cooper's voice was being broadcast, Erin paused to listen. She realized the spot must have been recorded earlier. She had just spoken with Cordelia.

"This is Cordelia Cooper. I don't know what you've heard about Planned Parenthood, and I'm a member, but my interest, my goal, is that every child who arrives in this world is a wanted child. I'm speaking on behalf of our Save the Child Foundation. Stop in and visit with us. There is no pressure on you to make a decision. The information is free. There are couples waiting to adopt. When that happens, you really save two lives—"

By the time Erin reached the street the simmering at her armpits had halted. She inhaled a deep breath and allowed a hint of a smile to animate her features. She would allow Alex his temporary triumph. *Enjoy it while it lasts, turkey. Until tomorrow.*

She strolled to the savings and loan awash with mixed emotions. Investing in the radio station reflected a monumental change in her life. She had no time for misgivings, for guilt feelings, for wondering if she'd made the correct choice. She had to remember that every situation in life had a beginning and an end. For the loan officer job at Washington Savings she had been prepared. In an earlier job at the bank she began by preparing all the forms, applying herself, learning more every day. When the bank's loan officer wanted to play golf, go fishing, or attend conventions, she had eased into the position on a part-time basis. Soon customers were coming to her. It was said of the late loan officer at Washington Savings and Loan that he had served with General Washington at Valley Forge and his heart had remained cold ever since. As logical as it was for Henry Leighton to hire her to fill the void, he needed someone to say no if prudence dictated. She had discovered early on that Henry had other motives. He had proposed marriage at least twenty times. Of one thing she was certain, she did not wish to be a Mrs. Henry. Her mother had mentioned that Henry was the right age, a personable, clean-cut man from a good family, on the way to becoming wealthy. She had explained to her mother that Henry had inherited only forty percent of the business. He hadn't identified the other stockholders, but mentioned that if the other stockholders acted in concert they could replace him.

"You would make a lovely couple," her mother had insisted. "He's a nice-looking man."

Erin had planned what she would tell Henry Leighton now. She gestured for him to sit at his desk and confided, "If things come down the way I expect, I may need to tender my resignation."

"You're not leaving town?" His expression deepened from concern to disappointment.

She smiled faintly. "No. Nothing like that."

Not leaving town. He sucked in a breath and grinned with relief. "For a minute there you had me worried." He had never confided to her his plan to expand the business with a branch office. Of course he would want her to train new personnel, or perhaps manage a branch office.

Erin went on, "If you are interested in me staying part time, I might be able to work out something."

"Interested, Erin? That's an understatement. I'll be happy to work something out. If you could work even a half day, I'd appreciate it. Gosh, I knew this would happen some day. You're not going back to the bank?" *Not getting married?*

"No. It's something I've been working on; another job. A position where I have a financial interest. I'll tell you more when I'm certain."

She's not getting married! "Working two jobs would mean putting in a lot of hours."

"It's only time, and I have time on my hands. A lot of people work sixty or seventy hours. Pharmacists, for example."

Him again. "Don't talk about pharmacists to me." He didn't want to think of her friend R-ex for even an instant. "You know I think the world and all of you." He hesitated in order to regroup his thoughts and mused, "Maybe if you are exposed to my charm on only a part-time basis I'll have a better chance." He placed a finger to his lips and twitted, "If I fired you—"

Erin saw "that look" and said curtly, "Don't talk nonsense."

"It wouldn't be nonsense if you married me—" He broke off abruptly when he saw her frowning. Her hands had come to rest on her hips.

"I'll keep you informed."

Erin attempted to phone Cordelia to explain her terse conversation, but Cordelia did not answer her phone. They had missed seeing each other by only five minutes when Erin walked to Washington Savings and Cordelia parked in front of Schecter's shoe store.

"Is it that time again?" Eloise Schecter asked.

Cordelia laughed. "With all the dancing I'm doing, it's a wonder I could stay away this long." She glanced searchingly at Herb.

Herb grinned. "I'm still on the wagon. Thanks to you and Jake."

"No," Cordelia said sharply. "Thanks to you and your own will power. And good common sense."

Herb bobbed his head. "You know what I mean."

He remembered how it had been. He had been totally besotted when his tearful wife phoned Jake Cooper, sobbing, "We can't make the payment this month. Herb is drunk again."

Jake had come to the store, grabbed him by the collar, and given him a swift kick in the butt. "Straighten up. You're coming with me!"

He'd found himself locked in a cell in Jake's barn where he sobered, and suffered withdrawal, and endured three square meals a day liberally laced with wine or brandy. Although his meals were tasty at the outset, in a short time he couldn't bear the sight of food laced in alcohol. Then nutritious food began to arrive.

"How long are you going to keep me here?" he cried. "You can't do this. It's kidnapping. I want to see an attorney."

In response, Jake had brought out Judge Lars Jennings Strand. They paused to talk outside the barn where Herb could hear.

"Judge," Jake posed. "You know Herb Schecter. If his wife asked a friend to lock him up till he gets dry, would that friend be in trouble?"

"I don't see how," said the judge. "He's drinking himself to death. We'll bury him in sight of a year. I'd look on it as a kindness."

"Dead within a year? I guess I'll have to find a new man for Eloise and the kids. You know I have to protect my investment."

"If he doesn't want to save himself, his wife ought to have somebody lock him up."

"Come in for a snort, Judge. I've got some bottled in bond that's mighty tasty. Say, are you going to run again?"

All during their conversation, Herb remembered that locked inside the barn there hadn't been a peep out of him. Jake explained later, "I allowed you to hear not only an attorney but also a judge. Maybe if you shape up, Eloise may want to come out and pay you visit. She could come out some evening. You could spend some quiet time together. But it's time you'll have to earn."

"And see me like this? And embarrass me?"

"She's seen you worse. Falling down, stinking drunk. I figure she's entitled to a last look of what you might look like if you tried."

Jake didn't tell him that he'd been spending at least a half day at the shoe store, teaching Eloise how to set up books, how to apportion advertising, how to write copy, how to run promotions. Herb would have been totally demoralized if he realized he wasn't needed, that Eloise could run the business without him.

The evening she came to visit him, Eloise mentioned that Jake was helping her in the store. No one intruded on their privacy. At the appointed time Jake knocked politely and allowed Eloise to leave.

"I'm ready to go home too," Herb had insisted. "I've learned my lesson.

"Maybe you have, and maybe not. We'll see."

Jake brought in a pint of whiskey and a half-dozen bottles of beer. "If you can resist the temptation, we might reconsider. That is, if Eloise wants you back."

Later, Jake inspected the bottles. The caps appeared intact, but close inspection revealed the beer bottles had been filled with water.

Jake shook his head. "I guess you ain't learned your lesson."

Herb remembered. Eventually he had been able to resist temptation. He hadn't taken a drink since.

"Your husband put me through hell, Cordelia." He helped her slip into a new pair of shoes.

"You put yourself through hell," Eloise countered. "But not as bad as the hell you put me and the kids through."

"How do you like the shoes?"

"Fine. I'll take them." Cordelia reached into her purse for a pen and began to write in her checkbook.

"We're keeping up our end," Herb said. "The tradition you started—giving shoes to kids who couldn't otherwise attend the prom. We kept up the tradition you started with Erin Ames. If you hear of anyone who needs prom shoes, you let us know."

"Will do," Cordelia said. "I like the way you handle it." Her voice lowered. "By the way, don't ever mention anything about that to Erin. And don't mention that I even know about it, or so help me I'll come in and skin you both alive." She laughed heartily.

Not long after Cordelia returned home, Erin called to apologize for her terse phone call. She didn't reveal she had a plan to bring Alex to his knees. That could wait until she succeeded.

The next morning Erin decided Alex had gloried in victory quite long enough. She walked into his office accompanied by Orville Keane.

She said, "This is my attorney."

"We've met," Alex acknowledged.

"I understand there's some dispute about the stock," Orville began.

"Not that I know of," Alex said blandly. "We had a little misunderstanding. For a while Erin was under the wrong impression, but that matter is settled."

"It's far from settled, Mr. Barca," Erin said sharply.

"You're representing Erin?" Alex charged.

"I am."

"How can you do that?" Alex demanded. "You are the corporate attorney. You are the attorney for Cordelia Cooper. How can you represent Erin as well? Isn't that a flagrant conflict of interest?"

"No, I represent the *situation,*" Orville said evenly. "All the parties are aware and have given their permission. If even the slightest hint of a conflict arises, I shall recuse myself. Now, I understand your position is that Erin purchased twenty percent of the corporate stock of this station."

"That's correct. There's really nothing to understand." Alex shoved out his chin. "That's the way it is."

"You couldn't be mistaken? Think it over a minute."

"No sir. Absolutely not. I don't make mistakes." Alex realized his absurd overstatement. "At least not about the sale of KNDA stock."

"Could you possibly have forgotten—with all the activity of starting up?"

"Absolutely not," Alex insisted. "I have an excellent memory. We went over the agreement several times, the last time being when she presented her check. The check was for twenty percent. I'm certain the check contains no such notation."

"Twenty percent?" Orville pressed. "There's no mistake?"

"Absolutely positive," Alex asserted. "I'm as positive as I can be."

"Definite?"

"Definitely."

"I have something I want you to listen to," Orville said. He reached into his leather satchel and brought out a small player-recorder and pressed the play button.

Erin spoke up. "I think you will remember our final meeting at J's Pizza place. I think you will remember our conversation."

They listened.

Alex paled. *The bitch was wired!*

He heard Erin say on tape, "Now let's go over the details. You told me there wouldn't be a finder's fee."

"That I did. There will be no finder's fee."

Erin's voice continued, "Gertie, bring us a couple cocktails. The usual. On me. Now, Mr. Barca, I'm handing you a check. It's for a one-third interest in Radio Station KNDA, is that correct?"

"Yes, a one-third interest. Why the formality?"

"Do you wish me to date the check on the fourteenth or the fifteenth?"

"The fifteenth will be fine. Make it out to KNDA Escrow. I'll see that you receive your stock certificate promptly."

Orville turned down the volume. His expression hardened. He held Alex in a penetrating gaze. "Well?"

Alex swallowed with difficulty and rubbed sweating palms. Attempting a look of sheer innocence, he managed, "I'm wrong. I'll say it. I'm wrong. I don't know how I could have made a mistake like that, but I'm wrong. The transaction apparently was for one-third. I'll have to make that right."

"A moment ago you said you were certain. You hadn't made a mistake. You hadn't forgotten. You insisted it was definite. In a court of law that's perjury."

"W-Well," Alex said nervously as beads of perspiration formed on his brow. "Anyone c-can m-make a m-mistake."

Orville said, "You did. You made a big one." He turned up the volume on the tape recorder and heard Erin say, "Gertie, we need some refills over here."

"You certainly know how to do business."

"Whatever else might be said about me."

Orville switched off the recorder. He saw Alex staring at it in longing contemplation, debating. Orville quickly withdrew the recorder and returned it to his satchel. "We have a proposal. We will see that this recording remains in a safe place. Next, Erin comes to work for the station—at her current salary. You will cooperate with her in scheduling so that she may continue at her present employment on a part-time basis. Further, don't even think about making life miserable for Erin. There will be no retaliation, no harassment of any kind. *Do you agree?"*

"Yes, yes," said a pale and stricken Alex Barca. *Bitch.*

"I do so want our relationship to be amicable, Mr. Barca," Erin said. "I can start in a week. As far as I am concerned you merely had a memory lapse."

"A memory lapse. Y-Yes. Yes." Alex felt his hands trembling. "I don't know how this could have happened."

With the tape in their possession there was nothing he could do.

Orville demanded, "Can you live with these terms?"

Alex said in a whisper, "Yes."

Orville continued. "I wouldn't advise looking for the tape. We have numerous copies in safe and strategic locations. If anything happens to either of us—"

"I understand," Alex said

Orville walked Erin to her car.

"Do you really have copies of the tape?" she asked.

"No."

"Make some," she said. "I want one for my bank lock box and one at home. You also need an extra. There's more to Alex Barca than meets the eye. We can't have him getting any ideas, not after you fed him one."

"Oh, I don't think I fed him anything he didn't think of himself. All right, I'll have copies made."

Erin drove at once to the residence of Cordelia Cooper, knocked twice, and entered. "Hey," Erin exclaimed excitedly. "Let me tell you how we backed Alex Barca into a corner and peed all over him!" She laughed.

"Come in. Come in, girl. Tell me all about it. I simply love the way you express yourself. Sit here, child."

In the serenity of his office, a disturbed Alex Barca buried his face in his hands. Muttering, he lowered his hands, made a fist, and drove it into his palm. "Bitch. I wish I'd never met you, bitch!"

Chapter Five

Public service announcements served a valid purpose and promoted rapport with radio listeners. However, nothing could be more boring for an announcer.

Downbeat reminded himself to read the announcement with interest. "Here's an urgent message from Luella Brown for her sister Evelyn. Come home at once. It's my night to wear the girdle."

Alex Barca leaped out of his chair as if spring activated. He waved Downbeat out of the broadcast booth. "What kind of stupid trick was that?" he shouted in unrestrained fury. "It's pure idiotic cornball. Do you really want this job? One more break like that and you're through. Understand?"

"B-But it's written down," Jackson said. He held out the pink telephone note.

"Yeah?" Alex retorted. "So what? Any damn fool can write a note. Do you believe in three dollar bills? Shape up or get out."

Downbeat swallowed with difficulty. "Sorry, boss. I'll try to do better." *Ask me about nine-dollar bills.*

"You'll do more than try." Alex continued to rave. "You will do better or I'll kick your ass out."

Doris felt his humiliation and could not look at Downbeat, fearing it would add to his discomfort. Jennifer Otley averted her eyes because she wanted no part of anything disagreeable.

Downbeat remembered he was on a tenuous one-week guarantee, in effect no guarantee at all. With every new job there came a confidence that he could remain sober. Even when the ax had fallen and he'd been discharged, for nearly three years he had managed to remain sober. However, if something outrageous happened, something totally unfair, like being kicked out of broadcasting, he wondered if he could handle it without Nola. She had always been there to make rough spots smoother. How could he possibly endure a transition attempt alone? Alex had been treating him in a snide and demeaning way from the outset. There was no reason to expect that would change. He could expect the worst from Alex Barca. Something about Mr. Alex Barca bothered him. He decided to call on friends around the country to confirm his suspicions. Downbeat realized he had two choices. He could do nothing. Or he could muster his troops. He could circle his wagons. The corners of his mouth raised slightly and dissolved the look of dejection that anguished his large, cherubic features. He asked himself, "How do you circle one wagon?" Unaware that the use of self-deprecatory humor had lifted him beyond crisis, he realized he was not without resources. There might be a way to save his job if push came to shove. It was an avenue that cried out for exploration. He had to meet with Erin Ames. His urgent call to her at Washington Savings and Loan reflected more than quiet desperation.

"It's urgent business. Meet me at six-oh-three in the parking lot of the Ice House Restaurant."

Erin arrived a punctual two minutes late. As soon as she turned into the lot, Jackson stepped out of his car and approached her window.

He looked around furtively. "This place is too visible. We need to find a more secluded spot. Would you like me to drive?"

Before he could say "You wanna flip a coin for it?" Erin said, "I'll drive. Get in."

Jackson ran around the back of her car and had not properly seated himself and closed the door when the car lurched forward.

"Nice wheels," he said.

"It's a compromise," Erin said. "I should drive a Cadillac, but I can buy two new Buicks for the same price. Heels are hard on floor mats. When the floor mat goes, I buy a new Buick."

"That's very practical."

"Maybe not."

Erin drove to the highway and doubled back along the bypass to Miss Kitty's Saloon and Steakhouse. "This place isn't visible?" she teased. "Perhaps we will blend in with the travelers."

"I had to talk with you," he said, as worry furrowed his brow. "Thanks for indulging me."

A hostess seated them and presently a waitress appeared. "Would you like a drink before ordering?"

Erin said, "I'll have an Erin."

"Oh hi," the waitress said as recognition dawned.

"Diet Coke for me," said Jackson. "I'm on the wagon." He found it difficult to refrain from asking, what's an Erin? He had an answer when the waitress placed a beer in front of Erin, beer in a tapered pilsner glass into which had been dropped a single maraschino cherry.

Erin responded to his puzzled and somewhat bemused look. "It was meant to be derogatory. I won't explain it. Use your imagination. I think I have risen above it—and turned it around."

"That's what I did with my habit," Jackson said indicating his Coke. "Turned it around. I've been sober for nearly three years. I'm a reformed alcoholic."

"I didn't know. Sorry. I shouldn't have ordered a drink."

"Relax. I'm glad you did. Every time someone takes a drink within my reach I chalk up another victory."

"Congratulations."

"This is nice," he said. "I'm glad I didn't ask you for a date. You would have said no."

"You don't know that."

"Yes, I do. Look I'll get to it. I don't know what I'm doing at the station." He halted and began again. "I said that badly. Of course I know what I'm doing. What I don't know is, why I'm here. What is Alex Barca's angle?"

"Angle? I don't know." Erin paused. "Does he need an angle?"

He didn't tell her a friend had warned him about Barca's unsavory reputation. He'd kept his eyes open. "He's running the station on excess power—way beyond what the FCC authorized. Sparks is following his instructions. Is Alex deliberately trying to bring the FCC down on us? Calls are coming in from other stations. The secretaries have been ordered to tell callers that we are operating appropriately. They're told to say the manager isn't here, take their phone number, and say he will call them back. He never does. I'm afraid the government is going to come in here and close us down. It might take a year to reopen."

Erin frowned. "I see." In worried concentration now, she remembered that Barca could not be trusted. She had experienced that on two occasions.

Jackson spread his heavy hands. "My information is that Cordelia Cooper owns half the station, you own one-third, which leaves only one-sixth for Alex Barca. What's his angle? I've been around long enough to know he must have an angle."

"Maybe not. Maybe he's trying to settle down in a sensible small town like Clarinda."

"Alex? Nonsense. If he runs the station into the ground, does he think he can pick up the pieces for ten cents on the dollar?"

"Hmmm."

"What I mean, Erin—may I call you Erin?"

"Certainly."

"What I'm afraid of is that I'm set up to be the moth in his flame. A patsy. Am I going to be the guy who carried the message from Barca to Sparks? All I have is a lousy one-week guarantee." His hand came out toward her and quickly withdrew. "I need to know where I stand when push turns to shove. You and Mrs. Cooper control eighty-three percent—what I mean—I'd really like to stay and make my home here. Glenn Miller is my cup of tea. I don't want to go to some daytime religious station for minimum wage."

"I don't blame you." She regarded him and saw deep-seated anguish. "I will—"

"Stop," he said in a terse whisper, reaching out and touching her arm. "Don't move."

"What is it?"

"Speak of the devil. Alex Barca just walked in. He saw me, turned around, and left. He had a woman with him. I only caught a tiny glimpse of her back."

Erin deadpanned, "Probably his mother."

"Are you implying that I'm your father? Thanks."

"No such implication. I'm not good at veiled commentary. I usually say what I mean straight out."

He smiled and said, "I heard that about you. I've been talking to people."

"I hope I'm not the talk of the town."

"No. I heard you are a woman who is confidence personified. A no-nonsense person with a sense of humor. You don't make excuses. You make personal sacrifices. You are comfortable with who you are. You don't put on airs. All that spells C-L-A-S-S in my book."

"Oh my. That's some load. Did people really say that?"

"Not exactly. It's my interpretation."

"Are you making a play for me? Me, the plain Jane?"

"Don't I wish. You're out of my league."

"No I'm not. You're buttering me up."

"About Alex," Downbeat resumed with a worried expression. "What is he up to? There has to be some reason he's blasting beyond authorized power." He suspected Alex was contacting distant merchants, but it wouldn't be prudent to reveal his suspicions. It wouldn't be wise to know too much.

Erin said, "You have piqued my interest. There is no one I can ask about you. I'll accept your version of you."

"It's no secret," Downbeat said. "I've had my Sunday kind of love. When Nola—died—" It was still difficult to say *died.* "It flipped me. I thought I could find the answer in a bottle. It wasn't there. Now I have to live with a rotten one-week guarantee—because I'm a drunk with a bad rep—you can see why I'm worried."

"You must have loved her very much."

"That's putting it mildly. How deep is the ocean? I didn't know it then, but she could walk on water. I still talk to her. Sometimes."

"I can relate to that."

"No matter what I did, no matter where I went, she was there for me. She looked after me day and night. She knew what I needed before I could put it into words. Me the word master. She devoted her whole life to me. What did I give her in return? Nothing."

"Wrong," Erin said with sudden force. "You gave meaning and purpose to her life. You gave her a reason to love. You *were* her life. If she was here now, she would tell you that without Downbeat Jackson, her life wouldn't have amounted to a hill of beans in this crazy world. Listen, I've been down that road. I know what I'm talking about."

Jackson brightened. "Somehow I think you do."

"I read somewhere that a person who won't let go of the past is scared of the future."

"Or the present," he said. "Listen, I'm glad we had this talk."

Conversation lagged as each became a captive of their own thoughts. Each quietly wondered about the identity of the woman who had been with Alex Barca. Obviously Alex had recognized them before his hasty departure. Alex would be thinking about conspiracy. Now he would be wondering what scheme they were hatching, what conspiracy they planned.

Before they left the restaurant, Erin promised, "I'll do everything in my power to see that you stay at the station."

"Thank you," Downbeat said. "I knew I wasn't wrong about you having class."

Erin dropped him at the Ice House parking lot near his car. "I'm glad you invited me," she said matter-of-factly.

He hesitated before stepping out. "Stop at the station. Tomorrow evening would be a good time. I have some ideas I think will interest you."

"Will do."

A wonderfully sensitive man, Erin mused. He had loved deeply. It made her think about Captain Gaylord Haversham. Had he loved her deeply? Had he been aware of her love? Certainly she had loved him deeply, without reservation. Would she ever be able to love in that wonderful, magical way again? She knew the unhappy answer and banished the question. She remembered that after their meeting she'd expected the dashing captain to phone. He hadn't called that night or the next. Or the next.

More than two weeks passed before he phoned with a romantic outburst. "Erin, I love you."

"I think you just crossed the line."

"I know it. Can you see me backing up? I'm stepping back, going back, way back. Now I'm shouting, 'Erin I love you.'"

"I love you too." Had she uttered those words? Had they slipped past her lips? Wasn't it absurd to believe that one could fall in love during an evening of dancing and a breakfast the morning after? "I think I just crossed the line too."

There had been daily calls and within a week he said, "I have an invitation. You can say no." She discerned the tension in his voice. "I want you to fly to Denver for a week of glorious sex. Now I've really crossed the line."

Did he expect her to slam down the phone? It was crazy, totally absurd, but she heard herself say, "Okay. I'll come to Denver but that doesn't mean I'm committed. There may be a line you cannot, you dare not cross."

"Understood. You will come?" His voice soared. "Gloryosky!"

She could not believe she had agreed to fly to Denver. Yet, there was something about it that made her feel exhilarated. The whole idea seemed so delightfully naughty. Of course it was wrong. But how could something that felt so right be wrong?"

Her mother knew it was wrong. Belle Ames remonstrated. "Don't go."

"But I want to," Erin said.

"What about the new pharmacist? The one you call R-ex?"

"He's just a friend. He doesn't know how to have fun."

"Listen, girl. Life isn't just a bowl of cherries. The pharmacist will have steady work all his life. You'll never be poor."

"But I would have to listen to him explain that the money we spent going out is more than the profit on a bad prescription day. R-ex equates everything with money. He can't get beyond nickels and dimes."

"Oh? What do you know about this Captain Haversham anyway? I really don't think you should go."

Erin felt vapors of uncertainty coiling up within her. Her mother was right. She knew nothing about the captain. He might have a wife and a half-dozen kids.

"Considering your parents," Belle said, "This rebellion should not be surprising. I'm sorry to say it is."

"I know, Mother. Like father, like daughter."

"You certainly are your father's daughter. I'll say that much for you. "And your mother's. I raised you pretending we had a generation gap. Usually we didn't. You were so like me that it sometimes scared me."

"Mom, I know Grandfather disinherited you for marrying my father. When Grandfather died, you and your mother finally reconciled. Sometimes I wished you hadn't. Especially when you sent me to Atlantic and Grandmother tried to make a lady out of me."

"Well, it was only a hour's drive and I wanted you to know your grandmother. And all the while I thought we succeeded. There are those who contended that I marred wrong. At least I got married. Running off with a guy you hardly know is—" Belle sighed heavily. She closed her eyes and dark clouds came ghosting into her thoughts. She at once opened her eyes and stared directly at the glowing lamp. Through the years she had developed psychological tricks to help her cope with reality. "I just wish you wouldn't." Her hand raised. "Before you tell me you are in love, that this may be your only chance, let me tell you that I know exactly how you feel. I know all too well that if you are really in love you shouldn't allow anyone or anything to stand in your way." Her mother regarded her levelly, eyes unwavering, hands on her hips now. "Would it be possible to wait until you are absolutely sure?"

"I am sure, Mother."

A faint smile crossed Belle's face. "I knew you would say that. Well, I've done my duty. Go off and meet this Romeo who has a wife and ten kids."

"You've never shirked your duty, Mother. You've never shortchanged me."

On the plane to Denver Erin wondered if Captain Haversham had a wife and fourteen children.

All thoughts of wives and children evaporated when Captain Gaylord Haversham met her at the airport. He gathered her in his arms, and he must have known when his lips met hers that she, too, wanted him desperately, that no impediments remained.

"Hello you," he said, sucking in a happy breath.

"Hello yourself," she managed.

The removal of a barrier did not mean she had relinquished all control. She would not allow him to tear off her clothes any more than she wanted to rip off his. She was too much the lady to allow him to mess with her private garments. Not when she could remove them herself.

She had planned the moment a half-dozen times. "Don't lie to yourself," she advised herself. "You've been thinking of nothing else." *How many times?* "At least forty dozen times."

When they arrived at their room in the Brown Palace, she stopped and pointed to a chair. "Now you sit down and stay put while I freshen up. There's the line."

She prepared herself, dabbed perfume on her wrists and behind each ear. Wearing only high heels and the wildest net stockings she could buy, she marched into the middle of the room, placed her hands on her hips and slowly turned, her features frozen in a glowing smile.

"Ta-da," she sang. "What you see is what you get."

He rushed over, whisked her off her feet and placed her gently on the bed.

"You certainly know how to fly," she whispered before his lips closed hers.

She slipped out of her heels. She did not think of three wives and seventeen children.

There was something amazingly aeronautic about the way he leaped, like an airy glide. On the following day when he caught her and they fell across the bed, the bed collapsed.

Now they were laughing so hard they almost forgot why they were there. Almost, but not totally.

"Let's go shopping," he said later. "I want to buy you something. What would you like?"

"Heels."

"I might have guessed," he said.

"There was a time when I didn't have shoes."

"Ah, a slipper psychosis," he said, grinning. "A princess can't dance without slippers. You know I love the way you dance."

"You can't know what it means to have only one pair of flat clodhoppers. You can't wear them to a prom."

They went shopping and he purchased not only heels but a ball gown and accessories also. He said, "How about a negligee?"

"Oh no," she insisted. "I can't accept anything personal—unless I'm married."

They laughed awkward laughs. Each would recall the moment with lingering doubts. *Should I have said something else?*

"I get it," she said as they strolled to the hotel. "You want to see me parading around in clothes."

"You found me out," he said.

They discovered the bed had been repaired. Management never acknowledged that it had been damaged.

"If you like a parade," she said later, "how about this?" She modeled his pajamas.

"Not fair," he said. "I can't wear yours."

On the next shopping trip he purchased men's pajamas in her size.

"I love the way you dance," he said. "You're the only girl I've met whom I can't trip."

"There have been others? I suppose you meet—and dance with quite a few."

"At least six."

"Only six?" *Is that how many children you have? Go away, Mother.*

The glamorous week of dining and dancing, of loving, extended to ten wonderful days. He promised to phone when she returned home, but she did not hear from him for days. *Why didn't he call?*

The days of distress caused Erin to asked herself why she had gone running after him like a hungry puppy, as if he were the only man in the world. *He is the only man in the world.* She wondered if he really had a wife and three kids. Yet, there was something about him she could not deny, an open honesty.

Erin trashed the memory and snapped out of her reverie. The meeting with Downbeat had given her rising concern and she dutifully went to the station the following evening as he requested. Downbeat was there alone, and she seated herself and listened.

"Who can name the tune that won a gold record for Glenn Miller in 1942? The first person who answers correctly will receive a plain old black record suitably mounted in an attractive artistic frame and a couple dollars cash."

Cordelia Cooper had framed the records purchased at Abe's Antique shop, adding lettering that reflected her artistic prowess.

The fourth caller correctly identified "Chattanooga Choo Choo." "That's right," Downbeat exclaimed, slapping the table top with his leather baton. "Stop at the station during regular business hours and claim your prizes. Now for the next prize we will take only the first and fifth caller. How many years had it been since anyone sold one million records?"

The prize went unclaimed.

"You should have picked up on my hint of the first and fifth caller," Jackson said with a chuckle. "The answer is fifteen years. Now we separate the amateurs from the pros. Who can name the artist and the tune that sold a million records in 1927?"

Several listeners guessed, "Caruso."

"No it wasn't," Jackson said, whapping the table. "All right. Contest over."

Another call came in. Erin recognized the voice of Cordelia Cooper. "I won't accept a prize but I thought you might listen to a few notes of the original record."

She held the phone near the phonograph as it played Gene Austin's "My Blue Heaven." "Originally there were more than a million sold. How many are left?"

"Well, I don't know. One for sure."

"This is Cordelia Cooper. I like what you're doing."

"Thanks for calling, Mrs. Cooper. This is for you. Sit back and listen to a version without any disturbing scratches. Folks, here's Glenn Miller with 'My Blue Heaven.'"

Jackson came out and greeted Erin warmly. "Mrs. Cooper sounds like quite a lady. I'd like to meet her some time. Okay. What I have for you is a practice reading of an announcement."

"Me?" Erin said, surprised. "I have no radio experience."

"You will after tonight. The first rule you need to remember—whenever you step into a broadcast booth, assume that every word you utter goes out on the airwaves. If you remember that you can't go wrong."

"I don't know if I can be an announcer."

"You won't know unless you try. Keep your voice low. Let me hear you read this aloud. Wait till I set up another record."

He played "Stardust."

"Two signals," he instructed. "When I point to you, you start reading. If my palm goes up, you stop. No excuses, no explanations, no asides."

Jackson pointed to her and Erin read until his palm raised. He played another record and indicated for her to start at the beginning. The recording of "Blue Hawaii" faded and Jackson covertly flipped a switch. Erin was unaware that she was on the air until well into the script. She made a face and continued to read.

"You tricked me," she said when it was safe to talk.

"I warned you. I told you everything you utter in a broadcast booth should be treated as live."

She waved a scolding finger. "Bad boy." Secretly she was pleased with her performance.

Alex Barca heard the broadcast as he returned to Clarinda. He had departed early in the morning for Council Bluffs and Omaha. There he called on merchants and professionals in an attempt to sell advertising. He talked about sectors, vectors, and demographics and he'd made numerous sales.

He told merchants, "Normally you expect a radio station to draw business to the hub where they are located. But with our power—we are heard north into

Canada and west beyond Denver. With this package you will have people knocking on your door from all directions."

Armed with a portable radio, he tuned in KNDA as he talked and more than likely the prospect heard an ad for Abe's Antique store in Omaha, which Alex had instructed the new young announcer to run at frequent intervals, "as a favor to Cordelia Cooper."

He selected businesses catering to seasoned citizens inclined to listen to Glenn Miller music. A funeral director, reluctant to sign up for a year of spots at knockdown prices, was told, "We will give you an exclusive package. Yours will be the only funeral home in Council Bluffs that we ever mention."

Approaching the outskirts of Clarinda now, Alex marveled that it had been a particularly rewarding day. He'd been tempted to deposit the fistful of checks in an out-of-town bank, but reconsidered and decided to deposit them locally in Citizens State Bank, with withdrawal limited to only his signature. From time to time he would withdraw small sums and carry them to the Page County State Bank where the station maintained an account. Realistically, some cash had to be deposited for spots he'd sold. The sound of a familiar voice suddenly grabbed his attention.

"Hello. This is Erin Ames. For those of you who completed our survey cards at the Super Valu Supermarket, we say, 'Thank you.' And we have good news. For those of you who asked for a free trading post, you will be pleased to learn KNDA is starting just such a program next week. Here's how it will work. Call our special hotline number during the show; describe the item you wish to sell, the price, along with your phone number. When buyers call you direct, you may describe your article in more detail and inform them where you live. Limiting your call on the air will allow more people to take part. No cars, real estate, or garage sales please. Stay tuned for details."

Alex swore. "What the hell is she doing on the air?" *Damn her.*

Erin was still seated in the broadcast booth when Alex burst into the studio. Jackson had started "Tuxedo Junction," and he and Erin came out to greet Alex.

He glared at Erin. "What were you doing on the air? You aren't even on board yet, and already you're trying to take over. I won't have it." *That's what they were cooking up last evening at Miss Kitty's.*

"It was all my idea, boss," Jackson said. "She's local. She has a reputation. And she can read. She's a natural."

"I don't care about that," Alex raved, arms waving.

"Did I do something wrong, boss?"

"You sure did. You're supposed to clear these things with me first."

"I tried, boss," Jackson said with a shrug. "I tried four or five times this afternoon. I couldn't find you anywhere. The staff didn't know your whereabouts."

"Well don't let it happen again. Or you're out of here."

"If everyone gets sick," Erin reasoned. "You will need backup. Someone in reserve who is able to run the equipment—keep KNDA on the air. Besides, I have a vested interest in continuity."

"And you don't get sick?" Alex shot back, sneering.

Erin spoke in a calm but forceful tone. "I don't get cholera."

Alex muttered under his breath as he fled to his office.

Jackson confided in a whisper, "You didn't make any friends by doing that. Now you can see why I want you on my side. I may be gone by the end of the week."

"Oh," Erin said with a hint of whimsy and a twinkle in her eye. "I rather doubt that."

"What's that Alex said about you coming on board?"

Erin said, "Yeah, but keep a lid on it."

Downbeat's smile began to build until his face glowed. "This is my lucky day. My angel has arrived."

Chapter Six

Cordelia Cooper's car, like three others before it, had been equipped with an auxiliary hand brake. She called it a bastard brake because it lacked legitimacy and in no way could be considered standard equipment.

With the car moving forward, Cordelia tested the bastard brake, a ritual established years before Jake Cooper died. If it made good sense to follow his recommendation then, it certainly made compliance doubly important now. It had been years since she drove beyond the jurisdiction of Clarinda's police Chief Wilbur Wendinger. Cordelia took pride in her driving record and the fact that she had never had an accident. Late yesterday evening, after she read her first commercial, Erin had stopped at Cordelia's house to excitedly inform her, "Alex Barca is broadcasting in excess of authorized power. Some of us are afraid the government will swoop in and shut us down. It might take a year before we can get out of the dark."

"That isn't the half of it," Cordelia said. "The FCC can levy a fine that could bankrupt Midas."

"People are calling in complaining. Our receptionists are taking phone numbers, telling the callers Alex will call them back. After that, nothing happens."

"I'll make something happen," Cordelia declared. "I'll go right down there and take those calls."

"If you do that," Erin reasoned, "Alex will think one of the ladies phoned you. He will fire one—or both."

"I see what you mean."

"You need to be there," Erin theorized. "When a call comes in, when a complaint is made."

"Yes. Yes, I have it," Cordelia exclaimed. "First thing in the morning I'll call to see if our manager is in. If he isn't, I'll go down to the station to deliver some of the records we purchased at Abe's Antique store. I've been framing them, adding some artwork."

"They make lovely mementos when added to the cash prizes," Erin said.

The following morning, an energized Cordelia parked her car in front of the station. Doris helped her carry in an armload of framed records. The moment Downbeat Jackson saw Cordelia, he came out of the broadcast booth to greet her.

"I've been wanting to meet you, Mrs. Cooper," he said, pumping her hand. "Excuse me a moment." He returned to the booth. "This is Downbeat Jackson and 'Live Jive,' coming to you from KNDA, Clarinda, Iowa. Just sit back and relax, smile and dial, one eight hundred, Pennsylvania six five thousand. That's one eight hundred seven two six five oh oh oh… You're there. We're here."

Within minutes, the special on-the-air phone rang. "Hey, Downbeat. I haven't heard your cheery voice since you were on KFYI in Phoenix. We miss you."

"Thank you. Who is this?"

"May I keep that a secret for now?"

"All right, Mystery Man, where are you?"

"On a cell phone. I heard you as I was heading west on Interstate Eighty. I made the connection. I wanted to say hello, Downbeat."

"I appreciate that."

"Play something and talk to me off the air."

"That sounds mysterious, Mystery Man."

Off the air the caller reported, "I have a lot of little-known material on Glenn Miller. One of these days you will run out. How would it be if I called you from time to time?"

"I'm not sure we can pay you—much."

"With a Glenn Miller format, I'm not sure you'll be on the air long. Why don't we wait a couple weeks and see what it's worth?"

"Fine by me. Sounds like a plan, Mystery Man."

"Okay, you'll hear from me."

In the waiting room, Cordelia waved for Jackson to follow her during an interlude. She at once accosted the engineer. "What's our power at the moment?"

Sparks looked around furtively. He knew he couldn't snow Downbeat Jackson. "Maximum power, ma'am."

"How many watts?"

Sparks hesitated. "Er, ah, fifty thousand watts."

"We're only authorized five thousand watts."

"Mr. Barca told me to broadcast at the max. That's all I know. Every station I ever worked for ran at the max. I couldn't have misunderstood."

"I don't doubt that Barca told you. What's your name?"

"Sparks. They call me Sparks."

"Don't give me that. I mean your real name. The name that appears on our employment records."

"Humphrey Poulton."

"And your social security number? Now put this ship on a proper heading. Start sending at five thousand watts."

"All right. I understand that you're the president of the company. I was only doing what Mr. Barca directed."

"Have you worked with Alex Barca before? Where did you work last? I mean your regular job. I mean your permanent address."

"Michigan, ma'am."

Later, Cordelia would pause and wonder which of her numerous questions he had answered. Was his answer truthful?

At the next break, Downbeat reported the change. "KNDA, broadcasting on the government-assigned power of five thousand watts. Clarinda Broadcasting Company, a Jake Cooper station, Cordelia Cooper, president."

Jackson expected Alex Barca to be tuned in, wherever he happened to be. At that moment Alex had stopped to call on a prospective advertiser and had switched off his car radio. Straining Las Vegas odds, Alex missed six consecutive station breaks. His cell phone buzzed and he picked up the receiver. "Yeah, who's this?"

"Hump. The old lady came in and made me tone down the power. It's over. She's still hanging around. Do you want me to cut and run?"

"No. Get back to work. We'll play it out. I'm turning around. I'm on the way back."

Behind his thick lenses, the soundman's eyes twinkled. He loved giving a performance.

In his car, Alex removed one hand from the wheel and shook a clenched fist. "Damn. Just when we were getting started." His face contorted, he decided the best thing to do was stall. He would confront the old lady and deny. Deny. Deny! No doubt about it, he had to knuckle under to the Cooper woman and allow her to remain in control.

Alex heard Jackson's new station break as he approached the limits of Clarinda. He parked behind the studio and hurried in. "I heard the spot. Bring me up to date. Ah, Mrs. Cooper," he said with a benign look of innocence. "I'm glad you decided to pay us a visit."

"I'll come right to the point," Cordelia said snappishly. "We have been sending signal at fifty thousand watts. The ladies tell me we have received numerous calls complaining. I took one such call myself."

"Yes, yes," Alex said nervously. "At first I assumed the callers were crackpots. Sparks is in charge of power. He came to us highly recommended. I can't imagine he would be broadcasting over the legal limit. I planned to return the calls today. That's why I'm back. I've been out beating the bushes and it's an uphill battle." He accosted the soundman. "What's the problem here, Sparks?"

"Like you ordered, I've been running at max power, fifty thousand watts. What you said."

"I never told you to max the equipment."

"That's wha[illegible]tions do. They run at max power. That's the standard for the industry. Exce[illegible]aybe at night."

"But we h[illegible] an older set. I *distinctly* remember telling you five thousand watts."

Sparks shook his head in disagreement. "That's not what you said."

"I can't have someone around who isn't able to follow orders," Alex said. "You're the engineer. It's your duty to follow specs and see that we stay on the air, level and uninterrupted. We've had a little down time."

"That's to be expected with these old tubes."

"No excuses allowed," Alex said in a dictatorial tone. "I'm letting you go. Stop at my office and collect what we owe you." Alex turned and marched to the office, back stiff with defiant anger.

"It ain't fair." Sparks followed in his wake. "I don't know why I should take the blame. I did what you told me."

Cordelia and Downbeat Jackson exchanged glances. Alex perspired heavily. Sparks had taken the fall. Maybe he was safe—for the moment.

"There are times when engineers are fired if the station goes off the air a second time," Downbeat said. "I think we have been silent three times. But not for long." He could see the firing weighed heavily on her.

Cordelia had already decided not to undermine Barca's authority. If he left town, he would evade the spreading net she felt would drop over him. Why hadn't Chief Wendinger reported back to her? She had to admit that Alex Barca knew how to run a station. Right now the station needed a good manager.

Sparks burst out of the office raving. "It ain't fair." He gestured with chopping motions. "It just ain't fair. I shouldn't be fired for following instructions." He faced Cordelia. "I'm not lying about following instructions. I'm not lying." He ripped open the envelope, took out the bills inside, and flipped the torn envelope into the wastebasket.

When he had gone, Cordelia realized it appeared awkward, but she swung to the wastebasket and retrieved the envelope, carefully touching only a corner. She placed it in a file folder.

"If you want his fingerprints," Doris said, "he left an empty Coke can on the ledge." She gave a self-effacing shrug. "My son has given me a lot of grief—and quite an education."

"Thank you, Doris. That's a splendid idea." Inserting a pencil into the slit in the can, Cordelia dropped it into a plastic sack.

She paused when Downbeat added a trailer to a break. "Serving the heart of the Mo-Kan-Neb-Ia area."

An irritated Alex Barca ran out and confronted him. "What the hell is that?"

"An acronym, boss."

"I know what an acronym is," Alex asserted. "We're located in Iowa. If you're going to use it, Iowa must be first! And I do mean first!" He quickly withdrew.

Downbeat went directly to the mike and interrupted Glenn Miller's "Frenesi." "What I meant to say—serving the Iowa-Mo-Kan-Neb area, the heartland of America." He raised his eyebrows in an expression of injured innocence, shrugged, and reached for his handkerchief.

Cordelia drove directly to the police station where Chief Wendinger received her politely, if not with enthusiasm.

"Now, Wilbur, I don't want anything less than the state crime lab on these prints. Lift and match."

Chief Wendinger asked a series of questions and said, "But this man has done nothing criminal."

"Call it an old woman's intuition." She didn't tell Wilbur that Sparks had been sacked by KNDA for broadcasting beyond FCC limits.

The chief hemmed, "Well—"

"Indulge me. I'll stand any expense. I feel like I'm in the movies and can't get my feet on the ground."

"Well," he stalled. "I guess it wouldn't hurt. You never can tell what he's been into."

"He mentioned coming from Michigan. Have you heard anything concerning Alex Barca from Michigan?"

"Not yet. I expect to any day."

"All right, then. Keep after them 'til you get results."

The chief waited until Cordelia left before he shoved the exhibits she had given him into the bottom desk drawer.

"No rush," he told himself. He had more to do than answer to the whims of Cordelia Cooper. He turned to his secretary and explained, "She's got too much time on her hands."

"And too much money," Ellen joked.

Ellen Iverson provided a humorous counterpoint to Chief Wendinger's dedicated routine. A tall woman, her nose was too long and too pointed to be beautiful—a nose as sharp as her wit. Her shoulders were slightly narrow, her hips wide—ideal for child bearing, her doctor maintained. "Never again," she told her doctor after the birth of her only child. The delivery had been normal, but too painful for Ellen. Millions of woman had experienced the same agony and cried, "Never again." Ellen meant it. She informed friends and relatives that if she ever became pregnant again, she would (1) have an immediate abortion, (2) have her husband castrated, (3) file for divorce, (4) take all his money, (5) make him pay an outrageous child support, and (6) make him wish he was never born.

Her husband lent support to her view. "She really means it."

Their decision had little effect on the Iverson family. There were already more Iversons in Clarinda than anyone else, a fact not lost on the chief. With Ellen's contacts within the Iverson family she was worth more than any two officers when it came to picking up rumors from the street.

"And too much money," agreed the chief.

"How can anyone have too much money?" Ellen asked soberly.

"But you just said—"

"I didn't say anything."

As she drove away from police headquarters, lines formed on Cordelia's brow. "There is something in Michigan, I just know it." Why had Alex Barca selected a radio station in Clarinda? She doubted that it concerned what was being broadcast. If Alex wanted to send a message all he had to do was run an ad in the classifieds or pick up a telephone. When she drove past the supermarket, she noticed Sparks using the telephone. He was probably calling his wife to tell her the job had ended. Cordelia could not have guessed that his collect call had been made to an administrative agency in the nation's capitol.

"Agent ex-nine," Sparks said in a metallic voice. "Our boy is up to his old tricks. Broadcasting over specs. He's changed his MO though. No stock swindle here. He owns one-sixth of the operation. I can't figure it. He might be going straight. He might be getting tired."

"We couldn't be that lucky."

"Why do I keep thinking he's in for one last score before he slips away to Brazil?"

"Are you hanging around?"

"No. He fired me. I'm outa here."

"Fired?"

They shared laughter until the line clicked.

The man in Washington spanked the buttons on his phone.

"Hello?"

"Hey, I just had a call from our mole in Clarinda."

"Hunh? Oh. Yeah."

"Apparently our friend is at it again. Broadcasting more watts than authorized. That much is predictable. But there is no evidence of a swindle. He has changed his MO. Now listen, when a tiger changes his MO and becomes a man-eater, he's dangerous. If our friend has become unpredictable, he's dangerous."

"So?"

"So there is just two things you can do with a blackmailer. You can pay him, and pay him, and pay him, or—you can stop his clock."

"We haven't given him any money."

"What we've done is more dangerous than money. We knew early on—we talked about it then, we knew it couldn't last—that some day we would need to do something serious. It's getting too dangerous to keep covering, to keep running interference. Do you want to wait for a congressional investigation?"

"What *is* he doing?"

"I really don't know. I can't figure. He owns part of the station. He's hired only locals except Downbeat Jackson, who's a reformed alcoholic—and as solid as apple pie on the Fourth of July. The president of the station is an elderly handicapped widow. I suppose it's too much to hope that he's putting down roots and going legit."

"Out of the question. Once a tiger—"

"I think it's time for you to call Mack the Knife."

"Where am I going to find someone like that?"

"It will be too late after we see our names in the *Washington Post.*"

"That's for sure. I think the place to look is Kansas City. I could put out feelers. But that will take time. It will mean sticking our necks out."

"What do you mean 'our necks'?"

"I mean yours and mine."

Sparks had left the pay phone at the supermarket. He'd collected his gear and on the way out of town found himself in a warm and jovial mood. It wasn't every day that he could collect twice for the same work. He had enjoyed his brief stay in Clarinda. He couldn't wait to be called again. As a final gesture he listened to KNDA, where Downbeat Jackson was saying, "Serving the Iowa-Mo-Kan-Neb area, a Jake Cooper station in the heart of the nation." He smiled as he visualized Downbeat slapping the desk with his bull dick stick. He could not know that at that very moment Downbeat had reached for it.

Peering out of the soundproof booth, Downbeat could not believe what he saw. A scraggly youth had opened Doris's desk drawer, removed her purse, and rummaged inside. He withdrew a twenty dollar bill. At the adjacent desk an apparently unconcerned Jennifer sat listlessly filing her nails, jaws working over three sticks of Dentyne.

Jackson flung open the door. His leather baton raised and came down like a whip, cutting the young man's hand. The quirt raised and fell again.

Keith Gordoncamp yelped in pain and dropped the bill. Jackson scooped it up and returned it to the fallen purse.

"It's my mother's," the young man squealed.

"All the more reason to ask permission," Jackson said, continuing to stand guard with the baton.

"What's it to you?" Keith said with a surly snarl. He brought his bleeding backhand to his mouth and sucked blood. "Mind your own business."

At that moment Doris returned. "What's going on?"

"I caught him stealing from your purse," Downbeat said.

Doris glared at her son. "I told you never to go into my purse."

"But I have to have twenty bucks," Keith wailed.

"I told you no," Doris scolded.

"How about five then?"

"No!"

Keith glared at Downbeat. "I'll get even. So help me, I'll get even."

"No you won't," his mother said. "What you will do is go out and get a job."

"Says who?"

"Says me. Says I. Now get out of here before I call the police. I thought you had put this delinquent behavior behind you."

Keith departed vomiting curses. An apologetic Doris turned to Downbeat. "I'm sorry for making a scene. He's been good for so long. I thought he was over it." Her eyes lowered to the leather baton. She raised her gaze and appraised Jackson with renewed interest. Clearly he was more than a clown. He had substance.

Jackson plumped to Jennifer's desk. "What are you, an accomplice? Why didn't you get off your dead butt and do something?"

"None of my beeswax. I know Keith is her son. I thought he had her permission."

"No you didn't," Jackson charged. "You haven't had an original thought since you got here. You just don't give a damn."

"No skin off my nose," Jennifer said.

Jackson had reached the sanctuary of the booth when Alex approached. "What's going on out here, Decorah?" he demanded, using her correct name.

"Nothing," Doris replied. "My son tried to borrow money from my purse, and fortunately Downbeat stopped him. Keith didn't have my permission."

"You tell your son to stay away from the studio," Alex blustered. "From now on this place is off limits for him. If he can't stay away, you'll have to find another job. Got it?"

"Yes sir." Doris risked his further ire to show that she was on top of the situation. "Would you like me to advertise for a new engineer?"

"No," Alex said. "We've had our shakedown cruise. The station is up and running. We don't need a replacement. Downbeat can handle those duties." There was little about running a station that Downbeat did not know. "I know how to engineer a station," Alex said with angry emphasis.

Alex turned and started scolding Jennifer. After a moment he realized he should have originated his tirade in the privacy of his office, but it was too late. "You're being replaced," he said. "Your job here is through."

"What?" she flared.

"You're through here."

"I'm being fired?" she declared, totally incredulous. Her face reflected more animation than any time since she arrived.

"That's the size of it."

Jennifer leaped to her feet. "What for? Just because I didn't stop Keith from looking in his mother's purse. Hey, I thought he had permission. She never warned me to keep an eye on her purse."

"This has nothing at all to do with Decorah's purse. You are simply being replaced. Nothing personal."

"Nothing personal," she recoiled. "How can you say that? After the way we were." She bit off her outburst and continued to probe. "What's going on, Alex? Where do we go from here?"

"It's out of my hands. The stockholders—"

"After what you promised?" Jennifer realized she was shouting at his fleeing back. "Replaced," she sniffed. "Well, we'll see about that. He hasn't heard the last of me." She turned to Doris, misty eyed. "Who's replacing me? Who by?"

"By whom," Doris corrected. "Do you own one-third of the station?"

"No, but—"

"Use your head, girl." Doris focused on the man at the mike and smiled.

Downbeat grinned back, covering an uncertainty swirling in his depths. Alex was in a firing mood. Would he be next? "Something old, something new, something borrowed, and something blue," he caroled. "Here's something borrowed. It's the sweetest version of Duke Ellington's 'Take the A Train' that you will ever hear."

Jennifer clawed some things from the desk drawer and plunked them into her purse.

At the first opportunity Doris would inform Downbeat that his technical talents made him more valuable than ever before. She realized she was staring dreamily and broke her trance. "Cream always rises to the top, honey."

Chapter Seven

Erin arrived at KNDA without fanfare. Alex made no introductions or explanations. Hadn't she already mouthed off to staff that she owned a one-third interest? After all, in this hick town everybody knew everybody else.

Erin seated herself at the vacant desk. With a split shift, come-and-go employment, she predicted that it would only be a matter of time until Alex made trouble. Accordingly, she prepared log sheets and requested that Doris also maintain a record of her time. "I know it's a lot of bother. I'll try to make it up to you."

"No problem," Doris said. She would probably need Erin's help in the near future, a feeling heightened when she saw a grumpy Alex Barca bearing down on them. She hastily slid papers over the log sheet and breathed a sigh of relief when Alex proceeded to the adjacent desk.

"I want you to go out and sell some advertising," he told Erin. "You ought to be good at that."

"Why, good morning," Erin said cheerfully. "No one wants KNDA to succeed more than I—boss. After all, I have a vested interest."

She gathered materials and set out. As Erin strolled around the city square, she became aware that it would be possible to stop at nearly all of the establishments and hear the same tune. The new disc jockey, Tom Berringer, in a brief test program, specialized as he said, "in music beyond Glenn Miller." At the moment he played, Tommy Dorsey's "I'm Getting Sentimental Over You."

Like Erin, the young announcers Alex hired had other jobs. Berringer worked in a furniture store. An active member of the local thespians, radio announcing provided a natural extension of his talents. Dan Pulliam held down a job at the newspaper. The editor of the *Clarinda Herald-Journal* allowed, "Okay, as long as it doesn't conflict with your work here."

Erin selected a restaurant, made a casual entrance, and eased into a booth. "Good Morning. Coffee, please. Black."

In a few minutes the proprietor, wearing a stained white apron and rolled-up sleeves, slid in opposite.

"Well, I see you're holding down two jobs now."

"Not exactly," Erin said. "One is part time." On her first morning on the job was there anyone in Clarinda who did not know?

"Out selling advertising then?"

"Supposed to be."

"Don't need any."

She knew he would say that. She could probably guess with a high degree of accuracy his opinion on nearly every local issue. "I wonder," she posed. "If I sell every restaurant in town, isn't there a cancellation factor? What I mean is, don't they cancel each other out to some degree?" She had baited him; however, there had to be a kernel of truth in what she said.

"That's what I always say," he agreed. "The media has us over a barrel. In all my life I have never purchased a single ad that paid for itself. The media has us bamboozled. They tell us we are dead if we don't advertise. Look at all the advertising that is done and what for? Clarinda is half dead anyway."

Erin wondered if he ever paid his chamber of commerce dues. She guessed he didn't and was content to merely ride along on their wagon.

"The only time we hear from the politicians," he said waspishly, "is three weeks before the election. The rest of the time Des Moines doesn't know we exist. Except, of course, in April during tax time."

"Perhaps you shouldn't consider an ad," Erin said. "Until you have something special."

"More opportunities all the time," he said with sarcasm. "Since the radio station started up, I can't get any work out of my people. All they want to do is swing and sway."

"I heard that," objected a young woman. "It's not true. We've got the place spic-and-span." She regarded Erin. "We love the canned music. It will have to do until the real thing comes along."

Two ideas surged into Erin's thoughts in rapid succession and she could not decide which to pursue. Then it became clear. She rose quickly and said, "I'll get back to you. Call me if you have something special."

Surprised, the man observed, "Now that's the softest sell I ever had. What she said, 'Call me.' Isn't that supposed to be my line?"

Erin's pace quickened until she was almost running as she approached the Sports Bar operated by Ben and Sarah McAllister. They had a history. It began the first day Erin came in for coffee. Ben stood behind the counter pontificating. "We named the place Sarah's Sports Bar. That way, when I kick off, Sarah doesn't have to change the name."

"Maybe she will," Erin quipped. "She might want to call it Ted's."

Ben's color turned six shades redder, and he exploded indignantly, "Do you know something I don't know?" He stormed to the kitchen.

Erin heard him shouting at Sarah and quickly departed. How could she know that Sarah had once been engaged to a man named Ted? Three days later Sarah phoned her at the bank and asked her to return. A contrite Ben slid a donut and a cup of coffee across the counter. "On the house."

Sarah said, "Would you answer one question?"

"If I can."

"Why did you say 'Ted'?"

"I just picked a name out of thin air. I might just as well have said Billy, Bob, or Barry."

"See?" Sarah said to Ben. "Not just your ordinary Tom, Dick, and Harry from her."

When Ben retreated to the kitchen Sarah whispered, "I'm glad you said Ted. Ben has been giving me a lot of special attention." A squeaky giggle escaped her.

With that experience behind them and a longtime friendship established, Erin knew the plan she had in mind would interest the McAllisters. It would benefit them more than KNDA.

Now, slowing at last, Erin swung open the door, approached Ben, and said breathlessly, "Have I got a deal for you!"

Ben stepped back one step and regarded her with interest.

"It's special," Erin gushed. "And for you a natural. Some night you feature a special dinner of Rocky Mountain oysters. With that meal, everyone gets to drink a free Erin to start."

"Here in Clarinda? Isn't that pushing the envelope?"

"It would get you talked about," Erin admitted with the hint of a smile. "Isn't that the purpose of advertising?"

Ben debated. He teased with a chuckle, "I might be willing to go along if you served the first Erin."

"I can do that," Erin said, unfazed. "Why not? I could bring another couple from the station. You could conduct a drawing. The lucky couple wins two free dinners and gets to sit at the KNDA table. Another prize might be the first Erin drink to be served."

Ben became serious. "Have you pitched this to any anyone else?" He knew that the first such promotion would score like gangbusters. Whoever did it would have dibs on a repeat. Anyone else who tried it might bomb as being a copycat.

"No. I haven't even talked to anyone else."

"Well, don't. I want this."

"Then we'll shake on it," Erin said. They shook hands and she started to leave.

"What about a contract?" he asked.

Erin called over her shoulder. "You'll get it in due time. We need to work out the details."

Ben turned around and grinned. "What was that that just hit me. Who was that masked man?"'

Erin called Doris and Downbeat into one of offices formerly used by car salesmen and exploded her brain child.

"Great," Downbeat said, at once impressed. "I wish I had thought of it."

"Yuck," Doris said, making a face, "I don't see how anyone can swallow those things. Yuck."

Downbeat tossed back his head and laughed. "Wait a minute. Selling an ad is one thing. Having us stars appear is something else, a personal appearance." He remembered where he was and tempered his enthusiasm. "Of course here in Clarinda, what is that worth?"

"Maybe four free dinners," Erin said.

"You won't catch me eating Rocky Mountain oysters," Doris said.

"So who invited you?" Downbeat retorted.

"Listen!" Erin said almost shouting, lowing her voice, spreading her arms and singing, "It will have to do—until the real thing comes along."

A moment of silence and Downbeat cracked, "What did they put in your breakfast food? Canary seed?"

She ignored him. "We have to bring in the Glenn Miller orchestra."

The idea struck his fancy. Later he would tell Alex, "The idea hit me like a ton of bricks." Of course they had to bring in the Glenn Miller aggregation. "Great idea. There are ghost bands touring for Artie Shaw, Tommy Dorsey, and Glenn Miller." He raised a finger for emphasis. "Two things. One, we need a hall. Two, we need the band's schedule. I doubt if we can afford an air mail special. But if they are playing in Davenport and Denver and there's an open date between, we might get them to drop down to Clarinda. Why not? Erin, will you let me run with this?"

She beamed. "I think you already have."

"The Glenn Miller band here?" Doris mused. "Wouldn't that be something?" Of course the Glenn Miller band sometimes appeared at the annual Glenn Miller Festival.

In an ebullient mood, Downbeat clasped his palms together in a prayerful attitude. "Say, kiddo," he said, directing his remark to Doris. "While we're on the subject of celebrations, how would you like to have dinner tonight with an over-the-hill announcer?"

"I don't know any over-the-hill announcers," Doris shot back. "I really should say no after the way you put me down a few minutes ago about not being invited."

"You're being invited now," he said. "Erin, help me out. Give me a recommendation."

Erin nodded. "He's good company."

"Okay, I accept," Doris said. "Pick me up an hour after I get off work."

Downbeat went joyfully skipping toward the broadcast booth and when he was out of earshot Doris admitted, "I was hoping he would ask me. What can you tell me about him?"

"He's trying to stay on the wagon." Seeing Doris's somewhat crestfallen look, Erin explained, "He told me he's been dry three years. He still misses his late wife awfully."

They paused to listen to an incoming call from the mystery man.

"Yes, Mystery Man," exclaimed Jackson. "What do you have for us today?"

"There were always song pluggers around Glenn Miller. How much did he pay for the upbeat signature of World War II, the jitterbugger's national anthem, 'In The Mood'? I dare the station to pay the same sum as a prize."

"All right," Jackson said. "We'll throw it open. The caller closest to the sum will win. I'll get the answer off the air from the Mystery Man. We'll run the contest ten minutes."

Calls came in and people estimated ninety-nine dollars and one hundred one. A steady listener thought Downbeat had tossed out a hint by running the contest for ten minutes and said, "I'll guess ten dollars."

"Not quite right, and time has run out. You are the closest. The answer is five dollars. Glenn Miller paid five dollars for 'In The Mood.' And what a bargain. Thank you, Mystery Man."

Alex appeared at once. "What if the price had been a thousand dollars?"

"It wasn't," Downbeat said lamely.

"It might have been," Alex charged. "You committed the station before you knew. You didn't get the answer from Mystery Man until you committed the station."

"Not a problem." *There goes the job.* "I've been around," Downbeat said, seeking a confident tone. "I knew the answer all the time."

Alex shouted angrily, "Be careful after this!" He turned, stopped, and demanded, "What are we paying Mystery Man?"

"Nothing yet. We'll work that out later. He's real reasonable. Nothing in writing."

"Good!" Alex returned to his office.

Downbeat swiped a heavy hand across his sweat-beaded forehead and resumed. No one had a clue as to the turmoil churning within him. He'd survived another barking confrontation. No one could mistake the happiness in his voice. He looked out, saw Doris, and found comfort in her presence.

The day wore on.

At home in the evening, Doris waited in her living room, peering out of the curtains now and then. When she saw Jackson's car she hurried out to meet him.

Downbeat surmised, "Keith is home."

Doris bobbed her head and they left it there. She liked Downbeat but she had to know if he still had a problem with booze.

Moments after they were seated in Miss Kitty's restaurant she said "I'd like a beer. How about you?"

"Make it an Erin for my friend," Downbeat instructed the waitress. "Diet Pepsi for me."

Presently the waitress returned with a tapered glass of tap in which had been dropped a solitary cherry.

"This is an Erin?" Doris questioned.

"Yes," Downbeat replied. "A local favorite."

Doris ordered another and when the meal arrived she noticed conversation had become stilted. In this social setting Downbeat had no problem with liquor that she could determine. Then suddenly she became aware that she might have a problem—he might not be impressed with her. She had already fortified herself with Dutch courage. She would measure her words. She would put on a happy face and be very careful.

As if concern had become contagious, Downbeat thought he had failed to made a slam-dunk impression with Doris. If it had been an interview, his glib repartee would have carried the day, but this was his private life. He became aware that serious doubts were swirling within him, serious enough to demand a slow start. Somehow he had fallen off his game. *Don't compare,* he chided himself when he encountered a fleeting thought about Nola. He couldn't expect bells to ring. Not ever again. "I'm having a good time, Doris," he heard himself say.

"I'm having a good time too," she admitted. "In fact, such a good time that I had found myself woolgathering, exploring serious possibilities. Isn't that just crazy?"

They did not linger after dinner and when he parked in front of her house they exchanged perfunctory thank yous. He reached for her hand and held it. "I'm not going to kiss you," he said. "I'm not ready. A kiss should mean something special." He had kissed Nola a thousand times without thinking—because he thought she wanted to be kissed as he hurried out the door.

Doris sensed his pain. "There's something to be said for that point of view." She withdrew her hand and stepped out. She stood staring at her hand a long moment after he drove away. She started up the walk.

As soon as she stepped inside Keith confronted her. "I don't want you to go out with him again."

Months of denial, pent-up emotion, suddenly exploded in unthinking reflex anger. In that moment of uncontrolled rage she raised her arm and backhanded him sharply across the mouth. Her ring drew blood.

"You hit me," Keith wailed. "You never hit me before."

In control now, Doris reveled in the advantage. "It's been long overdue. Attempting to steal from my purse is the worst thing you've ever done. I thought you outdistanced all that delinquency. It's time you started acting like a man. Acting like a brat and bully is not acting like a man. You think you're running things. You're not. I'm in charge of this house. Not you."

Keith fled to the sanctuary of his bedroom. He lay there in agony, wondering why the world was beating up on him. This couldn't go on. He had to do something. He had to get even.

At work the next morning, Doris greeted Erin. "I didn't know you were a celebrity, girl. Last night I drank two Erins."

Erin stretched out her limbs in a feline preening motion and chortled. "It's Clarinda's favorite drink of moderation. If you stretch the meaning of the word favorite. How did things go?"

"Okay, I guess."

"Wanna have some fun?"

Doris listened and in a moment they stood up and rushed toward each other, fists clenched, arms flailing, pretending to be slugging it out. Erin picked up a hand lettered sign and flashed it at Jackson.

FIGHTING OVER YOU!

It was the first time in living memory that anyone could remember Downbeat Jackson breaking up on the air.

Doris faced Erin directly. "My grandmother used to say that many a true word is spoken in jest. Do you want him?"

"No," Erin replied. "But you wouldn't think you won if you didn't get some competition."

The answer pleased Doris until she had second thoughts. Competition had a way of getting out of hand.

Alex Barca came marching toward them with a look of discontent. "What's going on?"

"Not a thing—boss," said Erin.

He looked around and saw nothing amiss. Wearing a look of even deeper discontent, he returned to his office.

"May I have that message?" Doris asked.

Erin waited till Alex was out of sight and handed her the FIGHTING OVER YOU! page. She watched Doris fold it into quarters and tuck it inside her purse.

"Someday that will make a nice souvenir."

After a time Erin said, "I have one stop, then I'm heading back to my old job. I'll call in my time."

"Got it," Doris acknowledged.

Erin stopped at Schecter's Shoes, a place of pleasant memories. Herb and Eloise played an influential role at a critical stage in her young life, allowing her to outdistance insecurity. Even they did not realize how their generosity resulted in a burst of self-assurance. Erin smiled tentatively. She had not known then where her newly found confidence would lead.

She remembered that with the high-school prom only a week away, she'd felt wretched, outcast, and ignored, expecting to spend the rest of her life totally alone, when she received the surprising phone call from Eloise Schecter. "Can you keep a secret?"

"Y-Yes," Erin had said with hesitation.

"Then come to our shoe store."

She had trudged to Schecter's and Herb had fitted her with prom shoes. "They're yours," he said. "If you can keep a secret."

"Who's paying for them?" she had asked.

A beaming Eloise Schecter said, "Now that's our secret. One that we must keep. Promise not to tell anyone about the shoes."

"I promise," Erin said. She wondered who would buy her shoes but maintained a discreet silence.

At that point a hectic pace had begun with her mother sewing a prom dress. Belle Ames had skill accenting colors, adding buttons and bows to a rather plain frock.

Her newly found confidence had not gone unnoticed. Clarence Sanders phoned and asked for a date. The laughter in the background should have warned Erin that something was wrong. On the evening of the prom, Clarence never appeared.

"I'm not going to let you sit here mooning. Not after all the effort I spent sewing a gown," Belle said.

Her mother dropped her at the high school at the last possible moment. Prom night always started with a banquet, which meant everyone attended whether they had dates or not. When the dance began, Clarence had the nerve to ask her to dance.

Erin smiled timidly and said, "Thank you." In the middle of the first number she said in a loud voice, "You stood me up, creep." She stopped dancing. Her arms went up and down. "That's all you get," she said even louder and left Clarence standing alone in the middle of the floor, completely frustrated, the laughter of classmates ringing in his ears.

"You did that?" her incredulous mother asked when she told her what she had done.

"Simply saying no would not have been adequate," Erin said.

Buoyed by the happy memory, she greeted the Schecters warmly now and said, "You've made a lot of kids happy through the years. Maybe it's time you blew your horn."

"I don't think she'd appreciate that," Herb said.

"She?"

"Her," Herb said quickly, gesturing toward his wife to cover his gaffe. "She keeps saying the best thing we can do is keep our gifts confidential. Most of the recipients keep our secret. It's been a good program. We prefer to keep it quiet. We rely on a couple of teachers at the high school to keep us informed. If you know anyone who needs prom shoes, Erin, don't hesitate to give us a tip."

Erin sold them a short series and when she stepped outside, Eloise playfully punched her husband. "You almost let the bunny out of the bag. Watch your mouth."

"I thought I covered it rather well."

"You wouldn't be of much interest to me if Cordelia Cooper skinned you alive."

They shared a laugh.

Outside, Erin waved at Eloise before she started down the street to the old stand.

Henry Leighton fidgeted and said, "Am I glad to see you."

"And good morning to you."

"Yeah. Good morning. I don't know how to break this to you," he said. "There's probably no good way. I'm in a bind."

"Not another audit?"

"Nothing like that. This is family business. My brother-in-law is building a house and needs a loan. I don't want to handle the transaction. It's a no-win situation with the family. If I turn him down, one group is upset. If I give in, it won't be fair to some relatives I turned down in the past. But if I turn it over to you, I'm off the hook."

"Brother-in-law," Erin said. "Not the obstreperous one I sued for slander after he called me a lezzie. Not Ned Sunderman?"

Henry smiled wanly. "The same."

"You really know how to hurt a girl." She clutched her chest as if she had been shot. "What makes you think I could be impartial?"

"It doesn't matter what you do. I'm off the hook. Don't you see? More or less anyway."

"Let me think about it. You know you're the boss and I'm the employee."

"Don't be that way. You know how I feel about you."

Erin attacked paperwork that had accumulated while she worked at the station. Her thoughts drifted and she wondered if Henry's reluctance to handle a family matter, his indecision, was one reason she had spurned his proposals of marriage. Of course he hadn't asked since she threatened, "If you don't stop with the proposals, I'm going to quit and go back to the bank."

Erin swiveled around in her chair and called to him. "All right, Henry. I've thought it over. I'll do it. But you have to explain it to him—and the family—up front. He has to know what to expect."

"Thanks," Henry said with obvious relief. "You don't know what this means to me."

Two days later Ned Iverson, Henry's indiscreet brother-in-law, appeared, looking somewhat distraught. He crushed and rubbed his cap with such intensity that Erin felt it might be shredded.

"I'm sorry for what I did," he stammered. "Sorry it caused you grief."

"I'm sorry too. That's two of us in a sorry state. Let's put it behind us and get down to business. If you think I am going to turn down the boss's sister's husband for a loan, you have another guess coming. You'll get your loan. Now all that is left is to work out the details."

Erin cut the usual interest rate—three-quarters of one percent on a thirty-year fixed mortgage. When the documents were inked, she could not tell which of the men exhibited the greatest relief.

"I could fall in love with someone like you," her boss said later.

"Don't start," Erin warned.

"I won't," he said. "But I have to maintain my competitive edge. I guess I'm doing almost as well as that pharmacist. Who shall remain nameless."

"Which reminds me—" Erin said, breaking a thought.

"Seriously," Henry said. "Do you believe it's true, what people say, that somewhere in the world there is someone for everyone?"

"Absolutely. Let's think of the perfect mate as a coin. Say a nineteen sixty penny. If a person keeps his head down, eyes glued to the sidewalk, he has a good chance of finding such a penny one day. Yet, think of all the flowers, birds singing in the trees, faces of friends such a person would miss seeing. Or think of it this way. A fortune teller told a guy he will meet his mate on a bus. He rode a lot of buses after that but he always sat with old ladies because they slept a lot and he liked to doze. He missed a lot of possibilities."

Henry placed his hands on his hips in imitation of her and smiled indulgently. "Darling, are you talking about me? Or could you possibly be thinking of someone else?"

"Perhaps," Erin said. "Perhaps I was preaching to the choir. And talking about myself all along. You'd better keep an eye on me."

"I'll certainly do that." He looked her up and down with playful lechery.

"Stop that."

He grinned. "Would you close? I want to go home and work on my Whippet."

"Sure." She knew that while restoring that fifty-year old car he formulated some of his best ideas, such as the College Club, which allowed families to earn a higher rate of interest on long-term savings. "Then you're not going to the impromptu chamber of commerce meeting Andrew Seligman has called? What's that about?"

"You ought to know," Henry said. "You started it. Rocky Mountain oysters. At least that's what I hear. You should cover it."

"I'll just do that."

Chapter Eight

The Clarinda Chamber of Commerce, like its numerous counterparts across the country, had as its purpose the attraction of industry, increasing merchants' sales, generally promoting business, and the creation of a favorable business climate. Andrew Seligman had been secretary of Clarinda's chamber long enough to collect a cadre of friends and a contingent of constant complainers. Under his leadership membership had increased 6.8 percent and the mountain of chamber debt had been entirely eliminated. A couple of hardware dealers questioned in jest whether this achievement alone might not be justification to seek his resignation and replacement.

Seligman had come from a town smaller than Clarinda, and it was grudgingly acknowledged that sooner or later he would be climbing the population curve to a larger town with a greater war chest and a commensurate increase in salary. Clarinda had been an exceptional training ground for a war lord masquerading as a serf. There were those in town who seriously meant to keep him at that modest level. Seligman enjoyed the fellowship of other chamber secretaries, and the moment they became inattentive, he liked nothing better than tempting a business interested in their town to come to Clarinda.

Andrew Seligman had several favorite sayings. One was, "I made a believer out of him." Today he used the other one. "I didn't call this meeting."

Erin strode into the office and looked around. All the chairs were taken and several people were standing.

"I'm surprised to see *you* here," a man said. "I hear you caused the problem."

Erin retorted sharply. "I didn't call this meeting."

"Time to get started," said Seligman.

Erin removed a notepad from her purse and began taking notes. And quotes.

"We've had a complaint about the upcoming Rocky Mountain oyster festival."

"It's beneath the dignity of the town."

"I didn't know we had any dignity."

"Didn't the Lions Club have a Rocky Mountain feed two years ago?"

"Where is Ben getting them from—a local farmer?"

"A restaurant can't serve meat that isn't government inspected."

"You mean if I go deer hunting, I can't serve venison in my restaurant? That sucks."

"It's true. I think it's true."

"So it's a public health issue."

"That might be one way to stop him. And the station."

"They're probably shipped in from Omaha and inspected—"

Erin cleared her throat and directed her remark to Secretary Seligman. "The complaint you received. Was it from a paid member of this organization?"

Seligman hesitated. And swallowed. "Well, no."

A dissident said, "Do you realize that the radio station has done more to put Clarinda on the map in three weeks than you've accomplished in three years?"

"Why are we entertaining a complaint from a nonpaying nonmember? I've had it with this blamestorming. I'm out of here."

Erin followed.

She wondered how many eyes covertly focused on her destination. Which of the members expected her to go running to Ben with a report of how the chamber had handled the complaint. She fooled them.

Instead, she placed the call from home. "Ben. I just attended a rump session of the chamber. It would be a good idea if the Rocky Mountain oysters came from a government-inspected source. Save the packages, in case someone schedules a raid at the beginning of the evening."

"You expect that?"

"No. I expect us to put Clarinda on the map."

She sat thinking about unreasonable suspicions. Was there any way a person could guard against the shattering of great expectations without indulging in paranoid suspicions? At what point did the common sense of being on guard turn into unreasonable suspicions? Maybe it had to be lived. What did one have left after expectations crashed? Only experience? Only memories?

She stared at the phone and remembered that long-awaited call of long ago. Following the delightful time with Captain Gaylord Haversham in Denver, she had not heard from him in days. Then he called.

"Hey, Ducks. Meet me in LA. We'll fly to Hawaii and get married."

"In my pajamas? Do you realize I'm sitting here in my pajamas?"

"I thought you might be stubborn and say something like, 'I haven't been asked.' Well, I'm crossing the line. Darling, will you marry me? I bought you a negligee. You know, a personal item."

"Are you going to quit talking and allow me to say yes?"

Erin remembered. Hadn't she said, "Yes, yes, yes!"

She'd told her mother the wonderfully exciting news.

Belle said, "Good. I guess your captain isn't married after all, and doesn't have ten kids."

"No, Mother. Apparently not."

They plotted a conspiracy, a conspiracy of silence, based on events in Belle's past. Part of the conspiracy had been grafted from a travel agent's ad. "Don't tell us where you want to go. Tell us when you've been there." There would be ample time to tell friends after the honeymoon.

The bank agreed to the sudden-notice vacation and Erin soon found herself waiting in LAX. The joy of waiting, the joy of anticipation, turned into utter frustration.

"Where is he? Doesn't he realize if he doesn't get here that we will miss our flight?"

"Sorry, we can't hold the plane any longer."

"I'm sorry too," Erin said.

Every few minutes she returned to the counter. "Have you heard anything? Any message for me from Captain Gaylord Haversham?"

"No."

After a couple times it was unnecessary to ask. When she approached the counter they attendants merely shook their heads. There was no way to check his incoming flight. He had been scheduled to arrive on a military plane. And take a taxi to LAX

She waited an hour. One hour became two. She had added the person at INFORMATION to her quest. The gentleman had received no messages. "At least you still have your bags," he said. "They aren't on the plane heading for Hawaii."

She made a reservation at a nearby hotel and left her address with both the airline and Information. In the loneliness of her room she came to grips with what she dreaded. She hadn't wanted to acknowledge what had grown to become the dreadful, undeniable truth. He wasn't coming. The time for blind, unreasoning denial was over.

She remembered vaguely that sometime or other he had mentioned that relationships should be terminated quickly, like a knife cutting through butter. Maybe he did have a wife and six kids. Betrayed, feeling totally invalidated, a torrid seething rage ripped from her depths and rose within her. She regarded her own image in the mirror and saw only him. "You son of a bitch," she cried. "You rotten son of a bitch. You stood me up."

Tears coursed down her cheeks. Her shoulders shook to her sobs. She felt empty now, completely drained. An ice cold and dreadful hand closed over her heart. She spoke to herself words that would be chiseled in stone. *I WILL NEVER PUT MYSELF IN THIS POSITION AGAIN!*

She returned to Clarinda. "Ma," she sobbed, using a term for her mother she thought she had outgrown. "I allowed myself to be deluded. I guess he has a wife and six kids after all. I feel wretched. I feel like a—" She couldn't bring herself to say the word. At length substitutes came bursting out. "Like some hooker. Like some cheap street woman."

"You can't say you didn't bring it on yourself."

"Don't, Mother. I'm already devastated. You can't know how I feel."

"Can't I?" Belle's voice raised with her eyebrows. "I know precisely how you feel. I've been there."

"You, Mother?"

"I don't want to talk about it."

Erin prepared to tell the staff at the bank that the vacation had all been a swindle, that some crook's chicanery had been discovered, resulting in cancellation, fortunately before they went winging off to Hawaii.

Belle admitted to telling only her best friend about Erin's planned honeymoon, which ultimately needed to be followed by a denial.

"It's probably all over town by now," Erin said. "A denial will be futile, but do it. It will give the tantalizing tongue telegraph something to untangle."

"I understand how you feel, dear," Belle said consolingly.

"How could you?" Erin said, sniffing. "At least you married the man of your dreams. So your family disowned you. You had a victory to cling to. You had your man. So it didn't work out. Grandmother finally came around. I recall our trips to Atlantic—how she tried to make a little lady out of me. I guess her efforts were in vain. With you, it all worked out in the end."

"You don't know the half of it," Belle said. "What end?"

Then came the terrible news of the captain's plane crash, followed by another flood of tears. Thoroughly ashamed of her vile outburst at the hotel, riddled with guilt, Erin sank into the depths of depression. Cursing him had been stupidly unfair, as unfair as being poor. She struggled with a terrible reality.

How could she possibly live without him? "I can't live without him," she cried over and over. "How can I?"

"You go to work," her mother said. "You put one foot ahead of the other and put a smile on your face. You go to work and pretend that nothing has happened."

Hopeless and helpless, she plodded to work, a fixed expression on her face, hoping somehow to outdistance not only grief but self-denigration. SHE'D BEEN UNFAIR!

She was being punished. She worried that the pervasive wretched feeling would never leave her.

"You go to work," her mother said. "You put one foot ahead of the other and go to work. This too shall pass."

The days passed slowly. She went about her tasks mechanically, and slowly she put the worst of it behind her. A month of concern and suspicion led to confirmation after two months. What she felt inside might realistically alter her dreary life. What had happened, what she felt inside was to be expected and gave her great joy. Her heart soared. If she had been deprived of the love of Captain Gaylord Haversham, she would not be deprived of their love child. She longed for the child—his child. She had never before considered a child to be a living memorial. She wouldn't go slinking off to some remote town to have the child. She would bear the captain's child right here in Clarinda, look everyone straight in the eye with a Go-Straight-To-Hell look if they gave the slightest hint of according her censure.

She made plans. No way would she find herself in the same destitute situation that had befallen her mother. The future of little Gaylord—or Gayla—was assured. She had the house and a secure job. Her mother would be there to lend assistance.

She wondered, would she experience morning sickness? She smiled at the idea of walking into a restaurant, appearing positively pregnant, seating herself next to a single man and chatting with animation, reaching out to touch his arm in an overfriendly gesture. What would people think? Their reactions would certainly be interesting.

"So when are you going to tell me about your pregnancy?" Belle demanded.

"When I'm sure," Erin replied. "I suppose you expected me to return pregnant all along."

"The thought crossed my mind. One plus one is still three, given the right equation."

Friday morning began with uneasiness. Erin suppressed her nausea at breakfast with toast and orange juice. The thought of lunch lost its savor. By late afternoon the rippling within her had become insistent, a raging tide destroying everything in its path. The spontaneous abortion occurred late that evening, dashing her hopes, her every dream. Possibly the result of an endocrine imbalance or some mystery of nature, no hospitalization required, Erin returned to work promptly Monday morning, "putting one foot ahead of the other, a smile on her face."

She had played the game. She had taken a hefty swing at the ball and solidly connected. She had broken into a run for first base, only to hear the umpire say, "Foul ball, strike two." Then she just stood there and took a sizzling fast ball. The umpire said, "Strike three. You're out!"

No longer expecting the captain's child, she had only a tale of romantic experience, little more than a fading memory. She told herself it was fate, retribution—punishment. She was being punished for playing a game she should not have played, for thinking ill of the captain, for calling him vile names. She felt herself slipping back into the quagmire of depression and vowed not to sink into the dismal depths. She immersed herself in work. Was it fate, a reprieve, that brought a check in the mail? The captain had made her his beneficiary. Not long after the twenty-thousand-dollar insurance check arrived, she received a larger check constituting the rest of his remaining assets.

If fate had taken a hand, it had to be for a purpose. She would make the money work in his memory. The money would be a growing monument to him. She set about investing with a vengeance. Half of the funds went into companies with household names, companies whose stock prices had plunged, including Chrysler, IBM, and K-Mart. She reasoned that if the government didn't want Chrysler to fold, it wouldn't fold. To supply balance she invested in a little-known company, one with a future in the computer business. Microsoft emerged and began to move. She added her own savings.

"Unlucky in love, lucky in investing," she told her mother when she mailed money to the Piper Jaffray brokerage firm in Omaha.

"Actually you were very lucky in love," her mother pointed out. "At least you didn't stay pregnant."

"Are you saying you regretted having me?"

"Never. Not for an instant. To the contrary. I never regretted having you. I hated not being able to provide for you the way I wanted."

Erin withdrew her hand from the phone and halted her reverie. *Onward and upward.* Building on her early investment successes, she had enlarged her horizon by investing in KNDA. She thought of Doris who would frequently assert, "Life is basically unfair." Doris had a way of coming to grips with reality. She continued to show up; she continued to play the game. She assumed that about now Doris would be at home, waiting for Downbeat Jackson to call for her.

Erin had guessed correctly. At the moment, Doris was fussing around the house. She knew the matter had to be addressed sooner or later. She also realized that later had arrived. Later was *now.*

"Keith," she called out. "Come in here, please. I want to talk to you."

Keith swaggered in and said, "You hit me. I don't like that. You are never going to hit me again."

"I hope not," Doris said. "I hope it doesn't become *necessary.*"

"What do you mean? Necessary?"

"I want you to remember that slap. It signals a new beginning." She raised both hands with scolding index fingers extended, bobbing in unison to indicate she was doubly serious. "Let's talk." She faced him directly. "We have had our share of trouble and I admit I made some mistakes. I withdrew into my shell. I abandoned virtually all social contacts. I allowed my grief to feed on your anger. That's over. Over. I have a good job now—one that I can be proud of. It's a new beginning. I'm out and about. I think I pushed you into being the man of the family. Well, you're not. You're my son and from now on you are going to act as such. And respect me—"

They heard a knock at the door.

"That's Downbeat Jackson," she said. "I want you to go and meet him. Open the door."

"Aw, Ma, do I have to?"

"You have to, if you want to live in my house."

"He hit me too."

"Well, you had it coming. Now open that door."

Keith opened the door with a scowl and muttered a surly, "Come in."

Downbeat extended his hand. "Good evening, Keith."

Keith glanced at his mother and didn't wait for her gesture. He forced himself to say, "Hi."

Downbeat noticed that for all his reluctance Keith gave him a good, firm shake.

"Come in," Doris said. "Sit with us. Keith and I were having a discussion. He mentioned that you hit him. I hadn't gone into that. I was just ready to start."

Keith stared at the floor with downcast eyes.

"It wasn't you I was hitting," Downbeat said. "I was hitting a thief who was stealing from my good friend."

"I could have had permission. Then what?"

"The way you were acting? Give me a break. If you had permission, I would be on my knees now, asking you to forgive my stupidity."

"You want me to get on my knees?" Keith said in a belligerent tone.

"Of course not," Downbeat said, turning up his palms. "I'm just trying to explain how it came down. It wasn't the good you, the you that I know you can be, that I swatted. It was the bad you, greatly in need of correction. As they say, it was nothing personal. Nothing personal at all."

Keith grimaced. "Do we have to talk about it?" He looked at his mother. "Why is he horning in?"

"Because I invited him," Doris said firmly. "Wise counsel should be valued and appreciated—by anyone with a grain of sense." She mounted a hopeful smile and asked Downbeat, "Do you think my son can get a job? I was going to tell him he needs to go out and get a job."

"He can get a job—if he tries." Downbeat said. "If he works at it."

"With my record?"

"That's a broken record," his mother said. "It's an old record. It's a juvenile record. I keep telling you that." She turned to Downbeat. "What's your take on it?"

"Let's see what Keith has to offer," he said. "All right, first the negatives. An old juvenile record. Lazy. Lacks motivation, needs a push. In the plus column—he's sound of wind and limb. Fairly good looking. Well muscled. High school graduate."

"Top fourth of his class," Doris said with pride.

"There you go. Intelligent," Downbeat said. "Basically a good kid. In the neutral column, a third-class con man. How that plays out remains to be seen. It's up to you, Keith. It seems to me you have something to offer. You will need to get a job sooner or later."

"Hunh?"

"Your mother is a fine-looking woman. One day she is going to be sitting at her desk at the station, when in walks a corn broker from Illinois who wants to marry her and take her with him to Chicago."

"Mom?" Keith said with total incredulity.

"Yes, your Mom. She's a fine-looking woman."

Keith looked at his mother as he hadn't in a long time. He had to admit that she was far from ugly. She was a fine-looking woman. "Mom, would you do that?"

"Quicker than you can say red-eye special."

Her words stung Keith and he reverted to being a brat. "I don't like you moving in," he said to Downbeat.

"I'm not moving in. I was invited to sit at this table—by your mother—someone you ought to listen to. Each man is the architect of his own disasters. Like I said, you're basically a good kid."

A sullen Keith pretended not to hear and stalked toward his room.

"Ready?" Downbeat asked.

"And able," Doris said.

"Did you leave out willing?" he teased.

"Complaining already? Quit while you're ahead. Let's go."

Within minutes they were seated in the same booth in Miss Kitty's restaurant. Doris said solicitously, "Would it bother you terribly if I ordered an Erin. Just one?"

"Be my guest. I've licked my booze problem. It's just a day-to-day grind now." He laughed timidly. "There is one thing I miss. I need to remember everything now. I need to use my head." Seeing a puzzled look, he explained. "There is only one advantage to being a drunk. You don't have to remember anything. You can always pretend you forgot."

"Isn't that interesting. Something so dreadfully bleak still has a positive. That's what I need to look for in Keith."

"He will make it if he gets off the dime. There's good stuff in him even if he doesn't realize it. If he can overcome his doubts—"

"You think?"

"I'm sure of it."

"That's good to know."

"I've been waiting to get serious with you," he said. "I guess I shot off my mouth back at the house."

She reached out and covered his hand. "Corn broker. Chicago. I read between the lines, even if Keith didn't. Maybe I'm moving too fast. Are you that corn broker? Or am I assuming too much, too fast?"

"Maybe I'm the one who is assuming too much. I know that I'm full of corn."

"I suppose I have competition—right there in the station," Doris said, significantly raising the tapered glass.

He nearly blurted, "Out of my league." How could he phrase it so she wouldn't feel as if he'd lowered his sights to include her? He regrouped. "It has to click before it's right."

Her hand remained on his. "What I mean to say, Downbeat, I don't know why you'd want to take on a whole new set of problems as well as the ones you already have. One set is more than enough."

"It's no good being alone," he said. "Like the song, sometimes I wonder why I spend each lonely night."

"A person should have to battle only one big catastrophe in a lifetime. You battled your demons and won. Oh, I know they're still lurking in the shadows. Despite what you said, I feel the worst of my problems still lie ahead. I noticed how well you handled Keith. I doubt if he would ever accept you as a father figure. He's starting to resent me."

"He'll get over it. The last thing I want to do is come between you and your son. With two sharing the load, it might just be easier."

"It might work."

"It could."

"If we took it slow."

"One step at a time."

"Sure."

In the morning, when they met at the station, they acknowledged each other with a glow of affection, then went about their business in a calm, mature, rather disinterested manner.

"Congratulations," Erin said in a quiet voice totally without emotion.

Doris replied equally without emotion. "The log of Starship KNDA. Erin Ames aboard."

Presently it was time for the Trading Post. On the first day, Downbeat had positioned a platter of "I'll Never Smile Again" in case the program encountered dead time due to a lack of callers. The disc had never been played. From the outset, the Trading Post was a glowing success but not without a problem.

Downbeat cleared his throat on the air—he never did that unless ready to launch a tirade. "Folks," he began. "KNDA offers its listeners a sincere apology. For several days the same person has initiated the first call. Now there is nothing wrong with ambition, but we have learned that this caller has a business selling furniture and antiques from her home. KNDA will not knowingly accept an ad for the Trading Post from any business. We have a ten dollar Buy-Sell show in the afternoon strictly for that purpose." He made a mental note to thank Erin for the information. "All right, I'm ready for the first caller."

"Hi, Downbeat. I want to buy a square washtub with legs—metal legs."

"Sounds like work to me," Jackson quipped.

"I'm not going to use it for laundry," the caller said. "I have a special project in mind."

Jackson chortled. "Now you're not going to tempt me to ask what for."

The Trading Post program attracted the attention of Police Chief Wilbur Wendinger. In his office, the chief said grumpily, "He's talking about Beulah's Barn. We all know that she's a fence. Now the thieves have got a show of their own."

"Weren't you listening? He turned her off."

"Yeah, yeah. Crooks can still advertise what they stole. And if someone wants a girl's bike, one kid will steal it, another kid will contact the buyer. For instance."

"Do you want to assign an officer to listen?"

"No. Next thing you know he will be involved with buying bargains. I think I will listen myself. You know what they say, if you want something done right, do it yourself."

"Does that including kissing?" Ellen asked. She held back a hyena laugh and donned an expression of mock solemnity.

"Depends where it's directed," said the chief.

Chapter Nine

Lonica Barca read the sign. CLARINDA 2 MILES. It was just like Alex to hide in a sleepy little town in a state that grew nothing but corn. The Corn Ball.

"Clarinda," she mused, allowing the word to play off her tongue in song. How sleepy is Clarinda? The town had to have some life if it had a radio station. They probably rolled up the sidewalks at half past five, long before the sun set. Maybe folks sat on their porches sipping coffee or tea. Did anything really ever happen in Clarinda? Probably not. Probably not.

She would make something happen. "This time," she warned herself, "don't go storming in, all bellicose and bluster, shouting accusations at Alex." She'd done that last time, in Michigan, and blown it. Confronting Alex had given him time to flee. This time she would slip into town quietly. This time she would opt for a private attorney instead of a county attorney. This time she would nail his hide to the wall. This time she would win.

The automatic station finder on the car radio pulled in the strong signal of KNDA. She heard the announcer say, "For a long time Count Basie called it 'Sign Off Number.' One night the show was running late and the harried announcer shouted excitedly, "It's one o'clock! Jump!" From that time on, the tune has been known as 'One O'Clock Jump.' This is KNDA, Clarinda, Iowa. A Jake Cooper Station."

"Strictly cornball." Lonica sniffed. She reviewed the facts to be related to her attorney. Last time she tracked Alex to Michigan, confronted him, and he'd skipped before the county attorney could file for child support under the Uniform Reciprocal Enforcement of Support Act.

An apologetic county attorney murmured, "Sorry. Until a parent is served, we are powerless."

Serve the documents first.

To remain a woman of mystery and to avoid detection, Lonica donned dark glasses and draped a scarf across her face when she drove past the station. It would be her luck to see Alex standing outside, have him recognize her and skip. She didn't see Alex. Of course he might be here anywhere. She maintained the disguise as she parked near Orville Keane's office, a name she had selected out of the yellow pages.

When his secretary informed him of the presence of an out-of-state client, Orville dropped what he was doing, ran out to the waiting room, arm outstretched, ready to eagerly pump her hand. He rushed her into his office with the queen-bee treatment. "I'm delighted to make your acquaintance. Now what is it I can do for you?"

"Do you know Alex Barca?"

"I've met him," Orville said.

"I want you to sue him for child support, past, present and future."

Orville listened to her tale of woe and asked, "How ever did you find him?" She seemed better at it than the police might be under similar circumstances.

"I had a friend in Michigan who told me that requests kept coming in from Clarinda, Iowa, requesting information about Alex Barca. I put two and two together, verified his presence by using Ma Bell, and here I am. Is there any way we can get him locked up before the hearing?"

"Not with what you've told me thus far. Let me ask you this. Assume you have two choices. One, you receive a check for child support every month, mailed to—" He raised his eyebrows.

"Bellefontaine, Ohio."

"Two. You receive a check every month mailed to Bellefontaine, Ohio, but first some big galoot beats up Alex. When he's lying there, you come along and kick him in the groin with your pointed-toed shoes. All hypothetical of course, but which alternative would you really like?"

"The kicking. That was a dumb question."

"I know. An absurd question, but I used it to ascertain your level of devotion to the cause."

"He hurt me and I want to get even. I want to hurt him back if I can. I'm mad as hell. Does that explain it?"

"I understand. All right," Orville said. "We can get him served. I need to explain what might happen. Worst-case scenario, he runs again. But this time we get a warrant. When would he get arrested? Who knows? Perhaps in a month. Maybe not for a year. Your children might be in college before he's located." He saw her ready to erupt and raised a silencing palm. "Hear me out. I'll finish this bad probability and go on. If he's found in another state, there is the costly matter of extradition. Or you could travel to that state and initiate a reciprocal action. In the meantime he would probably be released. Away he skips again. Let's foreclose all that. If you have patience, I think I can eventually bring home the bacon."

"In the meantime, who feeds my children? Not feeding children is criminal."

"I agree," Orville said and made a note to tell the judge in argument that Alex not feeding his children was really criminal. He took a breath. *Domestic relations. Parents sniping at each other, using kids as pawns. Kids became ping-pong balls batted back and forth. This is a helluva way to make a living.* He quickly stifled the thought. "It will take at least a month after he's served to get him into court."

Her shoulders lowered to an expelled breath. "You make it sound hopeless."

"Hear me out. Not if you have patience. I'd like you to give me a couple months. I'd like to consolidate this case with a possible criminal matter. If that happens, we can hold him. Maybe."

"A crime. You suspect Alex of a *crime?* Really?"

He uttered a noncommittal, "Ah. Well." He waved his hand in an airy, vacillating gesture. "Put it this way. Alex is too clever by half. If we dig, it wouldn't surprise me if we found something criminal."

"What about costs? What's this going to cost me?"

"I like a person who is direct," Orville replied unctuously. "Not a cent up front. The court doesn't like fat old attorneys taking a bite out of what is due the child. We will just let the court determine what I should have after I collect." He didn't tell her he knew Alex owned one-sixth of KNDA.

"Not a cent up front?" Lonica said. "That's too good to be true."

Orville continued. "In the meantime, use what you expected to pay me to take care of the children. I have to level with you. I represent the radio station and a couple of the stockholders. There is a remote possibility of a conflict of interest. If that arises, I will let you know. We can transfer the file to another law office here in town. I'm pretty sure I can get them to give you the same deal."

"Do you think I should get another attorney now?"

"No. Not now. I'll file the case and get your ex-husband served and—"

She cut him off. "Ex-husband, nothing," she erupted. "He's not my ex-husband. I'm still married to the son of a bitch."

"Well," Orville said, mind racing toward another fee. "In that case we could represent you on the divorce. Would you like me to file for divorce at the same time?"

"If you think that's best."

Orville rubbed his hands together. "Failure to provide child support. Child abandonment. Child neglect. We might try for a charge of child abuse. It's thin for a criminal case, but before the right judge, who knows what might happen? Did Alex ever hit you or the children?"

"All the time. He's a nasty little bastard."

"Ah, now we have something. Real criminal activity.

"It didn't happen in this jurisdiction, but we need it to hold him in custody. Now try not to be impatient. I need time. The judge I prefer doesn't get back from vacation for a while. Then we need time to see what Alex has been up to."

"You've shown more spark than I've seen in a long time. And the price is certainly right."

"All right, have a seat in the conference room." He handed her a yellow pad. "Write down everything you can recall about the beatings. Date, time and place. How many hits and to whom. And the circumstances. In the meantime I'll have my secretary prepare some sworn complaints for your signature."

When the papers were signed, Orville repeated, "Do you understand that I'm not going to serve Alex right away? There may be criminal matters we need to pursue. I can't imagine that sly old Alex hasn't cut a corner or three someplace."

"All right," she said. "I'll go along with it. But if Alex escapes before you get him served, I'm going to hold you responsible."

"I know." He knew exactly what she meant. Aloha on the steel guitar and farewell to his liability insurance. He prepared an additional agreement of understanding that stated Lonica Barca agreed to waive time for immediate filing to allow for further investigation. A clause allowed her to rescind and initiate immediate action.

Orville's secretary interrupted. "I need to collect a filing fee."

"I knew it was too good to be true," Lonica said.

"Not for me," Orville quickly interposed. "It's for the court. They charge for filing documents."

"Well," Lonica admitted, "it's better than an exorbitant retainer."

Orville's last words to her were, "Try to be patient."

In the solitude of his office, Orville leaned back in his luxurious chair and realized he faced a dilemma. If he explained the matter concerning Alex Barca to Cordelia Cooper, she might go off like one of the firecrackers that local kids crossed the Missouri line to obtain. Relative to a possible conflict of interest, he had an obligation to tell Cordelia; however, that could wait until after Alex had been served. In the meantime, he didn't want the case compromised by Cordelia's precipitate action. He knew he needed inside information. He made a compromise of another kind. He picked up the telephone.

"Erin. Hello. I have copies of the tapes you wanted. Would it be possible for you to stop at my office to pick them up? We also need to discuss another matter."

"Will do."

He had his pitch prepared. "Erin, I know you've had experience with audits. First when you worked at the bank, and later at the S and L. I'll get right to it. I want you to conduct an audit of KNDA. Very quiet. No one must know about it."

"Did Cordelia ask—?"

"No," he said quickly. "Heavens no. Be particularly careful not to mention it to her. Or anyone. This is extremely important and not without risk."

Erin came away from the meeting intrigued, almost fascinated. She mulled attorney Orville Keane's request. Although he had been her attorney and would be again, attorneys had to be dealt with at arm's length. She had to remember he might have an agenda of his own. He had advised her not to speak to Cordelia about an audit and had warned her about the risk. That is the way she would play it. However, it didn't make sense to terminate her friendship with Cordelia. The two of them represented more than eighty-three percent of the voting stock, a quorum, a majority, which meant a meeting of the two of them would certainly be more reasonably *constituted* than the last chamber of commerce fiasco.

"Still single?" Cordelia challenged when she saw Erin flouncing toward her on heels.

"After hearing this from my mother, after all these years, I finally got her to stop. Don't tell me that now you're going to start." Erin laughed. Cordelia's taunt made traditional sense. Sixty years ago the salaries of women in Clarinda were so low that marriage was looked upon as an economic necessity. Certainly that was no longer true.

Cordelia suppressed a grin. This girl could think on her heels. It would be difficult to disarm her. "Your mother is the lucky one. I suppose she is even lucky at bingo."

"A cut above average. She wins frequently."

"Constantly." Cordelia smiled.

"May I change the subject? I love working at the station, Cordelia. The way I look at it we may be living on borrowed time. We have Mr. Barca, two ladies, a professional announcer, and two part-time announcers. When we add up the salaries, utilities, and routine expenses, it appears that the handwriting is on the wall."

"You figured that out?" Cordelia shifted uneasily.

"The station is presenting itself like an Omaha network station. I don't know how long we can carry it off."

"Which means—?"

"There are two ways to go. Cut back on staff or sell more advertising. Actually there's a third way—a merger with a cash-rich business."

"Do you have something in mind for a merger?"

"No, it is just a reasonable statistical possibility."

"I've been worried about something else," Cordelia said. "Why hasn't the government come around and shut us down? Why haven't we received a belated cease-and-desist order? Why haven't they levied a fine? After blasting with megawatts, I can't understand it. Knowing how keen the government is on exercising power—and grabbing taxpayers' money—I can't understand it."

"Hmmm," Erin mused. "Maybe we should count our blessings."

"It's as if gravity has been suspended. The government doesn't go around conferring blessings."

Erin seized the opportunity to tease. "What about you? Has some rich farmer stopped by and decided to roll you out of here?"

"No," Cordelia answered. "They're too afraid of being shot."

The way she said it, Erin assumed she had a weapon handy. "I thought they'd probably be afraid of Buster."

"That too. I'm glad you stopped in. I will mull over the possibilities. Maybe I'll think of something."

On her next visit to the station, Erin spoke to Downbeat Jackson. "Suppose KNDA wanted to merge with a company that would compliment our business, and in addition could provide a security blanket. What kind of company would you suggest?"

"It's that bad?" he said soberly. "Off the top of my head I would say media. A newspaper, television, even cable. I could check around."

"On the QT," she said solemnly.

"Right."

Doris intervened. "Are you two discussing the nutsy nosh?"

"It's not a nosh," Erin countered. "It's a gourmet feast."

"Not with those things. Yuck. Listen, let's get serious. Erin, what are you wearing? We have to be color coordinated. A clash with my appetite is one thing—and about all I can stand. I suppose you're going as Cinderella."

"Remember what your grandmother said about speaking in jest. I'll probably go as a pumpkin." *Reminds me I need to invite R-ex, my friendly pharmacist.*

"The boss has been strangely silent," Doris said.

"He hasn't been invited," Erin said.

Downbeat predicted, "We'll hear from him when our campaign gets rolling."

They had previously conspired not to talk about the event when Alex was present. It was their way of fending off censure for offenses real and imaginary. As predicted, when the spots began to run regularly, Alex appeared and demanded, "What have we committed the station to do? You mentioned an appearance by station personnel."

"The station is committed to absolutely nothing. I can show you the contract. With an entirely private agreement, on her own time, Erin will emcee the opening. That's what the client wants. She has generously agreed. Did you know she has a drink named after her—long before you and I came on the scene?"

"I knew that," Alex snapped. *The bitch has a drink named after her? What next?* "Very well. Carry on."

"Carry on?" Downbeat questioned when Alex had gone. "What are we, some military outpost? Who does he think he is, some top sergeant?"

"Oh, much higher than that," Erin said without emotion.

"You've got the swagger stick," Doris observed.

"And I'm going to use it," Downbeat said. "He went into the booth, made a station break, and whapped the table top twice. "Listen. if you've never enjoyed Rocky Mountain oysters and have always had a hankering to try them, come join Erin Ames and some of her KNDA friends at Sarah's Sports Bar and Restaurant. And remember, if you buy the dinner, you get an Erin free. That's *an* Erin, not *the Erin.* Don't be square. See you there."

"About color coordination," Doris persisted.

With discussion came consensus: blue—light blue.

Erin squeezed into a blue sheath, combed her hair up in a beehive, and sprayed it with "shellac" to prevent a single strand from straying.

She planned to arrive early. Ordinarily at this hour a cannon could be fired down the street without danger of hitting anyone. Tonight, couples in animated conversation streamed into Sarah's. Erin walked in and saw the mayor and his wife seated with attorney Jerry Kessler and his wife. She identified chamber members who had tried to prevent the event. *Hypocrites.*

The building was somewhat wider than the average store, and Ben and Sarah McAllister had taken advantage of its depth by providing a space for dancing behind the kitchen. The tenant in the adjacent business did not need the depth of that building to conduct his business. An opening had been cut in the walls to allow dancers to use the rear portion of the next-door building as well. Tonight there would be no dancing. The entire L-shaped area had been filled with tables and chairs.

An enthusiastic Ben explained he had hired a bouncer "to inhibit catcalls."

Pharmacist R-ex arrived and stared at Erin's face. "You're wearing makeup! Since when?"

"Well, hello. Since I went to Omaha and decided to try some non-allergenic stuff. So far it's working. Just what the saleslady promised. No reaction." She remembered that she had never called for the hypo-allergenic lipstick that had finally arrived. R-ex would probably sulk and become noncommunicative. To prevent a dismal mood she played the ever-reliable close-to-his-heart card. "Here's your ticket. It's worth twenty bucks!"

Attired in a powder-blue suit and wearing a lovely corsage, Doris arrived on the arm of Downbeat who purchased a ticket that would not require her to eat "those things." They had already decided that when Downbeat received his free Erin he would slide it across the table to Doris. A free Erin was included only with "those things." Doris had been warned that if she said "Yuck" even once during the evening, something dire would happen, not excluding having an Erin poured over her head.

"Look," Downbeat exclaimed, "There's Keith. He decided to come after all." He strolled over and handed Keith the ticket originally intended for his mother.

Ben banged a spoon on a glass. "I want to thank you all for coming. What a crowd! Have a great time. If you get out of line, we will be sure to capture you on film." He pointed toward Sarah, busily engaged with a camcorder. "Now, Erin, come over here and draw the first Erin. The winner is one of our regulars, Stan Nothwehr."

"Good evening." Erin smiled and made eye contact with the crowd. "It has been said that life in the fast lane here in Clarinda is really a dirt road. I think we have laid some paving tonight." She tilted the glass, held it under the spigot, and pulled back the tap handle. With great ceremony she dropped in the maraschino cherry. She held up the glass and kissed it before sliding it toward the waiting winner.

"That's right," someone shouted. "Kiss it good-bye."

A young farm couple won the privilege of sitting with them at the KNDA table. Olaf Larson farmed near town. Active in the regional politics of the Sons of Norway lodge, his wife, Inga, had written a couple of cookbooks featuring traditional Norwegian fare, which gave Erin an idea for another promotion.

Presently people were saying, "Wasn't this fun? Where has the time gone?"

Doris said "It is time to—" She halted, mouth agape, when Chief Wilbur Wendinger and a deputy accosted Keith.

"I ain't had no beer," Keith said. "None at all." He had agreed with Downbeat at home that beer wouldn't be a good idea. He had not yet reached the age of twenty-one.

When the officers hustled Keith past the KNDA table, Downbeat rose and said, "He hasn't been drinking."

"This ain't about drinking," said the chief. "We had a complaint from your station. Mr. Barca went out back where he parked and found all his tires flat."

"Alex wasn't there when we left. What time did he park?"

"According to my man, about ten or fifteen minutes after seven."

"Then it couldn't have been Keith. He has been here since quarter to seven and he hasn't left. You will look silly if you arrest him for something he didn't do." Downbeat glanced at Ken's wife who had pointed her camcorder at them.

Chief Wendinger directed a question to Erin. "Was he here all night?"

"He was here all night," Erin said.

"Go back and sit down," the chief told Keith with a scowl. "It looks like you're off the hook."

"He was never on," Downbeat observed.

The chief muttered, "C'mon, Earl. Maybe he had somebody else do it."

"Thanks, man," exclaimed a relieved Keith. "For going to bat for me."

"You're welcome," Downbeat said. "But I didn't do it *for* you." He hesitated. "What I mean, I did it because it was *right.* You happened to be standing in the right. Lincoln said something about standing with a man when he's right. I'm happy to do that any time."

"See?" Doris said with raised eyebrows.

Keith returned to his friends.

Doris regarded Downbeat. "Well?"

Downbeat said, "Well?"

Erin added her, "Well. Now we have a chorus."

"Alex has four flat tires," Doris said with ample sarcasm. "Now isn't that a shame?"

R-ex said, "Do you have a ride home?"

"Yes," said Erin.

"I thought so. Thanks for the ticket."

When he had gone, Doris said, "There's a live one. All he needs is resuscitation."

"Behave yourself," Downbeat said.

"See you in the morning," Doris said.

"No," Erin said. "I'm at the other place."

It would not be a quiet morning.

Clarinda awakened to the chatter of birds, mostly sparrows. Early-morning risers chattered over coffee cups. Housewives in chenille bathrobes chattered on their phones while husbands wolfed down breakfast. Ben McAllister attempted to reach Erin at the station but learned she had begun the day at her other job. The phone rang at the savings and loan long before business hours, and Erin answered.

"Erin," Ben McAllister raved. "We had an overflow crowd last night at outrageous prices. What a bang-up evening. Wow. Folks were still coming after you left. We need to talk about the next one."

"Obviously."

"I've given it some thought. It can't be too soon or the novelty will wear off. If we put it off too long, someone else with grab it and run with it. I could be left in the dust. Can you help me keep this promotion exclusive?" He paused. "Well, sort of exclusive."

Erin's pen moved as she spoke. "I can give you a RADIO exclusive. I figure your KNDA advertising budget should be dramatically increased. Perhaps as much as fifty percent. It need not be tied to this event. You might want to cut back on newspaper advertising. I can protect you with a penalty clause to prevent our station from accepting any more Rocky Mountain oyster ads. Ouch. That's too broad. We couldn't foreclose a charity. Not much chance of them doing that. As for me, that will continue to be a separate issue. If I am such a celebrity, in addition to four free tickets, how does fifty dollars hit you?"

"Have you heard of Babe Ruth? Another home run! Write it up. Can you do it today?"

"Exactly what I had in mind. The early bird gets the worm."

"Worms. I was squirming last night when some of those big shots arrived. For a minute I thought they wanted to be present at the lynching. Just when I started to relax, in comes the chief and Deputy Dog. I tell you, Erin, my heart was in my throat."

"You can't quarrel with success."

"Amen."

Erin strolled to the station where Doris happily reported, "The phones are ringing off the hook. I have three leads for you, people who want you to call on them."

"Great. But it will have to be later." Erin smiled hopefully. Perhaps with increased revenue the station could keep its head above water.

Downbeat plumped by and said, "We have a chance to get the Glenn Miller band. Some doctors in Des Moines are sponsoring a Saturday night bash. There is a good chance we can get the band before they continue to Oklahoma City."

"Do we have a hall?" Erin asked, but Downbeat had gone to the mike. She retrieved Ben's old contract, made a copy, whited-out portions, and made a copy which she would use for the new contract.

Alex Barca received a phone call from Chief Wendinger. "What kind of problem have you had with Keith Gordoncamp?"

"No problem," Alex replied glibly. "I have never met Keith."

"What's going on here?" groused the chief. "Do you know it's a crime to file a false report?"

"I do. I have never met Keith."

"I'm listening. It better be good."

"Apparently—I didn't see it—apparently Keith came into the station and attempted to remove some money from his mother's purse. Apparently a scuffle ensued. Apparently there were words. Later, I issued an order to Decorah that her son was never to set foot in the station if she valued her job. I'm for law and order. And decorum at the station. Have you arrested him yet?"

"No," said the chief. "Tell me, when did you park your car?"

"Like ten after seven. Maybe fifteen after."

"That's what's in Earl's report."

"You haven't arrested Keith?"

"Not going to," said the chief.

"Why not?" Impatience etched Barca's voice.

"He's got an alibi. Maybe a couple dozen. Including three members of your staff. Have you got a second choice? Anyone else who might be mad at you? An enemy?"

"I don't have an enemy in the world." *My staff alibied the no-good brat?*

"Good-bye then." The chief replaced the phone. *Pipsqueak.* He said to his secretary Ellen, "Did you know Doris Gordoncamp's real first name is Decorah?"

"I knew that."

The chief directed his attention to the radio. Downbeat responded to a question from the Mystery Man. "Listeners, can you identify the mouthy musician who was fired twice by Glenn Miller?"

"Not Alex Barca," suggested the chief's secretary.

A radio listener suggested, "Ray Eberle."

"No," said Downbeat. "That was a good guess though. But not the right one."

"I guessed Ray Eberle because he was missing when the band went to Hollywood to film *Orchestra Wives.*"

"Good reasoning. Glenn and Ray had a contract dispute. Ray wanted something extra for appearing in a movie. That didn't happen. By the way did you notice Jackie Gleason playing bass fiddle in that movie? Now the next caller."

"Ray Anthony," a woman guessed.

"Right on," Downbeat cheered. "You are the winner. You're always a winner when you listen to KNDA. Now give a listen to a tune from *Orchestra Wives.* Here's 'At Last.'"

Downbeat stepped out. "Where's Erin?"

"Gone again."

Erin lost no time in returning to Sarah's Sports Bar and sat down with Ben to execute new contracts.

Ben shook his head. "I still can't get over last night. I'll bet you could name some of those characters who came to see me shut down. Hunh?"

Erin smiled. "Now you know I can't comment on that. We have to settle this. I agree not to appear for Rocky Mountain oyster galas for other people. I may appear for other *events,* christenings, weddings, funerals, a raccoon barbecue." She snickered.

Ben thought her teasing might conceal more. "Is that what you're going to promote next?"

"Not for sure." She wanted to tell him about the Glenn Miller band but decided to wait. "Thanks for giving me the business."

"Thanks for making my business." He crushed an alien thought about someone giving her the business.

Before returning to the S and L, Erin stopped at the office of attorney Orville Keane.

"There is nothing amiss," she reported. "The station books balance to a dime. There is one thing that is interesting. On a number of out-of-town accounts, the spot ads, Alex paid for them with cash. Sure, the ads were at giveaway prices, but we are just getting started. The money came in dribs and drabs, in cash, which prompted me to ask the musical question, 'Where is he getting the money?' He hasn't been out of town when the money comes in."

"Good girl. Keep poking around. I wouldn't look under his mattress."

Erin uttered a borrowed word. "Yuck!" She reminded herself not to get into the habit.

Alex wasn't the type to store money in a mattress, she decided. He was too prissy—unless he wanted to use the money in a hurry. Following intuition, she greeted friends at the Citizens State Bank.

"Does KNDA have an account with you?"

"Yes," replied the teller. "Do you want statements mailed now? The account has a no-statement order."

"No. Leave it as is. And don't mention that I've been making inquiry."

"Sure thing, Erin."

Erin telephoned Orville Keane from her office in the S and L. "I found it. A KNDA account at Citizens State Bank. Withdrawals are on Alex's signature only. No statements are sent. It looks suspicious."

"And it looks legal," Orville said aloud. "There is nothing illegal unless—and until—he taps into the account for his own purposes."

"On the way out of town," Erin speculated.

"You said it. I didn't."

Erin said, "If you were thinking of nabbing him with his hand in the cookie jar, it would be necessary to determine where that money came from. Anyone can set up a KNDA account with their own money—"

"Don't do anything else for now," said attorney Keane. "But if you sense anything in the works, call me day or night."

It would not be difficult to determine receipts. All that needed to be done was telephone the accounts—talk about satisfaction—inquire how they paid, ask them the sums on their checks. Easy. But Orville said, drop it for now. She turned up the volume on her radio and heard Downbeat say with abundant cheer, "Wouldn't it be wonderful if we could get the Glenn Miller band to come to Clarinda?"

He's got them!

Chapter Ten

Alex Barca realized that being in command frequently resulted in loneliness at the top. A staff need not love their leader, but it was imperative that they functioned as a team. Lately the group had become more distant as they exhibited an us-versus-him mentality. Competition, he would remind them, meant magazines, newspapers, and television—not management.

Staff meetings would allow him access to feedback he might not otherwise receive. Lately, station projects had resulted in his remaining on the outside. On the other hand, if he insisted on being included in all decisions, certain worthwhile projects might not see the light of day. It meant walking a fine line. He could not allow the others to know his sadness about exclusion, nor would he tell them how really well they were doing.

They assembled in the largest office with Alex standing in the open doorway. "We need to be considered an integral part of the community," he began. "We're not strangers here as the *Herald-Journal* suggests. That's why we're apportioning membership. Erin Ames is already a member of the chamber of commerce. I've been a member of Rotary before and Downbeat holds an active membership in the Lions." He looked at Tom Berringer. "You can discuss with Dan Pulliam which of you will join the Kiwanis. Now, any news?"

Downbeat said, "Andrew Seligman dropped by one day and wanted to know if there was anything in the pipeline that we wanted to place on the chamber calendar."

Alex shot back, "Is there anything he has that he wants to calendar with us?" He refrained from mentioning that he and Seligman had gotten off on the wrong foot. They'd crossed swords at their first meeting, and each had attempted to take the other down a peg. The result left a bad taste.

Erin said, "I heard that Seligman made some unkind remarks about KNDA. I don't understand that."

"Keep on top if it," Alex said, hoping she wouldn't dig into it. "It's clear Seligman can be a pain."

He's not alone. "We're flying high now," Erin said. "We can't overlook the fad effect. When I'm on the street I no longer hear only Glenn Miller music. Folks are reverting to old habits. Other stations. Maybe it's Miller mood fatigue."

"Man can't live on peaches alone," Downbeat observed. "I'm getting requests for other than Glenn Miller. The issue is, will we be responsive to our listeners? If we are not, there goes our Arbitron."

"We already have a partial answer," said young Tom Berringer. "My 'Beyond Glenn Miller' show fills the bill with its you-asked-for-it format."

"What it's about," Alex said sharply, "is money! Money! We need sales. It's a constant and continuing effort. Anyone leading the pack has worries. If he stops, the hungry hounds in second place are up his tail. We need to expand our lead."

"Well said," Downbeat agreed. "Out west when they talk about leadership they say it pays to look back now and then to see if the crowd is still following."

Alex impaled Downbeat on a steely stare. "I hear you're planning a Sunday night bash. I suppose you're bringing in some squeak-and-squawk country-and-western outfit. We dare not court disaster. Keep me informed."

"I'll let you know, boss. As soon as I have anything."

"Meeting over. Get back to work. And sell!" Alex stalked to his office.

"Stick around," Downbeat whispered to Erin. He closed the door when the others were gone. "I hired the Glenn Miller band!" he said beaming.

Erin's hands found her hips and she gave him a look in imitation of Alex Barca. "You mean you hired the Glenn Miller band without having a hall?"

"Sure," he said, eyes atwinkle. "For years McNabb's at Carroll didn't have a roof. And that other place—I can't remember—Swing under the Stars. We can always pitch a circus tent."

"We need to play this cool," Erin said. "We already have an annual Glenn Miller festival. I remember the first one, back in '76. Glenn's younger sister, Irene Miller Wolfe came in to honor her brother's memory. Ben Zersen, the banjo player in Glenn's first high-school band, arrived. I stood there with the crowd at the birthplace house when the Lion's Club and National Federation of Music Clubs dedicated the bronze plaques on the stone. At the beginning, folks just came because they wanted to be here. Now, every year they come by the thousands. We don't want to appear like we're usurping their thunder."

"Right. We'll try to keep our celebration separate. We'll try to establish our own identity. We'll just have a dance with the Glenn Miller orchestra. That's happening all over the country."

"There will be a difference," Erin noted. "At the annual festival everyone knocks themselves out for a week, working day and night. This dance will be for our own pleasure and enjoyment."

"Good point. Perhaps I can include that in my spiel."

Doris swung open the door. "Can anyone get in on this party?"

"Later. We're going out to see the local Sy Schribman."

"Who?"

"Rudy Wagoner. The owner of Cordelia's Ballroom," Erin supplied.

"C'mon, sweetheart," Downbeat said lustily in his imitation Bogart voice.

As they hurried out, neither of them saw displeasure clouding the face of Doris Gordoncamp. She scowled and muttered, "This competition is getting out of hand." She thought about inflating Erin's hours, getting her in trouble, but Erin would straighten that out with Alex. A raving Alex might fire her. No, Doris decided, it would be better to swallow her pride and not tangle with Erin Ames, who, after all, happened to be a *stockholder*. She sniffed and shrugged in resignation. "Life is basically unfair."

Downbeat rehearsed on the way to the meeting. "We need to play this close to the vest. We can't allow some bartender to slip in ten of his friends and their families. We risk a loss on the band. We're entitled to a cut of the profits on liquor. We furnish the tickets and the ticket takers. We need a joint inventory of the liquor."

Rudy Wagoner, the second owner of the Cordelia ballroom after Jake Cooper, had not bothered to change the name of the hall. It would have meant losing name identification.

Rudy, a man of middle-age and conservative bent, listened to a replay of what Downbeat had rehearsed. He bobbed his head and said, "Sunday night is not my favorite night. It's hard to attract a crowd on Sunday night."

"You can't lose," Downbeat enthused. "Instead of an empty hall on Sunday night, you will have half the profits on drinks and there is no risk to you on the band. We expect an overflow crowd. We could go another way. KNDA will rent the hall for cash."

"Nooo," Rudy said, drawing out the word. "I'll take a flyer on half the liquor. It's always easier to divide a profit than it is to split a loss. A loss can be a problem for me, and as I see it there is no way for me to take a loss with half the profit on the booze guaranteed." He'd heard rumors that the station might fold, just like when Jake Cooper had it. "It's none of my business, but do you have an underwriter for the band, other than the station?"

"Erin here," Downbeat said. "She's our angel."

Erin summoned an effort to retain her composure, not to show shock, dismay, and a touch of anger.

Rudy's face brightened with the hint of a smile. "Well, if Erin is backing you, include me in. Erin can come out and help me count kegs and cans. So, Mr. Downbeat, what band have you got? One coming up from K.C.?"

"Glenn Miller," Downbeat said smugly, as if trumping a king with an ace.

"Mensch," Rudy said, clapping a hand over his mouth.

Downbeat wrote out the agreement and signed. Rudy signed and Erin signed where he'd written "Glenn Miller band appearance fee guaranteed by Erin Ames."

"Let Erin know how many tickets you need for staff. She can negotiate that part."

"Me negotiate?" Erin objected when they were under way returning to the station. "You sure played fast and lose with my money."

"Don't worry. I'll give you my hold harmless agreement in writing and I'll work the rest of my life to pay you back if need be."

"I'll take that in writing," Erin said.

"Somehow I knew you would," Downbeat said without emotion. "Now it's up to me to put it over."

When they returned to the station, Downbeat interrupted Tom Berringer and asked him to read a message. "We interrupt this regularly scheduled program for a special bulletin. Can you imagine it in your fondest dreams? Radio Station KNDA is bringing to Clarinda what many of you have requested. You've been waiting for the real thing to come along. KNDA is proud to announce the appearance of the Glenn Miller Orchestra!"

In the chamber of commerce office, Arthur Seligman flew into a rage and hurled an ashtray across the room. "What are they trying to do, dilute our Glenn Miller festival?"

In the back office at KNDA Alex Barca leaped to his feet, his face growing a shade redder with each advancing step. He waved his arms and shouted to Downbeat to get out of the broadcast booth.

"I thought you were going to keep me informed!"

"I was," Downbeat said with a totally innocent look. "I was on the way to your office when I passed the mike and we just had to tell our listeners and advertisers. This news is hot. It's going to sell advertising, boss."

Alex stormed. "What are we on the hook for? What's our exposure?"

"None. Only our reputation," Downbeat said, beaming. "I have a hold harmless agreement—*in writing.*"

"Who's dumb enough to do that?"

"Erin Ames."

"Her again," Alex said, gritting his teeth. He whirled and marched toward his office. Suddenly he turned. "This means an all-out, no-stops campaign. Get on it!"

"I'm on it," Downbeat shouted happily. He bent down and said to Doris, "Before I forget," he made a grandiose gesture as if sweeping off a derby. "Would you do me the honor of accompanying me to the Glenn Miller dance and celebration?"

Happiness rippled up her spine and settled in a warm pool over her heart. "I would do you the honor, sir." The pool drained and she wondered if Erin had declined. *Don't do this to yourself. Stop acting like Keith.* She mounted an anemic smile. *Well, it's easy to see where Keith gets it.*

At Washington Savings Erin made copies of the agreements with Rudy Wagoner. She addressed her employer. "Okay, Sport. How would you like to take me dancing—to the ghost band of the one and only Glenn Miller?"

"Really?"

"Really. KNDA is sponsoring the event. Well," she paused. "In or out?"

"In," Henry Leighton said, wondering if a certain pharmacist had to work that evening. "You know," he posed. "It would really be an event if I got down on one knee in the middle of the dance floor and—" He halted when he saw her upraised palm. "Okay, I'm shut. I'm not saying it."

"Be prepared to dance," Erin warned. "You're going out with a high stepper."

"Don't I know."

At the station, Downbeat covered every angle. "Folks, we know that Sunday night dancing isn't everyone's cup of tea. We're not trying to interfere with your religious practice, and we don't want you hung over Monday morning. Heh-heh-heh. But we are thoroughly overjoyed to be able to bring in the Glenn Miller band. Now if you want to celebrate with KNDA staff, tickets are on sale at the station. Advance ticket purchases are at a savings. If you wish to reserve a table, that will cost you. We may see people from Des Moines, Omaha, and Kansas City. To make reservations fair and equitable, table assignments won't be decided for a couple of weeks in order to give outlying listeners a chance to mail in their checks. Stay tuned. Now here's Marian Hutton to sing that rare wartime ditty, 'The Five O'clock Whistle' and to explain why it never blew."

Because of the publicity, people began arriving from neighboring Missouri, Kansas, and Nebraska on Sunday afternoon.

From Kansas City, Dirk Lowe Bartle arrived alone. Born to wealth, he had disappointed his family early on. He'd wanted to be an actor for as long as he could remember. When he followed his dream, the family saw to it that he would not share their wealth. He'd run the gamut from New York to Hollywood to New York, where he had also been known as Dirk Lowe and Lowe Robart. His soap characters had always been short lived. Now, back in Kansas City for a role in *They Die By Night,* he had used the family's connections to work his way into the organized seamy side of life to make his character real. A friend mentioned an opportunity to play Glenn Miller and when he made contact, he had been told where to obtain a major's uniform. Half the fee had been paid in advance, and while that satisfied him, appearing in Clarinda might have a fringe benefit that would satisfy him more. The Glenn Miller band appearance meant a big box office. He couldn't plan anything on strange turf, but he could certainly keep his eyes open. Accordingly, he drove around Clarinda to learn the lay of the land, and how best to plan a getaway. He wasn't due at the ballroom until well into the dance.

In contrast, many KNDA staffers arrived early. Downbeat, Doris, Erin, and Henry Leighton sat at a table near the entrance, a position Downbeat called "a working location." From this vantage point, it would be easy to assist with problems that might arise, a strategic location to conduct business. The proprietor would know where they were, Downbeat could glad-hand, and Erin would be able to greet friends. Yet, of all the reasons presented, one succinctly stated by Doris counted for more than all others combined. "So we don't have to put up with Alex Barca." Alex and his date were seated in a choice location near the bandstand.

Downbeat noticed the large number of singles, not all of them young. He wondered if they had come stag to save money. Doris explained, "No, they come to meet people."

"In a community this size?" Downbeat questioned. "Aren't they meeting the same people all the time?"

"Tradition," Doris explained.

Downbeat excused himself to jabber with the sidemen.

"We were in Des Moines last night," explained the musician who played the Willie Schwartz clarinet lead. "We were sponsored by doctors, a semiprivate affair. The leading surgeon of Iowa told us he always wanted to be Peanuts Hucko. Imagine! Not Jimmy Dorsey, Artie Shaw, or even Woody Herman. Peanuts Hucko! Go figure."

At length Downbeat returned. "Nice crowd."

"It's finally happening," Erin said.

The band opened with "Moonlight Serenade." Downbeat noticed the crowd no longer fell reverently silent for that long moment. Here and there a member of the American Legion or Veterans of Foreign Wars allowed his thoughts to drift back to a time when at a young age he had been caught up in a war.

"In California," Downbeat said, "the minute a famous band started playing, young people would rush toward the stage and hover near the band. Sometimes the standing crowd occupied half the floor. Especially when either of the Dorseys played."

"Let's dance," Doris said.

"As Benny Goodman would say," Downbeat joked. "Let's dance." Did he imagine for a fleeting second that Erin would rather dance with him? He watched her glide into Henry Leighton's arms.

"We should do this more often," Henry told Erin. "You're the best dancer I know. Where did you learn?"

"That's a long story." Erin didn't tell him how she polished her only pair of shoes and came to the hall and waited around to walk in with a family. One night the ticket-taker's hand reached out. "How many families do you belong to?"

"I don't have any money," she said unhappily. "I want to learn how to dance."

He stared into her depths with eyes that could penetrate a plank. "Wait here," he said sharply. She dreaded that he would call the police but when his replacement appeared he said, "C'mon. You said you want to learn."

Erin took a breath and told Henry, "I became acquainted with a man called Uncle Pete. He took tickets. An older gentleman, short, about five foot six, he was the best dancer I ever met. Girls would come up and ask, 'When are you going to dance with me, Uncle Pete?' When he had to go back to work at the door, if he saw someone he could trust, he would hand me off. 'Mel, here's a nice girl to dance with.' How did you learn to dance?"

"Nothing as exciting," Henry said. "Lessons."

Erin remembered how she would wait for a circle two-step, a mixer that required a change of partners. She remembered tall men who lifted her off her feet, a short fat guy who reeked of stale sweat, and guys drenched in Old Spice. She learned a lot of them couldn't dance well. But she learned to dance. Erin smiled at the memory. At the end of the set she and Henry joined Downbeat and Doris.

Downbeat observed, "The band is good, but not as good as Glenn Miller. Today, musicians just play. When Glenn had the band, the blending of the clarinet lead an octave over the saxes created a special mix. The guys played as if they had been grabbed, you know, like the notes were straining, two percent sharper."

Henry said, "You have a good ear."

It wasn't long before the bandleader, often called Slider, said, "Something old, something new, something borrowed, and something blue. Here's a tune that's old, but very new for the band. We borrowed it from a bandleader who is here with us tonight. How many of you know that your own Downbeat Jackson had a very successful band? His theme was 'Whispering.' I know there is no one who can lead 'Whispering' as well as Downbeat Jackson. Come up here, Maestro, and lead this band."

Downbeat leaped to his feet and pelted toward the stage like a Pop Warner kid rounding third. He raised the baton and "Whispering" issued in the best rendition Downbeat had ever heard. Eyes moist and tears welling, he found himself in an epiphany. "Listen, Nola," he whispered. "It's me again." When the "Zeke Zarchy" trumpet section triple tongued, tears flooded over the rim and coursed down his cherubic face. He blinked. *Man, this is the most.*

Slider saw he was overcome and when the song ended, whispered, "Stay for one more?" He announced to the crowd, "Let's have Downbeat lead the band one more time. Here's 'At Last.'"

By the time the song ended, Downbeat had composed himself. He spoke into the mike, "You don't know what this means to me."

He hurried to the table feeling a warm and fuzzy optimism he hadn't felt in years. He looked at Erin and stretched out his arms. "Come dance with me."

The band played "Sunrise Serenade."

"I haven't felt so thin in years," Downbeat exclaimed. "Look at this crowd, Erin. We pulled it off."

"You pulled it off."

"I couldn't have done it without you."

"Thank you, sir." She closed her eyes and momentarily thought of Captain Gaylord Haversham. When they returned to the table, she murmured another "Thank you, sir" and traded pleasant smiles with Doris.

Each of them wondered if clouds were gathering. What lurked behind their polite smiles?

Doris said, "My turn."

Henry excused himself and walked toward a door designated MEN.

Keith marched the length of the hall for a duty dance with his mother, and seeing Downbeat dance her away, he had to stop awkwardly or continue. He continued.

"Hi," he said clumsily. "I don't suppose you'd like to dance with me."

"I would love to dance with you," Erin said. "Let's hit the floor, Dude."

"Hunh?" For him the phrase meant something else.

"Isn't that the term you young people use for dancing?"

"Well, maybe. Not exactly."

Following a dreamy number the band launched into an up-tempo Harry James favorite, "Two O'Clock Jump," and Keith said, flustered, "What do we do now?"

"We practice," Erin said. She demonstrated a basic step and Keith quickly mastered it. "No, don't look at your feet," she said the way Uncle Pete would say it. "It doesn't matter if you take two steps or three as long as we're dancing in the same direction. Maintain tension in your left arm. That's how I will receive the message of what you intend to do."

Presently Keith spun Erin out and whirled her back. She enjoyed teaching Keith. "Thanks for asking me," she said, directing her eyes toward Jennifer Otley seated across the hall. "There's a girl who would like to dance with you."

Keith grinned. "A homecoming queen shouldn't be neglected. I think I will ask her."

"Great idea."

During an interlude, when everyone returned to the table, Downbeat raised a glass to his lips and took a long swallow. He blinked. "It's spiked," he cried. He wanted to spit but dared not splatter his friends. "S-Some idiot spiked my Seven-Up!" He felt mule kicked. The alcohol burned within him.

Erin plunged a hand into her purse, grabbed a throat lozenge, and popped the bubble. "Here, take this." She ran to the bartender and demanded a glass of water. She ran back. "Here, rinse your mouth with this."

Downbeat's look of anguish dissipated. "Who would do that to me?"

"Probably someone who thought it was a treat," Henry suggested.

"Or a treatment," Doris added.

Downbeat took another swallow of water. "With friends like that who needs enemies?"

The band resumed and Erin said, "Now it's your turn to dance with me again. How do you like the lozenge?"

"It tastes terrible. Do you actually use them?"

"Only when I have a sore throat. Now listen. You didn't fall off the wagon. You didn't reach for a drink. You only had a little cough medicine."

"You almost have me convinced."

"You *are* convinced," Erin asserted.

"I know what you're trying to do."

"It's more important that you know what you're going to do. Take the high road."

Erin sensed Doris's discomfiture and when they returned she said, "Your turn."

Doris lost no time in dancing away with Downbeat.

"I think Doris was a little put out with you," Henry Leighton observed.

"She's laughing now."

When the couple returned, Erin slid another lozenge across the table. "One to grow on." She reached out and touched Doris on the arm. "Look, there is Keith dancing with Jennifer. They make a nice-looking couple."

"Yes, they do."

Downbeat heard it first—a crowd murmur emanating from near the bandstand. He guessed that two young men had faced off and were ready to trade punches. He searched for where he'd last seen Keith.

Over a babble of voices they heard, "It's Glenn Miller!"

A man resembling Glenn Miller strode on stage.

"Did you plan a skit?" Erin asked.

"No," replied Downbeat.

Henry asked, "Why the impersonation?"

Doris shushed him. "A Glenn Miller impersonation? This is bad taste."

From the outset there was no doubt the man was an impostor. If alive, Glenn Miller would be well past eighty. The impostor appeared to be half that age. Whomever it was had researched the role. The rimless glasses were correct. Likewise the WW II Air Force uniform complete with major's bars and crush cap.

Accepting the baton, the impostor spoke into the mike. "Thank you, what a thrill it is to be back in this dump. I mean a real downer." He raised the baton, led the band in a few bars, and silenced them abruptly. "If you ever bring my band into this crazy town again without my permission, you'll have to deal with me. I'll level this dump. You guys stink. The whole town stinks. You're all trying to live on my name and my fame. Get a life of your own. The best thing I ever did was move out of this rat's nest." He waved at the leader. "Come back here and get your stick. These guys stink. They aren't fit to play under my name. You're all fired. I'm putting the bunch of you on report. Latrine duty for a month. Clarinda is that latrine. Start cleaning!"

He tossed the baton at Slider, who stood flabbergasted.

Stepping down from the stage, the impostor spoke to a burly youth, "Lead the way, sergeant. Get me out of this hell hole."

Those near the door heard a car rev and watched it disappear into the night.

Downbeat immediately ran toward the bandstand. When he passed where Alex and his girlfriend were seated, Alex gave him a withering look. Rushing on stage with frantic breaststroke gestures to quiet the crowd, Downbeat pleaded, "I'm sorry to interrupt your fun. Please let me assure you that radio station KNDA had no part in the sorry performance you just observed. We have no information about it. We do not know why anyone would disparage the band or Clarinda. As always, we are asking for your help. If you know anything about this shameful appearance, please give us a call. In the meantime, please enjoy the rest of the evening."

The burly youth who had cleared a path for the impostor had drawn a crowd. "Don't look at me. I don't know anything about this. There was a look about him. When he asked me to clear a path, I just did."

Before his car reached the highway, Dirk Lowe Bartle slowed and darted between a line of cars, slowed again and made a circuitous route in and around the sea of cars. He parked and waited. He put the car in motion and found another spot. Apparently no one had bothered to watch him. With the Glenn Miller band performing, who cared about cars? He changed out of the uniform and a short time after intermission, when a ticket was no longer required to gain admission, entered the hall with a group of young people.

Downbeat's disclaimer helped, but did not dispel the tarnish. The high point of the evening had passed. "Alex shot me a dirty look. I know he thinks I had something to do with this."

"That's Alex. I'm worried about something else," Doris confided. "The money. Call it a premonition. Have we made arrangements for an armed escort?"

"In Clarinda?" Henry said. "This isn't Detroit. If you're worried, I'll carry the cash."

"No," Erin said. "We need a plan."

"I could carry the cash," Downbeat said.

"No," Doris said. "I'd be worried about you."

Erin lowered her voice. "I have a plan."

Unaware that someone else had taken a keen interest in the receipts, they rose to dance when the band played "Moonlight Serenade," the last dance of the evening.

According to plan, Downbeat walked to the ticket booth, accepted the nearly empty cashbox and casually strolled out with it under his arm, followed by a watchful Officer Eastman.

Erin stopped at the ticket booth to say "Good night" and walked out with the receipts in a bag, mostly concealed by her purse. She drove to Washington Savings where Henry stepped out and unlocked the door. Erin ran inside and placed the money in the safe.

"We make a good team," Henry said. "I'd like to make it more permanent."

She wanted to say, "Not now, Henry." She knew the drinks had dissipated some of his restraint. "It's something to think about seriously," she said with a laugh.

Downbeat halted in front of Doris's house. She leaned over and kissed him. "Now, be careful."

"I will. I don't think we have anything to worry about. After all, I don't have the money."

"You look like you do," she said. She could not dispel a haunting worry.

Downbeat drove to the station, parked in front, and approached the door, key in hand. From out of the shadows a dark figure crept up behind him, hit him over the head, grabbed the cash box, and sprinted into the darkness.

Officer Eastman, who had dropped back to cover Erin's deposit at Washington Savings, continued toward the station on routine patrol and found Jackson lying there. Despite Downbeat's protest, "I'm all right," Officer Eastman took him to the hospital and immediately phoned the chief.

"I knew it," complained Chief Wendinger. "I watched a movie and just got to bed. What is it this time?"

"Downbeat Jackson got hit on the head. They robbed him of the cashbox. Fortunately they didn't get any cash." He outlined the diversion.

"Take care of him," Chief Wendinger said, stripping off his pajamas. "I'm on the case!"

He drove directly to the home of Doris Gordoncamp and parked nearby. Presently Keith arrived and parked. The chief sped up, hit the brake, and leaped out. "Just keep walking, Keith. Right into the house."

Doris appeared in her chenille bathrobe. "What is it this time?" She failed to hide her indignation.

"I'll ask the questions. Where have you been, Keith? Since you left the dance hall?"

"I took Jennifer Otley home. We stopped for a malt first, then I came home."

The chief called Jennifer Otley who verified what Keith told him. "Go to bed," he told Keith.

"I know you have a job to do," Doris said. "But I get damn tired—"

"I know what you mean," said the chief. "I have a job to do."

"And I know you need to search our car. Go ahead. I'll wait."

The chief exited and returned presently. "All clear."

"As I knew it would be," Doris said pointedly. So what's the problem? Can you tell me?"

"Your friend Downbeat what's-his-name was hit on the head and robbed." He raised a calming hand. "Don't worry. He's okay."

"I knew there would be trouble," Doris said. "I felt it. I think Erin felt it too. It was a premonition. We came up with a plan—I just knew there would be trouble. So there was no robbery."

"It's still robbery," explained the chief, "even though the thief got only a cashbox and a roll of tickets. Well, thank you, Decorah, I'll be on my way."

As soon as the chief left, Doris called Erin and reported that Downbeat was in the hospital. Erin drove to the hospital at once and found Downbeat waiting for a police car to take him home. Officer Eastman had been called away.

"I'm okay," Downbeat told Erin. "Don't worry about me. I'll get along somehow."

"Come on, I'll take you home."

"I'm glad the crook didn't get the money," Downbeat said. "I certainly don't want to spend the rest of my life paying you back."

Erin laughed. "You mean I can tear up your note?"

"That's what angels do," said Downbeat.

Chapter Eleven

Doris arrived at work early because she wanted to discover the extent of Downbeat's injuries. She learned more than she wanted to hear.

"I'm okay," Downbeat reported. He turned to Erin. "Thanks for giving me a lift home from the hospital. I really appreciated that."

You picked him up at the hospital? Doris scolded herself for not driving to the hospital. She forced her mouth to utter, "I'm glad you were there for him, Erin."

Downbeat looked up from the news copy and said, "I can't read this. It's a black cat for an announcer to read an item where he's mentioned. You'll have to do it, Erin."

"Me?"

"I don't see anyone else around here."

Doris hid her face. *You don't see anyone else around here period.* She muttered under her breath. "I hate talent."

Erin seated herself at the microphone. "This—is Erin Ames—with the news. Clarinda police are searching for the suspect who robbed KNDA staffer Downbeat Jackson. In a brilliant diversion, Clarinda police prevented a possible robbery of the receipts of the Glenn Miller dance held last evening at the Cordelia Ballroom. Chief of Police Wilbur Wendinger explained that although the thief managed to get only an empty cashbox, when apprehended, he will still be charged with robbery."

Listening at the police station, Ellen gave the chief a verbal elbow in the ribs. "Did you hear that?"

"I heard, I heard. You know," he pondered. "I think there is some connection between that phony Glenn Miller and the robbery."

Ellen reacted. "Are you saying that Glenn Miller stole the Glenn Miller dance receipts?"

"He was angry enough, according to the dance patrons. He cussed out the band and the town. That's motive. Like everyone else around here, he had opportunity. Okay, call the station. I'm going to need written statements. I'll stop there by and by and pick them up."

Ellen phoned and spoke to Doris. "You should have seen the chief grinning from ear to ear when he heard the newscast. That grin might stay on his face all day."

Until he picks up my statement. Doris said, "I'll tell the staff."

Following the station break Downbeat came on. "As I was saying when I was so rudely interrupted by a Pearl Harbor attack from some lowlife creep. It reminds me of the time I sat down and wrote 'Jukebox Friday Night.'" He felt he had to explain at least part of the joke. "I only missed it by one night." If the listeners couldn't identify "Jukebox Saturday Night," that was their problem.

He began singing blurbs, absurd lyrics. "Moonlight succumbs you. It goes in your ear. You are my sunburn, my only sunburn. That's from my days in Phoenix. I went to the hospital. There's where I met the girl from Emphysema. I couldn't make time with her. You know those hospital gowns. Yes, we have no pajamas. We have no pajamas today. Heh-heh-heh. Ah yes, I told the Doc. Try to dismember the one correct member. From that old gangrene of mine. Lay that hypo down, nurse, lay that hypo down. Heh-heh-heh."

Erin jumped up and stood in front of the glass panel, frowning. She drew a hand across her throat. "Cut it."

Downbeat rolled on. "I'd rather have a bottle in front of me than a frontal lobotomy." He stopped "All right, seriously folks, enough already. I've been acting crazy to let you know that I'm really all right and darn glad to be alive. Let me share something. Last night I had the greatest thrill. They called me to the stage to lead the Glenn Miller orchestra with my old theme song, 'Whispering.' Those triple tonguing trumpets were something. I need to tell you that theme wasn't only mine. Long before I used 'Whispering,' it belonged to Henry Halstead who worked out of the Muehlback Hotel in Kansas City. Later Henry sold the band to Phil Harris, who you remember appeared on the Jack Benny program. Halstead is credited with making the first short sound film of a band in action."

Red faced, Alex appeared shouting, "Time for a staff meeting!" He directed his rage toward Downbeat. "You don't fool me for a minute with that butter-won't-melt-in-your-mouth routine. I know you're behind this Glenn Miller hoax.

You're trying to get back at me. I know you did it, and if I could prove it, you'd be long gone."

"That's unfair," Erin spoke up. "I worked with Downbeat on this event from the get-go and a stunt was never discussed."

"You can't watch Fat Farley all the time," Alex said with a sneer. "I suppose you're sleeping with him too?"

Doris felt her lips draw down. Her eyes blazed. Ready to release a tirade, she felt Erin's restraining hand.

"I wouldn't," Erin whispered.

Alex waved a scolding finger at Downbeat. "I suppose the best we can expect from you is a Band-Aid, eh, cornball?" He stormed to his office.

"Why is he so upset?" Downbeat asked.

"Go ahead. Answer the man," said Chief Wendinger, who had entered quietly. "I'd like to hear the answer to that myself."

No one replied and the chief continued to the office in the rear.

Alex looked up with a smirk that he quickly extinguished. "You're not here to sell me tickets to the policeman's ball."

The chief asked, "What was that sorry Glenn Miller performance all about last night?"

"Search me." Alex squinted. *That's a dumb remark.* "I mean, I don't know a thing about it. It was a complete surprise to me. I raised Cain with my staff. So far they deny everything. Maybe you can get something out of them." He drove a fist into his palm.

The chief gave him a look of disgust. "Will you sign a complaint?"

"I don't think so," Alex said. "As I see it, the station was only embarrassed. It's the community that was slammed. Have you got a lead on who flattened my tires?"

"Not yet."

The chief withdrew and would have closed the office door behind him, but Doris met him there and they shuffled back and forth, allowing them to hear Alex say in a barely audible voice, "Hick dick."

Unfazed, the chief kept walking and approached Downbeat. "What do you know about the Glenn Miller impersonation?"

"Only what I saw. Excuse me, I'm on the air."

The chief spoke to Erin. "Alex said he raised Cain with you all."

"More than raised Cain," Erin said. "To quote an old saying, methinks Alex doth protest too much."

"I see what you mean," said the chief. "I'll keep that in mind. By the way, the engineer you had here for a while, what's your impression of him?"

"Average to unsavory. I always thought he was closer to Alex than he let on."

Armed with the statements of KNDA personnel, the chief returned to the station and pulled out his lower desk drawer. He removed the plastic bag Cordelia Cooper had given him to send to the state crime lab for fingerprint analysis. He decided it would be a good idea to do that now.

At the station, Alex Barca pulled out the center drawer of his desk and opened an envelope into which he'd placed a woman's handkerchief. He'd found it lying near his car the night his tires were flattened. He knew someone with the same initials as those on the handkerchief. Obviously, the creep wanted him to draw that conclusion, but he, Alex Barca, wasn't born yesterday. Anyone could plant a handkerchief. Perhaps he should have given the initialed handkerchief to the officer who took the report. Perhaps he should have given it to the chief. Still, it couldn't be considered evidence. No telling how long it had been lying there or by whom it had been thrown. *It's not really evidence.*

Alex felt certain that the chief had overheard his crude remark. Oh well. A sudden thought made his head jerk. There were people who might give an order for more than a mere embarrassing episode. If they wanted to do that, they'd get a pro. Certainly the man who appeared was a pro. It was entirely possible the boys at Com-Com in Washington were tired of being used and were sending him a message. He reached for the phone and quickly stopped. His lips moved. "Don't call from the station." A call to the nation's capital would leave a trail. He'd call from a pay phone. On second thought, what would he say? "Got your message. Now what?" *You are just upset. Forget it.*

It was time to energize the staff. "Hit the bricks. It's time to go out and sell, sell, sell."

The Mystery Man called and Downbeat apologized for putting him on hold momentarily. "If we seem a little disjointed, it's because we're buzzing around, coming down from the big Glenn Miller dance last night. During the dance, in walked a man wearing a U.S. Army Air Force major's uniform, crush cap and all, looking very much like Glenn Miller. He took over the band—"

"What?" exploded the Mystery Man, unable to control himself. "Can you hold the line another minute while I delve into my files. Play something."

"What lit his fire?" Downbeat said on the air before introducing "Don't Sit Under the Apple Tree With Anyone Else But Me."

An excited Mystery Man returned. "We had the same occurrence here in Phoenix in 1974. And again three nights later in Dallas. Listen, Downbeat, would you be amenable to having me prepare a report on these matters? Be forewarned that it will take some air time, not the usual hop, skip, and jump."

"We'd like nothing better. We'll pay what it's worth."

"Quantum meruit? Okay. You're on."

"Thank you, Mystery Man," Downbeat said. "We will look forward to receiving your report." The phone buzzed disconnect and Downbeat said, "Folks you heard it the same time I did. Stay tuned for exclusive reports from the Mystery Man."

In his office, Alex Barca scowled and rose from the chair. Reconsidering, he plunked back down.

At the police station, Chief Wendinger observed, "It's like a balloon. The more hot air you blow into it, the bigger it gets."

"Hot air?" Ellen questioned. "You've already taken the temperature? Wonderful thermometer you have there, chief."

The editor of the *Clarinda Herald-Journal* debated whether the situation could be compared to proving a negative. The paper decided to add to the publicity by reporting KNDA's success with the Glenn Miller dance, questioning the identity and motive of the Glenn Miller impersonator. The *Herald-Journal* opined, "We haven't heard the last of this."

Nor had the community heard the last of the Mystery Man, who became the nexus, the energized nucleus, for the station's activity. Station personnel awaited the report of the Mystery Man as much as their listeners.

"This is the Maestro of Mystery, speaking to you live from Arizona. Yesterday, you remember, we mentioned the strange unexplained appearance of Glenn Miller in 1974. At that time, the question on everyone's lips was 'Could it really be Glenn Miller?' Reporters scrambled for records. Miller was born on the first day of March, 1904. That would make him seventy years of age.

"People offered explanations. Several suggested amnesia. Could Glenn Miller somehow have survived the war and suffered amnesia? Listeners suggested Glenn Miller might not be easily recognized in England.

"K-Tune, as we called the sponsoring radio station, found itself inundated by phone calls. Was that really Glenn Miller?

"Paul Harvey reported the surprising appearance on his radio program emanating from Chicago. He reported that a man wearing a major's uniform strode onto the stage during a lull between sets, picked up the baton from leader Dick Williams, and directed the band in two numbers.

"Said the erstwhile Miller, 'And now a tune you've been waiting for. Here's Jerry Gray's arrangement of "String of Pearls." Following this, Miller said, 'Thank you. Now you will enjoy dancing to an up-tempo number. Here's "Johnson Rag."'

"Dick Williams overcame his initial shock and approached him. Miller surrendered the baton and hurried off the stage. The crowd parted. Miller paused, signed two autographs, and disappeared.

"Your Mystery Man rushed forward but the crowd prevented him from reaching Miller in time. All I can say is, from where I stood the man looked and sounded like Glenn Miller. Remember, this was years before folks kept seeing Elvis Presley, still alive at the time. Back to you now, Downbeat."

Downbeat ran the report at intervals all day, taking care to report that Mystery Man's "coming to you live" only applied to the first broadcast. In twenty-four hours Mystery Man returned.

"Hi ho, this is your Maestro of Mystery, coming to you from his chalet just two short blocks from the heart of beautiful downtown Glendale, with another bulletin.

"Radio station KTUN featured music of the thirties and forties. Although a limited success financially, K-Tune made money on the Glenn Miller band appearance. The station manager capitalized on community interest and dispatched everyone who could be spared to sell advertising in this million-man milieu. Engineers labored loud and long to complete the connection for a simulcast via phone lines with KAAM, Dallas, where the band appeared three nights after they had in Phoenix. Simulcast. Remember this was 1974.

"Was this idea just plain luck or pure preparedness? 'It's happened again,' Paul Harvey reported in his frenetic style from Chicago. Phoenix residents heard it live when Glenn Miller walked onto the bandstand in Dallas. Dick Williams handed him the baton. Near the end of the song, two guards approached Glenn Miller and led him away. No one could have been more mystified than Dick Williams, who had agreed to lead the band for only a few days. Your Mystery Man had not heard of Dick Williams before, or since, for that matter.

"Interviewed during intermission, Dick Williams confirmed his final appearance with the band. 'Tomorrow it's Morrow. No pun intended.' The next day

Buddy Morrow would take over leadership of the band. Dick Williams went on to say, 'This Glenn Miller was not the same Glenn Miller who appeared in Phoenix. The Dallas Glenn Miller is shorter, stockier, and has no burn scar on his cheek.'

"From the outset, everyone more or less agreed that this impostor was a copycat. The mystery remained. Who and why? What about the two uniformed men who took him into custody? Where had they taken him? Some hospital for amnesiacs?

"In Phoenix, competing stations joined the feeding frenzy. KOOL, KMEO, KOY, and KLFF became involved. Well, KNDA listeners, we won't keep you in suspense. The Dallas Glenn Miller turned out to be an unemployed makeup man and actor, attempting to get a job with a company filming a picture in Dallas. That's history without the histrionics, just the facts, ma'am. Until the next rude interlude, this is Mystery Man saying ta ta."

Alex Barca made a face and said to Downbeat. "He's more of a cornball than you. Have you been sending him your breakfast food recipe?"

Downbeat grinned. "The Breakfast of Champions."

"It's good stuff," Doris said. "I can't wait for the next installment."

She had only one day to wait.

"This is your Maestro of Mystery. To help bring dates into memorial focus, Marilyn Monroe died August 4, 1962. The appearance of Glenn Miller at the Del Webb Townehouse in Phoenix occurred twelve years later. Elvis Presley was still alive and had three years to live. That's enough time frame.

"The fact that the Glenn Miller who appeared in Dallas turned out to be a copycat seeking a film role in no way rendered the Phoenix appearance a hoax. In what might seem a strange turn of events, a retired state senator from Kansas called station KTUN and said, 'A preponderance of evidence tends to prove that Glenn Miller was genuine. I would like proof beyond a reasonable doubt. In order to put my money where my mouth is, I'm sending you a check for one hundred dollars to hire a private detective. Maybe others will do the same.'

"The idea proved contagious. K-Tune listeners responded, even stations waiting for K-Tune to fall on its face. The rolling snowball became an avalanche.

"The detective they hired had impeccable credentials. Under his direction, K-Tune offered rewards for the two autographs recently signed at the Townehouse as well as those written prior to the war. Both recent autographs were discovered. A nationally accredited expert happened to be in Phoenix testifying on a forgery trial, and he agreed to make the comparison.

"Now K-Tune disc jockeys phoned members and associates of the original Glenn Miller band and asked them to listen to a tape recording of the recent Phoenix appearance that a rival station had made to air on their late-night news. The following is not a complete list, but the names your Mystery Man wrote down at the time: John Best, Zeke Zarchy, Jim Priddy, Paul Tanner, Willie Schwartz, Ray McKinley, Rolly Bundock, Kay Starr, Tex Beneke, Jerry Gray, Billy May, Al Klink, Bill Finnegan, Ray Anthony, and Marian Hutton.

"As one might expect, after listening some said, 'That's him.' Others said it was not. Some said, 'I can't be sure.'

"There were the usual crackpot calls. Who pays attention to them? Before it was over, everyone would.

"Now the station decided to have a voice print expert make a comparison with pre-war recordings. I recall an announcer asked each expert if he'd stake his reputation on the result. Both replied, in effect, 'Every time I make a comparison my reputation is at stake.'

"It had been agreed that neither expert would know of the other's decision. What did they decide? Yes? No? Or maybe? The answer to that will need to wait until the same time tomorrow."

Alex Barca came to the front and motioned for Downbeat to step out of the booth.

"Great. This Mystery Man stuff is absolutely great!" He pumped Downbeat's hand. "Use excerpts to hype tomorrow's broadcast and I want a blurb on every newscast. Take care of it. I'm hitting the pavement. Now is the time to sell, sell, sell." He hurried out.

Downbeat stared at his hand and jibed, "What got into him? I feel like I pulled the brass ring."

"Feedback from out there," Erin suggested.

"He likes what you are doing," said Doris.

"That alone makes me suspicious. Isn't there some sage in history who said, 'Beware of Barcas bearing gifts.'"

"I think that's Muppets bearing curds and whey."

"Hit the pavement," Downbeat said with a pseudo-Barca expression and mock severity.

The Mystery Man called the same day, explaining that he had a conflict. "I can't call tomorrow. You will need to tape me. This report is somewhat lengthy. Let me know when you're ready."

"All set," Downbeat said.

"Mystery Man speaking. The question remains, Was the Glenn Miller who appeared at the Townehouse in Phoenix the real Glenn Miller?

"Arlys Kwan answered that question. At the time, *Arizona Republic*'s leading columnist Arlys Kwan frequently appeared on public television. Five-eighths Chinese, one-fourth Irish, one-fourth Danish—hold it. If you totaled that and came up with one and one-eighth, it is no error on our part. Friends and foes, fans and detractors, generally agree on one point. Arlys Kwan is nine-eighths woman.

"I hold in my pecan husk–stained fingers her now-faded column. The lead line read 'TWO EXPERTS SAY GLENN MILLER LIVES.' With that pronouncement, crackpot calls to K-Tune increased in number and intensity. A man with a scratchy voice blamed the station for bringing Glenn Miller back to life. 'He ought to stay dead, real dead.' Did anyone bother with crackpot listeners?

"Sally Markham, a middle-aged secretary, received a call from Scratchy, as he became known to the staff. A caring person, Sally saw an opportunity to score points. She fell for Scratchy's promise that he could lead her to Glenn Miller. She set out to meet him with wide-eyed naiveté. What a tremendous scoop she would have! A long-time secretary, Sally's efficient notes, left behind, would provide a vital clue—when they discovered her body.

"The station detective informed the police. Together they went to the bar where Sally was to meet Scratchy. The bartender had no recollection of the meeting, but he knew an old musician with a scratchy voice and directed detectives to a rooming house. The landlady stated, 'He's back in Veteran's Hospital.'

"Meanwhile, K-Tune staffers met and for the first time exchanged reports as a group. At the first mention of Glenn Miller band's appearing, Scratchy had offered—asked—demanded to lead the band. As time passed his demeanor became more threatening. With the murder of Sally Markham, one thing became clear, each of them might be marked for murder.

"*Republic* journalist Arlys Kwan, of course, did not have this information. When Scratchy telephoned her as Mel Evers, inviting her to come to Veteran's Hospital, promising he'd take her to see Glenn Miller, she snatched up pen and purse and left the office flying. She met a man who led her to a recently painted deserted wing and was strangling the life out of her when police detectives arrived. Arlys managed to mash a spiked heel into the man's foot, giving a detective a clear shot.

"The wounded man lived two hours, long enough to relate that he had for a short time played with Glenn Miller and had been fired. During the war, in

London, he auditioned to become part of the Air Force band. Glenn recognized him and said, 'I never get myself in a position to fire a man twice.'

"The wounded man managed, 'He's responsible for me being sent to bomb Germany, getting shot to hell with flak. My voice is gone—plate in my head—constant pain. All Glenn Miller's fault.'

"Evers kept talking about the firing of Ray Anthony. 'Can you imagine. Firing the kid when the band came to his hometown? Then, later, firing him again.'

"Evers died as he lived, swearing to keep Glenn Miller dead. It's a miracle that the police arrived in time. The man had checked into Vet's Hospital as Sy Schuster, the name he used when playing for Charlie Barnett. He used the name Don Bauer when he played for Bob Chester. He also used the name Mel Evers and Hap Fischer.

"What of the experts? The handwriting expert maintained the writing exemplars had been mixed, that he only received actual Glenn Miller autographs. The voice print expert said, 'I'm human. I knew I would eventually make a mistake.' Arlys Kwan intimated he was a Glenn Miller fan and 'more than anything wanted to find Glenn Miller alive.' Her banner headline, 'CRAZY KILLER PLAYED WITH GLENN MILLER,' continued, 'The worldwide headache didn't stop when the war ended. For Mel, sometimes known as Sy, Hap, or Don, his headache ended in a deserted room.'

"Now, to borrow a phrase," said Mystery Man, "you know—the rest of the story. We'll go back to my contest tomorrow. For now I leave you with a penetrating musical question. Just who is YOUR Glenn Miller?"

A trickle of calls that remained fairly constant prompted Downbeat to ask if the station should run a contest. Doris opposed the idea with a comment, "Wouldn't that be in bad taste, after what we heard?"

After a one-day hiatus and a taped broadcast, Mystery Man returned. "Are you ready to play 'Name that Band'?" Here's the clue. The band sounded so much like Glenn Miller that when Glenn finally came to his area, dancers demanded, 'Why are you copying his band?' Name that band leader. Do you have a prize for the winner, D-Jay?"

"We sure do," Downbeat Jackson replied.

Mystery Man continued, "Listeners will have until I sign off. Back for a moment to our thrill-packed serial. With the murder solved, station KTUN found itself without a mission. Someone had the idea to phone former band members and ask if they remembered anyone with the names the killer had used. Not one of them did. The station managed to salvage an interesting interview when they caught up with Tex Beneke at Pottstown, Pennsylvania. They talked about Hal McIntyre and Charlie Spivak. Tex remembered when he drove all night from Detroit to New York to join the band. With Sally Markham dead, work at K-Tune no longer seemed fun. One announcer transferred to a Scottsdale station. Another moved to KSUN in Sun City. The station's days were numbered. Well, that's history.

"Now, has anyone identified YOUR Glenn Miller? What was his motive? Have you asked *cui bono?* Who benefits? Round up the usual suspects. Love. Lust. Lucre and Loathing."

"No." Downbeat cracked, "Don't quit your regular job."

"Whose toes have you guys at the station trod on? Who had to even the score? By the way, has anyone guessed the name of the band that sounded like G M?"

"Not yet," Downbeat said.

"Okay, D-Jay, the contest is over. Of course you know it's Bob Chester. I mentioned him yesterday. I thought someone might pick up on that."

"His theme was 'Sunburst,'" Downbeat added. "Thanks for calling."

Downbeat stepped out during a break and asked, "Who held a grudge against the whole town?"

Erin said, "It can't be love or lust. It must be someone who wanted to even the score."

At police headquarters, KNDA listener Chief Wilbur Wendinger turned to Ellen. "There you have it. Love. Lust. Lucre. Loathing. Write that down."

"T-H-A-T." Ellen spelled the word. "That!"

The chief gave her a steely look.

Chapter Twelve

As a young woman, Cordelia Cooper knew she had been spiteful on occasion. Most of these lapses of etiquette or breaches of decorum had been righted long ago or obscured from memory by the sands of time. Since Erin had come into her life, one poignant memory lingered and, in fact, grew undeniably persistent. She had to meet Belle Ames face to face. Cordelia knew she had mellowed. She hoped that Belle had likewise mellowed. Paying Belle a visit might expiate some of the guilt, might have little effect, or might, indeed, have dire consequences.

She had struggled too long with indecision. It was time to accept the risk. She would visit Belle Ames. *The most she can do is throw you out.*

Belle Ames heard a car halt in the street and saw Cordelia Cooper laboring toward her front door on crutches. She nevertheless waited for her to knock. With a haughty well-what-do-you-want expression, Belle said, "So have you come to take Erin away from me, too?"

"I don't blame you for being mad at me," Cordelia said. "Is it all right if I come in?"

"Come in. Sit."

"I don't know where to begin," Cordelia said.

"You with no words?" *You, the loudmouth.* "That's difficult to believe."

"I often wondered what I would say. On the way over I planned exactly what I would say. That doesn't fit now."

"You could start by saying 'I'm sorry'."

"I am sorry. But would you be surprised to know that I rather expected the same from you? For years I wanted to hear that from you. Now it no longer seems important."

"Well, Erin is your buddy now, so it seems." Bitterness etched Belle's voice.

"About Erin. I want you to know I did nothing to encourage her. I mean, nothing to encourage the initial contact. It all came about because of the radio station. I have to admit, after that I never once discouraged her from seeing me. In fact, I encouraged it with open arms. I truly enjoy having her around." Cordelia hesitated, swallowed, and began anew. "You can be justly proud of Erin."

"I am proud of her. After all, she is my daughter." She glanced at Cordelia. "She has her faults."

"Don't we all?"

"So what have you told her?" Belle asked pointedly.

"Nothing. She never wondered?" Cordelia pressed. "With a father whose red hair would light a barbecue, she never wondered how she inherited none of his traits?"

"Erin was too young to remember him. I haven't belabored the facts. Marrying that jerk cost me a relationship with my own father. He disowned me. I didn't get back with my mother until after he was gone. Who knows about genetics? Just because he had red hair doesn't mean that Erin would."

Cordelia had a verbal jab on the tip of her tongue and with an effort closed her mouth. Why didn't the woman come right out and admit that she played fast and loose? Cordelia lowered her voice. "Sometimes I wonder what would have happened if I had swallowed my pride—but I was madder than a wet hen. I insisted that Jake Cooper fire his beautiful secretary who was so much competition. That was all my doing, you know."

Belle said, "You were mad? I was red-flag-waving-at-a-bull mad. Do you know what it's like to raise a child without a job? Do you know what it's like to be knocking on doors and turned away? The job I had with Cooper Motors was a good one. It was a long time before I got back on my feet. God, I hated you."

"About as much as I hated you," Cordelia admitted. *As it turned out, I would have traded places with you in a heartbeat. You were the one with that wonderful child.* "With all that hating, it's a wonder Erin turned out the way she has."

Belle admitted, "I wasn't always successful. We were so poor." She stared into the distance. "One year before Christmas, Erin came home from school all fired up. She wouldn't be restrained. She had to go to church and give money to the poor. She was too young to be out selling candy and Christmas cards, but she couldn't be stopped. On the proper Sunday she wrote, 'For God,' on some of the bills she contributed. She felt like a million dollars. A few days before Christmas the minister knocked on our door and left an envelope. When we opened the envelope out fell the bills on which Erin had written, 'For God.' Erin was shattered. 'Oh God, Mother,' she cried. 'We're poor!'" Belle's eyes misted. "That shattering experienced haunted Erin for years. Kids teased her about her Salvation Army clothes. Kids can be so cruel. Somewhere along the way she decided not to be poor. The rest you know."

Cordelia sniffed. *Prom shoes. That's all I did. I'll have to pay for that in the next world.*

Belle said, "For a long time Erin lost her sunshine."

"She certainly put sunshine back into my life," Cordelia said. "I must say it's to your credit that you never told her. She doesn't know about us."

"That wouldn't have been productive. You haven't told her?"

"As you say, that wouldn't have been productive."

Belle remembered her manners. "Would you like some tea?"

"Thank you. I'd rather have a beer."

"You won't get violent?" Belle smiled waspishly.

"Probably not. No guarantee. You could probably outrun me without much effort."

"Did you know there is a drink named after Erin?"

"She mentioned it," Cordelia said. "I think it's fantastic. Did you know that when she was in the bank, on her first job, Jake used to go in just to talk to her? He didn't want me to know, but he couldn't keep it a secret. Every time he went into the bank it was as if he went to a party. He'd always have a joke for her or some word of wisdom."

Belle nodded. "Erin would come home and ask me, 'Mom, did you know that nice guys don't finish last? Jake Cooper says they never even get started.'"

"That's Jake all over." Cordelia raised a palm. "When I came in, what you said about me taking Erin. You know at her age I can't take her."

"You can utilize her time. I'm a jealous woman."

"You never did what I did out of jealousy," Cordelia admitted. "Did Erin ever—?"

Belle set her chin and interrupted. "I really don't wish to discuss Erin. In a minute I might say something for which I'll be sorry. I dare not risk losing Erin—with you in town."

"No danger of that," Cordelia said. "Maybe I said too much."

"Now what?" Belle asked. "Where do we go from here? Never in my life did I think you'd be knocking at my door. I guess that's another secret I need to keep from Erin. She's accused me of keeping secrets."

"Well, I'm not going to tell Erin I was here eating crow. Of course she might just say, 'That's nice. I'm glad you visited my mother.' Come to think about it, for a woman of Erin's quality, it's strange that she never suggested my meeting you."

"She never suggested my meeting you either."

"Do you suppose she knows something?"

"I don't know. I can't be sure. I was so mad I might have said something back then. When she and Jake were trading stories at the bank, I might have let something slip about how I wasn't thrilled with you. She learned to be secretive working at the bank. On second thought, as a child she always kept to herself." Belle halted. "Now I'm talking about Erin and I said I wouldn't. Maybe it's the beer."

Cordelia raised her glass. "Could be. Thank you for mine. I do like a brew now and then."

"I can tell you one thing, if you enjoy it too long you won't need to worry about telling Erin. She'll be here and catch us red-handed."

"Then I'd better go. For what it's worth, I'm glad I came. It would be all right if sometime you came to visit me. After all, I owe you a beer." It surprised Cordelia that her smile came easily.

"I'll think about it. I'm glad you stopped in."

"I should have visited you ten years ago. Make it twenty. Thirty. I could have helped. I should have."

"Water over the dam. I would have been too proud to have accepted. Too stubborn is more like it."

"I guess we've cleared some air." Cordelia rose and moved toward the door. "Take care of yourself. I meant what I said about coming to visit me."

Cordelia clicked toward the car and said "Hi there" to a small girl playing nearby.

The girl was still playing there when Erin came home. "Who was that crippled old lady on crutches who visited your mom?"

"I have no idea," Erin said. *What was Cordelia Cooper doing here?*

"Well, Mother," Erin demanded when she walked into the house, "What was Cordelia Cooper doing here?"

Belle had thought about an explanation for several minutes, and yet now that she heard the question the answer came with difficulty. "It was a courtesy call. That's all."

"What did she want?"

Belle hesitated. "Nothing really."

"Well, what did she say?"

"Nothing. Just small talk."

"What do you call small talk?"

"Just conversation. We just visited. I didn't take notes."

"She wasn't selling magazine subscriptions or Girl Scout cookies. It had to be something she couldn't say over the phone. A letter wouldn't do. It wasn't a thank you note. So what did you talk about?"

"Are we playing twenty questions?"

Erin continued to press. "What was so important that it had to be discussed face to face?"

"You're making a mountain out of a molehill."

Erin's voice sharpened. "How long have you known Cordelia Cooper?"

"For some years, I suppose."

"Where did you meet her?"

"I don't remember."

Erin placed her hands on her hips, brows knit in stern appraisal. She knew her mother had been forced to sell her car to buy groceries when she was a baby.

When Jake Cooper learned of her plight, he allowed her mother to use a series of old trade-in vehicles. She had always believed that Jake Cooper's charity had been based on need. "Cordelia didn't think you still had one of Jake's old trade-in cars?"

"Whatever made you think of that? Why would I have one of Jake Cooper's old junk cars? Honestly!"

"That's a good question, Mother," Erin said levelly. "Why don't you answer it?"

"I'm not going to rehash the distant past."

Frustrated, in a rage now, Erin stormed toward the door. "Where am I going?" she shouted. "Out! What am I going to do? Nothing! Who am I going to see?" She slammed the door behind her.

"I know who you're going to see," Belle muttered. "Heaven help her."

As Erin drove, her anger abated and allowed her to become analytical. If her mother wouldn't tell her, perhaps Cordelia would. At least Cordelia didn't have thirty years' history of keeping things from her. She selected the same route Cordelia had driven less than an hour earlier.

At that time, Cordelia realized she had assaulted the posted speed limit and obediently slowed. "Drat the woman," she fussed. She felt her suspicions were well founded. She had led Belle up to the point where it would have been easy for her to acknowledge—to admit—what she knew to be true.

Belle had been disinherited because she married wrong. What would her family have done if they knew the child she bore was not that of her husband? Why would she have told Erin the truth? Even now, Erin might blame her for all the years of poverty, elementary school through high school. Erin might well disown *her*. Such a rift could lead to sharing a confidence with one friend, which might lead to common knowledge. Belle had been right in not risking the airing of dirty linen.

Cordelia remembered how she had raged when a so-called friend informed her how much Jake liked walking up behind his shapely secretary, inhaling her perfume, and staring down the front of her blouse.

"Get rid of her," she had screamed at Jake.

If it happened today—Cordelia couldn't imagine it. Today she didn't have legs—she tried again. If they were all younger—and she knew what she knew now—she'd turn a blind eye. What? Unlikely. She'd rant at Jake—"It's her or me. Make up your mind." No, she wouldn't. She would never put Jake in the position of having to choose. More likely she would warn him. "Some night when you're asleep. I'm simply going to kill you. Is your insurance current?"

She sniffed. For all her fury she had never threatened Jake with an alternative. She knew he might leave. She had to realize she was his new wife—his second wife, who in no way could replace the woman he lost to leukemia, the woman he loved.

Arriving at home, Cordelia realized the exertion of the afternoon had sapped her energy. She seated herself. Her eyes became heavy lidded and she dozed.

She awakened to the humming vibration of a car on the drive.

Erin rapped twice and stormed across the threshold, eyes narrowed, mouth tense, back stiff with anger. Cordelia at once sensed her irritability. "Erin—"

"You visited my mother," Erin charged.

"Of course I did. Sit down. Relax. Take a load off. What's troubling you, Erin?"

"You visited my mother," she repeated.

"Of course I did," Cordelia repeated just as calmly. "Why should I not? It was long overdue."

"Why did you visit Mother?"

"Just a friendly call. What did she tell you?"

"Nothing. That's the problem. She told me nothing. She stonewalled. There's no reason for her to do that unless your visit was important."

"Important?" Cordelia scoffed. "Just two old hens talking. Not much to it, but for us, important. For us time is running out."

"What did you talk about?" Erin insisted.

"Erin. Do you know what you're asking? I rather resent you coming here, prying into what is none of your damn business. Didn't your mother point that out?"

"None of my business?" Erin shouted "I'm sick and tired of being told it's none of my business. There's a connection between you and Mother. There's a reason for this conspiracy. I know it. I don't know precisely what it is but I'm going to find out!"

Cordelia's voice sharpened. "Erin, it's none of your business. If we talk tulips, that's our business. If we talk nasturtiums, that's our business. If it's zinnias, that's our business. How dare you attempt to censor your mother. How dare you attempt to censor me."

"Get real."

"All right, this is real. Really real. I'm worried about your investment in KNDA. You're riding high now with all the publicity about the Glenn Miller band and the Mystery Man calling in from Arizona. When the furor dies, what we face is a tough proposition. Possibly bankruptcy. The way I see it, we're living on the ripple effect. I don't want you or your mother mad at me if you lose every dollar you invested. Now are you satisfied?"

"I'm a big girl. I went into KNDA with my eyes open. There's more to life than stacking up money."

"I know it, but do you know it? In the beginning I was delighted to have you aboard. I'm not so sure now. We could face bankruptcy."

"We're not bankrupt yet. If that is your chapter one I would like to hear the rest of the story. You're holding something back."

"Are you calling me a liar?"

"If the shoe fits—"

"Get out," Cordelia shouted. "I'm tired of your insolence. Get out!"

"I'm gone"

"Good riddance." Cordelia blinked to double vision. Objects went out of focus. Everything became a blur. At the moment Erin slammed the door, Cordelia heaved herself to her feet. Heart pounding, gasping for breath, she tottered on rubber limbs for an instant and pitched forward on her face. She screamed as loudly as she could, but her ears heard not a sound. A spasm twisted her features. The corners of her mouth quivered. She clawed with both hands and lay still.

Erin drove down the drive. Her anger dissipated to the return of reason. She realized she had just alienated the largest stockholder of KNDA. If Cordelia joined Alex Barca—the unbidden thought jarred her—she knew she had to apologize. She had to make amends and she had to do it now. Why had she been so reckless, so abysmally stubborn? At the end of the lane she turned, socked the car into reverse, turned in to the driveway, and headed back to the house. She halted, knocked twice, and entered. She saw the sprawled figure.

"Cordelia!"

In the turmoil of her thoughts, Erin decided calling an ambulance would take too long. She bent down and pulled Cordelia into a sitting position. Approaching her from the rear, she reached around her in a hug and using strength she didn't know she had, dragged Cordelia, her heels bouncing up and down, across the rug, then across the porch to her car. She tugged Cordelia along the front seat and propped her up the best she could.

Buster whined and wanted to jump in. "Not now," Erin said.

She put the car in gear and sped toward the hospital, with Buster in pursuit. Driving through stop signs and red lights, she attracted a police officer. She waved for him to follow. He drew abreast, saw the apparently lifeless form of Cordelia Cooper, and shouted, "Follow me."

Officer Sullivan spoke into the mike. "Emergency. Get a doctor to the hospital. Cordelia Cooper is unconscious. Get a doctor to the hospital!"

Hearing the call, Chief Wilbur Wendinger ran to his car and turned on the siren.

Erin braked and halted near the emergency entrance.

"How long has she been like this?" asked a nurse.

"Ten, fifteen minutes. No longer."

They placed Cordelia on a gurney and wheeled her inside. Erin saw Buster running toward them and intercepted him just as Chief Wendinger arrived. She explained—not the quarrel—that she'd discovered Cordelia lying on the floor. "Somebody has to take care of Buster. I guess I'm elected. What do you think about me staying at her house?"

The chief mashed his lower lip in contemplation. "I dunno. Listen. Let's do it this way. Stay there tonight. Take care of her dog. We can see which way the wind blows in the morning. One bit of advice. Don't snoop."

"Didn't plan to." She tugged Buster toward her car. "C'mon, Buster."

She decided to face another eventuality. She drove home and apologized, "Sorry, Mom." She forced the words to come out. "I had no right to pry." Then in a flurry of words she blurted, "I put Cordelia in the hospital." She explained what she had done.

"It just goes to show," Belle said, "what comes around goes around."

"I'm going over to house-sit and take care of Buster. I owe her that much."

"You have to eat," Belle observed.

"I'll take along a TV dinner and heat it over there." Erin saw a melancholy look come over her mother's face and wondered if she, too, felt some responsibility for what had happened.

Belle said, "I think you should go and take care of her place."

Upon arriving at Cordelia's house, Erin allowed the dog to run, heated the TV dinner, and thought long thoughts. For the many questions, she reasoned, there were only more questions and no answers.

In the morning at the hospital, the doctor told her, "Getting Cordelia here promptly made all the difference. The first hour is critical. She's awake now and is her usual cantankerous self."

When Cordelia saw Erin she demanded, "Are you the one who scuffed up my shoes?" She gestured toward the floor. "Look at them. They look like they've been through the war."

"Look at you. You look like you've been through the war too."

"I'm alive and kicking. They told me you saved my life. You came back for me."

"I came back to apologize. I acted completely horrid. I'm sorry. Really sorry."

"If it's time for apologies," Cordelia said, "I have to play a couple sour aces. I'm sorry too." She stretched out her arms. "I could use a hug right now."

They hugged and sniffed and wept. And refused to admit they were emotional.

"I stayed at your house last night and took care of Buster," Erin said.

"How is Buster?"

"He misses you. He's in the car. They won't let me bring him into the hospital."

"Tell Buster I miss him too."

"I didn't bring your crutches. That's on my to-do list for next time."

They talked pleasantly and Erin said with a shrug, "Well, I have to get to work."

Cordelia asked, "Did you find the tire in the downstairs bedroom?"

"I never looked. Chief Wendinger told me not to snoop."

"What does he know? What I could tell you about him."

"But won't. What's the business about a tire?"

"Jake put it there. One night years ago, he received a phone call. A man said, 'I need a tire.' Glenn Miller made a quick trip to town and had tire trouble. Short of cash, he wrote an IOU. The old tire hung in the barn for a while. Finally it became a cherished possession along with that IOU. Glenn sent Jake a check years later which Jake refused to cash. That's a cherished possession too."

"Buster and I will look after the tire. And the rest of your things."

"Stay away from the barn though. It's haunted. I mean it." Cordelia's mind leaped to something she'd been waiting for the right moment to ask. "Erin. Would you humor an old woman?" Her palm came up. "No questions. Just listen. Would you be so kind as to give me an eight-by-ten photograph of yourself? Like a graduation picture, full face, face inclined slightly to the right with just the hint of a smile. Would you do that for me?"

"All right," Erin said without hesitation. "That's one way for me to make amends." It was uncanny. She had been thinking about photographs too, photographs of Captain Gaylord Haversham. "You take care now. And mind the nurses."

"That'll be the day."

Erin smiled. "We have to try."

She walked to the car and saw attorney Orville Keane park in the adjacent spot. "You're up early," she said by way of greeting.

"Yup. It's a tough life. It's worse if you weaken."

She watched him for a moment, trudging toward the entrance, briefcase in one hand, vintage typewriter in the other.

"You have two choices," Erin told Buster. "I can take you home. Or I can take you home."

Buster barked once.

"First choice. Home it is."

Chapter Thirteen

The Glenn Miller band had flagged, like a horse run too long. Excitement ebbed and even the Mystery Man could not sustain interest. Conversation along Clarinda coffee counters reverted to traditional topics: the weather, the corn crop, the athletic rivalry with Atlantic. In an ironic turn of events, the caller who most wanted the station to fail had, by his actions, heaped corn husks on dying embers and inflamed not only himself, but even energized the dying horse.

"Frankly, I think it was all a put-up job," he charged. "You arranged for an actor to pretend to be Glenn Miller. Come on, 'fess up. You guys at the station planned the whole thing."

"No sir," Downbeat said with emphasis. "Did you see me run up to the stage and promptly deny it?"

"You'd do that if you planned it. Anything for publicity."

Andrew Seligman stopped pinching his nose and put down the small plastic container with a hole in the bottom which he used to speak through to further disguise his voice. "That'll show them."

He closed the chamber office and walked to Vaughn's Victuals for a cup of coffee. In less than three minutes Erin Ames entered and seated herself in the adjacent chair. For a long moment Seligman did not speak.

"Well, Erin," he said at length. "What are you trying to foist off on the unsuspecting public today?"

"Not a thing," she said politely. "I've been meaning to speak to you. KNDA is not your competition. We're not another chamber of commerce. We're just another business like the *Herald-Journal*."

"Says you."

"And our chamber of commerce dues are paid."

"Now that you work in two places I suppose you expect two votes."

"Certainly not," Erin said. Whoever suggested that?"

"I guess you still haven't captured the Glenn Miller impersonator?"

"We've turned that matter over to the police. How about you?"

"They won't touch it. Where's the crime?"

Seligman rose in triumph and swaggered toward the cash register. Returning to the office he flicked on the radio and grinned. A caller had Downbeat on the defensive.

"It had to be someone with a score to settle, an act of revenge," the caller reasoned. "Logic dictates that his revenge had to be directed toward KNDA. If we ask who benefited from the publicity, we find it is KNDA—or possibly the chamber of commerce."

"No!" Seligman shouted. "Not the chamber of commerce!"

Downbeat said, "Let me assure you, the presence of the impostor was a complete surprise to all of us here at KNDA." He saw Keith out on the sidewalk, waving to get the attention of his mother.

Doris stepped outside, spoke to Keith, and motioned for Downbeat to leave the mike when he had a chance. Tom Berringer replaced him.

Doris said, "Keith wants to talk to you."

"Okay." Downbeat went out to meet him.

"You did me a good turn," Keith said. "I need your advice. I know something the police would like to know. They're not exactly my friends." His voice firmed. "I'm not a snitch."

"C'mon," Downbeat said. "I'll buy you a Coke."

At the cafe, Downbeat listened. "Look, Keith, if you're driving a car and want to turn it around, you need to turn hard, one hundred eighty degrees. Turning a little bit at a time will eventually get you around but it takes forever. If you want to turn it around, do it. That's what I did with my life."

"Man, that's tough."

"Yeah. Rougher than a cob. Still, if you do what is right, it seems to get easier."

"It's about your Trading Post. A guy advertised a seven-inch Emerson TV. I'm pretty sure it was stolen. He tried to sell it at the pool hall. Somebody said, 'Put it on the Trading Post.'"

Downbeat stared into the distance. "Now you have me involved."

"Oh man, I didn't want to do that."

"We're all in the same boat. Now I have twenty-four hours to decide what I'm going to do."

Keith shrugged. "I have to go to the police, I guess."

"Not on my account."

"Hunh?"

"Keith, you have to drive your own bus. Do I have your permission to alert your mother? No telling who will call the station about that TV."

"Sure."

After their meeting, Keith reluctantly trudged into the police station and announced, "I want to talk to the chief."

"Now that's different," Ellen Iverson said.

Keith remembered that Downbeat had told him to look the chief right in the eye, never wavering. "Chief, I have something to tell you. A seven-inch Emerson TV has been advertised on the Trading Post. Vinnie Van Deventer tried to sell a small Emerson TV in the pool hall. That's all I got to say." He started to leave.

"Keith," the chief called.

Keith turned and saw the chief wagging a scolding finger at him. This time the chief wore a grin.

When he had gone, the chief observed, "I always thought there was some good in that kid."

"When did you think that? I'm the one who said there might be something good in the kid, deep down."

"You never said that."

"That's right," Ellen said. You never did."

The police arranged for a tentative buyer to call and look at the television set. Late that afternoon, Vinnie Van Deventer found himself locked in a cell, hard-pressed to explain how he came into possession of a small Emerson television set.

"It pays to listen to the Trading Post," Ellen said, unblinking.

Chief Wendinger squinted and directed his attention to the radio voice of Downbeat Jackson.

"In the early days of the Glenn Miller band, the musicians traveled in a fleet of cars. None of you will know that the guys called Chummy MacGregor's vehicle the Death Wagon, because he always drove sixty miles an hour, even across town to the drug store. I'm going to give the third caller a gift certificate to our local drug store, with no question asked."

Ellen's fingers moved over the telephone.

"You're the third caller," Downbeat said.

"Get to work," said the chief. "Haven't you got something better to do?"

"I'll split with you," Ellen said.

"You better."

Downbeat said, "Back to you, Tom Berringer." He relinquished the mike and walked to the conference room where Erin and Doris waited.

"I wonder who rubbed Andy Seligman the wrong way?" Erin said. "I just had a tense encounter with him at Vaughn's. I'd pay a quarter to know."

Downbeat reached into his pocket and handed her a dime. "Add my ten cents."

Erin kept his dime. "Cordelia Cooper expressed some worry about our cash flow. I can see her point. Jake tried to run the station on advertising only. We scored with the Glenn Miller band. How much advertising would we need to sell in order to equal what we netted on the dance?"

"Boo-coo," Downbeat said, slowly hyphenating *beaucoup*.

Erin nodded. "We get peanuts for advertising when the real money is in the event."

Downbeat remembered when his Jive Five band worked for a percentage of the gate. "Also a good chance to go broke. It doesn't pay to get greedy."

"You're right D-Jay," Erin said with a smile. "I heard the Mystery Man call you D-Jay. I'm thinking of a luau. A Hawaiian night, roast whole pigs, loud shirts, leis, syrupy music. Come barefooted if you like."

"Hey, let's run with this," Downbeat said, beaming. "I like. I like. Our lead-in is 'Blue Hawaii.'"

Doris said wonderingly. "If we could only run a lottery."

"Hah," Downbeat said. "If it don't waddle and it don't quack, it's not a lottery. It's a door prize."

Doris interjected, "Add two dollars to every ticket. Maybe three. Maybe four." She read from her notes. "Pigs and pineapples. Grass skirts and leis. Colorful shirts. A syrupy band and a door prize."

"Okoolihow," Downbeat said. "That's booze to you."

"Hawaiian Punch for you," Doris said playfully. "Or I'll give you a punch."

Downbeat regarded Erin. "Do you want to underwrite the cost?"

"Do I have a choice? If I take the risk, I should get a cut of the profit. There's a conflict of interest. Better talk to Alex Barca."

"Thaaanks," he said.

"We need to follow procedure," Doris reminded him. *Did he have to look at Erin that way?*

"I'll ask," Downbeat said and walked to the back office as if heavily laden, without his usual enthusiasm.

He returned, shaking his head. "Alex says no. We go with only the advertising." He looked at Erin. "He says you can't sponsor it."

By the time Erin walked to her second job at Washington Savings, she had an alternative. "Henry Leighton. How would you like to take me to Hawaii?"

His heart leaped and at once settled. He knew she was not serious. "What's the hook?"

"Tell you later."

She drove to the high school and presented her idea to the principal. "Classes are always looking for special money-making projects," Erin suggested. "Sophomores could sell Hawaiian Punch and other soft drinks. Juniors could sell Hawaiian shirts in advance. We need a band to play Hawaiian music. They also need to be able to play in the style of our favorite son."

The principal nodded agreeably.

"There's one thing," Erin said. "We can't hold the luau here at the high school."

"Why not?" objected the principal. "The annual Glenn Miller festival originated here. In fact in the early years we had an exclusive."

"The difference is," Erin explained, "the Glenn Miller festival is held when school is out. It's strictly an adult function, designed mainly to attract out-o-towners." She gestured for emphasis. "I know students attend, but this celebration will be held when school is in session. To prevent criticism we're holding it at the Cordelia Ballroom. We're obligated to Rudy Wagoner. If we held it here, it would probably be considered a school event. There'd be criticism about the liquor. How would we get a sponsor?"

"Criticism. Hmmm. I see your point."

"We might arrange to have the shirts available through Weil's Clothing store. All sales made in advance. It's a guaranteed money-maker for some class."

He smiled tentatively. "You seem to have thought of everything."

Thought is the operative word. I hope Weil's goes along. "Not quite," Erin conceded. "We haven't decided where to get the pineapples and coconuts—the Hy-vee or the Super Valu. We might have a strolling photographer. The band always needs money. I'll leave it to you to present the idea."

"Will do."

Mention of a strolling photographer reminded Erin she had an appointment at the Barb Hale studio. She phoned to say, "I'm running late, but I will be there."

The sitting triggered thoughts she'd been having about photos of Captain Gaylord Haversham. He grinned at her every time she opened her wallet. Early on, she had drawn strength from the enlargement on her dresser. Now she stared at the photo less and less. She had gone beyond mourning him. She had outdistanced the feeling of making a success of her life as a memorial to him. His photograph had reassured her, and for a time it had been a convenient all-supporting prop, a crutch. Of course, her reliance on the photo had been real. Was not a crutch the ultimate reality?

Primitive tribes believed that if they were photographed they lost part of their souls. She wondered if the flip side of that platter involved losing her soul if she stared at the captain's photo too often. One fact could not be denied. During the intervening years she had aged. The man in the photo had not. One of these fine days the man in the picture would appear more like a son. Someone might wander into the bedroom and say, "Oh, I see you have a son in the service."

"Silly," she admonished herself. She nevertheless removed the portrait and placed it face down in the bottom drawer.

Cordelia phoned from the hospital. "They can't stand me around here. They're kicking me out. Can you come and get me?"

"I'm on the way."

Erin had Buster at the exit when the nurse wheeled Cordelia out.

"That was thoughtful," Cordelia said. She and Buster held a reunion. "Erin, we have a lot to talk about."

"I thought you were supposed to rest."

"Rest. Smest," Cordelia said impatiently. "I can't help wondering why we haven't been hit with a federal charge."

"Not a word yet," Erin said.

"Why not? Is the FCC sterile? Of course not. Who's taking the heat off? Who's running interference? Three people have come to town since we began to glow. Sparks—he's gone. Downbeat Jackson. I can't imagine he wields any influence. That leaves Alex Barca. He showed up with way too much information. He wanted to buy into the station. He didn't quibble about the price. What is he, untouchable?"

"I see what you mean." Erin's eyes widened. "Witness protection program? That's a wild thought. If that's real, maybe we can hide under his umbrella until the rains come."

"That might be a dream. What I have to tell you now isn't. Years ago there were two classy ladies in town—notice I didn't say dames—yours truly and your mother. Of the two she was classier, more polished. I had rough edges and a mouth. At any rate, Jake married me. Your mother picked a man roundly despised by her family. Her family cut her off."

"Totally," Erin acknowledged. "Until Grandfather died."

Cordelia continued. "I was in my flower-and-garden period. District president and all that. One day I came home and learned Jake had hired your mother. One of my friends told me more than she should—that Jake had an eye for her. I made Jake fire your mother."

"So that's why you went to see her."

Cordelia's lips tensed before she spoke. "To say I'm sorry. High time it was, too."

"I see."

"Your mother is not overjoyed with me monopolizing your time. I do look forward to your visits so."

Erin nodded. "Mother and I discussed that. Really, there is enough of me to go around."

"I don't think she holds a grudge now. I can't blame her for being jealous of your time with me. I'm glad you got to meet Jake. She mentioned that."

"Jake used to come into the bank," Erin remembered. "One day he would try to marry me off. The next day he suggested I would be the first spinster to reach the White House. I told him I'd rather be a cuddle kitten to some dapper hero-type instead of a hard-bitten politician. Then he'd say I was a mite too tall to be cuddly. He always had a snappy comeback."

"Greet your mother for me."

At her very next visit, Erin presented Cordelia with the requested photograph. When she had gone, Cordelia removed her own picture from the hinged frame and inserted Erin's adjacent to that of her late husband. She stepped back to appraise them.

"Well, Jake," she said aloud. "There you have it. Look at that face. A Cooper if I ever saw one. The same mouth. The same nose. There ain't one drop of that red-headed scoundrel in that girl. Jake, you son of a bitch, why couldn't you have just admitted it? Sure, I know. You wanted me, and you figured if you opened your mouth you would lose us both. That doesn't say a helluva lot for me, damn you. But you were right, Jake. You had me pegged. I'm glad you loved me for what I am. Was, I mean. Funny the way things turn out. Like the man said, life is just a series of unrelated coincidences."

More than mere coincidence would enter their lives and that of the chamber of commerce secretary. With plans for the Hawaiian Holiday going forward, the phone began to ring in the chamber office.

"Andrew. What's the hot skinny on the Hawaiian Holiday?"

"What Hawaiian Holiday?" Out of the loop again. "Nobody tells me anything any more. Call the damn radio station." He mashed down the phone and flung a pencil across the room.

Another caller inquired, "Where can I get tickets?"

"Try the radio station." This time he flung the pencil holder.

Out of his rage came an idea that led to his assertion, "It was really my idea from the beginning. The station is better equipped to run with it."

When his world had been righted, his phone rang again.

"You remember me," said Dirk Lowe Bartle. "The man with the uniform?"

"I told you never to call me here," Seligman recoiled. "It's not a good idea."

"It's not a good idea stiffing me for the second half of my fee. And don't tell me you put the check in the mail."

"The check is not in the mail," Seligman asserted. "And it won't be in the mail until you return the suit. I received another bill." He had used his post office box to prevent the letter from being intercepted. "I'm going to deduct the rental from what I owe you. If you don't return the suit pretty soon, you will owe me."

"Clown." Bartle's voice became harsh and threatening. "You are playing with fire."

"Return the suit."

"Little boys who play with fire get burned."

"Return the suit."

"Have you ever been scorched?"

"Return the suit, damn you."

Seligman slammed the phone and turned up the volume on the radio. He switched from KNDA to KMA. He decided to return the bill with a notation. "Actor won't return the uniform. Quote me a sale price."

If he could have peered into the future and been granted three wishes, the first would have been, "I never want to see or hear from that actor again." For him, Dirk Lowe Bartle would prove to be a bad actor in more ways than one.

Chapter Fourteen

The day began filled with sun and promise. For Andrew Seligman, a phone call shattered the promise.

"Hi there, Chamber Dude. I noticed you paid for the suit. But you still haven't paid me." An icy calm rendered his voice doubly intimidating.

"Y-You wouldn't return the suit. It d-didn't make sense paying for the rental every day."

"I want to give you one last chance to pay me."

"Listen you," Seligman scolded. He did not know the man's name. "If I deduct what it cost me because you refused to turn in the suit, you really owe me."

"Try not to act like a producer. Maybe I'll call the radio station and inform them of our relationship. I'll mention that my motive is that you haven't paid me. Which you'd better do. I still have the suit so send me the loot, rooty toot. Don't try to scoot, or I'll give you more than the boot. So—is it the loot or the suit? Dare me to shoot? Hey, ain't that a hoot?"

Seligman heard a bone-chilling laugh. He found little solace in knowing that the impersonator resided in Kansas City, 130 long miles away. When the call ended, he found it difficult to concentrate on office duties. He looked at the clock and decided to have lunch. When he reached the sidewalk, he saw spectators collected near his car. On the dash rested a World War II Air Force crush cap. Clearly visible, hanging against a back window, he saw the jacket of an Air Force major.

He halted, mule kicked. *Oh my God! He's here in town! He's here!* He swallowed and glanced furtively up and down the street. "Did anyone see who put the uniform in my car?"

A couple said, "No." People shook their heads.

Seligman wheeled and bolted for his office, sweating profusely. His mind cleared. The best defense had to be an offense. He phoned police headquarters.

"Chief Wendinger," he gushed excitedly. "Someone planted a major's uniform in my car. I just found it. It's like the one from the Glenn Miller dance. Someone is still trying to embarrass the city of Clarinda and my office in particular."

"I'm on the way."

Before the chief arrived, Seligman checked the pockets of the uniform and covertly removed a business card of the rental agency. He wasn't born yesterday. The creep might be watching. The back of his neck tensed. He glanced about and saw only locals. Of course, the creep could be watching from a roof top through a telescope. *What rooftop, fool?* What began as a smile curved into a sneer as Seligman realized that he was frightened. *Scared.*

He saw the chief approaching and thrust the crushed, sweaty business card into his pocket.

"I'd better check the pockets," said the chief.

Seligman stepped back and watched the chief check the pockets and find nothing.

"I'll keep the uniform as evidence," the chief said before he returned to his office.

At headquarters, the chief wondered aloud. "What crime has been committed? It's some bad joke. There's something about this Seligman. I'll just let him stew for a while."

"He will either call you," Ellen predicted, "or he won't."

"Precisely."

Seligman need not have worried about Dirk Lowe Bartle seeing him remove the rental agency's business card. The actor was already on his way to do a publicity promo at an Atlantic radio station. Bartle wondered if the producer would arrange for an appearance on KNDA. If Seligman didn't pay—and he probably wouldn't—KNDA would be a beautiful place to explode his bombshell.

In the chamber office, Seligman reminded himself, "I'm a realist. Maybe it's time I made a believer out of myself." He looked for a bulletin. Clarinda wasn't the only town on the map. Now he remembered that the creep threatened to phone the radio station. He dialed in KNDA and heard a listener tell Downbeat, "I am in agreement with the previous caller. That Mystery Man knows too much about these phony Glenn Miller appearances not to be involved."

"There's one way to settle it," Downbeat acknowledged. "I'll phone him."

"Hello," a voice responded.

"Hello, Mystery Man. This is Downbeat Jackson from KNDA, Clarinda, Iowa. You're on the air."

"Er-ah, yeah. O-k-a-a-a-y."

"Because you know so much about Glenn Miller impostors, a couple of our listeners have suggested that our impostor is you. Would it be possible to reveal your identity and give us a statement?"

"All right, Downbeat. The mask comes off. I'm C O Lamp, and I live in Glendale, Arizona. I couldn't be your Glenn Miller impostor. I haven't been out of Arizona in the past four months and I can prove that."

"Scratch another suspect," Downbeat joked. "So what have you been doing?"

"A little writing."

"When are you coming to Clarinda to pay us a visit?"

"Whenever I'm invited. Could I be on your show?"

"Sure, man. Anytime."

"I've always wanted to announce. Listen to this." His voice became sonorous. "From Frank Dailey's Club Meadowbrook, high above the palisades in Cedar Grove, New Jersey, across the Hudson, on the Newark Pompton turnpike, just a half-hour drive from the heart of New York City, we bring you music for moderns, the dance sensation of the nation, Glenn Miller and his orchestra!"

"On second thought," Downbeat said. "Don't rush. Heh-heh-heh. You might take my job. Well, listeners, there you have it. Our Glenn Miller impostor is not our Mystery Man. The search goes on."

Off the air, Downbeat phoned Cordelia Cooper. "I picked up a couple of leads—folks who might be interested in purchasing the station. I could send them to you."

"Just give them to Erin," Cordelia directed. "Excuse me, Mr. Jackson. I have a visitor."

The young woman approached Cordelia with yard-long strides and stood anchored on tall heavy heels. Her taut, creamy skin over high cheek bones and a flawless complexion where what might be expected of a recent homecoming queen.

"Yes, Jennifer?" Cordelia said, recognizing the former station employee.

"They told me that you could help me get rid of a package," Jennifer said petulantly. Her jaws continued to work two sticks of Doublemint. "What with your interest in Planned Parenthood."

Package? Now they called a precious baby a package? "So you are expecting a baby," Cordelia asserted, at once trying to humanize the problem.

"That's it."

Cordelia's eyes narrowed appraisingly, focusing on garishly painted lips that moved with an animal gnawing. The young woman's body language reflected insolence and defiance. She decided to allow Jennifer to remain standing. "I hate abortions. If you had done your homework, you would know that."

"I also heard that if a person wanted to dump a package, you were the one to see. There is no one who can grease the skids like you."

"Then you should also know, nothing will happen today. Why do you want an abortion? Have you given any thought at all to the alternative?"

"Having a baby would ruin my life. I can't afford a kid. I don't have a job. There is no way I can afford a kid. My life will be ruined. I need to dump the package."

Cordelia felt annoyance rising within her like steam. The way Jennifer said package indicated it might be a borrowed term. "Has the father urged you to have an abortion? Has he agreed to pay—?"

"No," Jennifer said abruptly. "He doesn't know anything about it." It was a lie. When she told him the father had said "So what?"

"That's a must." Cordelia knew she had stretched the truth. Telling the father might only be a courtesy, but telling the girl that it was a must might result in delay. A delay would work in the baby's favor. "Have you told your mother?"

"No."

"Are you closer to your father? Have you told him?"

"No. He would kill me."

"So, what you desire is a quick abortion with no one except your selfish self being the wiser. Who's been advising you, girl? Some Kansas City hooker? Listen, the first thing you need to do is tell your parents. It may not be easy but that's my advice."

"I can't do that."

"So they fly into a rage. When they come down from the ceiling, they may be the most supportive parents and grandparents in the world. You can't just keep running, Jennifer. You stand here endowed with what can be the number-one blessing a woman can have. Having an abortion will leave a lifetime of scars. I'd give every cent I have—at least I would have at a younger age—to be able to trade places with you."

"But I don't want a baby," Jennifer said pouting. "I can't take care of a baby. Are you going to help me or not?"

"I've already begun to help you by giving you sound advice. All right, if you don't want to raise your own flesh and blood, there is an alternative that allows you to maintain your freedom. Opt to adopt. Place the child with someone who can provide all the advantages."

Jennifer's chin came out. "What am I going to live on in the meantime?" Helplessness gave way to anger. "Tell me that."

Cordelia detected the vulnerability that stoked her anger. "I think we can find someone who will help with the expenses and even a little more."

"In effect, renting my body."

"Crudely put, but in your vernacular, correct." *If you were my daughter I'd take you across my knee. Maybe that's what she fears from her own parents.* "Let me calm you down. One thing you have is time. Don't look on this as a tragedy. You are not in this predicament alone. Your closest help is your parents. Consider allowing them back into your life. The father of the child needs to be involved. If there is an adoption, he needs to sign off on it. *Not always true.* If there is no adoption, the law requires the father to pay child support. That can easily total fifty thousand dollars over the minority of the child. Now don't rush into anything. Promise me that you will allow me to explore other avenues."

"Well, okay."

When Jennifer had gone, Cordelia glanced at a stretched-out Buster. "So you like her too? I noticed you didn't open your eyes. Are you getting old, Buster?"

Cordelia bobbed her head confidently. Here she had been sitting, feeling sorry for herself, when people still knocked on her door. People still needed her. Jennifer might have a wretched abortion. Jennifer might also delay. "Well, Buster, maybe she will listen to me. Maybe she won't. In the meantime we have work to do."

She reached for the phone, unable to suppress a chuckle. "Erin, honey. Do I have a package for you!" She thoroughly savored the moment. "Stop by. We need to talk."

Speaking with Cordelia Cooper had emboldened Jennifer and at the desk adjacent to Erin's, Doris put through her call to Alex Barca.

Alex heard a sing-song, "Hel-lo, Da-dee."

"I told you never to call me here," Alex snapped.

"You told me a lot of things," Jennifer cooed. "Mostly lies the way it turned out."

"At least I never told you the check is in the mail, and I'll never tell you that. In the beginning, right up front, you agreed you were a big girl—you could take your lumps, you said. If it didn't work out, you'd take your lumps. That's what you said."

"I was thinking of emotions. That's what I meant. Not what you call a package."

"Have you made arrangements to dump the package?"

"Not yet. These things take time. A lot of time. Are you sure you don't wish to make another contribution, Da-dee? This one in cash?"

"No," Alex shouted. "And don't call me here again!" He slammed the phone and stalked toward the front.

"Listen, if Jennifer calls again, tell her I'm out. I don't want to talk to her."

Less than an hour later he answered the phone and heard Jennifer's voice. "Don't hang up, Da-dee, sweetikins. I have a lot of muscle on my side. Did you know a father must support his child? It's the law."

"You'd have to prove I'm that father. Who ever would believe you?"

"I don't need to prove anything. The DNA test will do it for me. It's only a matter of time before you are found to be the father. I understand support can run up to fifty thousand dollars and beyond."

"Yeah, yeah," Alex muttered irritably. *Who had she been talking to? She didn't have a brain of her own.* "Don't call me. I'll call you. Don't get antsy. It may take a couple weeks. And don't call me here again. I mean it."

"Oh, I won't," Jennifer said. "Unless you forget to call me back. Then you will see me in person. You will also see my lawyer."

Bitch. Anger rose within him, steam searing. Lawyers. He might have known. He ran to the reception area and demanded, "Who wants to get fired? Who put through that call from Jennifer?"

"Oh, was that Jennifer?" Doris said, surprised. "I didn't recognize her voice. She told me she was Susan Brown. How was I to know?"

Alex wheeled and stormed to his office.

Erin said, "Clock me out. Cordelia Cooper wants to see me."

"Take these with you," Downbeat said and handed her two envelopes.

Erin wondered if Cordelia wished to discuss the sale of the station or a possible merger. She was not at all prepared for Cordelia's poignant question.

"How would you like to be a mother?"

Taken aback, Erin finally recovered. "Do I get to pick the father?"

"No. You won't have that luxury. You also won't have stretch marks or morning sickness. The delivery will be painless and you will have a beautiful baby. How do you feel about adoption?"

"Something tells me—"

"—to consider it carefully," Cordelia finished. "I know single-parent adoptions aren't favored by agencies, but an arrangement with the expectant mother will override that. You have the time. You have the money, and I hope the inclination. You even have a baby sitter in the house who did a wonderful job with you."

"You make it sound too easy. You said a beautiful baby?"

"Almost guaranteed. It's what you'd expect if the mother has been the homecoming queen."

"Well, are you going to make me stand here or are you going to tell me who the mother is?"

"As if you can't guess," Cordelia said. "Jennifer Otley."

Erin at once thought of Keith Gordoncamp. "Did she name the father?"

"No, she didn't. She said he doesn't know. She hasn't confided in her parents."

Erin decided not to share her suspicions about Keith. She remembered Orville Keane's comparison of Cordelia's penchant for action to a Missouri firecracker. "This comes as a big surprise," Erin admitted. "I'm not sure how to handle it. I need to give it some thought."

Erin felt her pulse quicken. As she bade Cordelia farewell and drove toward home, she could think of nothing else. Cordelia's final admonition had been "Don't delay too long. One can never tell what Jennifer might do."

Erin knew she had to act. She wanted to drive at once to the Otleys, but Jennifer's parents would be home. Jennifer might have scheduled an operation for the morning.

"A possibility," Erin told herself. The situation cried out for action. She decided to see Jennifer in the morning, just as soon as her parents departed for work.

"What has you so excited?" Belle asked.

"Nothing, Mother."

"Hmm."

Erin had long ago given up hope of becoming a mother. She thought the whole idea had been laid to rest. To her dismay, the idea lurked near the surface. She had not been as well tuned to her emotions as she expected. How well did she really know herself? If she allowed any more surprises to excite her, the next thing she knew she might wake up married.

"Nonsense," she said aloud.

"What's nonsense?" her mother asked.

"Just something I heard at the station. I'm going to play hooky in the morning. If either job calls, just say I had something important to take care of first."

Jennifer's parents had not been gone for more than five minutes when Erin knocked at her door. Jennifer answered and recognized Erin. "To what do I owe the honor?" she said, repeating a line she heard on a television movie.

Erin didn't wait to be invited. She seated herself and said, "I might as well be direct. I'm here to discuss your pregnancy."

Jennifer flared, "Did Alex send you?"

"Alex?" Erin questioned. "Why do you think Alex sent me?"

"The station," Jennifer faltered. "The station. You certainly wouldn't be here on behalf of Washington Savings."

Now I know who the father is. "My coming here has nothing to do with the station. It's personal."

"Then how did you know?" Jennifer answered her own question. "Cordelia Cooper. Yeah."

Erin nodded. "I did speak to Cordelia Cooper. I'm here to offer you an alternative to abortion. Adoption. I'll come right to the point. I've always wanted a child. I'm in a position to help you financially. That removes the worry about medical care." Erin held back the suggestion of an out-of-town apartment.

"You?" Jennifer erupted. "What makes you think I would ever give my baby to you?"

"B-But—"

"Haven't you done enough?" Jennifer shouted angrily. "First you get me fired from the station. Now you want to steal my baby. What's with you?"

Erin reach out to touch her. "Jennifer, I'm sorry."

"You're sorry?"

"I didn't realize you wanted to keep your baby."

"Well, I do."

"The baby needs a good home," Erin said lamely. "I can provide a good home."

"So can I," Jennifer shouted. "Leave me alone."

"It's my mistake. I didn't understand—"

"Understand this. If I want to give away my own flesh and blood, you're the last person I'll give my baby. Now leave me alone. Good-bye."

"I'm sorry, Jennifer. I didn't mean to upset you. I know this is a difficult time." Erin regained her composure and said in a face-saving gesture, "If there is any way I can help, let me know. You know where to reach me."

"Good-bye," Jennifer shouted, arms flailing. "I'm keeping my baby! If you want to do me a favor, keep your meddling mouth shut." Jennifer could not believe her own words. When had she decided to keep the baby? When had she changed her mind? Jennifer broke down to wretched sobbing and when her crying abated somewhat she wondered if she would change her mind again. It all came down to money. But Erin Ames wasn't the only one who had money. Alex Barca had money. If he didn't call within ten days, she'd approach him at the station. Jennifer felt her eyes welling with tears once more. Now it would be necessary to tell her parents. She had to do that before they heard about it from someone else. Her shoulders shook to her sobs.

"Damn you, Erin," she cried. "Damn you, Alex Barca."

Stung by Jennifer's rejection, Erin realized she was in no mood to go to work. If she was going to play hooky, another few minutes would not matter.

She wheeled to a halt near Cordelia's carport and burst into the room. "You set me up," she charged. "Why did you send me to pour gasoline on the fire? Jennifer threw me out. She said I'd be the last person she would allow to adopt. She is keeping the baby."

"She's keeping the baby?" Cordelia exclaimed. "That's wonderful."

"It's my guess she's bawling right now. I feel like it too."

"Don't feel bad," Cordelia said. "Look at the good that came out of your visit. Look at what you accomplished. You saved a life. Perhaps two lives."

"What about mine? You manipulated me."

Cordelia smiled faintly. "It's all about growing up. Think how much you expanded Jennifer's horizon. Think how much you helped the *situation.*"

"I guess so," Erin said reluctantly. She decided not to tell Cordelia that the father of Jennifer's expected child was Alex Barca. The was no point in allowing her to ignite the fuse to that firecracker.

Chapter Fifteen

The Cordelia Ballroom had never been so luxuriously decorated. Energized by the profit motive, Clarinda High School students had outdone themselves. Sophomores were making money selling Hawaiian Punch and soft drinks. Juniors contributed not one, but two roving photographers. Advance sales of multicolored Hawaiian shirts exceeded all expectations. The well-rehearsed high-school dance band would receive a generous stipend. Syrupy island music oozed from pillar to port, accented by crests of laughter. Cynical students who expected a damper had not been disappointed by the principal's solemn warning.

"Remember this is primarily an adult event. Try to act like adults. Anyone seen drinking an alcoholic beverage will be dealt with severely."

"You'll be off the team," warned the coach.

"Deprived of all extracurricular activities," scolded the English teacher and drama coach.

No such restriction deterred Henry Leighton of Washington Savings and Loan, the primary sponsor of the event. Leighton insisted that Washington Savings have a booth adorned with slogans. "With systematic savings, your Hawaiian dream vacation will become a reality." On his own, he authorized South Wind Travel to build an adjacent booth in exchange for splitting the cost of the door prize, a fabulous Hawaiian vacation for two.

Pleasantly surprised by Henry's taking charge the way he had, Erin displayed greater surprise when he tacked up a placard. "Let the Big Kahuna take you on an exciting Hawaiian vacation." He flashed two tickets at Erin and said in a voice many could hear, "Romance begins in Clarinda. Erin, you're invited to accompany me on a dream vacation. Come with me to where the moon is on the sea. Share a heavenly night under the sheltering palms. Oh honey, come with me. Oh honey, come with me."

There he stood, barefooted, clad in a grass skirt over his shorts, naked above the waist, chest covered with leis, a Hawaiian straw hat tilted rakishly on his head. A cigar clamped between his teeth, tendrils of smoke coiled around his beaming face. "I mean it, Erin. Come with me to Fantasy Island."

Her hands raced to her hips. "Hen-ry," she exclaimed in a severe imitation of Henry Aldrich's mother. "Hen-ry Leighton! Have you taken leave of your senses?"

"No. This is the most sensible thing I've done all week."

"Have you been celebrating early? Have you been drinking?"

A student taunted. "If you have, you're off the team."

Henry grinned a silly grin. "I'm as sober as Judge Strand."

Erin walked away, simmering.

"Is that a no?" he called after her.

Henry, you fool, you've crossed the line. He had never done such a crazy thing before. It was crazy, embarrassing her in public. Students snickered. Erin felt her cheeks redden and they retained their heightened color. It would be a long time before she trusted Henry to sponsor another event. It would be a cold day. He had taken too much for granted. She looked for R-ex, hoping to seat herself at his side. She could not find R-ex. Perhaps she would sit with someone from Furst Construction or Robinette, whose customers Washington Savings had been assisting with financing. She did not see them. In the end, she sat alone.

Alex Barca made a grandiose entrance befitting a celebrity, shaking hands with people he did not know. His performance had been well calculated to create memories that would stand up in court. He glanced at his watch and noticed several others looked at theirs. In a few minutes he slipped out the side door and drove to the abandoned foundry.

Jennifer had already arrived. She stepped out of her car. "You're late, Da-dee."

"Don't start," Alex warned.

"I'm glad you came. We have a great deal to talk about."

"What's to talk? Talking is a waste of time."

"I don't think so."

"Well I do."

"You need to face the fact that you're going to be a father."

"Me a father?" He sniffed with scorn. "You'd have to prove it first."

"On the contrary, I don't need to prove anything. DNA tests will do that for me."

"Why can't you let it go? Why make a big deal out of it?"

"It is a big deal," Jennifer insisted. "A very big deal."

"Look," Alex said with rising irritation. "Why don't you just dump the package. That's all there's to it."

"Oh, no. That's no longer an issue. I'm keeping our baby."

"What?" Anger edged his voice. "You can't afford to do that."

"But you can. I'm keeping the baby."

"That wouldn't be smart. Not at all smart."

"Wrong, Da-dee. It would be very smart. The law says a father must support his child."

Insolent bitch. "You've been talking to an attorney. By the time I get through with you they'll think you slept with the entire football team."

"That's why we have DNA. That old defense won't fly any more. My lawyer says the DNA test can pick out the father, the real father, no matter how many men have been in the picture."

He hated her sassy impertinent look. "I'll say one thing for you. You sure had me fooled." He reached into his pocket and thrust a monogrammed handkerchief at her. "All the while I thought that Gordoncamp kid dropped this when he flattened my tires, in order to implicate someone else. It was meant to confuse me. It did for a while, until I realized it was you who flattened my tires."

"That's what you say."

"That's what I know."

"What you think you know will be fifty times harder to prove than me proving that you are the father."

"All right, bitch, one last warning. One last chance to drop it and walk away."

"No."

"You won't listen to good advice?"

"I have good advice. Legal advice. I'm keeping the baby."

That damned attorney. "All right," he said easily, "If you won't reconsider—" His voice had taken on an almost solicitous, friendly tone. "—then you will have to take your medicine. We will do it the hard way." His fist had drawn back and he drove a savage powerhouse punch deep into her abdomen.

Jennifer jackknifed, air whooshed out of her lungs. His knee caught her under the chin and threw her back. His arms moved like windmill fans. Brutal blows rained on her face. Blood dripped from her mouth and nose. She staggered to another punch into the abdomen. Alex delivered a well-aimed karate chop, a back-hand, and another chop. Jennifer tottered and fell on her face. Drawing back his foot, he drove a savage kick into her ribs. He kicked again.

"That's just a sample," Alex sneered. "Open your mouth again and you're in big trouble."

Jennifer didn't hear a word. She had lapsed into unconsciousness.

Alex returned to the ballroom. He walked past the ticket taker, averting his face as he displayed the hand that had been previously ink stamped. He strode to the bar and said to Rudy Wagoner, "Nice crowd."

Rudy nodded. "An impresario with no chance to incur a loss is a happy bird." With students selling soft drinks, he had held out for three-fourths of the profits on liquor.

An anxious Keith Gordoncamp approached Erin. "Have you seen Jennifer Otley?"

"No," Erin replied. "Are you and Jennifer an item?"

"Sort of. Mostly my idea."

"I know how that goes."

Keith crossed the room and asked his mother, "Have you seen Jennifer?"

"Not tonight."

"She's late."

"Women are always late," Doris said. "That's something you need to get used to."

"Right," Downbeat said as he came up carrying refreshments.

"Have you seen Jennifer?"

"No," Downbeat said.

"It not just because she's late," Keith said. "I have this feeling. Something's happened to her."

"Premonitions run in the family," Doris said. "If you are really worried, you need to act on it."

"Yeah, but—" He saw Jennifer's parents and hurried to their table. Without a greeting he blurted, "Where's Jennifer?"

"We were wondering the same thing," Malinda Otley said. "She left long before we started out. She mentioned something about stopping at the old foundry first, but that didn't make sense to me. I have no idea why she wanted to stop at the old abandoned foundry—" Malinda stopped talking when she saw Keith running for the door.

Keith set the car in gear almost before it coughed to life. He covered the distance to the foundry in little more than a minute. His eager eyes seized on Jennifer's car. Then he saw her. His eyes widened in disbelief. He focused again.

"Jennifer!"

A battered and bloody Jennifer crawled blindly, then collapsed.

With strength spawned by emergency, he scooped her up and carried her to his car. "I'll take care of you," he cried. "I'll take care of you."

He drove as if possessed. Her glanced at her. She hadn't moved. Her eyes remained closed. *Dead? Oh my God, no.*

Officer Thompson saw the speeding car and at once identified the driver. *Got him.* He leaped his vehicle forward and spoke into the mike. "The Gordoncamp kid. Busting reds. Doing at least ninety. I'm in pursuit."

Intersection traffic brought Keith to a halt. He jumped ahead while the light was still red. Now he saw the flashing light. He slowed and waved to the officer.

Thompson brought his vehicle alongside and heard Keith shout. "She may be dead! We have to get her to the hospital." Siren blaring, Thompson led the way, with an eagle eye on the rear-view mirror in case Gordoncamp made a sudden detour.

At the hospital, a nurse uttered words that answered Keith's prayers. "She's alive."

Officer Thompson contacted the chief.

Wendinger asked, "What's the scoop?"

"Jennifer Otley is in the emergency room. Bad shape."

"And Keith?"

"I cuffed him. Locked him in my patrol car."

"Don't be a damn fool. Get him out of there and turn him loose."

"What?"

"And don't take his statement. I'll do that myself. Get back on duty. Keith won't go anywhere."

Released, Keith immediately phoned his mother. "I found Jennifer at the foundry, all beat up. She's barely alive. They told me she came to and managed to say 'Save my baby.' I didn't know she was expecting a baby. The doctor gave her a sedative and she's out again. I'm going to stay here—all night if I have to. I see Chief Wendinger coming. Gotta go. Gotta talk to him."

"All right, son."

Doris at once found Erin. She flung up her hand. "I don't understand it. Jennifer's been beaten up. Keith was locked up and released. It doesn't make sense. Jennifer is going to have a baby. I'm worried that—" She stopped. Why didn't Erin react?

"I feel sorry for Jennifer," Erin said in response to the facial prompt. She thought of going to the hospital and realized she would only be in the way. "There's Officer Eastman talking to the Otleys now."

The Otleys left the hall. For a long time Ted Otley drove in steely silence, attempting to suppress the rage swirling within him. At length he found words. "Did you know she was pregnant?"

"No," Malinda Otley said. "She didn't say anything to me."

"So who's she been going out with?"

"Keith Gordoncamp. I didn't think that was special."

He remembered Keith asking about Jennifer and running out of the hall. "I'll kill him," he said through clenched teeth. "I'll kill him."

At the hospital, Ted Otley saw Keith talking with Chief Wendinger and lunged for him headlong, fists raised. "You!"

Wendinger stepped in his path. "Cool down. Honor the blameless man. Your first job is to see your daughter. She's going to be all right. Get a hold of yourself."

Adrenaline rush dissipated, Keith stared in wonderment. The chief had stood with him! He swallowed. Tears welled in his eyes. He did not want the chief to see him crying and looked away. At length he heard the chief say, "It's time for you to go in. I'll be with you every step of the way."

Ted Otley extinguished a frown. His angry slash of a mouth lifted at the corners. "I had you wrong," he admitted, glancing briefly at Keith, then looking a way. "The doctor says you saved Jennifer's life by going after her. By being there."

At a loss for words, Keith shrugged.

Malinda Otley looked at a battered daughter she could barely recognize. She sniffed and dabbed her eyes. "Thank you."

Keith sniffed backward, a habit his mother warned him to stop. "Unless you want to get sinus trouble."

"I'm going to stay here all night," he said.

The doctor spoke. "I talked to her briefly. I've given her medication to calm her down. I think we can save the baby. Twenty-four hours should tell the story." He had already repeated to the chief and her parents the name of her assailant: Alex Barca.

"I'm not going to arrest anyone until I talk to Jennifer myself," the chief said. "When she's lucid and not doped up, when she is herself." His gaze moved from face to face. "Okay, everybody. Raise your right hands. I'm swearing you all in as special deputies."

"Me too?" said Keith.

"Especially you," said the chief. "Now say your name and repeat after me. 'I promise to faithfully uphold the law as a special deputy and speak to no one about what I have heard, or what I suspect, or what I believe about this case for twelve hours henceforth.'"

County Attorney Richardson told him the ceremony would not permit prosecution if anyone violated his or her oath, but he knew from experience that taking the oath had been impressive. *They don't want to get on my shit list.*

Ted Otley whispered to his wife with a nod toward Keith. "If he's staying, we should too. But I have to be at work early in the morning."

"Go home," she said. "I'll stay here and keep Keith company."

"Now don't do anything crazy," the chief warned Ted. "Let the law handle it. Barca is under surveillance." He called to Keith. "Did you see Jennifer's purse?"

"No."

"Then it must still be at the foundry. I'll give you a lift, Ted. You leave your car here for your wife. You can drive Jennifer's car home from the foundry. If we can't find her purse, I'll drive you home myself. Her car is probably not locked either."

Ted looked back. "Who would have thought I'd be beholden to that Gordoncamp kid?"

"It took me a while to get used to him," admitted the chief. "They say he has a lot of good in him, if one can find it. That's what they say."

The chief spoke into the mike and raised an officer at the hall. "What's happening?"

"We're keeping an eye on him. Me and Eastman."

"Good. Now don't tip your hand. Just see that he doesn't leave town. I'm going home. Don't screw it up." *First thing in the morning I'll call Mrs. Cooper and tell her I'm arresting her station manager.*

Inside the hall, Officer Eastman sat joking with a group of students from a location that allowed him to observe Alex Barca.

All eyes turned to the stage. "Now the moment you've been waiting for," Henry Leighton said. "The fabulous door prize! A free vacation for two to beautiful Hawaii!" He stared longingly at the tickets in his hand. "There is nothing in the whole world I would like to do more than use these tickets myself." He located Erin in the crowd and their eyes met.

She cringed. *Oh-oh. Here it comes. He's going to propose in front of the whole crowd. Well he's not going to get away with it. I'll stand up and shout "NO!"*

Henry continued. "I guess we all have to give up our dreams now and then. But some lucky person won't have to give up theirs tonight—courtesy of Washington Savings and South Wind Travel. Draw the name."

A young woman reached in and read the card. "Keith Gordoncamp."

"Keith Gordoncamp," Henry repeated. "Is Keith Gordoncamp here?"

After a long moment Doris rose to her feet. "He isn't here. Keith is my son and I work at KNDA. He's family. The family of a second-level sponsor should not be eligible to claim the prize. Draw another name. Draw again." She sat down and whispered to Downbeat. "He's going to kill me."

"I don't think so," Downbeat said. "Doris, did I ever tell you that you're a class act."

"Not lately."

"You're a class act."

Henry Leighton announced the winner. "Mary Woldruff."

A squeal emanated from the corner of the room. The waitress made her way to the front.

"So who's the lucky guy?" Henry asked.

"I don't know for sure," she said with a giggle. "I've had my eye on a pharmacist."

Erin frowned and muttered under her breath. "Alex Barca wouldn't let me be a sponsor. I've been outflanked by Cordelia Cooper. I've been denied by Jennifer Otley. And I've been embarrassed by Henry Leighton." She rose and paused to tell Doris, "If I don't break a leg and have a flat tire, I'm going home. I'll see you in the morning." She had already decided she was NOT going to work at Washington Savings. Not before lunch. Not in the afternoon. Maybe not ever.

"See you," Doris said.

Downbeat waved farewell.

During his years in radio, Downbeat had become accustomed to short nights. He arrived at the station early and read the seven o'clock news the way it had been given to them by the police department. "A local woman, Jennifer Otley, was found severely beaten in the area of the old foundry. The police have no leads."

Alex Barca heard the news and grinned. He knew the report would be repeated at eight. The clock had not yet tilted toward eight when he entered the building and made his way to the office. He did not observe police vehicles collecting on the street out front. Moments after the news had been broadcast a second time, Chief Wilbur Wendinger casually strolled down the corridor to Alex Barca's office.

Alex looked at him and paled. *The bitch talked. Damn. I'm out of it for a while. My word against hers.* Got to get a mouthpiece. He opened a drawer and grabbed a checkbook. He held it up to show it was not a weapon and waited to be patted down.

"Alex Barca," the chief announced. "I arrest you for the attempted murder of Jennifer Otley. You have the right to remain silent. Anything you say—"

The staff watched him being led away and Erin phoned Cordelia. "We just lost a station manager. From what Doris told me Jennifer suffered a rather savage beating. She's all right, and so far there's apparently no danger to the child."

"I'm glad of that. So the snake came out of the grass. I suppose he's the putative father."

"That's my guess. Nothing official. The station needs a manager."

Cordelia thought about suggesting Erin, but Erin had a job at Washington Savings, and a potential interest there, a very large potential interest. "I vote for Downbeat Jackson."

Erin smiled. "I vote for Downbeat Jackson. I move we cast a unanimous ballot."

"Agreed."

"By the power vested in me, I declare Downbeat Jackson to be our new station manager. Cordelia, you can't know how much pleasure it gives me to vote Alex Barca's stock." A throaty laugh escaped her.

"I'm enjoying it myself," Cordelia confided. "Tell our new manager I'll be down to shake his hand one day soon."

"Will do. Bye, dear."

The endearment warmed Cordelia's heart. "Well, well," she murmured happily. "Imagine."

Doris had overheard Erin's side of the conversation and beamed with delight. She waited for Erin to make the announcement. They listened to Downbeat at the mike.

"This time we're looking for a senior citizen with a long memory. I'll give you two last names and I want you to give me their real first names. Here we go. Chummy MacGregor and Tex Beneke."

"Hello," a loud voice boomed. "This is Gordon Sinclair from the nursing home."

"You have the winning name?" Downbeat said. "Hey turn down your radio."

"Hah? How am I supposed to hear?"

"On the telephone," Downbeat shouted.

"Hah? Well, all right."

"So, Gordon, you have the real names?"

"I think so. John Chalmers MacGregor is the real name of the pi-an-ny player. As to Tex Beneke, I think his name is Harold."

"So, Gordon—your name is Gordon?"

"Yes, it's Gordon."

"You're absolutely right. Tex Beneke's real name is Gordon. You're our winner!"

"Hah? That's good."

A laughing Erin waved for Downbeat to step out of the broadcast booth. If Cordelia thought a handshake to be important, Erin decided, she would give Downbeat one of her own.

"What's up," he asked.

Erin said with elaborate formality, "The stockholders have unanimously elected you to be our interim station manager. Congratulations!" She extended her hand. He shook it briefly and brushed past her arm for a bear hug and a kiss. "Thanks, angel," he whispered, none of which escaped Doris. She gave him a thin smile and a weak "Congratulations."

The phone rang and Doris vented on Henry Leighton. "No," she said snappishly. "Erin will not be at work over there this morning. She probably won't be in all day. We've lost a station manager." She mashed the phone button.

A shocked Erin averted her face.

Henry Leighton's brows rose in befuddlement. "What brought that on?" *Now I remember. Last night at the ballroom. Erin couldn't take a joke.* "I wasn't joking," he said morosely.

In the *Herald-Journal,* news of Alex Barca's arrest would appear adjacent to the column reporting the success of the Hawaiian Holiday festival. The charges listed included attempted murder, aggravated assault, divorce proceedings, establishment of child support, establishment of spousal maintenance, nine counts of child abuse, three counts of assault on his wife, and possibly other charges. The editor did not know the charges alluded to by both County Attorney Richardson and Attorney Orville Keane included paternity and child support relating to the unborn child of Jennifer Otley.

By the end of the day a charge of embezzlement from KNDA would be added.

Orville Keane telephoned Erin in a voice that could not conceal his elation. "It appears that in his haste to hire the firm of Kessler and Albee, our friend Alex issued a check on a KNDA account for his personal use. Thanks for filing the charge and thanks again for alerting me."

"You're welcome. But the real thanks should go to the tellers at Citizens State Bank for immediately calling the matter to my attention."

"Yes, it appears that Jerry Kessler went straight to the bank with the check. Barca's wife is going to be happy knowing he won't escape this time. Thanks again."

Keane phoned Lonica Barca with the news. "We have Alex where you want him."

"Well, not quite where I want him. I'll make reservations. I want to see his face when they haul him into court."

At the end of the day Erin sagged onto the sofa. "What a day. The phone never stopped ringing. I really didn't need an excuse not to go work for Henry Leighton. Ooooo, sometimes he makes me so mad."

"You'll have to go back eventually. Like tomorrow."

"Don't remind me."

"The road to love," Belle observed, "can be a rocky road."

Erin's head snapped. She stared at her mother with a look of censure.

Chapter Sixteen

In the heartland of America, county-seat towns are often designed with a square at the downtown center. Rising from the square stands a monument: a tall stately courthouse, a smaller version of Eastern state capitols, with architecture reminiscent of the Greek and Roman.

Visitors standing in the atrium of the Page County Courthouse have stared up at the airy space beneath the spire and concluded the architect wanted light to flow into the center of the structure. It might be argued that all this heavenly space is intended as a reminder that justice flows from God. Clarinda residents are inclined to believe that justice flows from Judge Lars Jennings Strand who has been a District Court Judge for longer than almost anyone can remember.

Called Jens by close friends, when he was young and had opposition in the polls, Judge Strand realized he could not possibly remember everyone by name. He opted to concentrate on the names of the women, who early on were his most ardent political supporters. Through the years the law had changed and now the ballot contained a simple "yes" or "no" alternative to the question, "Shall Lars Jennings Strand be retained?"

Judge Strand found old habits difficult to break. He still greeted every juror by name on the second day of trial. "Good morning, Mrs. Sunderman. Good Morning, Mr. Thompson." Of course, now a list of seated jurors would be placed on the bench by a thoughtful long-time secretary. At Christmas each juror who had served during the year would receive his Christmas card.

When the tiny elevator door opened, Judge Strand happened to peer out from the depths of his second-floor office and saw Cordelia Cooper and Erin Ames. These names he remembered. Jake and Cordelia had been strong supporters. Erin Ames had at one time delivered his newspaper. If her name eluded memory, as it had on occasion, he would chuckle and say, "How's my newspaper girl?" He went out to meet them.

"Good morning, Cordelia. Good morning, Erin. Here for the preliminaries, I see."

"No," Cordelia said. "It's probably my last chance to see you wearing a dress."

"Same old Cordelia."

"Old is right. I may be the only gal in town who can name your predecessor. We won't detain you longer, your honor. We are here to see that you dispense injustice with an even hand."

"Injustice with an even hand," he repeated, savoring the concept. "I believe that is the best policy."

Cordelia whispered to Erin as they crossed the hall to the courtroom, "If you are a woman in this county, you can do no better than have Judge Strand hear your case."

The judge returned to study the complaints and motions for severance. "Jennifer Otley," he mused. "She sold me Girl Scout cookies. Yes."

Behind his back one secretary shook her head and whispered to the other, "Jennifer Otley never sold him Girl Scout cookies."

"What's the harm in letting him think she did? Are *you* going to correct his impression?"

"Not I."

The bailiff returned from an assigned mission. At the judge's instruction he'd moved a couple of reporters to find strategic seats for Cordelia and Erin. Presently he preceded Judge Strand into the crowded courtroom and said in a loud voice, "All rise. The District Court of Page County is now in session. The Honorable Lars Jennings Strand presiding."

"Be seated," said the judge. His gaze moved from one counsel table to the other. "Is counsel ready?"

"Yes, your honor," they all agreed.

"Well," Judge Strand observed jovially. "This is a first. A county attorney seated with a defense attorney."

After Orville Keane filed civil assault charges, County Attorney Lance Richardson filed criminal charges of aggravated assault, attempted murder, embezzlement and other criminal acts.

In the memory of court aficionados, there had never been a case where civil charges had been heard at the same time as criminal charges. For one thing, a criminal case required the unanimous decision of all twelve jurors. A civil jury could be composed of as few as six, a majority of whom had to agree. Attorney Jerry Kessler had generated reams of motions for severance of various criminal charges, challenging jurisdiction because the acts had not occurred in Iowa, let alone Page County. Richardson and Keane each responded to every motion and suggested that two juries might be empaneled at the same time, one to hear the criminal matters, the other to decide civil issues. At this preliminary hearing, Judge Strand would decide these issues.

"It is a privilege to sit with the prosecutor," said Orville Keene.

"It is a privilege to share counsel table with a learned attorney such as Orville Keene," Lance Richardson observed.

"Now that we have heard from the mutual admiration society," defense attorney Jerry Kessler said in a booming voice, "I beg the court's indulgence."

"Ah, I see we are missing the defendant-respondent."

"He's on the way, your honor. I beg the court's indulgence."

"I suppose there is no way to settle this matter?" the judge inquired. Among court personnel, his honor had a richly deserved reputation as "the Great Settler."

At that moment, the sheriff and police chief shared the honor of escorting a shackled Alex Barca to the defense table.

"Alex Barca is present," boomed Jerry Kessler.

"Considering the first motion," intoned Judge Strand.

Lonica Barca leaped to her feet and shouted, "What's going on here? That's not Alex Barca. That's not the no-good father of my children!"

Flashbulbs flashed, cameras turned to the excited lady. In the tumult of laughter and shouting, Orville leaned over and asked in astonishment, "That's not Alex Barca?"

"No," Lonica shouted. "That's not Alex Barca!"

All the while Judge Strand had been banging down the gavel, attempting to silence the crowd. The bailiff added his own cries of "Order in the court!" Alex Barca rose and gestured at Jerry Kessler. "I told you I wasn't married. I told you I don't have any kids."

"Sit down," boomed his attorney.

The gavel came down again.

"These charges are bogus," Alex yelled before he sat down.

The gavel came down repeatedly and at length silence ensued.

The judge stared at attorneys Keane and Richardson and said with utter sarcasm, "Would counsel like to have a recess?" The question was rhetorical. "Court is in recess until two o'clock this afternoon." He strode from the bench to his office and closed the outer door. He waved a scolding finger at his staff. "No interruptions! Not a word," he ordered, and closed the chamber door behind him.

The courtroom remained in chaos until Orville Keane ushered his witnesses into Richardson's office. He inquired of Jennifer Otley, "Can you identify the man in court as the father of your expected child?"

She nodded and he quickly dismissed Jennifer and her parents, "Until two o'clock this afternoon."

"You goofed," Lonica Barca scolded. "You have the wrong man. That's not Alex Barca. How could you have made such a mistake?"

Orville listened patiently and, when her anger had subsided sufficiently, said quietly, "You are the one who told me Alex Barca had been located in Clarinda. You told me that. You never showed me a photo. That's something you might have done. Look, there's plenty of blame to go around."

"How was I to know?" she countered. "Alex Barca is in the radio business. I couldn't allow him to see me. He did that last time and ran. How many Alex Barcas can there be?"

"That's what we'd like to know," said Lance Richardson. "What does your Alex look like?"

Lonica gave a description.

"Wait here," Orville said, "while I check a couple of sources of information."

He raced down the stairs and caught up with Erin and Cordelia outside. "The Alex Barca we know is a Dapper Dan. The man she described as her husband is more of a Stanley Kowalski slob. Shorter, he wears thick, round glasses. Does that ring any bells?"

"Sparks!" Erin exclaimed.

"Humphrey Poulton," Cordelia said. "That's how he was carried on the station's employee roster. I gave Chief Wendinger his prints to be sent to the state crime lab."

"You did?" Orville saved his why question. "Do you have a photo?" he asked. "I'm crossing my fingers."

"Yes," Erin said. "From our first day on the air."

"Call Doris at the station. Have her look in my desk and all around for pictures of Sparks. Ask her to bring whatever she can find. I'll take Cordelia home for a bit of a rest."

"You'll do no such thing. You'll take me to the station. I want to greet our new manager." On the way to their car they saw Doris hurrying to the court house.

Two minutes after Doris arrived, Orville Keane spread an assortment of snapshots and said to Lonica Barca, "Take a look at these. From the description you gave, Erin thought a man who worked at the station for a short time might be your husband."

Lonica took a look and at once exclaimed, "That's him. That's my Alex Barca."

"See? We're not as incompetent as you think," Orville said in his professional voice. "He was known as Sparks when he worked at KNDA. The name he used on the employment files is Humphrey Poulton. Does that name ring any bells?"

"No."

"You might as well go home. Maybe you can catch an earlier flight. I'll keep up the pressure here. It wouldn't surprise me if our Alex Barca knows a great deal about your Alex Barca. Maybe at an opportune time we can induce him to give us the information."

"Then all my charges will be dismissed?"

"Against our Alex Barca."

"If I ever get my hands on my Alex Barca, I'll kill him."

When she had gone, Orville Keane informed Richardson about the fingerprints and insisted that he phone Wendinger in his official capacity.

"Chief, we learned that Cordelia Cooper gave you some prints of the station engineer to be sent to the crime lab. What can you tell us about that? Lonica Barca has positively identified photos of Sparks as her Alex Barca."

"Er-ah, I've got the report," said the chief. "I'll bring it right over."

In a hurry to leave town, a determined Lonica Barca nevertheless made a stop at the radio station. "Tell me about Sparks."

Erin supplied a post office box and a social security number. Lonica departed in a manner that Downbeat later described as "hell bent for election."

Downbeat greeted Cordelia warmly. She shook his hand with formality and selected the first office for their visit.

"The vultures are circling," Downbeat reported. "I'm getting numerous offers for the station. I didn't know that news of Mr. Barca's arrest could travel so fast."

"That's radio," Cordelia said.

"Most of the offers are of a fire sale variety."

"Dump them. If you get any meaningful offers, Erin and I want to see them."

"Will do." Downbeat rubbed his chin pensively. "I'm thinking of hiring a new announcer." He paused. "It may be nepotism but Keith Gordoncamp needs a break. It's long overdue. He catches on quickly. I believe I can teach him all I know in a couple of weeks. In the beginning I'll assign him scut work—every dirty and boring job I can think of. If he sticks it out for a week, I'll pay him a dollar. Then he's on board." Downbeat halted and waited for a reaction. "Well, what do you think?"

"You're the manager," Cordelia said, pleased that he required Keith to earn his way. "Do it."

"It's time to go," Erin prompted.

Once they were outside, Cordelia said, "Our manager is really taking hold. I particularly like his humanity."

"Yes," Erin acknowledged. "He's a good teacher. Look what he did with me."

When they reached the car, Cordelia insisted, "Erin, I'm taking you to lunch at Miss Kitty's."

"You really should rest."

"Nonsense. I'm as strong as a horse," Cordelia said with a laugh. "I mean," she amended. "As thirsty as a plow horse."

As soon as they were seated at the restaurant, Cordelia ordered "a rye with an Erin chaser."

"Celebrating new management at the station," Erin explained to the waitress. "Skip the rye for me. Just give me an Erin. I'm still a growing girl—and I need to keep my wits about me."

"Implying that I'm dimwitted—or a half-wit?" Cordelia questioned.

"Absolutely not. I'm not skilled at reverse innuendo, the kind you hear at the garden club. If I say I like a dress, it means I like a dress. It doesn't mean I didn't like the one the person wore yesterday."

"Folks tell me that you do say what you mean right out."

Erin arched an eyebrow. "Have you been asking around?"

"There you go again, says President Reagan. Seriously, Erin." Cordelia felt she had met her match. "How do you feel about selling the station? It might mean that every employee would be replaced. A buyer would be stupid to do that, but it's certainly in the cards."

"I do have a concern. Downbeat has accepted the fact that we might sell and he's never given the slightest hint of opposition. He's been working with us. Everyone else has another job, except Doris. I'd need to read the fine print on any sale document. I have no basic opposition."

"Good. Jake taught me that anyone can buy right. It takes a special discipline to sell right. He always said, 'Sell when you are on top. Don't be a Jesse James. You want your buyer to make it.'"

"I remember him saying that," Erin said. "It makes sense." She noticed that Cordelia looked tired. "We don't need to return to the courthouse. I could report what happened later."

"Nonsense," Cordelia said, brushing aside concern. "In for a dime, in for a dollar. I wouldn't miss it."

When Erin and Cordelia arrived at the courthouse, they learned the attorneys had conferred and reached preliminary agreement.

Court resumed promptly at 2:00 P.M. Orville Keane rose and spoke. "Move to dismiss without prejudice all counts relating to Lonica Barca and her children."

"Are you in concurrence, Mr. Richardson?"

"Yes, your honor."

"Mr. Kessler?"

"Yes, your honor. Waive time from trial stipulate to a setting thirty to sixty days hence."

"So ordered," said Judge Strand. "Defendant is hereby remanded to custody."

"What?" Alex protested. "I can't make bond?"

"Don't even think of it," Jerry Kessler said. "In the judge's present frame of mind he might order the death penalty. I heard he has a gun under the bench."

Richardson whispered to Keane. "Jerry hasn't received his fee. He hasn't received any more than the initial retainer that constitutes the embezzlement charge. He needs time."

"Alleged embezzlement," Orville said out of habit. "I know how that goes. If I work out a solution, could you live with simple battery, restitution, and not much more than time served?"

"To avoid the kind of circus for which you're famous? Is the Pope Catholic?"

"Never met the Pope," Orville said.

"But you would have to hit Alex with a heavy monetary penalty," Richardson advised.

"Jerry won't like that."

"So you have your work cut out for you."

As Cordelia left the courtroom she felt a dreadful weariness. "I'm sorry, Erin. I'm all played out. I guess this old horse has plowed too long. I don't trust myself to drive home. I know it's an imposition, but would you drive me?"

"It's no imposition. I'll be happy to drive you home."

"I hate to be a crappie."

"Don't forget to take your medicine."

"Slave driver." She handed Erin her car keys. "Ask one of the boys in blue to drive my car home when they are through chasing suspects."

While Cordelia remained in the car, Erin stopped at police headquarters and relayed her request. Ellen Iverson spoke to the chief. "Here's a splendid opportunity to prove the Peter Principle. You always wanted to be a taxi driver."

"Is that a fact?"

"I'll bring you right back," Erin promised. It appeared that the chief wanted to say something but changed his mind.

Chief Wendinger led the way and after he parked Cordelia's car in her carport, he gazed at the barn. It brought back old memories. He remembered a photograph with Jake's handwritten admonition on the reverse, "Always do right."

On the way back downtown the chief remarked to Erin, "You know you did right today. Because of you, a lot of things were straightened out. Mrs. Barca has a lead on running down her husband. The police alone wouldn't have been able to put that together." He wondered if he should tell her that he'd given the county attorney the report on the prints Cordelia had asked him to submit to the state crime lab. He decided he'd better keep it under wraps. "Do you know why Sparks would be using an Alex Barca identity?"

Erin said, "I have no idea. We have him listed on our station records as Humphrey Poulton. That's all I know."

"Well, you take care."

Erin walked to Washington Savings. Ever since missing work the day after the Hawaiian Holiday, the atmosphere had taken on an aura of formality. In the days that followed, she and Henry went about their business as if nothing had happened. He did not wish to talk about her attitude. She did not wish to speak about the crazy way he'd acted and embarrassed her in front of everyone.

A totally alien concept caused Erin's lips to tip into a grin. It was a crazy idea, as crazy as the one upon which Henry had acted. She imagined flinging her arms around him and kissing him solidly to see how HE reacted. Of course she didn't. "That would not have been seemly," as her grandmother used to say.

Later she shared her runaway thoughts with her mother. She could not believe her mother's assertion that she might be in love with Henry.

"If you didn't love him, you wouldn't care," Belle went on. "You do more for him than you realize."

"I just do my job."

"You even approve of him restoring that old car. And another thing," Belle said. "Do you know how much he is like that captain you ran off with?"

"Mother, he's not at all like Captain Gaylord Haversham. Besides, you never met him."

Belle knew a great deal about the captain as seen through her daughter's eyes. "Hmm," she said, insisting on having the last word. "All Henry Leighton needs is a uniform."

Chapter Seventeen

To hire a hit man, a client would drop hints to longtime bartenders along Whiskey Row. If the client appeared worthy, he or she would be informed that Luckman, "the best in the business," would "get back to them." The client wasn't told that the call might come from Omaha or some other city. When the call came, the client would be told to place an ad in the Omaha *World Herald:* WANTED: RELIABLE CONFIDENTIAL MECHANIC, along with a phone number where he or she could be reached. Perhaps then the client would receive a call from Chicago or some other city and be told to send an outrageous sum of money to Mr. Lobo at a Mexico City Bank. Lobo, who had been convinced it was better to live and prosper, rather than reveal or steal, skimmed a thousand dollars off the top for the favor of sending the balance to a numbered Swiss account.

The Kansas City police knew about Luckman and had dispatched a decoy along the bars of Whiskey Row. They had a phone trace ready and, to their surprise, learned the call came from Denver. When told to send an outrageous sum of money to Mexico City, the KC cops lost interest. So had the standoffish FBI. Neither agency had ever been able to connect Luckman with a single homicide in Kansas City or anywhere else for that matter. Old bartenders could have told them that. "Luckman don't do Kay Cee." Some might add, "Hell, he don't hit anyone. It's all gas."

In his role as Luckman, Brock Lyden knew there were rules. He had decided early on that he would not be greedy. He limited his mechanic's work to not more than two contracts per year. He had excellent cover. He traveled across the country selling classy gifts to executives for corporate giving to favored clients. This had enabled him to call on clients in Albuquerque on the same day he intercepted a witness in the parking garage across the street from the court building. A twenty-two-caliber slug placed behind the man's ear obviated the necessity of testifying against the local land baron.

Victoria Lyden knew nothing of her husband's avocation. Her candy-greeting card-stationery-notions shoppe catered to the elite of Kansas City society. She never questioned their offshore trust holdings, the chalet in Switzerland, the house in New York rented to a family who allowed them to stay in the spare bedroom whenever they were in the city. A safe in the bedroom contained other nations' passports—necessary, Brock explained, to prevent creditors from latching on to their assets. And wasn't it fun to arrive in New York as the Lydens and fly out using a different name?

"How else could we enjoy the French or Spanish Riviera?" he would say.

In his gift business, meticulously kept separate from hers, Brock Lyden associated with a Newton, Iowa, firm that drop-shipped his order directly to the executives. He had no inventory but had acquired one when he extended his holdings to a bar supply company that he allowed someone else to manage. The new business provided access to bartenders. Victoria had opened a second shoppe bearing her name in Omaha, and considered purchasing a third outlet in Des Moines.

"Never get greedy," Luckman reminded himself as he nosed the Lincoln town car toward Clarinda. He loved to drive, and the car did not leave a paper trail like airline reservations.

Luckman never relished "the act" itself. He had no blood lust. He denied that a client ever hired Luckman; a client hired his pistol or his bomb. He had never hit the wrong subject or injured a bystander. He prided himself in his expertise. A professional had to be just that: a real professional. A professional had ethics.

He had to admit he enjoyed the thrill that accompanied the risk. He could not remember when he'd been sent to a town as small as Clarinda. In Clarinda there would be no risk, no risk at all. The whole operation had the aura of a simple Halloween prank. To make the contract interesting, perhaps he would work in daylight. He would pose as a Glenn Miller fan; his inquiries would raise no suspicions. He'd do his job and return to the city. He thought about wandering into KNDA. Sniffing with amusement, he decided he would not.

Long before freeways, when Highway 71 had been improved to accommodate vital north-south commerce, Jake Cooper had remarked, "A road don't care who drives on it."

On the same highway now, Dirk Lowe Bartle wondered if his oil-burning junker would make it to Hollywood. He'd decided to stop in Clarinda for one final attempt at collecting the second half-payment due for his Glenn Miller impersonation. Something told him Seligman would hang tough, but he'd have the satisfaction of making him squirm. *I'll get even.* He'd enjoyed the gig. He had been paid half the fee—if not the agreed sum. So the play closed early. *What else is new?*

He stopped at a pay phone and dialed the number of the chamber of commerce. "Hah," he said in a coarse, grating theatrical voice. "So you managed to pull the costume rental agency's card out of the pocket before turning the uniform over to the police?" He'd checked, there hadn't been a whimper at the rental agency. "That forces me to call the police myself—unless you have wised up and want to pay me. I'm in town again. I'm willing to stop at your office. You can have the satisfaction of handing me the money in person."

"No!" Andrew Seligman shouted. For a moment his mind boggled. He sucked in a breath. "I'm calling the police as soon as you get off the line. Don't come near this place. I'll have you arrested." He slammed the phone.

Bartle heard the phone buzz. "I have no interest in being arrested, Dude. I also know that you have no intention of calling the police."

Seligman slumped forward and buried his face in his hands. He swallowed hard and sniffed, aware that the time had come to make a decision. He spread brochures of opportunity on his desk. The Marshalltown search was too far in the future. He had no valid reason for rejecting Ottumwa. That left Fort Dodge and Spencer. The time had come to leave Clarinda. He sent two urgent replies. He knew the gesture might place him at a disadvantage in negotiations, but time was of the essence. Perhaps he could negotiate an automatic raise in a few months.

Spencer and Fort Dodge. Perhaps he could play one against the other. A bidding war would be wonderful. He stared across the room, not seeing the opposite wall, deeply immersed in a daydream. "A bidding war. World get ready. Seligman is moving up!"

Dirk Lowe Bartle leafed through the phone book. If he couldn't get the second half payment, he could definitely get even. He'd been in hundreds of "Don't call us, we'll call you" auditions. He knew success always depended on someone else. Today he would be a casting director. Maybe he would teach a lesson to Andrew, the Dude, Seligman. He dialed and heard a woman's voice.

"Clarinda police department."

A lady cop. "About that Glenn Miller uniform you have in property. Look in the lining, left side. You should find a card from the Benton Costume Rental Agency in Kay Cee. They will tell you who received the bill for the rental."

"Who is this?" Ellen Iverson pressed. She heard a loud click. "Whoever you are."

Dirk Lowe Bartle found a parking spot near Vaughn's Victuals and noticed the adjacent car also bore Kansas City plates. The luxury Lincoln generated "Cool wheels," and he wondered if he'd seen the car before. He adjusted his sunglasses and strode into the restaurant.

He recognized the customer seated alone at a table, not by name but by general appearance. It was more than the smoky glasses and slick threads—there was something about him. He had to be connected. Dirk slid onto the chair opposite with a perfunctory "Mind if I sit here?" Not waiting for a response he said, "How is the food here?"

"Generous portions," Luckman said.

Dirk didn't care about the food. His thoughts focused on the foxy wheels. The Lincoln would provide first-class transportation to Hollywood. The best part of the scenario, the guy across the table would never report it stolen. Dirk gobbled his food and had nearly finished when the man rose and left. He followed.

Dirk felt pleased that he'd made the phone call to the police. There might not be time to do that now. He remained far back, almost out of sight, as the Lincoln turned into a supermarket parking lot.

Luckman approached a phone and made a collect call to a number at the FCC in Washington, D.C. Ordinarily he didn't phone until he'd finished the job, but this time he had set it up for on arrival. Nothing could go wrong. He'd make his report and return to the city.

"It's all wired," he reported. The next time the old lady starts her car, in one hundred seconds the carburetor starts on fire. You did say you wanted it to look natural."

"I did say I wanted it to be an accident. Say, what old lady are you talking about?"

"The one who owns the radio station. I didn't know she was crippled. If I'd known that I would have upped my fee."

"I never said to hit any woman. I said, the station manager, the honcho. Alex Barca."

"You never gave me the name. Not the woman?" Luckman cringed.

"No, I distinctly recall saying the station manager. That's Alex Barca. What the hell have you done? The crippled old woman is a majority stockholder, that's all. You got the wrong party!" His voice had become a shout. "Now get it right! Your target is Alex Barca. Now take care of it!"

"It will cost you—" The dial tone sounded before he could say "—a little more money."

Deep in concentration, Luckman had failed to notice a car had eased to a halt adjacent to his. Dirk slid out, left his driver's side door open, and kept the junker's engine running to cover the sound of starting the Lincoln. The keys had been left inside while the man made his call. He slid behind the wheel, shifted quietly into reverse, and coasted out of the lot. *Fantastic wheels.*

His call completed, deep in concentration, Luckman walked to where he'd parked his car. A moment passed before he realized the Lincoln was missing.

"Damn." His head jerked from left to right. He failed to see his car. The door of the old junker hung open. He remembered seeing it parked next to his when he left the restaurant. This rip-off had been planned. He leaped inside and floored the gas pedal. The engine coughed and died. He lost precious minutes while the engine ground and finally coughed to life. He followed Route 71 south and realized even if he'd guessed right, his Lincoln would be miles ahead.

He'd been wrong about something more important. He had miscued on the old crippled woman. In all his life he'd never hit wrong. A professional never risked his reputation by hitting wrong or taking out more than the intended mark. He had to correct his mistake. He had to remove the hotshot from the old lady's car.

In the trunk of the junker he found only a flat spare tire and a green cashbox containing a roll of tickets. He needed tools.

At that moment, the luxury Lincoln continued north toward Interstate 80 with Dirk Lowe Bartle at the wheel. He had shuffled through papers in the glove compartment and discovered the identity of the owners. "Thank you, Brock Lyden: thank you, Victoria Lyden. I appreciate your gifty," he sang. "This car is really nifty." If stopped by the police, the first thing he would say was that he had permission from Cousin Brock. He remembered he hadn't been able to place the cashbox and tickets where Seligman would be blamed. There hadn't been time. A producer couldn't be expected to handle everything. A producer wouldn't be bothered with mere details. "Don't call me. I'll call you." He laughed a crazy laugh. Hollywood lay ahead. This time he would be a big hit. This time he would be a headliner. He would be a star. He bobbed his head. It was a great expectation but one well within the realm of possibility and entirely reasonable. He noticed the Lincoln's speedometer had crept twenty miles per hour over the speed limit. He slowed abruptly. The last thing he needed was to be pulled over by some stupid cop.

Luckman shopped at Easter's Tru-Value Hardware and purchased a flashlight, a screwdriver, and pliers. At a service station he purchased a spark plug. The porcelain would allow him to silently break a car window in case the old lady had locked her car.

He waited until well after dark, parked the junker at the mouth of the lane, and trudged up the hill to the Cooper house. It wouldn't take but a moment to disconnect the hotshot.

He found the car unlocked. "My luck is holding," he told himself. The old lady had prudently removed the switch key. He didn't need it. He opened the hood and yanked the fuse that led from the carburetor to the wad of plastique stuck to the firewall. Suddenly he heard footsteps, and a warning growl from a dog's throat.

"Okay, Buster," Cordelia said, her loud voice obscuring the click of the hood's closing. "I'll give you six minutes to run."

Luckman sprinted for the safety of the barn. A shaft of light from Cordelia's open door told him the dog was loose and in pursuit. Frantically he flung open the barn door, allowed it to swing shut behind him, and breathed a sigh of relief.

"Score one for me. Zip for you, pooch."

He flicked on the flashlight and saw steel bars. "What is this?" He played the beam around. He tried the door. "Locked! What the hell is this?"

Anger burned within him like a relentless sun on desert sand, obliterating reason. He shook the door. It didn't budge. "Heavy-duty locking mechanism. No way to compromise it."

He raised the beam, discovered a light switch, and flipped it on. The cell contained a sink with running water, a toilet, a mound of straw, a small table, a chair, and a cot with blankets. A thin layer of dust covered everything. He shook the bars and found them secure. He heard the dog whining outside.

In a few minutes the old woman called, "Buster. Here, Buster. Time's up."

"We won't be getting back to Kay Cee by eleven," Luckman told himself. In the morning he'd be able to attract attention and get out. He'd sprint past whomever opened the door. He shook the dust off the blankets and slept after dreaming of the splendid meal he missed.

By the time he woke, his anger had dissipated, replaced with thoughts analytical. "Why me?" He decided he could only blame himself. He had screwed up big time and this was merely part of that reality. He'd hit wrong. He'd prepared wrong. The hit might still go down. He'd removed the fuse from the hotshot. The end dropped to the engine block. It might still ignite; it certainly would if the hotshot flared.

"Damn. Damn. Damn. There were no windows in the cell, no windows on this side of the barn. To the far right where a window might be, straw bales were stacked to the ceiling. Bales filled the entire barn. To the left, beyond the bales he could see part of a dirty window. He read the faded, fly-specked sign that warned him if he started a fire he'd be the first to cook. No doubt about it, the place was a tinderbox. If the cell had a window he'd have punched it out and hung out a blanket.

Stop fantasizing!

By Saturday night his hunger had become intense. He tried not to think about Victoria, sitting down in an upscale restaurant, starting dinner with Gewürztraminer, then a small steak cooked to perfection, the meal topped off with lemon pie. Wine connoisseurs might not find his choice of Gewürztraminer appropriate. He knew what he liked. They could go to hell.

The dog came around and whined. He yelled and pounded on the wall but the woman did not hear. She had a loud voice. She was probably somewhat deaf.

He observed a grasshopper. The Japanese ate grasshoppers, didn't they? He lunged for it and missed. The grasshopper jumped through the bars with a single leap.

He wondered how long a man could live on bugs and water. A cricket eluded him. He wondered how long a man could live on only water.

He stirred around in the straw and found nothing. He looked at the straw in his hand. Why not? He rinsed a handful and started chewing stems. "No flavor. More filling." When he was a kid, folks sometimes said, "Go to grass and eat hay." Here he sat eating straw. How many BTUs in a ton of straw? There had to be some. Burning straw gave off heat.

Sunday morning breakfast consisted of two crickets, hastily washed down with water. He'd captured them by tossing a blanket over them.

Inside the house the old woman would be having bacon and eggs, toast and marmalade, and steaming hot coffee, while all he had—"Stop," he admonished himself. "Stop feeling sorry for yourself. Get past it." He advanced to another level. "You are not Luckman. You are Brock Lyden. When they find your body, you will be identified as Brock Lyden. That day," he resolved, "will be some time off."

He made a face. "If I call a cricket a steak, will it taste more like a steak?" *Stop thinking crazy.* He didn't want to think about the old woman going to church. He didn't want to think that her breakfast would be her last meal.

He'd guessed right about part of Cordelia Cooper's breakfast. She did have coffee and toast—buttered with cinnamony applesauce. But that had been hours ago. Cordelia decided to make a call.

"Erin. I'm sorry to bother you on Sunday," she said.

"That's all right."

"I've been thinking. About selling the station. I received a good offer. You would make fifteen percent more than you paid."

"Hmmm," Erin mused. "That is a good offer."

"The thing is, I asked myself, am I just growing weary of it all? I'm feeling so punk I didn't even try to go to church."

Concern etched Erin's voice. More than a week had passed since Cordelia complained of being weary at the preliminary hearing for Alex Barca. "Are you all right?"

"Oh sure. I'm just a little run down. The buyer wants to purchase control, all of it preferably. That means if I sell, I need either you or Alex Barca."

"You don't need Alex," Erin said quickly and without equivocation. "I don't think we should talk to anyone about this. If you are planning to sell, I feel inclined to do the same."

"I don't want to push you into selling, Erin. That's the last thing—"

"You're not," Erin insisted. "A good deal is a good deal. I need to read the fine print."

"I'm counting on you to do that," Cordelia said.

Chapter Eighteen

Clarindians have a strong work ethic and on Monday morning they dig in their heels in anticipation of the week ahead. At KNDA, Downbeat Jackson instructed his trainee, Keith Gordoncamp. "You will be known as Gordon Keith. I'll pay you the for last week." Downbeat produced a crisp, new one-dollar bill and signed his name across the face. "Here's your short snorter. You're a damn fool if you spend it. Look at George Washington on the bill, the greatest man our nation has ever known. He's all but forgotten now. Do you realize he fought nine battles to set us free? And lost six of them? He would have made one fine announcer." He didn't tell Keith that whenever Washington entered a room, all eyes turned to him—and only him—even when Jefferson and Hamilton were present.

Keith carried the bill to his mother.

Doris sat in stunned disbelief, happy, stunned disbelief.

"My first week's pay," Keith said with pride. For being tutored in radio he knew he should be paying Downbeat.

Doris had not totally outdistanced her disbelief. "I'll have it framed. This is one dollar you don't spend."

She remembered Erin would not be coming in because she planned to work at the S and L. She phoned Erin there and exclaimed, "I just had to call someone before I burst. Keith finished out the week and everything is fine!"

"I knew it would be," Erin said. She had already been at her desk for more than an hour and had reduced the to-do stack by half. No sooner had Doris hung up than Erin's phone rang again.

"Orville Keane. This is official, Erin. Alex Barca's attorney called me. Alex wants to sell his interest in the station—at the same price he paid. My guess is, Jerry Kessler is pressing him for his fee."

"Interesting," Erin said. "I need to make a call first. I'll get back to you in a few minutes."

She at once phoned Cordelia.

"I've been expecting your call," Cordelia said. "I have no interest in purchasing any additional KNDA shares. As you know, I'm more interested in selling."

"Would you delay contacting potential buyers for a bit?"

"Yes, I can do that."

"How are you feeling?"

"Punk. My vitality has deserted me. I should get in the car and drive down to the station. I have some urgent business to discuss with Downbeat, but I'm too bushed."

"You are trying to do too much. Why don't I pick you up later and we'll meet Downbeat as a team?"

"That sounds great. I'll stay put until you get here."

Erin returned attorney Keane's call. "Cordelia told me she isn't interested in purchasing any more stock."

"That's what she told me."

"I'm inclined to make a counteroffer to Mr. Barca. My offer is ten percent less than he paid for his shares. If he can get more, he has my blessing." *Who else would buy only one-sixth?*

Orville Keane succeeded in suppressing only part of a chuckle. "I'll call his attorney and relay your counteroffer."

He bobbed his head in admiration. The girl did not just fall off the turnip truck.

Within the hour Orville Keane called Erin back. "Mr. Barca accepts your counteroffer. Reluctantly, I am told."

"I'll put the money in escrow. Probably during my coffee break."

The moment Henry Leighton arrived, Erin said, "I need a quick loan. I want to buy the rest of the station."

"All right. Give yourself favorable terms."

"Don't you want to handle it? I'd prefer that you did. As soon as Piper Jaffray sends me a check from Omaha, I'll repay the loan."

"Why bother with all the paperwork?"

"Because life is ephemeral, a tenuous thing. We need to have documents properly in place."

"Okay, do the paperwork. I'll sign off on it. I'm glad you said life is ephemeral. I had the impression that you planned to live forever. Erin, it's later than you think. I've been thinking—"

"I know what you've been thinking. Don't start."

Henry flung up his arm. "One of these days, Alice. To the moon!"

"Honestly!" He could be such a boy.

In less than an hour Orville Keane appeared in the chamber of Judge Lars Jennings Strand with an ex-parte motion to place a constructive trust on all Alex Barca's holdings, interests in escrow, and bank accounts to prevent anyone from withdrawing funds.

Judge Strand glanced at the caption. "Oh yes, the Otley girl. She used to sell me Girl Scout cookies." He turned to his secretary. "Get Jerry Kessler on the phone, please."

"Jerry," Judge Strand said and explained the motion. "I'm granting the request. We need to take care of our own. I'll show your vehement, strenuous, loud objection."

Kessler put down the phone and muttered, "Damn," in his usually loud voice. The worst part still remained—meeting with his client in custody and communicating the order. Later he would tell his secretary, "Alex released a line of profanity that would shame a sailor. He turned the air blue."

"Just what you wanted to do."

"Don't say it."

Erin strolled to the Page County Bank and phoned Cordelia. "It's fifty-fifty now. You own half of the station and I own the other half. Let's not fight." She snickered with amusement. "Why don't we sell the whole shooting match? Frankly, now that you can offer the whole pie, I think you should hold out for twenty percent more than I paid."

Cordelia laughed. "I knew you would be difficult. That's what I'll tell the potential buyers. All or nothing at all. Now don't forget to pick me up."

"I'll try to make it before lunch."

No sooner had Erin returned to the savings and loan than a man asked to meet with her.

"Erin Ames," the man said, extending his hand. "I'm Paul Hoffman from Spencer, Iowa. I had business in Omaha and the committee wanted me to drop down and check on things."

"Oh?"

"I might as well be forthcoming. I've tried to ask questions around town here on the QT, but it isn't working. My job is to investigate a candidate for secretary of our chamber of commerce."

"Ah," Erin acknowledged. "Andrew Seligman."

"They told me you would be the person to ask, that you would be candid with me. I'm not one of those chainsaw consultants, an outsider brought in to reduce the number of applications. I am a businessman with a lot to lose. Whomever we select will affect my business—and others."

"I can tell you this. Mr. Seligman increased our membership nearly seven percent while he was here and he eliminated a monumental chamber of commerce debt. To get that done he may have had to be dictatorial. We didn't have a radio station when he arrived. When KNDA came to light, he looked on the station as competition. He'd been accustomed to not only having the town calendar, but running it also. The station ran its own calendar."

"They said you would tell it like it is. Is he a flight risk—you know the type, put down on Monday, start planning to leave on Tuesday?"

"No. He's diligent. Not an um-secretary."

"Come again."

"He's never referred to as 'Andy, um…our secretary.' There's no 'um' about him. Mr. Seligman is definitely a take-charge person. If you have any laggards, he will make believers out of them."

"I'm glad I stopped in. Thanks for being candid."

"Well, what do you know," Erin whispered when he had gone.

The man from Spencer reviewed his options. To meet with Seligman in person might give him the impression that the committee was desperate. If he met with Seligman and later something went wrong, he'd take the heat. He decided not to meet with Seligman until he met with the entire committee. He made a phone call.

"Andrew Seligman? The Spencer Chamber of Commerce calling. We are favorably impressed with your application. Would it be possible to meet with us tomorrow about eleven o'clock? Your wife is invited. We have a restaurant here I know both of you will like."

"Sounds good," Seligman said with enthusiasm. "We'll be there!"

When the phone connection severed, he cheered, "Yee Haw!"

He put down the receiver and now placed a call to his wife. "Cancel whatever you had planned for tomorrow. We're leaving for Spencer in the morning. Find someplace to park the kids." He wondered if he should call Fort Dodge. A passing police car reminded him that the police would probably be calling him soon, asking why he rented a World War II Army Air Force major's uniform. *Forget Fort Dodge. Burn rubber for Spencer.*

Chief Wendinger had discovered the business card concealed in the lining of the major's uniform in property. A mound of clutter accumulated on his desk and he had taken no action pursuant to the tipster's phone call.

"No use sending a letter to the rental agency," he told Ellen Iverson. "It's too easy to lie on the phone. Is somebody going down there for a ball game or something?"

"Not that I know of," Ellen replied. "There's a detective who owes us a favor."

"You take care of that."

"Me and my big mouth." She hiked the volume on the radio when she heard Downbeat say, "Now from that 1939 concert at Carnegie Hall, here is Glenn Miller with 'Stairway to the Stars.'"

Downbeat stepped out of the booth to sing along with Ray Eberle. Doris loved it but motioned for him to tone it down when the phone rang.

"This is Erin. I'm going to pick up Cordelia now. We'll be there soon."

When she parked near Cordelia's carport, Erin noticed a screwdriver and pliers lying near her car. She picked up the tools and placed them on a shelf. She'd warn Cordelia about trying to do too much.

Presently, they traveled down the lane in robust spirits. "You're buying lunch," Cordelia said. "You cleared thirty percent on the stock you purchased from Alex. All in a half day."

"We sold?" Erin exclaimed.

"We sure did. Like butter on pumpernickel. Sharpen your pen," Cordelia said, beaming. "We got the twenty percent. The money will be here tomorrow along with CEO Hansen from the Carleton Group."

When they arrived at the station, Keith stood out front, keeping the parking space open, telling folks who wanted to park, "This space is reserved for Mrs. Cooper." Now and then he looked at the card he held, upon which Downbeat had written "THIS IS THE NEWS," reading the words aloud, each time accenting a different word. Downbeat would examine him, asking which version was the best, requiring him to give reasons for his choice.

Keith's training fascinated Cordelia. "How is our budding announcer working out?"

"You tell me," Downbeat said. "Let's conduct a little examination. Keith." He beckoned for Keith to leave the broadcast to Tom Berringer. "Another examination," he said. "I'll pose a situation. You give me the answer."

"In front of everybody?" Keith objected.

"In front of God and everybody. Here's the drill. You're working for KDKA, Pittsburgh. It's the middle of winter. Snowdrifts up to the belly of a tall giraffe, icicles hanging from every wire. You've drawn a double shift. The guy who agreed to relieve you at seven never showed up. You haven't eaten since noon. That was a light lunch. Now it's three o'clock in the morning. You're down, feeling like you're trapped inside a black dog at midnight. What you wouldn't give for a drink." *Not that. Back up!* What you wouldn't give for a hot cup of Joe and a double cheeseburger. Who's listening at three in the morning anyway? Some trucker? Some guy who's wife has thrown him out? Who cares? Suddenly you look and notice you're off the air. What do you do?"

"I check the modulation monitor," Keith answered. "Is the carrier on? Then I go to remote control and see if the transmitter is on. If it isn't live, it usually means there's a power outage at the transmitter site. You mentioned all the icicles on the wire. I'd check with the power company. If the power company said they'd have the line repaired in an hour, I'd be tempted to sneak out and get that cup of Joe and a double cheeseburger, but I wouldn't. I'd probably call somebody to deliver a pizza or something. Why wouldn't I have done that earlier in the evening?" Keith stopped and looked around.

"That's more than I bargained for," Downbeat said. He turned to the ladies with raised eyebrows.

"You passed with flying colors," Erin said.

"Excellent," Cordelia intoned. "Keith is the reason I wanted to see you," she said when he returned to the booth. "Better get his name on the blotter right now. He needs to be an employee as of yesterday. Erin and I sold the station, lock, stock, and barrel. That's not for publication."

Completely bowled over, Downbeat couldn't mask his surprise. A thousand wretched thoughts swirled through his mind. *Just when things were looking good. Out again. What about Doris? He'd lose her.* "Oh Lord," he groaned. He groped for enthusiasm and grasped it like a low-hanging twig over rushing water. "Hey," he managed. "That is news."

Cordelia sensed his anxiety. "All current personnel will remain in place. I made Mr. Hansen promise that. And not just for a transition period." She nodded at Erin. "That includes you, Downbeat."

"So we're protected?"

"The point being," Cordelia continued. "To get Keith on board before the transfer."

Downbeat encountered mixed emotions and pushed the negatives back to his depths as he attempted to put a happy spin on the news. A heightened color ascended his back and neck and diffused across his cherubic face in a rosy glow. "That's wonderful." He tried not to gush and tell Erin that he was right about her being an angel and bringing him good luck. "Will we make the announcement tomorrow?"

"The funds are due tomorrow," Cordelia stated. "I'll leave it up to the Carleton Group, whether they want us to make the announcement or whether they wish a joint announcement."

Her well wishing continued to included Doris, Keith, and Tom Berringer. She addressed Erin, "Ready to go?"

"All set."

Lunch became a quiet celebration, starting with two rounds of Erins.

"You were teasing me earlier, about making thirty percent on my investment in a half day."

"I wasn't teasing," Cordelia said. "Just stating a fact."

"I've been doing the math. That's nearly twenty-two thousand percent per annum, the way brokers compute. I promised myself that one day I'd stand with the best of them." Erin gestured with both hands. "The best of them being my classmates. Now I look around and find that I'm still standing alone."

"You'll find that the wealthier you become, the more alone you'll be—unless you work to get back into the mainstream. It's no good being a trout out of water. When Jake died, I promised I'd keep the money rolling in as my personal memorial to him. It wasn't long before I knew in the depths of my heart that I loved it. It wasn't a memorial to Jake. It was a monument to myself."

"You too?" Erin leaned forward and covered Cordelia's hand. "I had the same experience. I finally realized I was doing it for myself." She wondered if she should confide about Captain Gaylord Haversham. Maybe her willingness to talk stemmed from the beer. There was something else she could talk about. "You know, to be poor is to be without. I mean *without.* As hard as being poor is, it is worse being left out. I knew the dress I wore to school had been worn by someone else. I prayed some upper-class girl wouldn't see me in her dress and make fun of me. I was afraid they'd call me a Gun Town girl. I remember coming home in tears. Some girls had said my clothes were tacky. I promised myself that someday I would have money. I think it started when Herb and Eloise Schecter gave me a pair of prom shoes and Mother sewed a special dress."

Cordelia remained impassive for a moment. *So the shoes did make a difference!* "I just realized something. And so should you. Being deprived didn't slow you down. You're better for it. Unlike a radio signal that's multidirectional, you had one direction. Straight up. You had a goal and you went for it." *Now convince yourself.* "If you'd had money you would have become soft." *Liar. That's just a lame excuse. That's phony justification.*

Erin nodded soberly. "That's a great deal to think about."

Cordelia closed her eyes and sniffed. "One can't change the past. The only thing you can do with life is get on with it."

"You sound like my mother."

"I do?" *That's the best thing you ever said to me.* Cordelia brightened. "This is turning out to be quite a lunch. Of course if you're interested in getting back to the mediocre pack, you can do that by giving your money away."

"Really?"

Cordelia stared into the distance, face impassive. "I guess you know that being a so-called philanthropist is even more lonely. All the adulation and attention is just a ruse to get your money."

"Now don't get cynical."

"What I am getting is tired. I'm fighting to keep my eyes open."

"It's the beer," Erin suggested.

"Yes," Cordelia said. "It's the Erins." *ERIN.* She sniffed again.

When Erin drove up the lane and parked, and Cordelia stepped out, Brock Lyden began yelling and pounding inside the barn. He'd been asleep when they departed. The women were chatting. Buster barked an enthusiastic greeting. The wind sent a spanking breeze in the opposite direction, all of which combined to make Lyden's cries unheard.

As Luckman he had learned that men are creatures of habit. The daring among them did not get bogged down by tradition, and even these nonconformists became mired in their own routines. Finding a predictable point in their routine had allowed one man, at that precise intersection, to gain a fortune, and the other to encounter total misfortune.

Here in the barn he noticed crawling insects also had a routine. He wondered if they spent their entire lives plodding along the perimeter. When they entered his cell, most of them sought refuge beneath the little mounds of straw he placed in their path. A blow with the flat of his hand provided a morsel to be quickly swallowed and at once washed down with water. *Wine. Tell yourself it's Chardonnay.* Since becoming trapped, he learned that an intact beetle tasted much better than one that had been smashed. *Maybe it's a Cabernet.*

Insects were not forced to compete in the complex dog-eat-dog world of business. Here, in the enduring barn, they enjoyed shelter from the storm. He realized he had been mistaken about their idyllic existence when he detected another descendant from Eden. The snake slithered along the trail in pursuit of the same prey that Lyden expected to sustain him until someone opened the door. He waited until the snake was well within the cell to make his move. Then he pounced.

He held up the fourteen-inch snake, admiring the pink racing stripe that ran along its squirming length. "You're a rainbow trout," he said.

He removed a small penknife from his pocket. He decided not to eat the head. For a moment he considered tossing the severed head into the toilet, but reconsidered and tossed it out between the bars.

"Professional courtesy," he cackled, ending with an outrageous laugh. A man could survive adversity a long time if he didn't lose his sense of humor.

Now began the cleaning and washing of the snake, the persistent washing and scrubbing with the wood-hard soap remnant that refused to lather.

"Trout almondine," he said, exercising mind over matter. He had never liked raw chicken, he reflected, as he washed down each segment.

After he had devoured the snake, he said, "More filling." He'd eaten lunches in high-class restaurants that weren't as filling. It amazed him how much straw tasted like almonds. He leaned back and contemplated. What reasonable explanation might Brock Lyden give for entering the barn? Would it play to report the modified truth? Would anyone believe he'd been pursued by a dog? He had no doubt he would be discovered sooner or later. It was a great expectation, well within the realm of possibility and entirely reasonable.

He turned out the light and slept.

Chapter Nineteen

In New York or San Francisco, Wednesday merely followed Tuesday. For Clarinda residents, Wednesday morning meant that more than half the week remained to complete the jobs they had planned.

For one Clarinda family, this particular Wednesday morning meant a great deal of work and the promise of a new situation. For the Seligmans, yesterday's 195-mile journey north on Highway 71 had been fruitful. The Spencer Chamber of Commerce committee had extended the hand of welcome and Andrew Seligman had been hired on the spot. On their return to Clarinda, they had scrounged every cardboard box the supermarkets would relinquish and packing had begun.

"We'll tell the kids it's a vacation," Seligman instructed his wife. "If you get pressed and absolutely must give a location, hint at Fort Dodge."

"Really, I don't see the need for all this secrecy."

"Really you would, if you knew all the facts.

Before the end of the day Andrew Seligman's words would take on increased significance.

Life had also taken on added significance for Brock Lyden. Last evening the dog had come sniffing around the door. He'd yelled and pounded to no avail. The barn had a dingy window on the far side. He turned the light switch on and off in three quick movements, followed by a rest. He hoped someone would see the signal, even the police. He had a logical explanation ready. Now he feared the switch would wear out. If the switched failed in the off position, he would be shrouded in darkness.

Someday, after he escaped, he would find the creep who stole his Lincoln. It had to be the creep who arrived in the old junker, the creep with guts enough to sit opposite him in the restaurant. He turned over a dozen scenarios in his mind. Who would follow him from Kansas City in order to steal his car? Every possibility resulted in the same answer. He hadn't been a target. The heist of the Lincoln had been a crime of opportunity, entirely random. *Likewise, someday, somewhere, when you least expect it, someone will come up to you and say, "Smile Turkey. You're dead."*

At that moment, rookie Officer Davison observed the old car parked near the mouth of the lane and dutifully recorded the plate number.

Daydreaming lulled Lyden to sleep and resulted in an erratic pattern that caused him to lose track of time. He would have, had it not been for his digital watch which now indicated WED AM 6:59:30. He watched the seconds leap to 3l, 32, 33…

In the house, Cordelia had awakened early. Stalking about, she realized the activity of the previous day had sapped her strength. She would not have been able to maintain the hectic pace of meetings at the station, the bank, and the luncheon, if Erin had not called for her, acted as her personal chauffeur, and returned her safely home.

There had been no surprises. Everything had proceeded as expected. At lunch, she had insisted on being the hostess and ordered two rounds of Erins before G. E. Hansen, the CEO of Carleton Group, offered to pick up the check.

"Nonsense," Erin said. "We'll flip a coin for it. Shall I match you or will you match me?"

"You match me."

"Heads."

"Heads."

"Like I said," continued Gerard E. Hansen, "I'll buy the lunch. And Erin, I particularly want you to remain as an employee—of ours."

"Agreed. I understand all the employees are staying."

"That's right."

Cordelia remembered she had told Erin later, "He knows a good thing when he sees it."

Now Cordelia abruptly halted her reverie. She labored for breath. Why wouldn't her lungs work? Deep breathing did not refresh her. She could no longer deny that she needed medical attention. She phoned the hospital. "Is my doctor still there?"

"Yes, he is."

"Tell him not to leave. I'm on the way. I feel absolutely rotten."

She picked up the hat Erin had purchased for her and changed her mind. She placed it on the kitchen table. She told Buster, "Now you be good till I get back."

She hobbled to her car. The motor turned over and she tested the brakes as usual. The brakes were good. She continued down the lane and smelled something burning. The smell of smoke intensified her nausea. She'd skipped breakfast because of nausea. She notice paint on the hood discolored, blistered, and charred. *The car is on fire*! She debated, panicked. *What am I going to do?*

She halted the car at the mouth of the lane near another parked vehicle. She had to get out. She had to get away from the fire. She opened the door, snatched her crutches, and hurried away as fast as she could. The pain in her arm intensified. She grimaced and blinked. She stared straight ahead and moved. Pain became unbearable. She hesitated, and slowed. She tried to breathe and couldn't. Completely nauseous, her vision blurred. She tottered. Her arms slipped out of the Canadian crutches. She pitched forward a split second before the deep, rolling thump of an explosion shattered the morning calm.

Numerous emergency phone calls reached the police and fire departments. Interrupted at home during breakfast, Chief Wilbur Wendinger issued terse orders. "Close the road. Keep people away. Don't touch anything."

His simple instructions were simply ignored. By the time he arrived at the scene it looked as if a herd of goats had stampeded through it.

The chief accosted rookie Officer Davison. "I thought I told you to keep people away from the scene."

"Some were already here. The firemen had to get up close to put out the burning tires."

"Just because they were here doesn't mean they can stay. Now get over there and move those people out. Are you just going to leave her lying there?"

"You said don't touch anything."

"For God's sake, put a blanket over her. Don't you realize who she is? Was?"

The fire chief approached. "This was more than an engine backfire."

"You could say that."

"Did you notice there isn't a speck of blood on her."

"I noticed that," Chief Wendinger said. "It looks like the fire is out. Time for your boys to leave—without you all compromising the crime scene any more than you already have."

"We had to put the fire out."

Officer Eastman examined the old car with its shattered rear window. A flying shard of metal had ripped a hole in the trunk. He retrieved a flashlight from his squad car and directed a beam into the opening.

"Hey, chief," he shouted excitedly. "C'mere. Take a look. See what I see? It's the cashbox from the Glenn Miller dance. Or one just like it."

The chief bent down. "Looks like it."

"Let's rip open the trunk."

"Let's not. Let's have you paddle down to the judge and get yourself a warrant." The chief had noticed the out-of-state plate. "How long has this wreck been sitting here?"

Rookie Davison realized he trembled between a rock and a hard place. It might be worse if he remained silent. "Since last Friday. I—I wrote it in m-my daily report."

"Now just how long are you going to let a vehicle remain parked on the public highway? What is this? Come to Clarinda for free parking week?"

"I—I thought m-maybe it was s-somebody visiting. The car weren't hurtin' nothin'."

"Aren't you a little hard on him, chief?" Officer Eastman asked.

"I know it. But if I chew around out his butt long enough, maybe he will start thinking on his own. That's where his brains are now. When we send him to the state officer's school, I want them to realize we know what we are doing down here in Clarinda. Did you get any pictures? With the crowd and all?"

"Quite a few. Curious people won't be able to deny they were witnesses if we call them."

"Davison," called the chief. "I want you to take some pictures." He'd make blowups and show the kid how not to handle a crime scene.

After all the measurements had been taken, the coroner had come and gone, phone calls had been made to and returned by the state crime lab, and a search warrant obtained, it was time to open the trunk of the old Missouri junker.

Eastman used a crowbar and pried open the lid. Wearing rubber gloves he cautiously opened the green cashbox. He saw a roll of tickets. "That clinches it."

"Yeah."

"I ran the plate," Eastman said. "It came back, Dirk Lowe Bartle. Occupation, actor."

"The phony Glenn Miller," said the chief. "Why did he leave his car here?"

"Maybe it ran out of gas," Officer Davison suggested.

"Why yes, Officer Davison," the chief said with ample sarcasm. "Maybe he ran out of gas."

Chief Wendinger squinted in an attempt to close off external stimuli and allow his thoughts to flow with less impediment. It appeared the actor had committed the robbery of Downbeat Jackson. In a wonderful leap of faith he also ascribed the murder of Cordelia Cooper to Dirk Lowe Bartle. Certainly it was within the realm of possibility and entirely reasonable.

"The importance of an old report cannot be underestimated," he would tell his men. No one knew how many green cashboxes existed in the surrounding four-state area, but when the first ticket on the roll from the trunk matched the last number contained in the robbery report, as derived from witnesses records, wasn't that a pretty good indication that this had to be the same cashbox?

The chief turned to Ellen and asked, "Did we receive a report back from the Kansas City detective who owes us a favor?"

"Not yet," Ellen reported.

"Tell him we have a homicide."

"I'll give him a nudge."

After being nudged, the detective called back.

Ellen reported to the chief. "I have the name of the man who rented the uniform in question."

"Dirk Lowe Bartle," said the chief.

"If you knew that," Ellen said. "Why did you have me call?"

"For verification," said the chief. "I suspected Dirk Lowe Bartle hung the uniform in Andrew Seligman's car."

"But can you also verify that the Benton agency sent the bill for the uniform to Andrew Seligman? Why would Andy pay?"

"I'll try to discover that now."

The chief stopped for a donut and coffee before he called at the Seligman home.

"Packing, I see," he said when he opened their door. "Going somewhere?"

Mrs. Seligman looked to her husband for a response.

Seligman had agonized over what he would say when the chief appeared to question him. He knew it would be a miracle if he managed to get out of town without being interrogated.

"I'm being blackmailed," he told the chief as sweat broke through his Right Guard deodorant and drenched his armpits. "I got off on the left foot with the radio station and thought it would be a good idea to add something to the dance. It was supposed to be a tribute. I couldn't believe it when the actor went bad. Can you imagine my surprise? First, I got bills from the rental agency for the uniform. Then came telephone threats from the actor. I finally decided to pay for the uniform because the actor wouldn't turn it in. The next thing I know the uniform turned up in my car. I called you right away. Then last Friday I received another threat. He said he was in town. I told him I was calling the police." *Is he buying this?* Seligman pretended to wilt. Actually it was not all pretense. "I should have called you again, I know. I should have. Fortunately nothing happened on Friday. I already had job applications out. I didn't want anything to happen to my family—"

"What does this man look like?"

"I never saw him. Except on the stage with the band. At that time, with the glasses and all, he looked a lot like, you know, Glenn Miller. I never even knew his name."

"How did you hire him in the first place?"

"I called an acting agency in Kay Cee. Word went out. Sometime later I got a call."

The chief said, "I'm not going to say, don't leave town. But before you go, leave a written statement of what you just told me, along with a forwarding address."

"I'll do that."

When the chief had gone, Seligman's surprised wife exclaimed, "What you told the chief—is it all true?"

"So help me. May God send down a lightning bolt if it ain't."

"The forwarding address you leave better not be Fort Dodge," his wife warned.

Seligman closed his eyes momentarily. *If you can't lie to your wife, who can you lie to? I wish we could have made it out of town.*

The chief personally contacted each man on the force and warned him, "Don't discuss details about Cordelia Cooper's death, not even to your wife. Don't talk about that junky old car. Got it?"

He and Ellen composed a carefully worded release which she phoned to the radio station. Doris received the message and handed it to Erin. In the broadcast booth, Downbeat saw Erin break down sobbing. "Take over," he shouted at Keith and hurried out to comfort her.

"It's Cordelia," Erin managed over her sobs. She handed him the copy.

"I'm sorry," he said helplessly. "Anything I can do?"

"N-No." She shook her head.

Downbeat knew that. He'd been there. There was nothing anyone could do. A person had to work through it.

At the mike, Keith dreaded the end of the record. *What can I say?* The record ended. He began timidly. "This is Gordon Keith." He saw Downbeat had returned with a bulletin. "Back to you, Downbeat."

"With an important news bulletin," Downbeat said and began to read. "Pioneer resident Cordelia Cooper was found dead near her home this morning. Police are investigating what appears to be a mysterious explosion of her vehicle. Her body was found nearby. No further details are currently available." Downbeat paused. "Cordelia Cooper was the driving force behind the establishment and recent activation of KNDA and was, until yesterday, its major stockholder."

Keith indicated he'd like to say a few words. Downbeat nodded and he began. "We will all miss her. I suppose many of us have a memory of her, even young people. One day in the supermarket a little boy looked at Mrs. Cooper and asked his mother, 'Who is that old crippled lady?' The boy's mother was mortified. She began to scold the boy. 'I am an old cripple,' Cordelia said in a voice heard throughout the entire store. 'You called it like it is. That's an important asset. That's what I like about our President. He tells it like it is. Reagan likes jelly beans. Why don't we follow his example?' Whereupon she removed a bag from a display, broke into it, and shared them with the boy, his mother, the checkout lady, and the next person in line."

"I imagine the lad will remember the incident for the rest of his life," Downbeat said. "If not, I'm sure his mother will remind him during the next few days. We need to play something appropriate now. I don't know what could be more appropriate than Glenn Miller's theme, the song he used to start a show and to sign off. To Cordelia Cooper as she ends her tour of this world and embarks on a journey to a higher and better realm. Here's 'Moonlight Serenade.'"

There were tears all around.

Downbeat wrote a note to Keith. "You used the word 'whereupon.' Good going."

In the barn on the Cooper property, things were not going well, not well at all. Brock Lyden heard the explosion. His stomach knotted and remained tight. He'd managed to yank the fuse from the hotshot. Why hadn't he also disconnected the other end? Why hadn't he just given the fuse another yank and pulled it out of the plastique? Would that have required more than a second? Sparks from the hotshot had ignited the fuse, or possibly the oily residue on top of the engine. Even if he'd jerked out the fuse, a possibility existed that the plastique might have exploded, sometime, downtown, and taken out several people. He pinched his eyelids shut and tried not to hear the distant quaver of sirens. Each nearing squeal drained him of his professional status. He'd been an idiot. He amounted to less than a bumbling rookie. He'd been stupid.

It didn't make sense. He'd tinkered with the car on Friday. Cars had been coming and going ever since. Now, on this Wednesday morning—wump. Obviously the cars had to have been different cars. He'd been pounding and screaming when he heard them, now cars came and went and he feared making a sound. It would not be a good time to reveal his presence. To succeed in life required timing. Preparation was essential. He'd botched the job. He scolded himself, "You're washed up as a professional."

Where was the second snake? Didn't every kind of creature have a mate? Had the second snake discovered the head of the first and reversed course?

For the first time he realized that light seeped out around the outline of the door. Why hadn't he thought of that before? He'd been stupid not to notice. It hadn't been the only dumb thing he'd done lately. He would leave the light on a while in the evening. Perhaps someone would see.

The disturbed embers of long-suppressed guilt emitted a gloom that coiled up within him like smoke and enveloped him in a despondent cloud. A familiar but long-forgotten refrain drifted into his mind. He hadn't thought about the song since he was six, not since his mother died. His lips moved as he remembered the words.

Jesus loves me
This I know
For the Bible
Tells me so.

He'd suffered a series of young and thoughtless 'stepmothers,' none of whom he respected. As he grew to manhood he vowed never to marry a woman he couldn't respect. He found Victoria and he'd been able to respect her. They had a good marriage.

An image emerged out of the solid wall of straw bales, the figure of an angel. Brock Lyden's eyes widened, his jaw slackened. He shook his head in disbelief.

Like a Dickensian ghost, the angel easily passed through the bars. This had to be a dream. He reached down and pinched his thigh. He felt pain. He wasn't dreaming. The angel was real. The angel pointed a finger at his heart and uttered a one-word indictment: "Responsible!"

"I know," Lyden admitted. He choked and swallowed. He attempted to mouth the word and it caught in his throat. He tried again. "I'm responsible—for everything. But I'm going to change," he added quickly. "I'm going to give up hits for money. I'll be responsible. No more contracts for cash."

The angel turned and strode through the bars and disappeared into the solid wall of bales.

"Just as soon as I get out of here," Brock called after the angel. "And that's a promise." He drew up short to a soul-shattering realization. He might not get out. Had the angel arrived to presage his journey into the next realm?

Worry furrowed his brow. Had he succumbed to the delirium of starvation? How could he be delusional when his thoughts remained so clear. Hadn't he read that when Ghandi went on a fast that brought him near death his mind always remained clear?

Cars stopped coming and going. He worked the light switch. One off, two off, three off, stop. One off, two off, three off, stop.

He stopped to pounce on an unsuspecting but genuinely invited guest, the largest green grasshopper he had ever seen. Perhaps it was a locust. How long could a man live on locusts alone? On one giant locust? He closed his eyes while he gulped it in two swallows, quickly followed by a dessert of straw bits and water.

Thank God for water.

He had a great deal to think about.

Chapter Twenty

Perhaps the day should have been Friday the Thirteenth due to the dismal way it began, but in Clarinda folks use the same calendar as Texas and Tennessee. Folks have learned to take the bitter with the sweet.

Before bidding farewell to Clarinda and setting out on the 195-mile trek north on Highway 71 to his new job, Andrew Seligman stopped at police headquarters and dropped off his written statement along with a post-office-box address in Spencer.

His wife remonstrated, "I don't know why I had to give out misleading hints that we were moving to Fort Dodge. When the children are enrolled in Spencer schools, the principal will write for their records. Then folks will know."

"In the meantime folks will have become accustomed to saying we went to Fort Dodge. That will become etched in stone. I doubt if the principal will say much." Seligman's heart warmed as if to a gentle caress. The new position meant more money. After a short time in a rental house, they would be able to afford a larger home. The stupid actor wouldn't be able to find them without a great deal of effort. He probably wouldn't bother. If he called, he would be told, "Go ahead, phone the police." Seligman allowed a smile to build. He'd proved his worth to Chief Wendinger, who had believed him down the line, hook, and sinker. "A reputation isn't just the thing," Seligman told his wife. "It's the only thing."

"I'm glad we're leaving town before the funeral."

"Yeah," Seligman agreed. "She was radio."

Along Clarinda coffee counters conversation centered on the funeral.

"Isn't the funeral sudden?"

"No. She passed early Wednesday morning. She doesn't have anyone."

"I wonder who will pay for the roof on the parsonage now?"

"She didn't pay for all of it."

"She paid for most of it."

Another chimed in. "The roof should last twenty years. Maybe by that time—"

Jerry Kessler's coffee had lost its savor. He usually drank his coffee black. Barely into the cup he added cream and sugar. He disliked his client. He hated arguing from a position of weakness. Worst of all, by the time Orville Keane and Lance Richardson were through, Alex Barca wouldn't have enough money left to pay his fee. Kessler didn't finish his coffee; instead, he trudged in the direction of his office.

At the end of the counter a couple of guys snickered. "There's ol' Jake Cooper laid to rest with a woman on each side of him."

"Didn't his first wife die of leukemia?"

"Listen," said the mature waitress. "I knew Jake Cooper. I'd be proud to be the third woman laid out with him."

"At least the kids will get out of school this afternoon. What do you suppose the band will play?"

Ministers preparing for the union service had the same concern. "I remember Cordelia telling me that funerals should be for the living. That's why when we laid Jake to rest, the band played 'A Nightingale Sang in Berkley Square.' That meant something to Cordelia."

"Where are we going to seat everyone? I mean, what if it rains?"

"It wouldn't dare."

"Maybe the band could play 'A Foggy Day in London Town'?"

"I wonder who gets all that money."

"I think 'My Country 'tis of Thee' would be better than this modern Glenn Miller music. We hear enough of that on KNDA."

A senior minister spoke. "I believe we will hear what the high school band has rehearsed."

"With this band director, who can tell?"

In his office, attorney Kessler made a dreaded call. He knew Orville Keane had rehearsed his presentation. He did not expect Keane's harsh opening barrage. "A jury will kill your client and serve him up on toothpicks."

"It isn't murder," Kessler parried.

Orville brushed the thought aside. "We start with this beautiful, young homecoming queen, an innocent girl with stars in her eyes. She joins the work force at KNDA and comes under the Rasputin spell of this out of town slicker. With his blandishments, he gets her pregnant. Does he propose marriage? No. Does he seek the alternative of a lawful abortion? No."

Kessler grimaced without speaking. He knew Orville favored legalized abortion, but by the time he finished emoting to a jury it would be ready to hang his client.

Keane rolled on. "What does he do? He tries to mur-der her and mur-der her unborn child. We sent you the photos. Doesn't her fair complexion really show up all those horrible black-and-blue bruises. Did you notice the swelling of her face? She's barely recognizable. If you take this case to a jury, it will definitely award punitive damages!"

Kessler was glad Orville could not see him nod in abject agreement.

"As to tort liability, we're not going to settle this case for a mere five times medical bills. Our child-support demand will be sixty thousand dollars."

"That's too high," Kessler said. "Fifty grand is more like it. Even that's high. The present value of fifty grand has to be less than forty-five grand. Usually a man has twenty years to pay child support. Child support should be left open."

"We're not going to risk running after Barca, trying to extradite him from some Brazilian jungle. Not when we have him by the short hair. Jens is not going to let off the bastard who beat up the girl who sold him Girl Scout cookies." Orville laughed snidely.

"I hear you. About that embezzlement charge. You can at least dump that. An out of town outfit bought the station. Let it be their loss."

"Wrong again, ol' worthy adversary. That asset never appeared on the sale. The money is owed to Cordelia Cooper's estate and to Erin Ames. And Erin is here to testify."

Kessler remember that Erin had signed the civil complaint. "Are you going to the funeral?"

"Yeah. You?"

"Yeah. I'll get back to you."

Orville softened his tone. "You might see if Alex has some money stashed out of town. It wouldn't surprise me."

Jerry Kessler knew what Orville intimated. It wasn't necessary for Orville to add "so you will get paid for your service."

At the end of the conversation, Orville thought negotiations had gone exceedingly well. Jerry thought negotiations had gone as well as could be expected under the circumstances.

Orville phoned Jennifer Otley. "I want you in my office as soon as you can get here. Your parents don't need to attend."

Jennifer Otley didn't appear to be pregnant when she walked into his office. He'd like to see her looking pregnant if the case went to a jury. He doubted that a jury would ever hear the case. The last place Alex Barca wanted to be was in front of a jury. He'd rather buy his freedom. But a lawyer could not depend on the whims and caprices of someone facing lengthy incarceration. Maybe Alex would want to roll the dice.

"Jennifer. How would you like to be an actress?" Keane opened. "This is about money. If there's even a hint that you might get married, you can expect child support to go out the window. The jury will know that the child will have a father. From now on, I don't want you to date anyone. No one. I don't want you to be seen around town with any single man—or a married one for that matter."

"I get it," Jennifer said. "Like a nun." She laughed a snuffy laugh. "A pregnant nun."

"It wouldn't be the first time." Keane stopped abruptly, aware that she had disarmed him. "I shouldn't have said that. If we get to a jury, this conversation is privileged and I don't want you talking to anyone else about it. If you want to be paid like a Hollywood actress, you need to get into the role and work at it. And don't ham it up. I'll work with you."

"I can do it," Jennifer said.

When she rose he watched her gliding a way. *Beautiful. Great body.* He squelched the idea. This time his mouth remained closed.

Jennifer realized that if she could not be seen with a man, she could still—briefly—visit with a man if he was part of a group. She strode into the radio station, greeted Erin perfunctorily—cooly but correctly—and bestowed a smile on Doris. Her mouth broke into a grin as she saw Keith Gordoncamp, now know as Gordon Keith, announcer.

"I can't see you any more," Jennifer said.

"Why?" Keith looked pained.

"Because. It's part of my case against Alex Barca. I'm playing the role of a maligned woman. Like in a soap. My attorney says that if I expect to collect any money, I must play this part. No men in my life. Isn't that a drag?"

Keith swallowed. "Yeah. How long is this going to last?"

"Until the trial is over or the case is settled, whichever comes first. Until I have a check in hand. That's what Orville Keane says."

"I understand."

Before she left, Erin called to her, "Nice seeing you again, Jennifer."

"Sure." Jennifer withheld a smile. "Thank you." She had to be hospitable. She wondered if Erin had blabbed about their meeting. Why should she? "Bye, Doris."

She beamed at Keith and knew he would phone her. She'd have to tell him no more phone calls. It wouldn't do to have her mother or father placed on the stand to testify, "Oh, he is calling her all the time."

"Oh darn," she muttered under her breath. She realized that until the case was settled she would have no life, no life at all.

In the office of the *Herald-Journal,* the editor faced a dilemma. Cordelia had passed away on Wednesday morning, scant hours before the postman delivered the weekly edition. Ordinarily the Monday edition constituted advertising and society news. Cordelia had been a societal dowager. Did that not afford reason enough to print her passing in the Monday edition? The Wednesday edition, a full week after her passing, would contain a more complete article.

Radio had an advantage. Minutes after the death it was able to broadcast the news. The newspaper had to wait. Early-bird radio might be turned to the paper's advantage, the editor reasoned. It would allow time to assess the reaction of the community, crystallize opinion, and using trenchant phrases borrowed from KNDA radio, provide the foundation for a splendid, no-controversial, entirely correct article. It meant a lot to be totally correct.

Wasn't that fair?

A first draft had already been written. *An era has ended. Clarinda's leading philanthropist and the town's erstwhile iconoclast has passed into history. Cordelia Cooper is dead.*

It would be wise, the editor decided, to carry pencil and pad to the funeral to record the comment of ministers and mourners faithfully and accurately.

The church filled rapidly except for the first two pews normally reserved for family. At length, both pews were occupied by people who hardly knew Cordelia Cooper.

In the open casket, Cordelia appeared to be serenely at rest, a splendid example of the funeral's director's art. She wore a corsage representing her love for flowers and her years with flower-and-garden clubs. In her hand she held the hat Erin had purchased for her on their trip to Omaha.

Erin and Belle were seated well back in the church, not in the first pew where they ought to be, Orville Keane reflected. He suppressed a smile. In a short time the whole town would know, which would give folks something else to talk about. He craned his neck. Some people were here because of favors rendered in the past. How many had come to express their grief? How many expected to get their hands on the Cooper largesse?

Good luck. He wondered if the woman who came in and cleaned the Cooper house expected a slice of the pie. What had happened to Buster? At least Buster didn't expect to get anything. Orville almost laughed aloud at the idea. Maybe Buster would benefit—

The service blended the traditional with the modern. Only a few were prepared for the enthusiastic high school band blaring with gusto at the recessional, "When the Saints Come Marching In." Ushers had been instructed to "move folks along." Mourners need no encouragement to move. They clapped their hands, swayed and marched to the beat, singing, "When the Saints Come Marching In." The colorful band director, always under fire from one critical group or another, gloried in the performance and kept repeating the chorus.

Leaving the church, Orville encountered Erin and her mother. "Nice turnout."

"Cordelia would have loved it," Erin said, shouting to be heard over the din.

Orville raised his voice. "Stop at my office tomorrow. There are some loose ends. By the way, where's Buster?"

"Outside, being cared for. I'm taking him with us to the cemetery."

"See you there."

People continued singing, "When the Saints Come Marching In."

"It's deplorable," proclaimed a woman who always resented Cordelia. "What is this, New Orleans?" Later, over a nip, she would lean toward a friend and whisper, "I always thought she belonged in a New Orleans brothel."

At the cemetery, Buster lifted a leg and vented an opinion of his own. He whined at intervals during the service and, as the casket was lowered into the ground, gave a long mournful howl.

"Very appropriate," someone said.

Erin dutifully met with Orville Keane on Saturday morning. He opened the file and announced, "Erin, you are the successor trustee of the Save the Child Trust, with full authority to act in the premises. You are also the successor trustee of the Cordelia Cooper Charitable Trust, with full authority to invest and disperse funds as you see fit."

"Trusts," Erin said. "It looks like I have my work cut out for me. I rather expected this meeting would concern Buster and what happens to him."

"He's listed under chattels of another trust. I'm glad you get along with Buster."

"He's a handful. Every chance he gets, he runs to the barn and whines, as if he wants to retrieve a precious bone. The barn is a magnet. It's difficult to call him away."

"Oh?" An ancient memory stirred within him, and Orville reached for the phone. "Excuse me." When someone answered he said, "Wilbur. Orville here. Pick me up. We need to take a ride."

It was not lost on the chief that he'd been called Wilbur, something Orville never did. "Is it important?"

"In my opinion." Orville replaced the phone and continued. "There is a pour-over will, Erin, that places any left over property in a trust. Cordelia was a whiz on obtaining tax benefits." He did not mention that working for the Coopers had enabled him to parley a country lawyer's business into a healthy trust business as well. "Erin, I'm making a pitch to be your attorney. Seeing as how she left everything to you." His smile congealed.

"Me?" Erin said, surprised. She resumed breathing. "I had no idea. I can't believe it."

"Well, believe it. It's all yours. You don't need to wait for probate. Go out and take control. But don't go near the barn until I straighten out one possible problem."

"Cordelia warned me to stay away from the barn. So this does concern Buster?"

"In a collateral way, perhaps. I'll be in touch."

Seeing he was anxious to leave, Erin walked out with him, feeling somewhat dazed. "Everything," she murmured. "Imagine. The house and the proceeds from the station."

Moments after Erin drove away, Chief Wendinger arrived. "What's up?"

"Erin Ames and I were talking. It's about a dog's persistent reaction. Do you remember when two boys went snooping in Jake Cooper's barn?"

The chief's head snapped.

"Unless I miss my guess," Orville said, "I think we will find the driver of that old car, parked so long at the end of Cordelia's lane, locked in the barn. The dog keeps nosing over there."

"I'll be damned."

"I should have said 'Erin's lane.' It's all hers now."

"You don't say." The chief spoke into the mike. "I'm headed for the Cooper place."

"Oh, if you're going out that way," said a calm voice at the station. "Check out the barn. We just had a call from a man who said his boy saw blinking lights out there on Thursday night. The boy has an active imagination. Last night the father saw it for himself. He thought it might be kids, then he remembered the funeral and wondered why kids would be snooping around the barn."

"I can give him a couple reasons," replied the chief. "I'll give it a look. Better send a one-car back-up."

When the back-up vehicle arrived, the chief approached the barn door and knocked. "Anybody in there?"

"Yeah," came a feeble response.

"Stay put," commanded the chief as he opened the door. "Are you all right?"

"I guess so. For a while there I thought I might run out of toilet paper." Lyden staggered but was able to walk.

"We will have the doctor check you over. This is attorney Orville Keane. Right now I have to tell you we are conducting an investigation. You have the right to remain silent. Anything you say will be used against you in a court of law—"

"I understand."

"Are you coming along to the hospital?" the chief asked Orville.

"Might as well. As I recall, I had to walk down this lane once before. Once is enough."

The chief glanced into the cell and directed the back up officer, "Tie a yellow ribbon across the door."

"Am I glad to see you," Lyden said.

When the doctor pronounced him fit—the prisoner declined a high-protein IV—and relished instead the light-meal alternative. Now at the station, he once more waived his rights and agreed to talk. "My name is Brock Lyden. You have my wallet and ID from when you patted me down. I sell corporate gifts. Last Friday, I stopped at the supermarket to make a phone call. When my back was turned someone stole my car." Truth was better than fiction, he'd decided. Besides, there might have been witnesses. Perhaps the thief had blundered into police custody. "There was this old junk car, door open, motor running. I jumped in and tried to follow. The thief got too far ahead and I lost him. I turned the car around and it died. I managed to pull over at the end of the lane. I saw a light and walked up the lane to ask the family if I could make a phone call. I hadn't quite figured out who I would call first when a dog took after me. I ran for the barn, got safely inside, and found myself locked in. The keys you found on me are from the old car. It was junk. The engine died on me a couple times. Even the spare tire was flat. All I found in the trunk was a cashbox containing a roll of tickets."

The chief acknowledged, "What you tell me may be true. In the meantime, Dirk Lowe Bartle, I'm arresting you on suspicion of murder."

"I understand," Lyden said with a faint smile. Dirk Lowe Bartle. That was a name he would remember. Dirk Lowe Bartle.

When the prisoner had been secured, the chief ordered, "Get me a photo of Dirk Lowe Bartle. Get me a copy of his driver's license."

When he had a moment, Orville said, "Do you remember that farmer in the eastern part of the state? He got tired of having his vacant farmhouse burglarized. He set up a gun. The burglar came back, got shot, recovered from the wound, and sued. The jury gave the burglar the farm. At least the value thereof. The farmer was forced to sell."

"I remember the case."

"There's no gun here. The room had facilities, a bed, a toilet, and water. The guy was obviously trespassing."

"It's still false imprisonment," said the chief. "But he can't sue a dead woman."

"Her estate is vulnerable. He was locked in for days after Mrs. Cooper died. That makes the new owner vulnerable."

"Erin too? I see. The room should have been checked every morning. Like in the good old days."

"Exactly." Orville returned the hint of a smile. "Erin didn't know the cell existed. That's a defense."

"It's a bag of worms. The man's story makes sense. He's a respected businessman. The description of him fits. His credentials look good. We learned he owned a Lincoln. That fits. He admitted being all over that old wreck, so we don't need his prints. We'll try to lift what there is. Maybe there will be others."

"I'd like to settle this case."

"Be my guest. It's up to Lance Richardson." The chief opened his desk drawer and brought out a picture of two youths in a cell. On the back Jake Cooper had written, "Always do right."

"Hmmm," Orville acknowledged. "I got one just like it."

Neither of them felt inclined to say more.

Chapter Twenty-One

Attorney Orville Keane leaned forward and told the prisoner, "Nothing much can be accomplished on Sunday. The county attorney is out of town. He has to sign off on this. Up front, I need to say I'm not your attorney. I represent other interests. You can hire your own attorney. Here's the deal. In a nutshell, you agree not to sue or bring any claims against Cordelia Cooper who died last Wednesday, or her estate, or her successors in interest, or the Clarinda Police Department, or the City of Clarinda. In return you get a solemn covenant in writing never to be prosecuted for the death of Cordelia Cooper. I also need to tell you there is an open robbery charge. Until the police find that person, the State can't go forward with prosecution. There is a possibility that you ordered him to do it, or aided and abetted in some way. Until they find that person, you are in the clear."

Brock Lyden's eyes slitted. *I doubt if they ever will find Dirk Lowe Bartle. Try not to look eager.* "That's all there's to it?"

"You walk as soon as we find the County Attorney."

"Hand me your pen."

"Until the County Attorney gets back in town you will have to stay put. Until then, there's not much we can accomplish."

Within minutes Brock Lyden disagreed. He had met the man in the adjacent cell, Alex Barca. Lyden wanted to tell him, "Man, you don't know how lucky you are! You're Luckman's first miss." He pondered briefly and spooked a plan to finish Barca. They'd nail him for that. *Remember, no more hits for money! It's over. You messed up.*

Lyden knew he shouldn't be thinking of the past, he should be looking ahead. The flood of guilt, the wretched feelings of failure dissipated. They lingered less and less as time passed. If his luck held, he would be released soon. He couldn't believe how events were working in his favor. Even if he received nothing in return, not to be prosecuted had to be like winning a lottery. He did not revel in these thoughts. At the moment his mind focused on something more fascinating. He needed to induce Alex Barca to talk so he could learn his speech patterns, his inflections, his intonation.

"Listen," Lyden said forcefully. "I'm going to say this only one time."

Barca reacted with rapt attention.

"You listened," Lyden said. "People always do when you tell them, 'I'm going to say this only one time.' They are so absorbed in listening they forget to formulate an answer. They're afraid they will miss something. It's a great line to inculcate fear. It's a splendid line when you are letting someone in on what you represent to be an exclusive deal. They'll bite every time."

"I see what you mean," Alex said. *I should have used the line on that bitch Jennifer.* He repeated slowly, "I'm going to say this only one time."

"Right on." *Man, you don't know how lucky you are!* Lyden forced the haunting deprecatory thought from his mind. "I'm going to say this only one time. And don't you forget it."

Alex pondered how different his life would have been if he's used the line on local merchants and never brought Erin Ames into the loop. *No, you had to do it the easy way. Which turned out to be the hard way.* He turned the line over in his mind.

Lyden smiled waspishly. Barca was imprinting the line. Perhaps he would remember to use it. Attorney Keane had been wrong about not being able to accomplish much on Sunday.

Working in his office, Orville Keane risked calling Erin this Sunday morning. He told her about the cell in the barn. "I can't explain all the ramifications. There are a lot of negotiations going on that are designed to limit your liability. I'm serious about continuing as your attorney. I'll explain in more detail later. First thing tomorrow, as soon as the yellow tape comes down, I'll have a locksmith modify the lock with a dead bolt. Remember, everything out there is yours."

"I can't believe Cordelia did this."

Erin repeated the line to her mother whom she had convinced to come along "to look at my new house."

"I can believe it," Belle said when she heard the phrase repeated several times. "Who else did she have? You were with her all the time."

"Not all the time, Mother. Don't start."

Belle cringed when she saw the hinged frame with the photographs of Erin and Jake Cooper in a prominent place in the bedroom. How very alike they were. Every fiber within her cried out to destroy the photos, to hide them before Erin could see them. Had she already seen them? Maybe she could just slide out Erin's picture. No, Erin had spoken about Cordelia's request. *Erin will miss it.*

Belle swallowed and, with a quavering voice that grew in strength as she went on, said, "Erin. Come in here. You wondered why she left you everything. Look at these photographs. Here are the two people who meant the most to her. You and Jake Cooper."

"Isn't that something," Erin marveled. She glanced at the photos and failed to see any resemblance whatever. "What's this?"

On the dresser she found a handwritten note and read it aloud. "This house is too big for one person to knock around in." Erin looked up. "For whom was this note intended? She couldn't have known her time was running out."

"Maybe she did."

"I'm still numb. You don't think she was planning to sell the house and move into a nursing home?"

"Get real. More likely she wanted to have someone move in with her. I wonder who that might have been?"

"Maybe she was forgetful and wrote notes to remind herself."

Belle scurried around looking for other notes. Who could tell what secrets they might reveal? She found several reminders.

"So what?" Erin reasoned. "She was getting forgetful. No big deal. What business person doesn't maintain a calendar or a day minder? That's good sense."

At length Belle relaxed. A crisis had passed. Now that Erin had inherited everything, would folks start wondering, putting two and two together? She devised an explanation she hoped would suffice. "Cordelia simply fell in love with Erin when they met at the radio station. I can't explain it. They were inseparable after that."

Belle had the opportunity to repeat her explanation more than a half dozen times before the week began. Rumors were rampant. Orville Keane had not sworn Chief Wilbur Wendinger to secrecy when he mentioned that Erin inherited everything.

Along coffee row, gossipers added rumor to fact, and fact to rumor. Already a hot topic, the news had not reached KNDA personnel. A bubbling Downbeat Jackson drew Erin aside and confided, "I'm going to propose to Doris on the air this morning. What do you think?"

"I'm not underwriting this deal," Erin said with mock seriousness. Then her face glowed. "Go for it. To help matters along, I won't be a third wheel. I have a full calendar. How are things going with Keith?"

"Plum peachy." Trust Erin to get to the heart of any problem. "I think I've won him over."

"So do I. You have my best wishes."

"Are you leaving?" Doris called.

"Yes," Erin replied. "I have everything sewed up around here. All I need to do now is wait."

Erin set out, totally unaware that her life would never be the same. She would become the subject of intense speculation and wishful thinking as the morning continued. She failed to notice the turning of heads as she entered the cafe for an early-morning cup of coffee. A farmer who had been in the high-school class one year ahead of her found the temerity to saunter over with his cup of coffee.

"Good morning, Erin."

"Good morning, Fred."

He hemmed and hawed, uttering inanities. "For the life of me I don't know why I didn't think of this before—like asking you out, I mean. We could go to a game. We could."

"Are you serious?" Erin said with some incredulity.

His face reflected a mixture of hope, pain, and confusion. "Yes, I'm serious. Should have been before. Am. I mean, I know you won't live in the country. But I'd be willing to move to town."

Erin suppressed a chuckle. "Aren't you crossing the stream in two leaps?"

"That's better than not crossing the stream at all."

"I'll think about it," she said solicitously, putting him at ease. Whatever got into him?

From across the room a man raised his cup and mouthed, "Erin."

She did not see all eyes following her as she exited and continued to the drug store. Seeing her, R-ex came pelting up, eyes aglow. "Erin. How nice to see you. I've been meaning to give you a call. We haven't been out for a while." His palm came up. "Don't say it. It's my fault entirely. I'll take the blame."

"I thought you were thick with a certain waitress."

"Yes and no. About like you and Henry Leighton, I guess. No big deal. How about it?"

"Do you have a particular event in mind?"

"No. Not particularly. I'm sure you could think of something."

"Maybe."

"We could go to Miss Kitty's. My treat."

"Why not. It's not as if we're strangers."

"We're good friends," R-ex insisted with enthusiasm. "Oops, there's a customer. Gotta run. Sorry. I'll be in touch. That's a promise."

It was nice being popular, Erin reflected as she continued to Washington Savings What a lovely way to begin the week. She enjoyed the balm to her ego. With all the attention she had received—was it the moon?—it wouldn't be beyond the realm of possibility for Henry Leighton to propose. She would slow him down before he entertained the notion. "Good morning, Henry," she said tersely as if she were his schoolteacher.

"Good morning. Is there anything you would like to do?"

"No," Erin said easily. "Not that I can think of." At least he didn't wear "that look."

Soon he asked, "Do you think we should have another party? Like the Hawaiian Holiday?"

"It's too soon."

"Would you like to review these loan applications?"

"Not now."

He said with more force, "Would you like me to turn on the radio, boss?"

"What? What do you mean, boss?"

"You're the boss now," he said. "I own thirty percent, but now you own forty percent. That makes you the boss."

"Oh? You mean Cordelia had stock? News certainly travels fast." Erin collected her thoughts. "Is that why you always managed the stockholder list yourself?"

He nodded. "Cordelia thought it would be a good idea. Insisted, is more like it. She had some stock when you started here, but in the last couple years if someone, some estate, wanted to sell, she bought. You didn't know?"

"Why would I know?"

"I thought she might have mentioned it."

"She didn't."

"Really?"

"The subject never arose." Erin glanced at the clock. She turned up the volume on the radio. "I want to hear this."

Downbeat played a Vaughn Monroe number and sang along with the Norton sisters. "I love you, there's nothing to hide." His volume increased with the chorus, "There I Said It Again."

Erin motioned for Henry to listen. She whispered, "He's going to propose."

Henry blanched. "On the air?"

"Yes."

"Isn't that a little farfetched?" he said with a crestfallen look.

"No."

"I think it's—" His throat closed. He couldn't speak.

"Yes sir, folks," Downbeat exclaimed. "I'm the kind of guy who likes to have a girl in my arms when I dance. Life is like a dance. I've been dancing single too long. I'm going to ask a woman to dance with me the rest of my days. In fact, hold on to your hat, I'm going to propose to her right now. I've grown more than just fond of you. Will you marry me?"

Henry found his voice. "Of all the nerve."

"Shhh." Erin could imagine Downbeat grinning at Doris from the control booth. "That's a good start," Erin said without a glance at Henry. "Let's hear more."

"I've heard more than enough." Henry glowered.

"Yeah," Downbeat said. "I do mean it."

The next thing listeners heard was Doris bursting into the control room, shouting, "Yes, I'll marry you!"

"You heard her folks, Heh-heh-heh. Now she's hooked."

A silence followed. "What a smoocheroo," Downbeat explained.

Doris spoke again. "He doesn't have the least idea who is really hooked here."

Erin laughed. There was no way Alex Barca could come storming up to the front, yelling, "What's going on around here? Get back to work!" Alex languished in jail.

She saw a relieved Henry had resumed breathing and beamed at her. She phoned the station. "Congratulations, Doris. You have my best wishes."

"You knew this was coming, didn't you?"

Erin laughed. "What makes you say that?"

"I know he values your opinion. He had to clear the on the air proposal with someone."

"With me? You forget that I am no longer a part of management."

"You could have given me a hint."

"Again my congratulations."

Henry spoke up. "Over here you are management." He took a call. "Would you like to speak to Orville Keane?"

Erin nodded. "Yes, Orville."

"Could you stop at my office? On second thought, I could come over there."

You too? "No," Erin said. "I'll stop by."

"Thanks. Make it a little later then. I need to stop at the lock-up. I'm still on the job for you. I'm off to meet with Chief Wendinger and Richardson. I'll explain when I see you."

Lance Richardson had been interrupted during breakfast at home. He continued to gripe about that as Orville Keane thrust a document at him. He read hastily and directed his attention to the chief. “Wait a minute. Lyden could still be involved in the murder of Cordelia Cooper. As an aider and abettor.”

“What murder?” Chief Wendinger said through a cat-in-the-cream grin. “The explosion didn’t leave a mark on her. The medical examiner says she died of a massive heart attack while walking away from her car. He wrote, ‘Death due to natural causes.’ How are you going to parlay that into murder?”

Orville nodded. “I know it. The chief knows it, and now you know it. Maybe we shouldn’t wait until the prisoner knows it.”

Richardson walked into the cell and asked Lyden, “Is this your signature? Do you understand the agreement?”

Lyden smirked. “I guess being wrongfully imprisoned raises the possibility of a big lawsuit.”

“So does murder. You trespassed. You had water and a toilet. I hear you didn’t even run out of toilet paper. We give up something. You give up something.”

“Fair enough,” Lyden said.

“I’ve given you a chance to withdraw. You haven’t, so I’ll add my signature. I’ll be back with your copy. In the meantime you can start processing out of here.”

Released, feeling stronger from the ample servings of food, his skin no longer cold and dry, Lyden made a phone call while waiting for the bus to Kansas City. When assured of his FCC contact in Washington, the party who ordered the hit, Lyden’s voice took on the quality of a voice he’d practiced. “This is Alex,” he said, imitating that voice. “I’m going to say this only one time. Cordelia Cooper is dead. The hit man you sent is dead. Now leave it be.”

Before the man on the other end could speak, Lyden hung up the receiver. Word would filter back to Kansas City that Luckman was dead. If they checked carefully, they would also learn that radio station KNDA had been sold and that Alex Barca was in jail.

Brock Lyden decided not to call his wife. She would worry. When he arrived at the bus station in Kansas City, he would take a cab home. Then he’d tell Victoria all about the strange barn. His eyes narrowed. He had unfinished business. Part of it involved calling his insurance agent, telling him that he needed a new Lincoln. Part of it involved something else.

At Washington Savings, Erin continued a hectic pace. The editor of the *Herald-Journal* phoned. “Could I get a quote. Can you verify that you inherited everything?”

Erin's eyes widened. Suddenly it dawned. *So that is what this attention is all about. Cordelia's money.* "That is what Attorney Keane informed me," Erin said slowly, measuring her words. "I would appreciate it if you limited my comment to the charitable trusts." Her voice sharpened. "I'm going to run the trusts on a don't call me, I'll call you basis."

"Yes, ma'am."

Ma'am? In that moment of dead silence before the editor replaced the phone, Erin clearly heard, "Another Cordelia Cooper."

"And proud of it," Erin shouted to no one.

She told herself that she was handling everything with her usual style and panache. She was in total control of her emotions and attitudes.

The fawning, she estimated, would end with the setting sun. Then would come a series of ill conceived, poorly contrived plots to obtain money, not the least of which would involve proposals of marriage. The number of proposals before she became abundantly wealthy had been limited. Perhaps she should appreciate those who had showed an interest in her, appreciated her, rather than her money. "All others to the back of the line," she said with authority.

She spun around in her chair and called, "Henry. Henry Leighton. You say I own forty percent to your thirty? You say I'm now the boss. Very well. Stand up." She did not wait for a response. She flung her arms around him and kissed him soundly, an awkward kiss with too much energy, too little emotion. She remembered his wide-eyed surprise. She felt him reach around her, felt his comforting arms. He kissed her gently and with great tenderness.

"Much better," she breathed.

"That's what I like to see. A friendly store," declared a man who entered.

Henry shrugged and grinned. "Her idea. She's the boss."

Erin blushed three shades redder and stammered, "I—I can't deny that." She tried to cover her discomfiture with a laugh. *Why did I do that? Maybe I have lost control.*

The customer's mischievous grin told Erin that he couldn't wait to tell everyone up and down the street what he had seen.

"I don't know why I did that," she told her mother at the end of the day.

"It was rather impetuous," Belle said. "For you."

"I'd better get both feet firmly planted back on the ground." Erin admitted.

"Whatever for?" Belle asked innocently. "I hear you can do whatever you want now."

"At least Henry didn't propose again."

"He didn't. What's ailing him? How many opportunities like that will he get? He certainly missed a splendid opportunity."

"Yeah," Erin said somewhat dismally. "He did miss a splendid opportunity. Do you suppose he has lost interest?"

"Now, whose fault would that be?"

"You think I should ask him?"

"He might think it's your turn now. Does he like the house?"

"The house? I thought after some renovating, you and I might move there."

"Don't look at me," Belle insisted. "I have a house. I wouldn't move there if you paid mc."

Chapter Twenty-Two

Orville Keane released a flow of legalese well calculated to confuse his client. The last thing he wanted Jennifer Otley to realize was that she had something to say about the settlement he had so laboriously worked out for her. He'd given the impression that the judge controlled the court, a not unreasonable conclusion.

"Your lifetime child support settlement is forty-seven thousand dollars. My fee comes out of that. It might be one-third—"

"That much? That's a lot."

"Or it might be nothing. The judge will decide." He had already submitted a request for two thousand dollars. "Let me say now that you won't get the child support money in hand. It will be placed in a trust and will be doled out for the child as needed. I have selected Erin Ames to be that trustee."

"I don't like her," Jennifer blurted, eyes flashing.

"I don't care whether you like her or not," Orville said in a burst of temper. "She has more brains than any three bankers you can name. She'll serve for nothing. Do you know how much an iron-hearted bank charges to manage a trust? Do you want a bank telling you what to do?"

"I certainly don't want Erin Ames telling me what to do either." Jennifer's lower lip became petulant.

"Do you want your trust to earn two percent and have the bank take most of that for fees? I guess you don't want Erin to make a fortune for you. Why in the hell are you mad at her?"

"She took my job at the station."

"That's a crock. Alex fired you. Not Erin."

"She wanted to take my baby. She wanted to adopt my baby."

"Which only proves that she cares for your expected child. Do you know the grief she would have to put up with to raise a child? When they tossed you together, did they leave out brains?"

"You can't speak to me like that," Jennifer flared, feeling very much like the trophy fish on the wall behind him.

"It's time somebody did. You made a mess of your life with Alex Barca. You want to blame Erin Ames for that. She has only tried to save your child—and you indirectly. All right," Orville said, still angry and not particularly caring that he'd lost control. "It's up to you. Tell me now. You'll have to tell the judge in a little while. Do you want to grab the deal, grab the package, Erin and all, or do you want to risk going to trial to battle some attorney as smooth as a ferret? It's your call. Name it!"

"I'm sorry," Jennifer said. "It's just that—" She sniffed but there were no tears.

"You're just upset. In time you'll like Erin. When the child is ready for college, you will remember this day as the best day in your life." He pressed a button. A door opened.

"Come in, Erin. Erin, this is Jennifer. Jennifer this is Erin. We haven't time to talk now. We're due at the courthouse."

They made quite a pair, Erin in polished heels, flawless legs, dressed in the height of fashion. Jennifer, as instructed, wore flats, no makeup, and a high collared dress that looked like it came out of her grandmother's closet.

Orville covertly winked at Erin. "I hope this is the start of a beautiful friendship." He'd accomplished one thing he hadn't expected. The ladies limited their conversation.

They proceeded to the second-floor courtroom of the Honorable Lars Jennings Strand. From the outset, Orville realized the judge was not happy with the settlement.

The judge glared over his spectacles at County Attorney Lance Richardson. "Sitting with the defense again, I see."

Richardson hesitated, debating whether to speak. He opted for bobbing his head.

Judge Strand looked for the girl who sold him Girl Scout cookies, made fleeting eye contact with Jennifer Otley, and almost smiled. He located Erin Ames and wondered what she had sold him all those years ago.

"Erin Ames," he said in a judicial tone. "As successor to the account at Citizens State Bank, do you agree to accept restitution in lieu of further prosecution for embezzlement?"

"Yes, your honor."

"I don't need to question the prosecutor," the judge said. He's already signed off on this." He glowered at Richardson and continued. "I see the Defendant has stipulated to a lump sum settlement for child support in futuro. He impaled Richardson on a steely stare. "How do you make a man pay child support if there is no finding of paternity?"

Richardson shifted uncomfortably. "W-Well," he stammered. He looked to Keane who originated the settlement.

Orville leaped to his feet. "In the overall scheme of things—in the interest of justice. Mr. Barca has a history of moving—"

"Harrumpf." The judge looked at Barca with disdain. "Are you aware that by paying child support, it may one day be considered tantamount to admission of paternity?" His gaze moved to the Girl Scout. "That being the case, the defendant might request visitation, temporary custody over the holidays and during the summer, finally full custody." He noticed Jennifer's eyelids leap. Her mouth became an open oval of surprise.

"I'm not going to accept the documents that indicate there is no admission of paternity," the judge said firmly. "Suppose I pen in the phrase that this settlement, in the overall scheme of things, is made in the interest of justice, whereupon this court specifically finds that Alex Barca is not the father of Jennifer Otley's expected child. Do you have any objection to that, Mr. Barca?"

Feeling the heat of an icy stare, seeing his chances for leniency slipping away, Alex uttered an audible "no."

In turn, Attorneys Kessler, Richardson, and Keane all said, "No objection."

Judge Strand approved the civil settlement for battery and asked Jennifer, "Do you have any ill effects from the horrible beating you sustained at the hands of the defendant?"

"No, your honor," Jennifer replied.

Alex slid lower in his seat.

"You are a lucky man, Defendant Barca. To have all these felonies reduced to a single misdemeanor. How do you plead to the charge of simple battery?"

"Guilty, your honor."

Judge Strand grilled him unmercifully to establish the factual basis for the plea and said finally, “I see there is no recommendation for sentencing. That lets you off the hook, Mr. Richardson.” He did not realize he had voiced an additional thought. “Sitting too long with the defense bar.”

Jerry Kessler rose. “Waive time for sentencing, your honor.”

“All right. I’ll go along with credit for time served.” The judge glared at Barca. “I’m not sure that my tacking on another month or two to the added recommendation would teach you anything. However—” He turned to Richardson. “What’s the maximum monetary assessment for a misdemeanor one?”

Richardson hesitated and nervously relied on the truth. “I don’t know off the top of my head. I’ll look it up.”

“Do that. Written memorandum on my desk in twenty-four hours. I’ll make my final ruling then.”

Orville slipped Richardson a note with the answer, but Richardson rose too late. “Your honor—” He stopped when he saw the judge walking out of the courtroom.

On the way to his office, Orville advised Jennifer to remain celibate—he explained the word—until the check arrived.

When he learned of the settlement, Keith Gordoncamp—now often referred to as Gordon Keith—exclaimed, “We can get a new set of wheels.”

“That’s right,” his mother said with sarcasm. “Spend the money before you get it. It’s a good thing Judge Strand protected your baby with a trust.”

“My baby?” Keith objected.

“Yours,” Doris asserted. “The judge said it couldn’t be Alex Barca’s. That’s the law. Do you see anyone else standing in line? If you want to date Jennifer—if you have the slightest intention of marrying her—you’d better give some thought to your baby.”

“That’s something to think about,” Keith acknowledged.

Two men appeared and asked to speak to Downbeat Jackson. He recognized the members of the Lions Club.

“Now that you’re getting married—” said one.

“That was a consideration,” said the other. “We had a Rotary member in charge of the radio station and also at the chamber of commerce. We would like a Lion in charge of the chamber now. We’re here to convince you to take the job. It would mean a lot to us to have a Lion in charge.”

“If you agree, the entire club will support you.”

Downbeat needed time to think. "Take pride in the Lions," he said. "I'm radio. Radio has been my life. I know that will end some day. You've certainly given me something to think about. I need to speak to Doris."

"That's a must."

"I'll get back to you," Downbeat promised.

As they departed he heard one man say to the other. "The pride of the Lions. He has a way with the language. I told you he was right for the job."

Having a way with the language didn't make it any easier to tell Doris.

She gave him an answer he didn't expect. "Follow your bliss."

At the adjacent desk Erin placed a free 800 call to her Piper Jaffray broker. "Set up accounts for the Save the Child Trust, the Cordelia Cooper Charitable Trust, and the Blessed Baby Educational Trust. Attorney Keane had advised her she had full authority to invest in Jennifer's court ordered trust as long as her actions were commensurate with sound business principles. "On that one you need to be particularly aware of your fiduciary responsibilities."

Erin did not notice Downbeat make a phone call, nor was she aware he had played Vaughn Monroe's "There I Said It Again."

What good was it being a manager, Downbeat reflected, if he didn't manage? He'd seen Keith moping around and he'd urged him, "Give the girl a call," but Keith had failed to respond. When he spoke to Jennifer he said simply, "Turn on your radio."

He'd been handing Keith "Thoughts for the Day," to be read on the air without rehearsal. As soon as the music stopped he killed the mike momentarily and said to Keith in an urgent voice, "Here, read this." He flicked on the switch.

Sensing the urgency, Keith began, "It may be outrageous, it may be contagious, yet it's my devotion, as deep as the ocean, and I ask on bended knee, Jennifer Otley, will you marry me?" He stopped short and gulped. "Hey!" He looked at Downbeat with a helpless expression that begged "What do I do now?"

Like a cat in the cream, a grinning Downbeat spoke in a mellow tone. "It worked for me. Maybe it will work for you." He set up "The Hawaiian Wedding Song."

The phone rang. Doris had been instructed to put the call on the air if Jennifer answered.

"Hi, it's Jennifer." she repeated. "The answer is yes. Of course I'll marry you."

"No," exclaimed Orville Keane, who had been listening to his radio. He lurched out of his chair. His objection had been pure reflex action. He hadn't given Jennifer his permission to marry.

"Yes!" Downbeat cheered and whapped the table with his tanned bull-penis baton.

The instant his "Whoopee" escaped him, Keith knew he'd blurted something that should not have gone out over four states. He'd goofed, but there stood Downbeat beaming.

"Well congratulations, Gordon Keith." Downbeat continued. "This calls for a celebration."

"Not a double marriage ceremony," Doris mouthed at him. It did not matter that Downbeat did not understand now, she would lay down the law later. The phone rang and the caller asked to be put on the air. Doris signaled and transferred the call.

"Yes," Downbeat said. "You are on the air."

"This is Henry Leighton."

Erin sat bolt upright.

Henry said, "It may be outrageous, it may be contagious. My ocean may be a sea. All I have to ask is, Erin Ames, will you marry me?"

Downbeat beckoned Erin into the broadcast booth.

At the pharmacy, R-ex attempted to pour an elixir into a bottle with a tilted graduate and missed. The elixir formed a spreading red stain on the counter.

Erin spoke into the microphone in what she hoped was a professional voice. "We interrupt this program with a news bulletin. This—is Erin Ames—with the news. An impetuous Henry Leighton proposed today to a fellow employee of Washington Savings and Loan Association. In order to prevent the business from being any further scandalized, Erin Ames responded with an enthusiastic YES! No wedding date has been set. We return you to the program in progress."

Along coffee counters it was said that six single guys threw down their hats and stomped on them in disgust."

Doris flung her arms around Erin the moment she stepped out of the booth. "I'm so happy for you!"

At the mike, Downbeat cracked, "If this keeps up we may have to charge for our proposal service. This is KNDA, the cupid station, Clarinda, Iowa."

At Washington Savings, Henry Leighton cheered so loudly that the young woman he and Erin were training clapped her hands over her ears. Henry ran to Sarah's Sports Bar and was going to say "Drinks are on me," but at the moment only one man lazed at the end of the bar.

"Ben, pour us a whisky," he said to Sarah's husband. "The good stuff. Erin Ames promised to marry me, right on the air. Isn't it fantastic?"

"Let's see," Ben McAllister posed. "We ought to be able to arrange some sort of celebration. 'Here Comes the Bride Night'? We have to do something."

Henry drew himself erect and challenged with mock indignation, "Are you trying to exploit my wife?"

"Every chance I get," Ben said with a grin. "Every chance I get."

Joyful exhilaration reigned at the station. Doris said to Downbeat, "Now I'm not going to allow three weddings at one time. I want you all to myself." She noticed Downbeat had become gloomy.

"I don't like it," he said. "It's a black cat for an announcer to read the news where the announcer is part of the news."

"It wasn't really the news. Erin is not a full time announcer. I thought it was real clever the way she accepted."

"But she used her own name on the air. It would have been better if she had just said yes and not pretended to be an announcer."

"It was an impulse," Erin admitted. "Perhaps I was swept along with the good news of Keith and Jennifer."

"Now Keith," Downbeat warned. "Don't you ever read anything in the news where you are mentioned. That's a positive black cat for sure."

"What could happen?" Keith asked. "Will somebody throw a bomb in here?"

"Be careful crossing the street," Erin said. "Anyway, it's too late to do anything about it now. Or should I hire an exorcist?"

"I never heard of that," Downbeat said.

"I'm going over and greet Henry," Erin said. "I think his proposal should be sealed with a kiss."

With Downbeat's warning echoing in her thoughts, her steps reflected a measure of caution. She couldn't help thinking about Captain Gaylord Haversham and the plane crash. What had she done then to summon a black cat? She had been pregnant for days. Then she'd lost the child. All this occurred long before she became associated with radio. A person didn't need to be hit by a bus to incur a tragedy. Sometimes all that needed to happen was to walk into a church and say "I do." People faced tragedies every day. It was ridiculous to be worried by Downbeat's silly superstition. On the other hand, Downbeat was not a lose cannon. He had substance. From now on she would never read a news bulletin in which she herself was mentioned.

"Cheer up," Henry said when he saw her. "The world isn't coming to an end because you're marrying me. It's a beautiful beginning. It's home-run time, touchdown time, rainbow time."

Erin extinguished the gentle frown but not the substance behind it. She came into his arms. Their lips met. But not their hearts? The kiss was contractual.

"Incidentally," Henry said, "Ben McAllister wants to celebrate our marriage in style."

Celebrating, but not for the same reason, Alex Barca had to admit he was glad that Erin Ames had not given him the shaft and simply allowed repayment of money. It might have been a great deal worse. Now all he had to do was kick time. He'd be out in a couple months. With his reduced status, he kept telling officers, "I've never been a felon. A misdemeanor is more like a traffic ticket." Constant repetition resulted in not only reduced tension but also preferential treatment. He borrowed a typewriter and cajoled officers into making copies. He persuaded officers to purchase envelopes and stationery for him and coaxed Ellen into making copies of his resume. Before long he received telephone calls.

At the station, those who overheard were nearly as spellbound as the callers when Alex said, "I'm going to say this only one time. Where can you find another station manager who can come to town and within weeks, cold turkey, increase shareholder value more than forty percent?"

Chief Wendinger overheard him importuning Officer Davison, asking to ride along. "I'll always be in your custody. I promise I won't run. We'll stop for coffee and Danish."

The chief knew it would only be a matter of time before he convinced the rookie. "You want to ride with me?" the chief said one afternoon.

Alex grinned until the chief stopped on the highway and handed him a two large plastic bags. "There's lots of bottles and cans and garbage that needs picking up. Hop to it. I'll be two miles ahead. After this, don't be planning anything with my deputies, see?"

Alex looked back and saw a squad car had moved in position a short distance behind him.

A half hour later, Jennifer Otley drove past the spot where Chief Wendinger parked. She approached the man picking up litter and slowed. He looked familiar. When she recognized Alex Barca, she made a face and stuck out her tongue. "Bye-bye, Da-dee."

Chapter Twenty-Three

Following his unexpected imprisonment in a Clarinda barn and his return to Kansas City, Brock Lyden learned that a bartender on Whiskey Row, a widower, could not afford to send his daughter to college. As if to prove the old adage that there is some good in the worst of men, he wrote a check for the first year's tuition and added, "If your daughter does well the first year, you don't need to worry about the second."

Remembering his act of charity sent a warm feeling spiraling up within him. Perhaps his good deed would count for something. He drove the new Lincoln, purchased with insurance company funds, to Las Vegas. On arrival he parked his car and purchased a one-way ticket to LAX.

Looking ahead, he told himself he wasn't violating a promise. Not technically. No money would be involved. This would definitely be Luckman's last tour.

He checked with booking agents in Hollywood and had little difficulty in locating the address of the man whose name had become indelibly etched in his brain. All he had to do was wait.

As the sun dipped into the shimmering blue Pacific, he saw his old car approaching, driven by Dirk Lowe Bartle. By the time Dirk thrust his apartment key into the lock, Lyden had reached his side and, with an index finger pressed into his back, walked in with him.

Dirk recognized him at once. "How did you find me?" He winced at the quick jab of a needle.

Dirk pleaded as Lyden tied him in a chair. "I didn't mean to take your car, Man. I-I can make it up to you. Take the car back." He paled when he noticed Lyden's surgical gloves. "W-What are you going to do?" he asked, worried. Wide-eyed and anxious, he already felt somewhat exhilarated from the drug.

"It's time for dinner, country style," Lyden sneered, and produced a carton of insects. "Swallow them. All of them."

"You want me to eat those bugs? I can't."

Lyden grasped Dirk's hair, jerked his head back, and dumped insects into his mouth. "It's easier to swallow with water," he said, pouring from a glass.

Dirk gagged often and the procedure took longer than Lyden expected. "Take the car," Dirk begged, realizing at last that more was involved than the car. *Payback.* But he tried again. "Just take the car. I can tell you who set me up. Gimme a break." He barely felt the second needle. He would never know why he had been forced to eat insects.

Lyden removed the rope and shoved Bartle to the floor.

He peered through a crack in the door and saw no one. Lyden slid behind the wheel of his old car. "There's nothing more gratifying than a reunion with an old friend," he said with smug satisfaction as he pointed the Lincoln toward Las Vegas. He sold the car for cash, "No questions asked."

Lyden drove around Las Vegas in his new Lincoln, selling executive gifts. He didn't gamble. Gambling was for suckers.

"No more hits," he promised himself. Even great hitters like DiMaggio eventually retired.

He'd been careless in Clarinda. He'd been stupid. And he'd been caught. Trapped. The angel had prepared him for a second chance. In the days ahead, he knew he would sometimes be bored. He needed something to challenge him from time to time. "I wonder," he mused aloud. "Should I take up golf?"

Chapter Twenty-Four

Before dawn, the entire eastern horizon appeared to be ablaze. At length a ruddy sun peeked over the rim and tipped Clarinda church spires with a rosy glow. The crimson light might have inspired Gordon Keith to play "Everything's Coming Up Roses."

Downbeat argued that great savings might be achieved by decorating the church and renting a hall for the wedding receptions only once, but Doris remained adamant. "I want to be mother of the groom, not just another bride. And with Jennifer's condition, the best thing we can do is get them married."

Invited guest Orville Keane no longer worried that Jerry Kessler might file a motion for reconsideration. He hadn't. The judgment had been paid. Judge Strand had signed orders releasing funds from the constructive trust imposed on Alex Barca's funds on the same day that Jennifer accepted Keith's on-the-air proposal. Orville wondered if any funds remained for Jerry's attorney fees.

When Keith indicated he needed more training at the station, Doris rewarded his "display of good common sense" by moving out of her house temporarily so the honeymooners would not be disturbed. At Erin's request, Doris would spend a week with Belle Ames.

"That's for keeping my time records," Erin explained. Now residing at the Cooper House, Erin had asked Henry to be her guest and bring his toothbrush and pajamas in order that they might discuss their future. In reality she worried about their compatibility.

Since Erin's acceptance of his proposal, Henry Leighton had been walking tall, receiving congratulations from friends and clients. Several men admitted they envied him.

When he walked into Sarah's Sports Bar for a midmorning cup of coffee, a concerned Ben McAllister did not hum a few bars of the "Wedding March" as he had before. His brow furrowed. "Have you noticed the weather? I think we are in for a storm, a fence lifter. A real gully washer."

"I doubt it," Henry said. "It's probably just another false alarm." The only thing on his mind was spending the night with Erin.

For her part, Erin worried that supper would be a disaster. After being together all day, would there be anything left to discuss?

Not long after she began working at Washington Savings, Erin had purchased a coffee pot, "to provide a measure of hospitality when I sit down with someone who requests a loan." Both she and Henry sometimes strolled out for coffee, "just to get out of the store." She knew Henry enjoyed coffee-counter banter. Today, she feared he wanted time away from her. She had to admit she felt uneasy about their impending wedding. Would Henry detect the uncertainty that haunted her? Having him stay over would certainly provide an opportunity to clear the air.

Outside, clear air appeared to be at a premium. All afternoon clouds shifted, collided, and mashed together as the cumulus drifts piled higher and higher. What had been light, fluffy marshmallows became dark pillows that threatened to dump their moisture on a parched earth.

"We need rain badly," Ben observed when Henry stopped for a late-afternoon cup of coffee. "But I don't like the looks of this."

As a curtain settling on the opening act of a play presages continuing melodrama, so the dark, ominous clouds settling on the horizon predicted a gathering storm. A customer viewing the golden backdrop to the tumbling clouds said, "That means good weather tomorrow."

"You don't know what you're talking about," Ben objected. "That's not the setting sun shining through. What you see is wind. And if that gold hue takes on a green tint, it means hail."

When they locked Washington Savings, Henry and Erin listened to the distant rumble of thunder. “I hope this isn’t another false alarm,” Henry said. “Farmers are hurting for rain.”

Buster greeted their arrival with a hearty tail-wagging and, when Henry bent down to pet him, Buster licked his hand, a response that did not escape Erin.

The evening meal did not go as Erin expected; it resulted in what she had feared. Melancholy came into her voice. “The philosopher who said that what you expect never happens is wrong. All afternoon I expected this meal to be a disaster and it certainly is a disaster. Have I run into a self-fulfilling prophecy? I so wanted to make a good impression.”

“It’s not that much of a disaster.”

“Then why do I feel as I do?”

“Pre-wedding jitters. You’ve been in a deep-blue funk ever since you said yes. You can take it back if you wish.”

“After what I said on the air?”

“Yes.” His eyes gently met hers and held. “Look, I know you don’t love me.”

His challenging words hung like an indictment.

“I do love you,” she said. “I’m sure of it.” She took a breath. “It’s just that when I married, I expected to hear drums pounding and bugles blazing. Perhaps sirens wailing.” She gave an uneasy shrug.

“Maybe I hear enough drums and bugles for both of us. You’re in love with the idea of being in love, rather than being in love with someone. I know I’m rather colorless.”

Her hand went out in a consoling gesture. “You’re not.”

“I’m practically invisible. I’m sort of a loner. In school I was always the last kid chosen. I tried collecting stamps. When I learned all I wanted to know, I gave it up. I switched to coins, but that’s a rich man’s game. When I go deer hunting, I’m happiest if I don’t bag a deer.”

She chuckled. “You’re pleasant and you make me laugh.”

“At me.”

“That’s not fair. I laugh because I enjoy you. I even like your persistence in restoring old cars.”

“I rather do enjoy putsying around with that.”

She had a tremendous surprise. She decided not to tell him about the collection of old cars hidden in the barn. She hadn’t seen them behind the double rows of straw bales, but Orville had opened a sealed envelope and provided her with a list.

Henry gazed out the window. "Have you noticed the weather. The sky is evil. We're in for a storm. Speaking of storms, I spoke to Orville and asked him to draw up a pre-nup. What's yours stays yours, what's mine is mine. A simple document, I told him." Henry waited for a storm to erupt inside the house.

Erin's eyes widened slightly. "You did that?"

He favored her with an anemic smile. "I decided to risk it. I thought it was something you might like. I have the notion that you feel somewhat trapped."

Maybe she hadn't fully appreciated the way he could take charge. "I'm not trapped. I'm going full speed ahead. By the time we get married, Doris and Downbeat will have had their wedding. Would you like them to stand up for us?" She'd already discussed it with Doris and Downbeat.

"Why not? I know my name turns you off. You don't have to be a Mrs. Henry or even a Mrs. Leighton. You can keep your own name."

"You've been talking to Mother."

He nodded.

"People aren't going to pay attention to what I like." Erin said.

"They'll come around. In time. You'll forever be Erin Ames."

"You're a dear. It's not the Leighton part," Erin explained. "Maybe I could be a Mrs. Hank. Mrs. Hank Leighton." She shook her head. "No. All right, you have me convinced. I'll keep my name." She hadn't realized the enormousness of the problem. She stopped to listen to the wind. "Hear that howling wind?"

"I'd rather hear you. Listen, hon. Remember that coffee pot you brought into the store? After the hot plate brings the pot to a boil, where can it go? I think marriage is like a pot. I'd rather have our marriage start with a low flame, then when passion brings it to a boil—what I mean, we'd have that wonderful feeling to look forward to."

"That would be a great expectation," Erin said. "And entirely reasonable." She had another worry. "We could develop exposure fatigue. We might get tired of each other. We're together all day. Or we were before I started at the station."

"And get along fine."

"Don't interrupt."

"Yes, ma'am."

"Stop that."

He sobered. "Frankly, my dear, I think you love me more than you realize. I believe that love will grow. I heard your acceptance. You're not the kind of woman who can be easily stampeded."

She did not reply. *I was—once.*

Downtown, folks scurried to their cars to beat the storm. Entertaining them on the way to their homes and farms, Dan Pulliam began a solitary vigil at the KNDA microphone.

He scoffed at a jurist's illogical charge that a woman with a short skirt attracts a rapist. Nevertheless fascinated, Dan would later call the Midwestern plains short skirted. The wheat had been harvested, and if the short-skirted plains did not invite a storm, at least the rain would be timely. He would not get to say "Raped by the storm."

What happened to the wind? The silence had become eerie, a dead silence when not a leaf stirred, an electric, breath-arresting silence. Had Dan been able to see into the future he would have preferred that it remained that way.

The KNDA building had been constructed a foot higher than its neighbors. Above the roof and toward the front towered a twelve-foot hollow pipe that Jake Cooper used as a flag pole. A patriotic man, Jake also flew a checkered flag when he wanted to offer folks "a sweet sizzling smoking deal." The pipe extended through a well-tarred opening in the roof and was anchored on a distant studding below. An electrician had utilized the pipe as a conduit for electrical wires connected to an outlet on the roof. His idea had been copied for antenna wires for several television sets. A television antenna toward the back afforded a splendid roosting place for birds. There were wires for a clothesline and wires no one could explain.

Suddenly the wind whipped through the antenna with gale force, creating a windsong. Cold frosty air from the nimbus strata came diving down into the hot cumulus layer, tumbling into a rolling turmoil, a cumulonimbus mass. Lightning flashed in protest, followed by the explosion of thunder. Random raindrops, suddenly ice cold, splattered on the sidewalk like bird eggs flung off the roof.

Olaf Larson ran for his pickup truck. Hair on this forearms stood erect. He glanced up and saw bolts of lightning, coming simultaneously from the left and right, hitting the flagpole. In an instant, zip-zip, two more direct hits came from the same two directions, then bam-bam, thunder so loud it made him wince. The building exploded. He ducked in time to escape the shower of glass and splinters. He leaped into his truck as hailstones pelted him like hard boiled bird eggs.

Inside the studio, moments before, Dan Pulliam had played an appropriate record and raced down the hall to the bathroom in the rear, planning to return before Lena Horne completed the song. He remembered his hair standing on end a second before he felt himself hurled against a wall. He recovered consciousness a short time after the fire truck arrived.

"That's the last time I play 'Stormy Weather,'" he muttered from his hospital bed.

The *Herald-Journal* printed part of what he had to say under a banner headline, LIGHTNING STRIKES TWICE, TWICE. Had not a young farmer been an eyewitness? The editor omitted Pulliam's comment that when he looked at his wet pants he said, "I guess I don't need to go to the bathroom now." Folks clustered around coffee counters generally chose to include that comment.

A few minutes after Downbeat Jackson arrived and surveyed the scene, he phoned Erin. "Are you all right?"

"Yes. I'm fine. Why?"

"You should see the station! What's left of it. It's a complete meltdown! Four bolts of lightning. The building is in shambles."

"Oh my God!" Erin's words came in a rush. "Was anyone hurt? Is there anything I can do?"

"Dan Pulliam is in the hospital—he's going to be all right, I think. The fire department put out several fires. I can't tell exactly where, they won't let me go inside. I can tell you we're out of business. It's back to square one. From the ground up. There's some of the frame left, especially toward the back. I need to call the company but there's no use trying at this hour. I'll wait till morning."

"Let me know if you need help."

"Erin, are you sure you're all right?"

"Yes. I'm fine."

"When I saw what happened here, with all the lightning around I simply had to call to see if you were all right. I couldn't help worrying, what with you reading your own news. Well, maybe the station took all of the black cat. Talk about splinters. We could start a toothpick factory."

"I'm all right." she assured him. "I'll be down early to survey the damage. There's nothing you can do. Be sure they cordon off the place. We don't want anyone getting hurt. Thanks for keeping me informed."

"I've got it covered."

Erin told Henry what had happened and moved to the window. Hailstones were melting under a drenching rain. Henry came up behind her, placed his arms around her, and kissed her neck.

"Ooooh" she murmured and slowly turned as a happy tingle ascended her spine.

"No drums or bugles?" Henry said. "It isn't thunder dear, it's only my poor heart you hear. Is that enough to keep romance alive?"

"Just about right," she said before his lips closed her mouth.

At length he said, "Where's my bedroom?" He knew there would be no fooling around before the ceremony.

A sleepless Erin lay in her bed, wondering about the curious mixture of destiny, luck, fate, and timing. Cordelia, the house, the sale of the station, and now this. Fortunately she still had a full-time job—and perhaps a wonderful future with Henry Leighton.

"Hon?" she called, using the same word he had used for the first time.

"Yeah?" he replied from the adjacent bedroom.

"Would you mind terribly if I called you Hank? Even at work?"

"No. Call me anything you want. Just not too late for supper."

"Oh you."

Perhaps she would call him "honey" at home. Thoughts in a turmoil, she could not sleep. Henry had described himself as colorless, yet he had a certain flair. She could not help making a comparison. She remembered the colorful Captain Gaylord Haversham. She'd had a youthful heart-throbbing fling with the captain. The dashing captain had been challenging, totally unpredictable, fun to be with. Henry, no Hank, was predictable, steady, reliable, and actually fun to be with. She knew she should not make comparisons. Then was then, now is now. Hank will work.

She remembered Hank's allegory of the boiling coffee pot. She wondered if she had married the captain, would the flame under the coffee pot have flickered and gone out? Would the marriage have endured? Knowing what she knew now, life would not have been easy.

Her mother warned her about "building castles in the air. Life is not a bowl of cherries."

A totally alien thought surfaced. She realized she didn't need to work a day for the rest of her life. She banished the thought. "Idle hands," her mother said, "are the devil's playground." She had never considered not working. Hank said he needed her. She had to manage the trusts. She would be needed to help with the station disaster. Disaster? Disaster means opportunity for someone. She had seen the Carleton Group balance sheet. They had dissipated nearly all of their cash in purchasing KNDA. Leveraged, in debt, she saw an equation for trouble. In the morning she would call CEO Hansen and inform him of the extent of damage. "We are totalled."

A cold, wet touch on her arm startled her. She stiffened. "Oh, Buster," she said when she realized it was his nose. "So you've put Hank to bed and now you're ready to tuck me in? Well, okay." She knew Buster had curled up on the rug in his usual spot. "So you think he's a keeper?" Could she go wrong if she married a man of whom Buster approved? Her smile faded when she fell asleep.

At dawn she heard Hank singing in the shower and listened. "I want a girl, just like the girl, that married dear old dad." Buster had abandoned this place on the rug and gone to investigate.

Momentarily Hank entered her bedroom, wrapped in a towel. "Good morning."

"You've crossed the li—" She halted abruptly. "Good morning," she returned with sudden force. "Sleep well?"

"Like a rock."

You are something of a rock. She ran her hand through disheveled hair. "I must look a fright."

"You look just fine to me."

"Want a companion?" he twitted. "I'm reasonably dry. I could dive right in..."

Her expression congealed beneath a frown. The urge to scold leaped into her thoughts and she forced herself to relent. It was not necessary to scold. He had already turned and departed. Laughter trailed in his wake. He's not as predictable as I thought.

"What do you want for breakfast?" he called out when dressed. "I'm an expert with the frying pan. How about a couple fried eggs, fried bacon, fried potatoes, fried onions, and fried bread?"

"What?" She recoiled in horror.

"Yeah. With fried green tomatoes. They call me the cholesterol king."

Only now did she realize he'd been teasing.

"I like a light but substantial breakfast," he said later.

Erin toyed with her cereal. Her thoughts were not focused on breakfast.

"I should have told you last night," Hank said. "I'm a fairly good cook, but you would have taken that as a criticism. I've been doing my own cooking. Do you realize that most folks our age have been married a dozen years or more?"

"Ummmm. Interesting."

"What's interesting?"

"I think I'll call my broker and short Carleton stock. With this disaster, I think it will take a hit."

He turned up his palms with a look of resignation. "Okay by me. It's your money."

"Not all of it. There are the trusts. About the cooking," she said. "I hope you don't show me up."

"I would never do that. It wouldn't be prudent."

They parked near the station in time to see a beaming, triumphant Downbeat emerging from the ruins, waving his leather baton. "I found it!" he shouted with enthusiasm. "Not a mark on it."

"Did you call Mr. Hansen?"

"I got him out of bed."

"There's nothing we can do here," Erin said. "Why don't we meet at our place?"

She and Hank continued to "their store."

Erin phoned Piper Jaffray and said to Bob, "I want to short Carleton Group. I think their stock may drop from current levels."

When the KNDA staff crowded into the conference room, Erin had already spoken to CEO Hansen. She reported, "Rebuilding is an option, but by no means certain. The board of directors will have to vote on it. Then contracts would need to be approved. The bottom line, we're off the air for the foreseeable future."

"Nuts," Keith muttered. "Just when we were getting a good start."

The two-man committee from the Lions Club came to speak with Downbeat.

"Strike while the iron is hot, I always say," said the leader.

"We're here to renew our offer," said the other. "We think you'd make a bang-up chamber secretary."

"It passed committee. You can go to work today."

Downbeat rubbed his large hands in a gesture that seemed more like grinding than indecision. "It's an ill wind that blows no good."

"That's what I always say," said the first delegate.

Downbeat turned to his intended with a questioning look.

"You're the boss," Doris said. "At least until the end of the ceremony."

"All right, I'll do it," Downbeat told the men. "If you will agree to three conditions. The first is, Doris comes along as my secretary."

"No problem. The secretary hires his helpers."

"The second is, I want the membership to know this may be temporary. I'm going to insist that the entire membership vote on me in a couple months. Remember, I'm radio. Next, I'm going to extend an invitation to every chamber member to attend our wedding. And no gifts. I'm blessed as it is."

"That's about five conditions," Doris said.

"It's a done deal," said the first delegate. "Just walk over to the chamber office and take charge."

"It's an ill wind that blows no good," repeated the other delegate as they left. "Why didn't we think of that?"

"We did."

Ensconced in the luxurious chair Andrew Seligman wanted to take with him but didn't dare to, Downbeat rose to meet a continuing stream of well-wishers. Several told him precisely how to run the office, to which he replied, "That's an excellent idea." He repeated the phrase so often he confided to Doris, "I might say it in my sleep."

In between visitors he phoned several Omaha radio stations. "This is Downbeat Jackson. I have two green kids who need a break. They're just starting out. They need all the help they can get. I'd consider it a personal favor if you'd give them an interview."

A serious-looking Keith and Jennifer approached Downbeat later in the day. Downbeat said, beaming, "I have some job interviews set up for you in Omaha. I want you to go up there, and don't pretend you know more than you do." It took him a moment to realize Keith and Jennifer had something else on their minds.

"You brought us together," Keith said. "We've been talking. You may flip when you hear this. We'd like your advice."

"What? That does flip me out. I have troubles of my own."

"We're serious," Jennifer said.

Downbeat scratched his prominent chin. He guessed they'd been in a big argument. "All right. Let's hear the problem."

They both spoke at once. Downbeat managed to separate Jennifer's, "He wants to handle the money. My money," from Keith's, "A man should handle the money."

Downbeat threw up two massive hands. "All across America, money causes more problems in marriage than all other problems combined." Downbeat had second thoughts. "I shouldn't butt into this."

"We want you to," Jennifer said. "You butted in with that on-the-air proposal."

"Yeah," Keith said.

"During my first marriage I allowed—Nola—to manage the money." Her name came easier to him now. "You go with your strengths. I've watched both of you and I've listened to your mother, Keith. Considering the two of you, Jennifer is the more efficient money manager. She didn't rush out to spend her settlement. You asked my opinion." He tapped Keith solemnly over the heart. "I think Jennifer should manage the money."

"What?" a crestfallen Keith erupted. "Aw, gee whiz."

"Management expertise comes with experience." Downbeat knew he'd hit a home run. "You don't go to a filling station for brain surgery. Go with your strengths. Be patient, Keith. Maybe in time you will learn what she knows."

Keith scowled and knew Downbeat spoke words of wisdom. He wanted to change the subject. "Tell us more about the interviews."

Doris had been eavesdropping and popped her head around the door frame. "Does that mean I get to handle the money too?"

Downbeat immediately emptied his pockets and handed her his coins and wallet.

She returned them with a kiss. "That's your allowance."

"Just one kiss? That's my allowance?"

"Don't overdo a good thing," she said, hoping the young couple would pick up on it. "Now you kids go out and talk about what Downbeat said. You are married now and you will have to work out your own problems. You're lucky, Jennifer. With that settlement for getting beaten up, you have a nice nest egg."

Keith exclaimed, "I know, Mom. I know. She gets to handle the money."

"Smart kid," she said looking him in the eye. "You catch on without having to be hit on the head. Lord knows, I wanted to more than once."

"Love you, Mom."

Erin arrived to discuss wedding plans with Doris.

Doris gestured toward Downbeat and joked, "He's the Secretary, big S. I'm little S. Guess who does all the work?"

Erin winked at Doris and spoke to Downbeat. "I have this problem, Mr. Secretary. I'm working in a respected business and my boss wants to marry me. He claims it's not for my money. What should I do?"

"Don't kid a kidder. What you should do is get out of here and let me get my feet on the ground."

Erin returned to the office to hear an excited Hank inform her. "You had an important call from Bob at Piper Jaffray. He wants you to call him back."

She placed the call. "You wanted me to phone?"

"Yes, Erin!" he exclaimed, recognizing her voice. The broker prided himself in that. "The Carleton stock you shorted has been in a free fall from twenty-two down to eleven. It looks like some insider is dumping it. It might be a good idea to close out your position. With the money you made you won't need to work the rest of the year."

"But you will," Erin countered. "Enter a buy order at ten and one-half for one hour. Move up to ten and three quarters for an hour. Then eleven for an hour and so on. Commit forty-five thousand dollars from the Blessed Baby Trust. Fifty thousand each from the Save the Children Trust and the Cordelia Charitable Trust. Then two hundred thousand from my own account."

"Got it. How high do you want to run your bid?"

"Thirteen. That's one of my lucky numbers. I'll get back to you."

Bob the broker wanted to commit funds of his own, but chose not to risk a conflict. He decided he would not buy until Erin's order had been completely filled.

Orville Keane encountered no such restriction. When he phoned Erin and learned of her purchases, he erupted, "You committed all the funds in Jennifer's Blessed Baby Trust? Isn't that playing fast and loose? It's court imposed, you know. You have a fiduciary responsibility."

"I'm not worried. In case of a loss I stand ready to replace every cent from my own account."

When their conversation ended, Orville phoned his own broker. "Buy Carleton Group."

Viewing stock activity, Erin raised her buy order to fifteen. The stock continued to inch higher.

The following day Erin received a call from Carleton CEO Gerard E. Hansen. At the outset she detected hesitation is his voice. "I don't know how to say this, Erin," he began. "None of us has a good excuse. The truth is no one thought of insurance. We didn't have insurance on the station." He left if there.

After a long and pained silence, Erin said. "I never cancelled our policy. I've been too busy. You should be entitled to collect on that. I'm sure that the policy is an asset the parties intended to transfer. If the insurance people are stubborn, I'll collect on the policy and endorse the check over to you."

"You'd do that?" he exclaimed, relieved. *Saved from the wrath of stockholders.* "That's wonderful. It's generous of you."

"My mother didn't raise a daughter to be a skinflint."

"Erin." Reassurance had entered Hansen's voice. "We have a vacancy on the board of directors. I'd like it if you would accept the position."

Erin emitted a tiny giggle, one she had used before with a devastating effect. "I'll hold you to that, Mr. Hansen. When is the next board meeting? Why don't I accept at that time, and after I've been seated, I'll deliver the check."

"I said it before. I'll say it again. I love the way you do business. I know you will make a significant contribution to the board."

By the end of the week, the price of Carleton stock had risen to twenty-three and she instructed Bob, "Sell everything except my own. Slowly."

Erin decided to keep a written record of the dates and times of all the transactions. She had entered all the buy orders before she knew about Carleton's insurance problems. Because her knowledge had been no more than public knowledge—and shrewd analysis—no one could accuse her of insider trading. As a prospective member of Carleton's board of directors she decided to hold her own stock for the time being. She prepared a written report which she delivered to Jennifer Gordoncamp with a copy to Orville Keane.

"The trustee is happy to report that the value of the Blessed Baby Trust has increased to more than ninety thousand dollars."

An excited Jennifer thrust the report at Doris. "It's already doubled! When I first read that I nearly wet my pants!"

They prepared for Saturday's wedding, oblivious of a scheme hatched by Downbeat and readily agreed to by Keith. When the minister asked, "Who gives this woman in marriage?" it had been agreed that Keith would answer, "I do."

When the time for the question arrived, Keith remained silent, raised his hand in signal, and most of those gathered, especially the Lions Club members, shouted in unison, "We do!"

The surprised minister could not restrain himself and said, "I've never seen a crowd so anxious to get someone married."

Chapter Twenty-Five

Downbeat said to Doris, "Stop the car at the burned-out station. You go ahead. I'll walk the rest of the way."

He strolled among the shattered ruins. "Nola. It's me. I've come to say good-bye for a while. I've beaten the booze monkey. I'm sure of it. All this time I was scared there was nothing for me after radio, but look where I landed. I'm secretary of the Clarinda Chamber of Commerce. And they came after me. Can you believe it? I feel resurrected. The way it stands, maybe they won't rebuild the station, but I'm building a new life. I've gotten married again. I should have told you sooner. I think you would like Doris. She's okay. Well, that's about it. Thanks for everything."

He walked a short distance and remembered he wanted to tell Nola that he would be a grandfather. He stopped. He decided that could wait, or maybe he wouldn't mention that. He had Doris now, and a new life. That had to be all a guy could expect. Was it his imagination, or did more people greet him now than ever before?

Doris could on occasion have a peppery tongue and she could also be marvelously understanding. She read something in his eyes and never once asked why he wanted to stop at the exploded radio station.

Before his midmorning break, the phone rang and Doris said, "It's the kids. They want to talk with you."

A thrilled Jennifer exclaimed, "I landed a job with radio station KFAB as a secretary, receptionist, gopher. I told the manager up front that I was expecting and it didn't bother him a bit."

"That's great."

"Keith wants to talk to you."

"Heh-heh-heh," Keith said in a fair imitation of Downbeat. "Gene Krupa was riding in a cab in New York City. The driver had on the radio. Gene listened to the up-tempo tune and said, 'Man, that'll never make it!' Then the announcer came on and said, 'That's Benny Goodman's latest release, "Don't Be That Way," the very tune on which Krupa had drummed with the band a few weeks earlier!' Hey, Downbeat, what do you think of that?"

"Don't quit your day job."

"That's what I called to tell you. I landed a job with KESY-FM. Tune us in at one oh four point five."

"Wonderful. Now talk with the boss and find out just what he wants. And lay off the cornball."

"It worked for you."

"Sure, sure."

"I'm letting Jennifer manage the money. Do you know she's written a thank-you note to Erin and asked for investing advice? Isn't that fab?"

"Watch your English," Doris said on the extension.

"I'm not on the air, Mom."

"You're full of hot air."

"Love you both. Bye now."

Doris went to the doorway. "Speaking of thanks, I owe you a big bucket of thanks for what you did for the kids."

"My pleasure," Downbeat said, beaming. "They're family."

"The people from the travel bureau and the Glenn Miller Preservation Society are here," Doris announced.

Some of his chamber duties were extensions of projects that he had already begun at the station. "Anyone can schedule a cruise to Hawaii," Downbeat declared. "We need to take care of our Clarinda people. Whether it's a cruise over, back, or around the islands, our people should get the bargains. Then we'll extend it to festival visitors. Deals they can't get anywhere else." He turned to the travel agent. "Can you work it out?"

"I'll give it my best shot."

"Doris and I are available to lead a honeymoon cruise. Erin has promised that she and Hank will be available to lead another excursion."

The GM Society rep said, "I'm not sure we can get the Glenn Miller band. They may already be booked."

"You're probably right," Downbeat acknowledged. "We'll get a name. We'll demand Music in the Miller Manner. There are enough musicians around LA who could put a band together. Off the top of my head, maybe Ray Anthony. Off the bottom of my head, I might even front an outfit myself. Downbeat Jackson and his Jive Five—count 'em—there's fourteen tonight!"

The GM Society rep nodded. "It wouldn't be difficult to handle. Visitors who register for the festival would be given a coupon redeemable on only our tours."

Moments after they departed Downbeat noticed a shadow in the doorway. He saw Chief Wilbur Wendinger approaching.

"I think we can close the book on the suspect who knocked you down and stole the cashbox," said the chief. "You know we found the cashbox and tickets in the trunk of an old car abandoned at the end of Miz Cooper's lane. The car belonged to an actor: Dirk Lowe Bartle. Today I received a call from a Kansas City detective."

"They caught him?"

"No. He's dead." The chief read from his notes. "Dirk was found dead in his Hollywood Hills apartment. The Los Angeles County medical examiner says death was due to an overdose of heroin and cocaine. The spiffy Lincoln he stole right here in Clarinda is missing. According to the police out there, it looks like a drug dcal gonc sour."

"I guess you can close the book. Thanks for letting me know."

"All in a day's work."

The chief had not revealed everything. The Kansas City detective had indicated that the Lincoln had been fenced to a shady character in Las Vegas and resold to a wheat farmer from Kansas. When Dirk's parents objected, "Dirk didn't do drugs. He hated drugs!" the detective ordered a copy of the autopsy report. The report confirmed that death had been due to overdose. The report also revealed that Dirk's stomach contained more than a cupful of assorted insects. The detective had asked, "What do you make of that?"

"Not a thing," the chief had said. "You can't trust these actor types."

The chief strolled to Washington Savings to inquire if the police department might be of assistance with anything for Hank and Erin's upcoming wedding. He interrupted Orville Keane who was reading a letter to Erin.

"Come in, chief," Orville said. "You're part of this. We received a letter from Lonica Barca. She wants to thank everyone in Clarinda who helped nail her husband. They nabbed him in Marysville, Ohio, only twenty-five miles from Bellefontaine, where he had another wife and family."

"Two families, twenty-five miles apart? Isn't that something?"

"It makes for an easy commute," Hank said.

Erin rewarded him with a look of censure.

Orville continued, "She says in closing that the judge out there has ruled she can keep the name Barca."

The chief chortled. "I'll be sure to tell Alex. That will make his day." A rumbling belly laugh followed.

The chief excused himself and Orville waved farewell. "I'll see you at Downbeat's chamber reception."

Flyers sent to the members listed in fine print, "Your paid-up chamber of commerce membership card is your ticket for admission to the reception and party."

At Sarah's Sports Bar, Ben McAllister stationed himself at the door and nabbed a couple of nonpaying nonmembers who had a habit of sneaking in but who became paid-up members, at least for the current year. Doris issued them membership cards.

An exuberant Downbeat proclaimed, "First, the business session."

"Don't make it too long," someone shouted.

"There will be plenty of time to party," Downbeat returned. "I need to give my slant on things. We've all seen Iowa towns decline in population. The time to work on the problem is not after the town has become a wide spot in the road but when it's thriving. I believe my job is to prevent Clarinda from becoming irrelevant.

"I've been listening. Right off I think we should change our organization name to coincide with this mission. We need to make our town attractive to industry. We've run a new name past some of you. The best one seems to be the Clarinda Association of Business and Industry. Does anyone want to make a formal motion to change our chamber of commerce name?"

"So moved."

"Seconded."

"All in favor say aye."

After the chorus Downbeat pronounced, "Carried."

"Don't those opposed get to say no?"

"Opposed, say nay."

"No nays? So be it." Downbeat couldn't resist a joke. "Have the record show it's umaminamimaminous. We are now the Clarinda Association of Business and Industry."

Downbeat resumed in a serious vein. "Folks, there's more to life than work. The Glenn Miller Festival is lots of fantastic fun. I've visited with some of you and it has been determined that from now on the date will be the second weekend in June every year. The Glenn Miller Preservation Society has graciously allowed me to say they have booked up the Glenn Miller band for the next ten years—if the band's schedule will permit. The band may be here two or three nights in a row during the festival. We're going to have some fabulous deals on cruises and vacations for our people. We're going to offer visitors to the festival packages that can only be purchased in beautiful downtown Clarinda."

The secretary of the Glenn Miller Preservation Society waved for attention. "I want to make an announcement too. Thanks to Downbeat Jackson, we are going to have Arlys Kwan, the nation's number-one female television anchor at our next GM festival. If you listened to KNDA before the meltdown, you know about Arlys Kwan. She will do a special here, so get ready for television crews. I think with Downbeat's help we might also get the Mystery Man. We're going to be busy!"

"Clarinda Association of Business and Industry," someone said. "That's CABI for short."

"Well," Downbeat said. "That's it. Party time!"

"Not so fast, not so fast," Erin interposed as she walked to the front. "Folks, if you don't know, I want to tell you. Downbeat is on the wagon for life. He's whipped his problem and I'm extremely proud of him."

Everyone started talking.

Erin banged on a glass with a spoon. The room quieted. "I know that not everyone enjoys something sweet. An Erin isn't for everyone. So tonight, at Sarah's Sports Bar, we feature a new drink involving that temperate beverage. Something salty." With abundant ceremony she dropped an olive into the beer. "What better way to start a tradition? I present the first Downbeat to Downbeat's first lady. To his lovely wife, Doris!"

Doris came forward and took a couple sips.

Downbeat joked, "She does all the drinking in our family."

"And don't you forget it," Doris said.

Downbeat overcame the public announcement and whispered to Erin, "Thanks, Angel. You squelched a rumor before it got started." He pointed to the glass Doris held and announced, "My drink is versatile. If the olive has a pit we have a Stoned Downbeat. With a stuffed olive we get the Spicy Downbeat, and with a ripe olive you get the real me, the Over-The-Hill Downbeat." He popped an olive into his mouth. "I like mine straight."

"You're not over the hill, Honey," Doris said.

"Just keep telling me that, I'll believe it."

"Yeeesh," muttered the bartender. "All those new drinks to learn."

"About your wedding," Doris reminded Erin. Have you selected a gown?"

"I think I'll just pull a suit out of the closet—"

"You will not," Doris charged, raising her voice. "You're going to do this right. Don't you realize you're history, girl? When they write the history of this town and put Cordelia Cooper on one page, you will be right there on the next page!"

Erin's voice sharpened. "Do you know what a bridal gown costs? To be worn only once?"

"As if you couldn't afford it. You're breaking my heart."

"It doesn't make sense."

"The lone holdout. All right. I give you mine. Jennifer will give you hers. Take your choice for the make-over."

A hand-me down? Oh, no! Erin decided at once that she would stop at the Traditional Bride Shop.

To her surprise, when she stopped the next morning, the lady in charge at Traditional had an offer of her own. "Will you will sell me Cordelia's wedding gown? I have been trying to buy it for a long time."

"I'll think about it."

Erin thought about it, but Belle decided it would be Cordelia's gown that she would be wearing. Erin found the gown in a garment bag at the back of Cordelia's closet.

Belle supervised the fitting the first time Erin slipped into Cordelia's wedding gown. All the while Erin fussed.

"Honestly, Mother, I've regressed. Here I am in hand-me downs again. Does the label read 'Salvation Army'?"

Belle said, "Oh shut up. The pearls on this gown are only real. You'll be the envy of every bride from New York to San Francisco. You know what Hank said? If you don't marry him pretty soon, he would ask me."

"I suppose you told him that if he did, you would say yes."

"In a heartbeat. He likes my cooking."

"Don't rub it in. I'm going to loan the gown to the bridal shop for display after the wedding."

"So you're going ahead with the wedding?" Belle joked.

"Yes, Mother." Erin felt as though control of the wedding had slipped from her grasp.

At the savings and loan, little mention had been made about the impending nuptials but at CABI, Doris kept asking people, "Are you coming to the wedding? You'd better if you know what's good for you."

Erin couldn't decide whom she would ask to walk her down the aisle. She had narrowed the field to Ben McAllister and Herb Schecter. When she stopped at Schecter's Shoes for a new pair of white heels, she made her selection. "Will you do it, Herb?"

"Be glad to."

"For the honor, I need your help in selecting a maid of honor to carry my train. I call it a railroad train. I want you to fix her up with a pair of shoes—shoes she can wear to the next prom. And we'll send her over to the bridal shop for a gown that I insist can be salvaged for the next prom. Mom will help with any alterations for the prom. Mom is taking charge of my life so I'm taking charge of hers. "

Herb and Eloise exchanged furtive glances.

"I think I know someone," Eloise said tentatively.

The Schecters exchanged glances again.

"Good," Erin said. "Does she have a name?"

"I was thinking of Annette Archer."

"Good. See if you can arrange it."

The refrain, "Something old, something new, something borrowed, and something blue," monopolized Erin's thoughts with such insistence that she began humming. As day of the wedding approached—would it ever arrive?—it seemed that everyone was making arrangements. She told Hank, "I'm about ready to elope."

He smiled indulgently. "If you do, I guess I'll have to marry your mother."

Despite confusion and anxiety, the moment of the wedding arrived. Herb Schecter accompanied her down the aisle and Belle responded "I do," when asked "Who gives this woman?"

After Hank lifted the veil and kissed his bride, the minister said, "It gives me great pride to present Henry Leighton and Erin Ames, husband and wife."

Most of the congregation did not pick up on the fact that Erin had retained her own name, but they would before they left the church. Photographs formal and informal required an hour and a half and Erin said, "I can't wait to derail this train."

She unhooked the caboose and handed it to her mother for safekeeping. Erin had planned that she and Hank would drive home "for a change of costume." Officer Davison had been designated to lead the way in a squad car, but when Hank's car did not arrive promptly, he took charge with a authoritative "Get in," and they rode home seated in the back of the squad car, an area usually reserved for prisoners.

"Call me when you're ready," Officer Davison said when he dropped them off.

"I have a surprise, darling," Erin said. "You know how you like working on old cars? There are several out in the barn. Look at the list Orville gave me while I change. It's in an envelope on the desk."

He opened the envelope on which Jake Cooper had written in his own hand, "To be opened in an emergency."

"I can't believe this," Hank called out as he eagerly scanned the list:

1930 Harley-Davidson 74
1938 Indian Four
1929 Lincoln, with extra gas tank used to transport Prohibition whiskey from Templeton to Kansas City
1948 Tucker, with headlight that turns with steering wheel
1958 Edsel
1935 Duesenberg

"Look at this!" Henry said exclaimed excitedly. "A Duesenberg! Do you know what a car like that is worth? Have you seen them?"

"No. They're behind several rows of straw bales, covered in plastic sheets, covered in canvas, jacked up on blocks, oil in the cylinder heads, more or less in mint condition. They never appeared on any inventory."

Amid the joy of expectation, the significance of that fact did not escape him. "We ought to go right out and have a look."

Erin picked up the key ring and tried to keep up as Hank hurried toward the barn. She inserted the key into the recently installed lock. "Wait a minute," Henry said, "I want to carry you over the threshold. I should have done that before."

"Into a barn?"

"Why not? It's different."

He put her down inside and the door swung shut. He flipped the light switch. "What in the world is this? A jail cell?"

"It appears to be," Erin said. "First a ride in a cop car. Now we're in jail. I wonder, what is strike three?"

He took her in his arms and kissed her, a lengthy breath-consuming kiss. "I love you so much," he whispered.

"Hank? What are you doing?"

He swept her off her feet and put her down on the mound of straw.

"Hank, What—?"

"Haven't you heard, strike while the iron is hot? Don't put off till tomorrow what you can do today, because if you enjoy it you can do it again. Lost time is never regained." His hands moved along her delightfully long legs. "I'm consummating the marriage," he said.

"Not now. Not here."

"Yes," Hank said.

"It takes two to consummate," Erin said as she kicked off her heels.

Hank had been expecting her to give him the "Do what you want with me" treatment. He'd resigned himself to Erin being as responsive as a bag of oats.

Erin allowed a long, bottled-up passion to soar free. She flung her arms around him and held him in the vise of her legs.

"Jeepers Willikers," he cried, as he thought of the man holding the tail of a tiger, unable to hang on, unable to let go.

"Ummm."

"Ummm."

"Oh, Hank!"

They collapsed, totally out of breath.

"I didn't know you could be so impetuous," she managed. She leaped up, eyes wide, and pointed at an intruder.

"Don't be afraid," he said. "It's only a snake. Just what you'd expect in the Garden of Eden." He advanced and the snake slithered away.

She almost said "Now look what you've done" when she observed all the wrinkles in her gown. Yesterday she would have scolded. "I can't wear this." She smiled and said, "I'll have to iron this while we wait for Officer Davison." She tried the door. It wouldn't budge. She used more force. "It won't open."

"Give it a kick."

"It won't open. We're locked in!"

"Really?"

"Really. Now look what you got me into, Ollie."

Hank examined the mechanism. "I think it will open if we just move this little lever. There." The door opened.

"I'm glad I married a man who is mechanical."

"Oh, I'm very mechanical," Hank said.

Erin found comfort in the arm around her as they strolled to the house. "I love the way you love me," she murmured. "It's exciting and yet comfortable. Of course, we will need to try out the bed." She laughed. "I can hardly wait."

While Erin pressed the wrinkles out of the gown and removed telltale bits of straw, Hank said, "When you're on the board at Carleton, you'll do some traveling. I'd like you to keep your eyes open for business opportunities—other S and Ls that might be for sale, or spots where we might establish branches."

"Maybe after the dance," she said dreamily, we can talk about it then. She imagined Downbeat telling the overflow crow at the Cordelia Ballroom, "Charlie Spivak played with Glenn Miller and Glenn financed Charlie's first band. The trumpet player has been rehearsing this number for a week. Here's Charlie Spivak's theme, 'Star Dreams'!" Erin halted her imaginative star dream and listened to Hank.

"Even small-town banks need to grow," he rolled on. "It's time we expanded. A network of small-town offices will prove interesting. Of course, it would mean work." He stopped when he saw her beaming.

"What is this, role reversal? Usually I'm the one who's driven and you're more relaxed."

"Is that a fact? Maybe you haven't been paying attention." Hank made an expansive gesture and stared into eyes as blue as Lake Okoboji. "It just illustrates how flexible we both are."

Erin smiled. "It's you and me against the world, kid. Leading the parade in our Duesenberg."

"We might actually do that," Hank said and combined lines from two classic movies. "Frankly, my dear, I think this is the start of a beautiful friendship."

Erin wanted to say, "It's a lot more than friendship," but decided Hank should have the last word.

Epilogue

Not long after he had arrested Alex Barca, Chief Wendinger ordered Barca's car impounded for safekeeping. Now, on the day of his release, the chief had the car brought round and handed Alex the keys. "Good luck on your next job. Always do right."

Alex responded with a sneer, accepted the keys, drove straightaway to a supermarket parking lot, and placed a collect call to Washington, D.C. "This is Alex Barca."

Unaware that months ago Luckman had imitated Alex, the man at the FCC said, "I'm surprised to hear from you."

"I'm going to say this only one time. I've served my time and I'm out. We should end it. Your hit man missed. I have made numerous copies of the documents. In case of my death they will be dispatched to police chiefs, the FBI, and Senate investigating committees. As I see it, you don't owe me anything. And I don't owe you anything. It would be stupid for you to send another trigger. It's over." He broke the connection.

The man at Com-Com exclaimed, "How could we be so lucky?"

Alex Barca started the four-hour drive up Route 71, north past Atlantic, past Carroll, past Storm Lake, to radio station KSPN where he had accepted the job as manager.

He'd outdistanced his troubles. Things could have gone down a lot worse. Lawyer Kessler hadn't grabbed the car the chief impounded. Kessler hadn't discovered his offshore account in the Caymans.

He tossed back his dark head in a thunderclap of laughter. Through slitted eyes, he read the road sign. SPENCER 7 MILES. A little hick town in the remote corner of a cornball state—who would think of looking for him here? Only a few miles from Minnesota, all he had to do was cross the boundary to escape an Iowa warrant. Spencer would provide a fertile ground for a man with ideas. There would be opportunities galore. Every summer the naive well-to-do congregated around Lake Okoboji and Spirit Lake. They would provide easy pickings.

At his new job he encountered the secretary of the Spencer Chamber of Commerce, Andrew Seligman, who had been unfriendly before.

"Small world," Mrs. Seligman wrote to a friend in Clarinda at Christmas. When Jerry Kessler learned where Alex could be found, he promptly garnished his salary for unpaid attorney fees.

Life for Alex had an unexpected upturn during the second summer when he met a wealthy widow. The couple moved to Key West, Florida, where a carefree Alex currently operates a bar. On the jukebox, the selections are limited to Glenn Miller hits and two from Les Brown: "Leap Frog" and "I've Got My Love To Keep Me Warm."

The friendly folks at Clarinda continue to prepare a Glenn Miller festival that is annually bigger and better than the year before. It is held on the second weekend of every June. Plan to be there.

YA ALL COME, YA HEAR.